That Which Lies Between

by Annabelle Delavigne

First published by No TabooOh in 2022.

Interior illustrations using Canva Pro graphics

A catalogue record for this book is available from the National Library of Australia.

1st Edition
ISBN Paperback: 978-0-6452930-1-2
ISBN eBook: 978-0-6452930-4-3

Author Contact
e: annabelle.delavigne@gmail.com
in: @annabelle.delavigne
w: www.annabelledelavigne.com

No TabooOh
e: sayhello@notabooh.com
in: @no.tabooh

Dedication

To all the women who need to be set free from the chains imposed upon them.

To the source of my strength: my mother, the one who has fought the world so that I could be free.

The value of things is not in how long they last, but in the intensity with which they happen. That is why there are unforgettable moments, inexplicable things, and incomparable people.

—Maria Júlia Paes de Silva

Prologue

It is said that our cells have memory. It is said that they store every touch, every sensation we have ever had in our lives. A smell or a sound is capable of bringing back an event that happened decades ago to the present. It's time travel.

A song can evoke the scent of the perfume, texture and warmth of the skin and the sound of your grandmother's voice telling you stories on the couch.

It can take you back twenty years and make you remember the colour of the rug, the glow of the dust particles in the ray of light crossing the window and marking the timber floor. You are reminded of the summer heat that broke your skin, the taste of a mango picked from the tree you climbed and happily hid between the wide, firm branches. That magical moment is when your cells are awakened, and memory becomes a reality. It is when reason disappears, and we act without knowing what we are doing. It is when we enter a crossroads of senses and discover what really matters and who we really are. It is when we come across the best of ourselves and how dark we can, or have already, become.

The same goes for everyone around us, because nothing human is exclusive to just one person, no matter where you are and what culture limits you; inside, we are all the same. We are, all of us, inevitably poisoned by life day after day until we no longer understand who we are. We pretend to like what we like, not knowing that we are fooling ourselves. There is always more than meets the eye—always. The signs are everywhere, but it is not enough to look for them. It is also necessary to feel, touch, smell, hear and allow yourself. Allow yourself to jump into the unknown, trusting that the truth about you and everything will be there.

The big question is, who would you be if no one knew who you were? What would you do? What would you like? Who would you help, if anyone? What would you eat? What would you work with? Where would you live? Who would you love? What would you allow yourself to feel, do and live if no one knew who you were? I know who I would be, and this is my story.

Tainá de Oliveira Drummond

1

'Coffee?' he says while cheerfully walking through the door of the meeting room, which is already open to half a dozen early risers. 'Who wants coffee? It's on the house!'

Luke throws out the most banal and commonplace words any mortal has ever heard in his life. *Coffee.* A simple, ordinary word, a symbol of relief to the poor souls who are not quite awake but are already in this meeting room at 7:30 in the morning on this winter Monday. *Coffee*, said by that voice, in that intonation, awakens me to a not-too-distant past that busts open the door of my sanity.

Suddenly, like someone who's heard a lullaby at eighty and felt their mother's skin, like someone who's opened a perfume and smelled their first love, or like someone who's eaten a sweet and transported themselves to their favourite holidays, I have no control over what my memory does to my body. My eyes close, and what seems like an electric shock puts my blood in motion, filling my heart so fast that it makes me doubt it has enough space to cope with such intensity. I feel a shiver behind my left ear, as if *coffee* is being said only to me, up close, with his breath tickling the skin of my ear.

My right arm rises, almost touching the back of my neck, and I can feel his hand going around my silhouette. Only memories. He is nowhere near me. My head tilts back. I take a deep breath and quickly come back to myself. Still, eyes open and aware of where I am, I can smell his sweat and feel the weight of his body on mine. In a meeting room, at 7:30 in the morning. On a freezing winter Monday.

Nobody seems to notice me leave the room for a few seconds. Seconds that brought me the memory of a night that marked my soul, like a slave experiencing freedom.

Luke and I have been together before, not romantically, of course. We see each other every day at work, but I never noticed his features until now. Until he said *coffee*. Until he said *coffee* like that. In a way that brought my past to the present in that mysterious moment of cellular memory taking over my logical brain. Because of this, my eyes stick to him, to the *coffee* man. Luke. His shoulders could be his, the masked man's—the other one. His shoulders seem big enough to nestle me like the other one—or *he*—had done last week.

Luke writes down the coffee requests with an ink pen. Gentle hands that may fool some into believing they are weak. I'm not one of them. I know they are the ones that held me up into the air and propped against walls. I shudder. The scratches on my back, arms and legs come alive again. I feel them burning just as they did in the salty bath I took after one of our unforgettable nights. I had forgotten about the scratches. I thought they healed. When will I meet you—him—again? Will I? His lips . . .

Maybe I could tell if Luke is my guy from his lips, but sitting four chairs away at this giant table, I can't notice the same level of detail that I could when we were at the parties. His well-groomed beard today could fool me from the roughness that exfoliated between my legs as he drenched me in a kiss. I would know how to identify his eyes if he looked at me with the same vehemence as him. The other one. Could Luke be him? Would he recognise me?

Luke's hair. If I could touch it, I would know if it was the same as his. Of all the people in Sydney, would he be the guy who knew me more than I ever knew myself? Could it be possible to not recognise the man I gave myself to, simply because I couldn't see his face?

Come out of it, Tainá! You're at work! Focus, creature! And so, distracted in this conversation with myself, I notice Luke is talking to me.

'Don't you want anything? Coffee, tea, water?'

'No, thank you. I'm fine . . .' I wonder if he didn't see my full water bottle right in front of me. I toast the air, lifting it a few millimetres off the table.

'You must like waking up early!' he says, and I smile awkwardly—a mix of flirting, embarrassment and confusion—sort of agreeing. I wake up early. I don't know if I like it or not, but I do, without an alarm most of the time. Perhaps always without an alarm.

The director soon begins his long speech, just as Luke hands the coffee orders to Lynette, our three-hundred-year-old receptionist, cheerful as only she can be. He, the director, says what a phenomenal team of architects, planners and engineers we are, and that we must work together to win this competition, as it will not only bring three years of income but open many more doors to new clients and new work. He shows us the schedule for the day. At the end of it all, we should have a conceptual direction for the project. The day unfolds between piles of butcher paper, pens, sketches, 3D visualisations, mathematical and financial calculations, coffee, sandwiches and a few toilet breaks. I must admit that, despite the tiredness, I am completely distracted from any other libidinous thoughts. There, amid all that creation, I am complete. I end the day satisfied, and it is only now, going back home, that my mind returns to the past again, more specifically to five weeks and four days ago.

2

I can't complain that my life is quiet and monotonous. I was born in Niterói, a city of just over half a million people, separated from Rio de Janeiro by the waters of Guanabara Bay. There, the feeling is that just one common acquaintance separates everyone. Though no one actually knows everyone, that is the feeling: cosy, supportive. It was ranked number four in the entire country for quality of life—if memory serves me correctly. Grandeur. The envious say the only good thing about Niterói is its view of Rio de Janeiro. Indeed, it is a stupendously marvellous landscape where the chain of mountains cuts the sky, ending in the water with the Pão de Açúcar—Sugar Loaf in English. Exclusive. For such exuberance and richness, there is something rather ambiguous: residents have a somewhat provincial mentality. Most people who are born there stay there, venturing out only for work, travel and maybe some entertainment. Truth be told, there are such wonderful places there that only a mad person would leave and never come back. The neighbourhood Itacoatiara, or Itacoa, as the locals call it, for example. Paradise on earth. Really. Every time you are there, you feel that time has stopped and that the hands of the most supreme force have graced you. It is impossible not to feel grateful when you are there. It is also where our family home stands at the foot of an imposing rock that cuts through the waters of the Atlantic Ocean.

I must have a screw loose, because as soon as it made sense, I left in search of other adventures and more interesting people. I lived in Amsterdam, London, Cape Town, Barcelona and now my address is Sydney. My life was never boring. Not predictable, either. But it is possible that I have reached a somewhat pendular repetitiveness. I can't explain why, but I'm bored. Maybe these changes around the world have put me in a state of constant euphoria, with so many discoveries to make in each place, that I don't know how to sit still anymore.

Despite the excitement, every move to a new city is effectively the same. First there is the settling-in phase, when you need to find a place to live, where the markets are, how to get to the doctor, how to use public transport, the difference between the dangerous and pleasant places. Everything is wonderful, and life is large. Then comes the acceptance phase. The euphoria of the new city calms down, and you spend your days comparing what you have here with what you had there, and vice versa. On a happy day, you accept the good things and overlook the bad. The wisdom in you, knowing that no place is perfect, allows you to be content. Unless you are having a bad day, terrible week or dreadful month, because the positives of immigration don't beat the problems, and nostalgia can turn your soul into a miserable being. I've never really given much thought to the cons of moving from one country to another. If one is miserable, you can always move again.

The problem with moving so often is realising that the world is all the same. Globalisation, I suppose. The work, bars, restaurants, streets, transport, and people are essentially the same. What changes is the weather and some local and linguistic peculiarities that make life richer with stories and folklore. Sometimes, I feel I'm the wind itself; a constant breeze for the trees, an incessant force of change that doesn't allow roots to grow.

Perhaps the doldrums I am feeling right now are, in fact, loneliness; in fact, I have never been so alone. Caio has always accompanied me in everything. Or rather, I have always accompanied him, and now he is not here. Perhaps I am spoilt, since I have lived with him for so long that I have not learned to be alone. Perhaps I simply can't adapt to a routine, spending my days in a nine-to-five job from Monday to Friday, or in my case, nine to nine, from Monday to Saturday. It's always the same thing: home to work, work to home, with some minor distractions along the way, like reading. It is hard to think that anyone could be bored in Sydney, though. There are so many things to do, so many parties, so many bars, so many new people to meet. Maybe I am getting old. Can that be so? Has youth passed me? I have completed the twenty-seven trips around the sun, and now I'm tired? Maybe what I've lost is the patience to start again. I prefer to stay still, reading my books in my corners. I have so many corners. Sydney is good for that. It has so many beautiful hidden, unique and forgotten corners and nooks waiting for someone to nurture them and make them feel alive.

Today, my corner is inside Kinokuniya, a very famous and modern bookshop with large steel-framed windows, ambient music and tiled floors. The opposite of cosy and secret, but somehow, the combination of books, sunshine and heritage enchants me. The Queen Victoria Building sits majestically between the window frames. It is easy for someone who lived in Europe to disregard the historical buildings in Sydney, as they are not that old and can be considered bastardised copies of the original styles back in the old world. That is true; I give that to them, but I like to see the architecture of the colonised countries differently. They are not products of the arts and years of cultural development that created the original ones. They are a sad reality of the pioneers, those adventurous people who were running away from a past they are not able to face. Their buildings are rushed copies of what was good of their previous lives before they hopped on those boats. I see these historical buildings as people like Caio and I, so I like them. This corner of the bookshop has been hugging me since February 15, two days after he left.

Lunchtime today is no different from the others. As usual, I pass by the crime section, then the romance novels towards the art section. Overcome by habit, I look at my watch to check the time in Brazil; in vain, whatever the hour or the day, I am unable to talk to Dad and get a recommendation for a good book. If I want to speak to him, it would be more productive to learn to pray or to become a medium.

I need to do some research for work. I want to look at fabric patterns to design some tiles in the lobby of one of my projects, a fashion magazine office. The art section always welcomes me, like a rich, childless aunt. Elegant and almost untouchable.

A book on a pile on a central table catches my attention. It is about Van Gogh, and I think of my mother. I'll take it to her as a Christmas present. *There are still six months to go before you get on that plane. Relax, Tainá—there's time.* I stop myself from buying it. I open another book on the works of the Louvre and see *La Liberté guidant le peuple* by Delacroix. My chest tightens. I remember the walks I used to take with my father to the museum, and when he told me that women make the best revolutions. I, protected in my world, never needed to make any revolution.

I send a photo of the Van Gogh book to Mum with my phone, only to get an almost instant message back of a little dancing doll, clarifying that she already has the same book. Glad I didn't buy it. The other promotional table has a bunch of graphic art books and some pretty silly stuff. I'm trying to avoid procrastinating by focusing on my search for a book that can inspire tile pattern ideas, when I suddenly catch a glimpse of a book with a matte white cover, textured paper and a very sensual image. Hiding its cover against my body, I look for its place on the bookshelf unsuccessfully. There seems to be only one copy of the book. I'm not surprised. It appears to be very unique. On autopilot, I take the book to my corner, at the window, where my favourite sofa is always waiting for me at 1:20 p.m.

I adjust myself so that my legs are warmed by the winter sun but in a way that the rays do not reach the pages. Somehow I feel uneasy openly reading a book as graphic as this in public. I scan the room to see there is anyone looking at me strangely. There isn't. Nobody seems to care what I do or don't do. Paranoid or not, I adjust my bag to hide the cover from others' eyes. Could someone from work see me here? I am mesmerised by the black-and-white illustration on the cover, which seems to have been hand painted and not printed. My fingers feel the texture of the paper and thick ink, reinforcing my theory.

The image is so intoxicating that it makes me forget what I should be doing, and I flick through the pages.

The drawings are beautiful. In one, the upper torso of a woman has proportional butterfly wings made using a rich pointillism technique. Her face is happy and content. She flies vertically on the page. From the waist down, her body is like that of a caterpillar surrounded by various crawling, disgusting creatures emerging from the damp, muddy and sticky ground of the forest. In the passage from caterpillar to butterfly, where a woman's sex lies, there is a man with his head embedded in her body. It is not possible to see his face, but he is facing her, hidden between her legs. His arms, wrapped around the woman's hips, run their hands up the lower parts of her back and bring her close to him. With his legs rooted to the forest, he doesn't seem to want to let her go, but I sense that her happiness comes from him.

Could he be the transformation, or is he preventing her metamorphosis? The man seems to create a barrier between the worms and the woman, a distance between anything that could attack her and prevent her from flying. With him there, she is less vulnerable. Could it be the pleasure he gives her that sets her free?

My phone makes a sound. I know it's the 1:48 p.m. alarm to remind me I need to stop reading and get back to work. I close the book. Look for the price. I can't find it. I go to the payment counter, and I look for a woman attendant. Little need to say why.

'Hi, excuse me, I can't find the price of this book,' I say, trying to avoid looking into the eyes of the girl, who seems young enough to still be a student.

'Hi! Let me have a look for you.'

She picks it up and starts typing on the computer. Meanwhile, I notice how immaculately dressed she is, mistress of herself with perfectly groomed red hair and a very slim waist marked with a belt. Her make-up is immaculate, her nails impeccably done and coloured in a deep wine. She interrupts my observation by letting out a grunt that sounds like trouble. I look at the clock, and it's already 1:57 p.m. She's taken nine minutes to look for it! I'm going to be very late. I'm never late. I especially cannot be late today. My responsibility takes over my vocal cords, and I tell her not to bother. I will be back tomorrow.

'The book doesn't seem to have been published commercially. There's no ISBN I can find. I can't find it or order it without one.' She puts it back on the counter, politely pushing it towards me.

'Can you order by name?' I ask, puzzled.

'The name is not getting me anything back, either. There's no author. There's nothing I can do. You can take it if you want.'

'No, it's not mine. It wouldn't be right.'

'Why don't I keep it for you and discuss it with my manager? Maybe we can figure something out. If you leave your number, I can give you a call.'

I place my newly arrived business card on top of the book, and like two magnets of opposite poles, my hand is stuck over it.

'When do you think you'll be able to talk to him?' I ask, worried someone else will take the book.

'Today.'

'What time do you close?'

Honestly, I don't know why I asked that question. I know perfectly well that they close at 6:30 p.m. I know that because I rarely manage to stop by after work, always tied up with some project to deliver in the evening. As usual, my boss will want me to change something because the client had a new idea and thinks we should redesign everything while keeping the same deadline. I don't want the owner of the book to come back, but I can't just take it. I'm not a thief. If I give the owner until 6:00 p.m. to come back, I can take the book without guilt. I'll leave at 5:45 p.m., come here and go back to work. That way, it'll all work out. Perfect plan.

I thank the attendant for her attention, and I activate my arrive-on-time mode. My legs seem to have gained a few extra centimetres as I stride like a frightened giraffe towards the exit. Suddenly, from behind me, someone calls out to me. A man.

'Thank you for finding my book!'

The clock stops just as I see him coming towards me. Taller than me, wearing a navy-blue overcoat, dark jeans and a light grey jumper over a white-collared shirt. He smiles charmingly.

His slender posture matches his sleek, freshly cut hair. The two-day beard looks like a style choice rather than sloppiness. He is probably in his early thirties. As he approaches with slow, firm, determined steps, I notice the silver wedding ring on his left hand. Married. Of course. My rush returns; it's 2:02 p.m. *How ridiculous of you to be late for a meeting because of a book!*

'Not a problem! Be careful not to forget it again. I have to run. Bye,' I answer while walking backwards, making my way to the exit. My only hope is for the manager to order the book, or I can try online. 'Thank you for forgetting the book!' I shout from afar, something totally not normal for me.

Haste has never made me polite, though I've never been late. Except today, except now. The meeting must have started already. I can't believe I'm going to be late because of a book. Irresponsible.

I turn away from him and speed up the pace to leave.

'Keep it!' His voice is like a tug on a rope that's wrapped around me, impossible to ignore.

'No, I can't accept it. I need to go. Really.' I turn to him to answer as quickly as possible, but I am sealed in place by the way he is looking at me: intensely. With every step towards me, his gaze strips me down as if getting me undressed. He is reaching for my soul. How is he doing this?

'You must. It's a present,' he insists, stretching his arms out, gifting me the book. His lips turn up slightly, and he looks spectacularly charming.

Time slows down. My heart beats faster with every millimetre he gets closer to me. No one has ever looked at me like that. Not even Caio. I can't escape giving my time to this stranger.

As he reaches me, my hands grasp the other end of the book—the only thing that separates our clothes from touching. We are close enough to make my boyfriend jealous if he were to show up right now.

'I can't. It's a very beautiful book. Keep it. I'll buy one for myself.' I pretend to be confident, but the tremble in my voice gives away how I feel. I'm pathetic. Frozen.

'It's not for sale,' he says, filling the air with mystery.

Why is it not for sale? His eyes are still fixed to mine, our jackets touch. I control my exhale not to give away my nervousness . . . it all feels like a cliff-hanger from my favourite series. I am lost.

'Please take it, or you'll be late for work,' he says, finally breaking eye contact, looking at my watch. Time is back to its normal, crazy speed.

'Yes, I will,' I answer, agreeing and noticing his wedding ring again as I look at the book. The spell is undone. I take a step back.

Get the book, Tainá. It's just a book, and you'll regret not getting it, I convince myself.

'Can I give it back to you?' I splutter. 'How about we meet here next Friday, same time?'

Why did I say this? He will think I'm asking him out. I have a boyfriend, for goodness' sake. *Shut up, Tainá!* I also make the mistake of catching his eye again.

He steps closer than before. Between us, there's only the pages of the book—which are not that many, maybe a hundred.

My inhale captures his earthy smell: vivid, saturated, rich and dangerous. It is—he is—like the warning sound of twigs cracking behind me on a forest hike. A hypnotic scent, impossible to ignore. His coat lightly touches my knuckles. It feels woolly, sophisticated, soft yet heavy.

'You don't need to give it back to me. It's yours for now. When you're done, pass it on,' he says quietly, almost whispering. The light breeze of his words stirring my hair around my left ear ignites a hurricane in me. I don't know where I am.

Guilt, irresponsibility and adventure bathe me like a summer storm at the end of a humid day. Quick and refreshing. He looks contented when I finally take the book in my hands.

'Read all pages . . . in order.'

I don't say anything but offer a quiet and puzzled thanks. I don't know what else to say. I don't know what just happened.

The rush of mundane responsibilities comes back, and the book goes into my bag. I look at my watch. Shit, it's already 2:06 p.m., and I still need seven minutes to get to the office. I'm very late! I've never been late. Shit, shit, shit! Leaping like a gazelle, I cut my way through the Victoria Galleries to get off at Pitt Street. As soon as I cross through the traffic-jammed cars, hearing some screaming from the drivers, I find myself stuck in the middle of a crowd watching street performers in front of Westfield. I make my way through and keep running until I reach the MLC.

The lift doors almost squash me as I squeeze myself between them. I wish my clients and my boss were here too, so we'd all be equally late, but they're not. I curse anyone who chooses an office on the sixteenth floor. Honestly, when you work so hard and don't have time to look out the window, what's the difference between sitting on the second floor or in the clouds if you don't have the time to be contemplating the view? They only pay a higher rent. I can almost hear my boss using my nationality to make stupid, general jokes, saying that Brazilians are always late. I'm not like that.

Someone should invent a lift that gets faster the more you push the buttons. Luckily for me, the lift goes straight to my floor. I see that all the clients and consultants are still at the reception desk; I look at Lynette, and she, of course, noticing my rush, gives me a golden tip.

'This way, honey; run this way.' She takes me away from them. 'That's the advantage of being in a round building, darling. You can always choose to go right or left.'

'Only you, Lynette. Thank you!' I smile at her in appreciation.

'She's not in a good mood. They had their managers' meeting at lunchtime. Get ready!'

'I will. Thank you again!'

I don't have time to go to my desk and get the printouts of the presentation I had prepared before lunch. I enter the meeting room with my bag and out of breath, frantically getting ready by turning on the computer and then the screen, logging in and opening the presentation while trying to hide my walking shoes. It's just my luck that everyone starts arriving, and no one notices I'm late except my boss. She notices the printouts are not on the table.

'Tanya,' she says so everyone can hear I messed up, 'can you get the hard copies so everyone can make notes during the meeting?'

No 'please.' She can't even say please.

'Tanya! I haven't heard that name in quite a while,' says one of our clients.

'It's *Tainá*, but most non-Latin Americans confuse it with Tanya. It's normal,' I explain smiling.

I don't have to look at my boss to feel her wrath. I can't get around letting her call me by the wrong name, even in front of clients. A different accent would be one thing, but not the wrong name. We've been working together for two months; she should know that Tanya is not Tainá. I can take her insults, but she won't take my name away.

'Beautiful name!' the magazine editor says. She is nice.

'I agree. I've never heard it before. Where are you from?' asks the director of the magazine, who turns up only at some of the more important meetings.

'Brazil,' I reply.

'We have a multicultural team here,' she, my boss—or, as I call her, *the cow*—brags loudly. 'We have people from everywhere! *Tayeenah* is Brazilian. A *super exotic* name!'

Against her will, but in the name of trying to please her clients, she corrects herself by trying to pronounce my name while asserting herself again as my manager. '*Tayeenah,* can you get the hard copies now? Please?'

'Sure.' At least she said please.

'Tayeenah,' the editor calls, 'I'm getting side-tracked here, but I hope you don't mind.' She looks at my boss for permission, who agrees. 'You might just be perfect for a photoshoot we are doing. There's a stunning dress that been lined up for an editorial, but we haven't found someone with the right skin tone and eye colour. No one seems quite right for it, but I have a feeling you might be just perfect. Do you mind coming by my office to discuss? I can call you or send you an email. Would that be okay?

Me, in a fashion magazine? This is embarrassing. What do I say?

'Yes, sure. Of course. Any time.'

I grab my bag, and on my way out of the room, my boss gives me that fake, hostile smile. 'Be quick,' she whispers as I pass her. 'We've wasted enough time already.'

I obey by going to my desk as quickly as possible—I need to remember to breathe. Besides what she asked me to do, I grab my notebook and my pens. Red, blue and black pens. A glance over at my bag shows the spine of the book. How could I have forgotten about it already? I quickly put the bag in the small niche under my desk to avoid anyone seeing the book accidentally.

'So, where did you go for lunch?' Fleur, my Canadian colleague, surprises me by appearing from behind a screen. The mother of two boys with the third in her belly—she secretly wants a girl—she is one of those people who is always smiling. She seems to carry no weight or problems on her shoulders, is always on time and always leaves on time. A perfect friend. She credits her enthusiasm and high energy to the fact that being at work, away from domestic activities, is like a holiday for her.

'I haven't eaten anything yet. Sorry, I need to run to that meeting. Chat later?' I reply, and she nods, agreeing.

The meeting lasts two hours. I leave it with a fried mind; I have so much to do. Why do people change their minds so much? It's 4:30 p.m. on a Friday afternoon. Our deadline is Monday at noon. Why can't my boss negotiate another deadline? I wish I could say something to her without her barking at me.

Sitting bent over and miserable with the prospect of coming to work on the weekend, I try to find a personal reason as an excuse for not being available. If I'm not available, she will find another deadline, right? Right. I invite Fleur to go out on Saturday, and despite her happiness being stamped on her face and in her voice, she declines.

'Going out without kids? Just the two of us?! Yes! But I can't do this weekend. My husband's family is coming on Sunday for a barbecue, and I need to prepare the house tomorrow. It looks like a hurricane has been through it.'

'Lunch on Monday?' I suggest, hopeful that I'll be able to finish the work on time and that, even if I miss the weekend, I'll at least have lunch on Monday.

'Perfect!' she answers at the same time her alarm goes off. 'Five o'clock! I'm going! See you on Monday, hun. *Au revoir!*' She grabs her bag and shuts down her computer in less than thirty seconds.

She leaves, just like that. Quickly and guilt free.

Two hours later, all I want to do is go home. It is dark outside, and it is depressing to hear everyone drinking and eating in the kitchen while I'm here working. So, I decide to go home.

I walk past them to wave goodbye and go to the changing room to put on my cycling gear. On my way out, my boss materialises like a drunken ghost. Not only do I work for a person who has no idea how much time it takes to prepare a project, but now she sees me in gym clothes.

'Still here? I thought a girl like you would be out there, in the clubs, dancing, having fun, picking up some *hunks* . . .'

Who knows why she's surprised to see me at work? I am here all the time. What does she mean by *I thought a girl like you* . . . ? Is this another insult?

'Yes, I need to finish what we discussed at the meeting this afternoon. Considering it takes around forty-five minutes to print the hard copies, if I come in on Monday at 9:00 a.m., I'll only have two hours and fifteen minutes before noon to design and prepare the drawings, perspectives and texts, and considering how often files are corrupted—'

'I get it. No need to go on,' she interrupts me. 'If you don't have anything to do this weekend, it would be good if you can go that extra mile . . .' Her arched eyebrow and cynical tone, as if I'm not dedicated to work, get on my nerves. I've been working every weekend; I don't understand why she does this to me.

'I'll come tomorrow, but I'd rather not come on Sunday.'

'Great! If there's anything you need, call my private phone, okay? I turn off my work one, you know. People can't leave me alone . . .'

I seriously doubt that.

'If I don't turn my work phone off, I can't rest. It's mental. These men . . . they can't do anything on their own.'

'What men?'

'You know . . . these guys who think they own the company, the buildings, the city!' She waves her arms everywhere.

It is exhausting to be next to her and her constant rants. Why does she look for enemies all the time? She writes her number on a piece of scrap paper she grabs from a random desk nearby. When she hands it to me, she asks if I'd prefer her to come in as well. Is she trying to imply that she is here to support me? You've got to be kidding me. As my mother always reminds me, *being alone is better than being badly accompanied.* So, I politely thank her for her availability and assure her that everything will be fine, saying I will call her if anything goes wrong or I need help. I won't call.

'All right, then, see you on Monday.'

As I walk towards the lift, she calls after me again.

'*Tayeenah!* One more little thing . . .' She walks towards me and in her normal voice—not drunk sounding—says, 'Next time you have to correct me, try not to do it in front of the clients.'

'Correct you? When did I correct you?'

'The pronunciation of your name . . .'

'I didn't correct the pronunciation of my name; I corrected my name. My name is not Tanya.'

'It's an affectionate nickname. Everyone has a nickname here, that's what Aussies do. See, *Aussies* comes from *Australian.* Diminutive.'

I can't believe this woman. I ponder if I need to answer anything as she continues.

'It looks bad to correct my pronunciation. It makes me look prejudiced against immigrants, which I am not. My great-grandfather was Italian, you know? You also have to adhere to the local culture. That's how we are.'

We? Does she mean Australians? I haven't met anyone like her. What kind of world does she live in? I wonder if it is worthwhile to discuss the matter. I judge it useless to argue with her, and I finally manage to leave in the lift's direction. While I wait, I sigh, looking at the office, not believing that I will be here tomorrow. Again. Working. My misery is reinforced by her unnerving voice beating in my ears again.

'Ah! *Tanyeah . . .*'

What's wrong with her? What is this *Tanyeah* now?

'Can you email me the presentation tomorrow when you're done, so I can see how far you've got it and proofread it?'

'Of course. If it makes it easier for you, you can call me Tai.'

'Tai? But then it sounds like Thai food. I don't want you to be associated with food . . . Men are disgusting as they are.'

What's wrong with her and men? I agree so she'll leave me alone. Men are not disgusting.

3

The ride home makes me realise how much I miss Barcelona. Here, I feel like a pest on my bike, small and annoying, like an ant. The cars pretend cyclists don't exist, buses rush us, motorbikes think they are equals. The streets are dark, and we have to wear so many safety gadgets that we look like a Christmas tree. It is the complete opposite from when I lived in Barcelona. We used to walk and cycle everywhere, including our unforgettable trip to the South of France. It was so safe and civilised. So romantic, so free, so . . . Miguel.

I get home in thirty-three minutes, four less than yesterday. The temperature outside is two degrees colder. The pride of having made better time and still having survived in this crazy traffic puts a sweet taste in my soul and a smile on my face. That's why, even complaining and afraid of getting squashed, I cycle. It's that lightness I feel when I get home. It's the cold skin contrasting with the warm blood pulsing.

We—or rather, I—live in North Bondi, at the extreme end of Ramsgate Avenue, where, between the sea and me, there is only air and a cliff. The street is a mixture of old, exorbitantly priced architectural splurges and even more outrageously priced new buildings. My flat belongs to the second group. I feel like an impostor walking into such an expensive place, but I'm lucky I don't have to live in the shantytown-like flats. Here, even the garage floor shines. Polished. I leave my bike in the well-lit and clean garage.

The flat is the same as I left it this morning, obviously. No one has been here. The table is clean; the cushions on the couch by the window still hold the shape I made with my body last night. The picture frame with Caio on the entrance console makes me wonder if he has a picture of us. I reach for my phone in my jacket pocket. No messages from him. He must be tied up at work. I ask for a photo of his place. I still have no idea where he lives.

The darkness of the sea through the window can be frightening to some, but to me, it causes a state of magical hypnosis. The horizon appears or disappears depending on the moon phase and, sometimes, the number of clouds in the sky. Without the moonlight, the water turns to sky, and the sky turns to water. How to know which is which? One reflects the other, but they never touch. Tonight, the waning moon and the clouds make the landscape equally enchanting. There are not two nights alike if you care to listen to them.

Would it be possible to see the starry, almost silver sky in a city like this if everyone turned out their lights at the same time? The horizon would be a silver line where the ocean absorbed the Milky Way, as it was back home.

The sound of the waves, the light breeze and this endless sea take me back to Itacoatiara. To home. Why did I leave? The claim of the sea against the land is the same everywhere. If it is calm, the ocean blesses us with that soothing, soft music that can settle the harsher hearts. But when it is angry, when it sends its waters in strong and agitated waves, its cry penetrates my soul. It has the power to bring out the anxiety and fear that live hidden inside of me.

Wherever you live, water and air will connect you with those you left behind. These elements have no roots to keep you stuck in the same place. They are fluid, like me. So, I breathe, and I swim. The waters of Southern Europe and South Africa were so different from the beach of my childhood, but here I feel at home. I don't know where this similarity comes from, since the colour, temperature, waves and smell are so different from where I swam as a child.

I feel as if Dad is still beside me, reading books in the hammock, listening to the waves, feeling the immensity of the sea and the calming breeze that used to make us get lost in time. There was no hurry or desire to return to the rush of the outside world. It was our world. Where are you, Dad? Could it be that you are there, in this endless sea?

If only I could jump into this darkness and find you, hold you, and tell you how much I love you. Come back here, come back to me. What were you thinking when you left? What's it like to die, Dad? Why did you go?

Why did *I* leave? *Because the worst death is that life not lived. Your soul is too free for you to stay here. Your little head is too curious to be content with seeing the same things every day. Flap your wings without fear because yours will grow every time one breaks.* I remember your words as if it were yesterday. You always brought me so much peace.

I was selfish. Why did *I* leave *you*? Now what? Me alone here, and you . . . where are you? Are you alone? I hope you're okay, Dad. What happens when we die? Can we find our parents, our family? Can you hear me? Is there a sea where you are? Did you meet your son, my brother? Did you find our Kadu? How is he? Kadu, was it you who called Dad?

Why wasn't I content to find a life well lived where I was born? I had everything. Why go out and explore the world? Why didn't I listen when they told me what really mattered? All I had to do was listen. I don't know if I wanted to listen. Tell me, Dad. Why does it hurt so much? If I have so many wings, why can't I fly? Why do I feel like a column? Stuck to the ground with steel and concrete?

How I wish I could fly and stay with you two! I wish I could bring Mum along. She doesn't seem to want to come here, and she doesn't seem to need me to go back. Her wings really do regrow, or perhaps they never get hurt. I'm sorry, Dad. If I'd been there, this wouldn't have happened.

I write in my notebook: *One needs to go back. Back to where their roots can feed them like a tree.*

Risk. Fix.

When you feel that your roots have turned to concrete, you need to go back. Back to the place where they are nourished by the earth beneath your feet.

Risk. Fix.

Just like trees, one needs nourishing roots. Dried, immutable, concrete foundations are only for buildings.

Risk.

Why do I even bother writing? It's pointless trying to be my own psychoanalyst. I keep feeling the same thing. Nothing. Nothing changes.

The delicate yet heavy tears run down my face, making their way to my empty chest. Just as the stars will die on the horizon of the sea and return tomorrow night, sadness will return tomorrow, in the same place and with the same strength. The same intensity.

The sound of the phone snaps me out of my trance. *Caio.* He seems to guess when I need to get out of my head, but I'd better eat first, then I'll call him back. I'm starving. I haven't eaten anything for twelve hours.

I don't know why they put such a big fridge in a one-bedroom apartment. Maybe it is to remind people how lonely their lives are if they live alone. I have half a dozen varieties of fruit, some water, salad and some noodles left over from last night's dinner. Otherwise it's empty.

I close the curtains, as I don't want to get lost again in what lies outside. It's time to get back to life. Back to the present. I send him a message: *having dinner, I'll call you soon.* The phone rings thirty seconds later, video call. It's him again.

'Hi, do you think I eat that fast?' I answer, smiling. It's nice that he can't wait to talk to me.

'I didn't see the point of waiting for you to finish dinner,' he replies, sounding busy with something else.

'I just wanted to talk to you without having to worry if my mouth is full of food. Are you working?'

'Since when can't you eat in front of me?'

'I can. I just don't want to. It's odd, isn't it?'

'Not really. It's not like we've never eaten facing each other.'

He's right, it has nothing to do with food. I didn't want him to call, so I wouldn't have to explain why I was crying.

'I miss you, babe!' he says. He seems sincere.

'Miss you too. How was your day?'

'The same old things. Work. You know how it is.'

I put a fork of salad in my mouth while hiding from the camera.

'What about you? What did you do? Who did you work with?' he asks.

'Same as every day. I ran on the beach in the morning—'

'Did the wetsuit fit?'

He interrupts me for a good reason. A few weeks ago, he sent me a wetsuit so I can keep swimming in these icy waters during winter.

'Where was my head? I forgot to say that it fits. Thank you. You are very generous, as always.'

'It was a pleasure. At least you can go back to swimming and surfing. Maybe sailing?'

'You know it will take time,' I say, almost crying again.

'Yes, I know. But at least you have the tools to swim in winter. If you want.'

I stop talking so I won't have to keep on this topic. There are too many memories tormenting me when I step in the water. I know Caio will try to make me dive in, be tough and forget it all. He never lost a brother and a father, so what does he know?

'I'll send you a song. I heard it at work today and thought of you.'

Caio sends the song by message, and I reply that I'll listen to it after dinner, but, at his insistence, I end up listening to it right then. The song, very famous, is about a guy who asks his girlfriend to marry him.

'Caio, what does this mean? You're asking me . . .'

'What do you think of the idea?'

'Not while you're in Singapore and I'm here . . .'

'If that's what you want, princess.'

'Princess? Since when? I'm not a princess.' Although, looking at my life now, I'm more like royalty than a commoner.

'You are *my* princess! I will give you the world. You know that.'

'You certainly took me travelling. I can't deny that.'

But has he given me the world? I shouldn't need him to give me anything. Should I? Is he really proposing over the phone, or is it one of his jokes? Do I want to marry—really marry—him? We are kind of married, right? Or aren't we?

'Big news!' he shouts. 'I've booked my ticket. I'm coming to see you!'

'That's great! When are you coming?'

'Next Friday! I'll come straight from the airport.'

'It will be so nice when you get here. We can . . .'

I see the book popping out of my bag and hear that man's voice near my ear again: *Every page . . . It is not for sale.* For an infinitesimal fraction of time, the image of Caio on the video turns into him, the guy from the bookshop. My brain is racing, remembering disconnected bits of what happened today. I can see his eyes fixed on mine; I smell his scent as if he is here. I inhale deeply. I have to end the call.

'Hi! Tatá, are you there? I think you froze. Hello?'

'Hi, I'm back. I think the connection crashed.' *I* crashed, not the phone. 'You know I love talking to you, but I need to get ready to sleep. I have an early start tomorrow.'

'You always wake up early. Tomorrow is Saturday, though. What are you going to do?'

'Work.'

'Who are you going to be working with?'

'Only me. Same project.'

'Only you? They can't expect you do to everything alone.'

'Just me. I prefer it that way.'

'It's hard to believe a company that big—for architects, that is—would put you alone on a project. They need to have more people helping you.'

'No, it's fine. I can handle it.'

'Well, you don't need to subject yourself to something like this—you know that. My salary is more than enough. You can stop working and come live here.'

'You are so kind, but it's not just about the money. I stayed in Sydney to try and have a decent career, and this office can help me get there. They're one of the best, so . . . I need to go tomorrow.'

'You need a career that respects you, that pays you properly and doesn't make you work overtime without paying you. How many Saturdays have you been working?'

'I don't know. It doesn't bother me too much; I like what I do.'

How I want to talk about all the overtime he did and still does, but there's no point in discussing that now. My new book is far more interesting than spending hours talking about work.

'Don't worry, there's not much to do in Sydney except go to the beach. And since you organised this awesome flat, I spend all night breathing the clean ocean air. Thank you. I really need to go to sleep now.'

'Well, remember that I only want the best for my girl. Good night!'

'Good night!'

'Tatá, I love you!'

'Me too. Sleep well.'

'Send me a photo with the wetsuit later. Miss you!'

'Okay, good night again.' I smile and hang up. I haven't tried on the wetsuit. I wanted to, but I couldn't. Now, I will have to, or he won't stop asking until I send him the photo he wants.

I wash the dinner dishes quickly, dry my hands on the kitchen towel and grab the book. It's 9:00 p.m. I have an hour before bed. Bath. Book. Bed. The basket thanks me for a few more items to wash, since there are so few in there. The hot water runs down my back, burning it just a little. It's the type of burn that makes me realise how cold my feet are. I've never felt so cold, not even living in Europe. The apartments here must be poorly designed. Soon I finish the shower, brush my teeth and, now finally warm, in my light-grey flannel pyjamas, I can get my book and sit in my favourite armchair in the bedroom.

I randomly open my new book on a page with a drawing of a woman lying face down on a striped beach towel. She wears only the bottom of her bikini; her body is round and youthful.

She looks at an open magazine between the sand and the towel. The image in the magazine is herself looking at the magazine, and it repeats in an endless sequence. The black-and-white drawing reveals that she is on a beach. On the edges of the paper, you can see marks of the feet that have walked there. She seems indifferent to what is happening around her.

Her inertia seems like a contemplation of herself. It makes me wonder what that image means. Are we so obsessed with ourselves that we only see us? Do we only see as *good* what we think is the same as us? Or would it be the opposite? She is so insecure that she needs to imitate what she sees in the magazine to think of herself as someone valuable? And that person in the magazine copies what they see in another magazine, and so on.

Do we need to see ourselves through the eyes of others to be interested in ourselves? Am I interested in myself? Who do I model myself on? Who could it be that Caio echoes? I am almost certain that my mother is an original example, so confident in herself.

I'm tempted to look for an illustration with a couple. I find one that takes place in an alleyway. There's a half-open corrugated metal door where empty plastic boxes have been left loose for milk deliverers to take when they bring in their next load.

The man in the drawing wears a structured winter coat, trousers and sleek shoes. His hair is short. His face is partially hidden in the woman's neck. I'd venture to say he even looks like the guy from the bookshop, and I can smell his fragrance again, and my breath deepens as if he were here. What has this man done to me?

The woman's mask covers her entire face except for her lips. Succulent lips. Satisfied lips. They drew the lace on the mask with a very fine pen. Bent over her body, he embraces her like a protective shell. His arms encircle her waist as she holds him with the legs that slip out of her overcoat. Her arms press their bodies against each other. Imagination completes everything else that happens under their clothes.

A more attentive look, and I notice the scene is framed by the glasses and beret of a police officer who seems to watch the couple. It is not possible to know whether the police officer is a man or a woman. The desire between the two is intense and passionate. Would I ever have the courage to do that? It seems so explicit.

I remember when I met Caio and wonder where our uncontrolled passion vanished to. We were once so spontaneous. Not quite as public as the couple in the image, but there was a time where our lovers' impulses couldn't wait for us to get home. Maybe the flame that united us burnt slowly. It faded in the faint smoke of the sleepless nights we spent connecting our souls with infinite caresses and tales of our lives. Maybe it died little by little, with each dirty dish, each packed box and each of my resignations from work. Our time in Africa was undoubtedly when we were more alive. Perhaps because we were so grateful after being so terrified or simply because it was the beginning of us. I wouldn't call me a princess then either, but I can certainly say he was a knight.

One day, as I was feeding my love for wildlife photography, an unexpected incident happened. A cheetah, the gentler of the big cats, almost made me her lunch. If it wasn't for Caio, she would have succeeded. It was the last photo I've taken of living things.

The book brings me back to the present. It seems to be alive, calling me with his voice—the bookshop guy's voice: *Read every page*. I feel as if he is here. Why did he choose me?

'What mysteries do you hold?' I ask the book out loud, running my fingers through the lines of the cover illustration. My search online yields the same results as the checkout lady: nothing. I will have to do what he said: read every page. Or find him again. Tomorrow, I will be there at 10:00 a.m. I hope he is there too.

*

Fate does not betray my intuition, and as soon as I arrive, I find him sitting in *my* corner. He is as clean, sophisticated and charming as yesterday. I smile. Mentally, of course. As soon as our eyes meet, they're glued to one another. He gets up and walks towards me. My legs, hard as concrete, hide the throbbing tremor inside, and they work hard not to disintegrate into cement powder with every step he takes. An irrational reaction. Reality blurs. I don't remember what I came here to do.

'I knew I'd picked the right person,' he says, close enough to notice my arrhythmic breathing.

How ridiculous am I? Control yourself, Tainá.

'The right person for what?'

'Come,' he says and turns around, certain that I'll follow him.

It could be the end of my life. A complete stranger and me, the perfect prey. I stand still in the same place, waiting for him to call me again, and, as soon as he notices my immobility, he comes a few steps closer and moves his arms in a gentle gesture, giving me passage, inviting me once more.

Something tells me, my body maybe, that this is not going to end well. Caio and I definitely . . . Caio . . . What am I doing? My curiosity walks side by side with my guilt, and I remain imprisoned by the desire to know more. I need the answers that surround this book and him.

His slow, focused walk, at the same pace as mine, adds to his chivalry. His hands, crossed behind his back, bring a certain sense of security. Maybe it's false; maybe he's a psychopath. What am I getting myself into?

We say nothing on our walk until we get to a familiar place just off George Street. It's the alley from the book's illustration. There is even a police motorbike parked on the main street where the light rail will pass.

'I see you've reached page 35,' he says, keeping his arms behind his body.

'I'm not reading the book in order.' I walk into the alleyway, not quite knowing why.

'You must read it in order, or it will be purely entertainment.'

I know books are not always for entertainment. The good ones serve a much bigger purpose: to make you think. But I don't feel like discussing this with him.

'Why should I?'

He follows me down the alley, but he is farther away from me and needs to use a louder voice for me to hear. The sound reverberates in a faint echo.

'You'll know.'

The silence reigns for a few moments as he comes closer to me, leaning one shoulder on the wall. His hands are now inside the pockets of his overcoat. 'It's for your sake, only yours.'

'Why me?'

'Because I know you will appreciate it. I know you feel trapped. But it's not a prison, it's a . . . cocoon. As cheesy as that sounds, you deserve to break out of it, to become the butterfly that lives there.' He moves his head, pointing his eyes and finger to my heart without touching me.

'It's pretty cheesy, but thanks.'

We stare at each other without blinking for an unmeasurable period. I try to enumerate all the reasons I should get out of here. The longer I stay, the more certain I am that I'm throwing away all that Caio and I lived together. The longer I stay, the more I feel I am jumping into an uncertain future. Can someone fight this force? All the logic cannot suppress what I am drawn to do. Instead of leaving, I reduce the distance between us to the thin layer of skin on our lips. My body responds to every move and every touch, as it has not done in a long time. My hands repeat on his body what his do on mine. It is automatic. I don't know how to describe the intensity. Everything seems colourful, guilt-free. I let him reach me under my clothes, and I no longer care if anyone is passing by. Let them see! What happens next words cannot fully explain. I give in to the craziness of renouncing myself. You can just feel when two souls become intertwined. I am as large as the universe itself. I surrender to the confusion of my senses: I breathe his taste; I drink his heat; I listen to his gaze and I hear his scent. I feel like

I have just started repairing some wings I didn't know were broken.

4

What have I done? I wake up sweaty, guilty and surprised.

My bed is empty, except for my duvet and all my pillows lying where I left them last night. Last night. There's no sign that anyone else has passed by, not even me. The bedside light is still on. I'm curled up in my blanket with my body aching from sleeping in my armchair. The phone tells me it is still half past six on Saturday. It was all a dream. I breathe out relief and disappointment while my head sinks into the pillow. Relief as betrayal in a dream doesn't count. Does it? Disappointment, well . . . Who wouldn't be disappointed knowing that their imagination is better than reality? The details fade away like in any unmaterialised dream, and despite my love for Caio, I know we may not last.

Maybe if he was here, I wouldn't need to test my loyalty and reputation. I reach for him in the place that he can be slightly closer to me: my phone. Nothing. Not a message, not a photo, not even an email. He is still away.

The morning sun lightens my face as I open the curtains and brings my mind back to normal. How amazing it is to have this view, this light inside as I wake? It feels like home. The few people on the beach make it an ideal day for running in the sand before it gets crowded with tourists. That's what I will do. I will sweat my problems away, rejuvenate in the waves and then I will be ready for work.

I send a message to my mother, who makes a point of ignoring me. I send a message to her neighbour: *Hi Ines, how are you? Have you heard from Mum*?

She answers quickly: *She left this afternoon, with a suitcase. She didn't say where she was going, she just said she'd be out until Sunday night and asked me to feed Fish & Chips.*

Fish & Chips? I ask, and she answers with an audio message: *The little fish she inherited from a friend who just passed away. Didn't she tell you?* I vaguely remember a photo with two fish. I admit I don't remember asking who they belonged to. What kind of daughter am I . . . I have to take care of Mum, call her more.

Thanks Ines, I'll wait for her to call me back. If anything happens, give me a call, okay? Good night! Sending kisses.

Nothing will happen, girl! You know your mum. Have a good day! Kisses! she replies and adds a dancing .gif in the end.

As I look up and see the cliff descending into the sea, I can't help but think of my brother. Another ghost. It would be good to have you here, Kadu. Why did you do that? Certain memories don't need to be recalled; they impregnate our cells as if they were part of our DNA. Just like I see my blue eyes every time I look in the mirror, I feel the pain and despair of that day. I try to suffocate, bury and concrete them away, but a small trigger—today, the Bondi cliff touching the ocean—is enough for the tears to overflow my face. I've been not dead for thirteen years.

No sound follows my tears, only pain. No pity, only longing. My body shivers and freezes. It's cold, despite the sun on me. I take a deep breath; I blink, pushing the last tear off my eyes; I close the curtains to break the trance. No city was as painful as here. Even Cape Town, so similar to home, didn't trigger this amount of loneliness. Maybe it was because Caio was with me. Maybe I didn't have time to feel this empty.

*

The sand that prickles on my legs quickly becomes the stairs of the walk from Bondi to Coogee, and I go much farther than I expected. I must have lost track of time. This doesn't happen very often—if ever. The entire run takes me seventy-five minutes, fifteen more than I wanted. It was worth it though; the painful memories came out in sweat instead of tears as I lay on the couch feeling sorry for myself. As inviting as the sea is now, I can't get myself to jump in. I know I am blaming work, lack of time and the cold temperature of the water. The truth is, however, that I can't get myself in the ocean since Dad passed away. The unused wetsuit collects the dust hanging on the back of my bathroom door. Why does Caio insist so much that I start swimming again? Why can't he listen to me?

I keep the warmth from my scalding shower by wearing three layers of clothes. I think twice before taking my camera. Staring at her—I treat my camera like a girl—I decide to leave our catchup for another day. She reminds me of when life had a bit more colour, when I could be called a semipro photographer during the time we lived in Europe. I don't see things as I used to, so my photos will never be as good as she's capable of. It's better to avoid the disappointment and take my book to read if I have some time. I take the 333 bus to the CBD.

To my surprise, the office door code has already been entered. Someone is here. Please let it not be *her*. I just need a bit of peace and quiet, which I will never get if she is here trying to *help me*. Her computer is on, but the screens are off, as are the lights in our area. She's not here, thank goodness. Someone must have left the door alarm off last night.

It's 9:20 a.m. The emptiness and greyness of this concrete box contrasts with the beautiful sunny day outside. Especially this winter sun, the kind that warms you up and makes you lazy. Not a day to work. But I'm here, investing in my career.

After almost an hour, not having figured out who was here before me, I hear a lively woman calling my name: 'Hi, *Tayeenah*!'

'Hi,' I reply. I don't know who she is but feel that I should, so I don't ask her name. I try to reciprocate some of her enthusiasm, trying to be polite without being fake.

'Stuck in here? I can already imagine the project you're working on.' She knows the manager I have. I can't stand the waste of time with small talk. 'Look,' she continues, 'I know you're new here, but let's talk. I think you might benefit from a new team, a new project. We don't want you to get scared and run away.'

Who is this woman, and what is she doing here?

'I won't run away. It's okay, she just has a lot of projects to take care of and—' Before I can say that I understand my boss's stress level, she interrupts me.

'She doesn't have that many projects. We know her, always terrifying the younger designers because she knows they won't say no. Do you want to change projects? What would you like to work on?'

A choice? I don't think I have ever had the chance to decide what project to work on. I'm smiling. What an odd surprise.

'It would be nice to work with master plans, housing development or schools. I've done quite a few schools before. Not here in Australia, but I really like designing schools.'

'Great, leave it with me! Let's talk next week. Put some time in my calendar, okay?' She says goodbye, reminding me to set the alarm when I leave.

It's 10:43 a.m. I have to speed up, or I will be here all day.

*

Three hours later and I'm making good progress with the design and the presentation, despite knowing I still have at least four hours of work to do, including some time to revise everything before sending it out to my boss. It's 1:39 p.m. The voice of my mother telling me I need to have lunch and the rumble of my stomach reminding me I haven't even had breakfast lead me to activate the security alarm and go down to the Domain to eat. The idea of sitting under a tree to eat is appealing, and I grab a wrap from the Lindt Café. A treat.

Saturday on Martin Place is empty, grey and suspicious. I'm waiting for some unwelcome surprise. The buzz and excitement of weekdays gives way to newlyweds and a few executives taking professional photos, tourist families, a group of teenage skateboarders causing the usual jitters with the noises of their manoeuvres on urban equipment. Beggars, such a normal sight in Rio de Janeiro, seem strange to me here. Unusual. In a country where unemployment is only 7 per cent, I wonder why these people live on the street. Prejudicially, I assume they must be schizophrenic. The idea of madness is more attractive than the thought that they ran away from a home where violence was normal. Why else would you be homeless? Sydney Hospital, which frames the east side of Martin Place, is like a magical portal, transitioning us from the concrete forest of the city towards the green, arboreal, joyful world of the Domain. I take some basic photos with my phone and send to Mum, saying I miss her. The time zone difference is rather difficult here: when I'm awake, she is sleeping, and vice versa.

I love sitting under the trees in Sydney, for they are old with long branches and perfectly located in clean parks. It's comfortable to snuggle up to them, even in winter. That is something magical about this city: there's greenery even in the coldest temperatures. Very different from London.

Caio would say that messages in dreams are esoteric ideas belonging to the dumb and foolish. He would say that it's just your brain organising what you went through during the day. He might be right, and if he is, I know that my brain or my hormones are organising a few thoughts. One is that I felt something for the man at the bookshop and the other is that I need to read the book in order.

Aligned in the middle-centre of the first page is the book title, *The Betrayed*. The next page shows *To You*, a generic dedication handwritten written in cursive letters. I try one more time to find more information on the book, author, publisher, but I find nothing again. So, I read the book in order.

Illustration 1: A woman looks at herself in an oval baroque mirror that was designed to hang on a wall. She can hold it in one hand, though it is disproportionately much larger than her. The woman, with her back to me, the reader, has straight, short, black hair. She is thinner than I would consider healthy. In the mirror, her image shows she has light, wavy, long, full, voluminous hair, full lips and an almost imperceptible nose. Her eyes are perfectly outlined by well-made eyebrows and seductive make-up. A corset grips her breasts tightly and makes her waist look much smaller than it should be.

The image in the mirror does not seem to match the person holding it. Is it a mirror or a frame around a hole in a wall, where there is another woman on the other side? The drawing is quite dark and does not answer my question. In tiny letters on the edges of the mirror are the words *Mirror, Mirror . . .*

I complete the sentence in my head, *on the wall . . . / Who's the fairest of them all?* So famous to anyone who has seen or read the modern version of *Snow White*. Kind of clichéd, cheesy.

When I turn the page, the phrase is not what I expected. The spread of two pages is covered with a bunch of arches like heads in a crowd. Only one is coloured in with ink. Next to it, something is written in miniscule font: *Who would I be amongst them all?* What are they trying to say? Are we so insignificant by being the same, or are we following everyone despite being different?

I observe who is around me. Families playing (which reminds me of Fleur's baby shower next Saturday. I still need to buy her a present), couples holding hands, friends sitting around having a picnic, a few people setting up a stage for an event, dogs chasing balls, people walking alone . . . *Who would I be amongst them all?* I, sitting under this tree, am as insignificant to that person walking on the other side of the park as they are to me. But, of course, we all think we are the special one: the coloured little dot in an equal and purposeless crowd. Are we all so unimportant? No, we cannot be. We are all unique, aren't we?

The next illustration is the image I saw last night—out of order—of the woman on the beach. The thoughts come again: Are we all so self-absorbed to only care for ourselves? Or are we that insecure we need to look like everyone else? I don't spend too much time considering this. I'm sure there will be a conclusion to this book. The visual story seems to jump from individual to relational. Now, a spread shows a man and a woman opposite in a sphere, interconnected almost like a yin-yang symbol. They are smiling. Out of them, as in an explosion, comes a bunch of happy little silhouettes. They look like children playing. They've scattered *From pleasure, pleasure is born* in fonts exploding like fireworks.

The next drawing doesn't need words to be read, as it touches me in a place I knew existed but never appreciated. A grown woman, wearing high heels, earrings, a dark-coloured dress and neatly cut short hair, which is flying in the wind while she holds a torn piece of paper. It is clearly a contract. There are some indecipherable lines and a signature on it. Part of it has fallen to the wind. Facing the grown woman, there is a little girl, wearing a balloon-and-flower-print dress, barefoot and without accessories. She looks like the adult woman, same type of hair, but longer, more natural, flying free in the wind. Both are sad. The girl is on the left-hand page, the woman on the right-hand page. This illustration is about the contract we have broken with ourselves. That part of us that always wanted to be happy and play forever, but as we become adults, we lose that innocent and true freedom.

I turn the page to avoid a life crisis before I even hit the middle of it. The torn contract now appears large on both pages, images of people having fun, jumping, rolling, running around without clothes, kissing and dancing, among other bodily satisfactions, spoilt by stamps that say *ugly, dirty, can't, wrong, behave.* There is no need to analyse these images too much. For the average person, it is enough food for thought: we are told that all that gives us pleasure is wrong.

The book becomes more explicit and adult from that point. A disturbing figure of a woman—once again—looking distant, apathetic, with a sad, lopsided smile and her hands on her chin, receives a superimposition of another face: transparent, like a shadow or a ghost. This other face screams and seems to want to get out, seems to need to escape.

I hesitate to continue. I ponder when I will stop reading the book to get back to work. It's getting late. I think that's enough reading for today; definitely a book that makes you reflect. Work awaits me.

*

It's 7:07 p.m. when I press send. That's it. My boss has the presentation in her hands now. My tiredness and my fear of going out alone at night make me call a taxi. I call my mother as soon as I tell the driver my address. Security measures. She doesn't answer—as our neighbour said, she's travelling. I try calling Bianca, my friend since forever, the one I can spend months without talking to, yet every time we meet it is as if we have never been apart. I feel bad for not having seen her more while we have both been in Sydney, but between my overtime and her work—social media goddess that she is—we have only met up once. She chatters with a contagious cheerfulness about all the things she will do around the world. It will be sad to see her leave again. It is only when I sit on the couch with my legs up that she makes me promise to meet her tomorrow for another goodbye.

*

Bianca is one of those amazing women who doesn't wait for anyone to give her anything. She goes after what she wants and usually gets it. Not always, but usually things turn out okay for her. She is about to go on a journey around the world to research the origins of foods and spices. She said she is expanding her brand to include healthy foods because one of her biggest pleasures in life is eating well. Her hope is to gain enough of a following that will allow her to attract sponsors and spend her life travelling. I've known Bibi, as those closest to her affectionately call her, since our primary school days, and while it's nice to have her in Sydney, I know she's just passing through.

I wait on the Bondi lawn. I can attribute my happiness over the past few months to our few yet rich endless afternoons, chatting and laughing over the ludicrous comments of her unfaithful followers. She tries to respond to all of them with warmth and affection. As she says: *I don't spread hate, I spread love and understanding.*

The only reason I don't have a heart attack after being abruptly hugged from behind as if I were a puppy is her shouting my nickname, Nanú. The name only she and my family use. Bianca appears with an unrecognisable look: short, reddish and curly hair.

'What's that face? You look like you've seen a ghost!' she tells me, overflowing with joy.

'A ghost who changed from blonde to redhead when she died,' I say, referring to the change in her looks.

We laugh like good friends do, freely. She tells me that her thing now is to be a brunette like me, or a redhead, because being blonde was too *démodé*. She asked her fans, and they voted for red hair. They said it would highlight her freckles. And yes, they were right.

'I wasn't born exotic like you, with that Amazonian Indian skin, those Nordic eyes and that perfect body.'

'I'm not going to brag about genes. There's nothing perfect about my body. It's a product of too little food and too much running. How much did you sell your blonde highlights for?'

'A wonderful price! A one-year trip around the world, alone, but with a team that sends me money every week and solves visa problems, gets tickets and things like that for me. If, after three months, I manage to increase my followers to one and a half million, they'll give me a crew!'

'A camera operator?

'I hope so. Someone to film will help me make more professional videos. Fingers crossed they choose a *he*, a hot and funny one.' She says giggling.

Bibi's freedom is admirable. Nothing seems to shake her self-confidence and the certainty that everything is temporary. The impermanence that I should accept.

'Why don't you come with me?' she invites me.

Maybe I should, but the idea of spending my days posting my life on social media makes me nauseous. She agrees with me on this, but she rebels when I say I want to stop moving around the world.

'Please, woman! Since when does Nanú stop moving around? That's not my friend!'

'I think I want to stay here, wait for Caio to come back and try to move things forward . . . I don't know. He kind of asked me to marry him . . .'

'Is that what you want?'

'I don't know. It's logical, right? We've been together forever.'

'And a day.'

'So, I should want to marry him.'

'Not necessarily. The time you spent together is nothing compared to how much is left for you two to live. Think *forty years*.' She opens her eyes wide, making fun.

'Before Sydney, I was sure. I think. I would have said yes.'

'Maybe Sydney is saving you.' She has that inspirational tone in her voice.

'Maybe, maybe not.'

'You can come with me, be my photographer! Use your camera again . . . But you can stay on your own. You are the only person who will be with you until the end. Know what you want.'

I rest my head on her shoulder, and she wraps her arms around mine. True friendship.

'What are you going to do with your flat in Kirribilli? You rented it for six months, didn't you?'

'Yeah. I'll do one of those seasonal rental deals. So, in case something goes wrong with my new enterprise, aka trip around the world, I can get back into the flat in a few days. I put it all in my business plan. It is easier to leave an apartment here with my furniture than sell everything and then have to buy it all again. When I come back, I'll buy another mattress, and that's it. I have a home.'

'What about Sean? You guys keep missing each other . . . ,' I ask subtly. What I should have asked is if they are together, as they don't seem to have a commitment to each other. When she is not travelling, Sean, her Scottish boyfriend, is the one who is not around. They have been *together* for almost three years, but I am not sure how much time they actually spend together. They always seem to be so in love, though.

'Get this!'

She laughs heartily and then explains that they agreed not to have any obligations towards each other, and that when the time came to settle down, get married, have children, etc., then they would see what they want to do, but it isn't time for that yet.

'How do you know it's not the time?'

'Because I want to go. I want to fly around the world and . . . it's my thing, it's for me, it makes me happy. It feels right. He doesn't want to accompany me, nor does he want to stay here. We have no obligation to anyone else. So why not do it if we feel compelled to? We will meet in Thailand next month. When I feel that the world we are going to build together is more interesting than the world out here, we'll see what we do. We love each other. I really love him.'

I know she does. I pause. Shaken and lost. *It feels right.* What is it I do that feels right? I stare at the infinity of the sea. She knows I'm absorbing her words and her energy. She waits long enough for my reflection to sink in before drawing my attention again. Her face appears between the horizon and me.

Holding my chin, she says, 'Nanú, it is as if something is calling me to do this . . . and it's not my followers, as you will say. It's something stronger than me. It's an excitement, an urge to go out screaming, running, jumping . . . I want to go out to play!' She holds both hands against her heart. 'You still remember what this is, don't you?'

I smile, delighted, drawing a connection with the scene I saw in the book earlier of the girl and her adult self. Of the stamps staining the happy, joyful and pleasurable moments. We hug and continue to reminisce about our lives together. She is like a blanket on winter days and the beach on summer days. She is the sister I have never had.

When the sun starts to cool down, I take her to the bus stop on Campbell Parade.

'Make sure you get back to swimming, okay?' She looks at me, holding my face to make sure my gaze doesn't stray from hers. That look of concern and reassurance; I know she knows exactly what I need. 'As always, call me! Text me! I will miss you, sister!'

'You call me too! Tell me where you want to be followed, and I will create an account. I promise. I want to see everything you're doing!'

She rolls her eyes, knowing I'm teasing her, and that making a social media account just for her would be a proof of love. We smile, knowing we won't see each other for at least a year. It's pointless holding back the tears. These separations hurt, but it's not the first and it won't be the last. By tomorrow, we will both be without this tightness in our chests, stomachs, legs, soul.

'I miss you already!'

As soon as the 333 departs, so does my friend, embarking on an adventure of her own.

Does it feel right to stay? It is impossible not to feel a twinge of envy. I wish I had half her confidence, charm and courage. I check my phone to distract myself from the emptiness left by this moment. There's no message from Caio or anyone else. I call Mum on my way back home, hoping that she has returned from her trip. Nothing. I text her friend Denise. If anyone knows where Mum is, it's her.

Hi dear! Your mother and I are on a retreat! They say it's spiritual, Zen. We laugh a lot, we sing songs! You should come next time! We can't check our phones, but I couldn't resist. I want to see the grandchildren. So, I'm sneaking out—guilty—and I saw your message.

I admire the patience that some people have to write these Homeric messages on their phones. Two more messages arrive, one with photos of the two in a group full of nature lovers. The other message explains what they did one morning: *We woke up early to sing to the sun and play crystal bowls.* I can't prevent a smile.

Thanks, Dê! Have fun! I'll talk to her tomorrow, I write back, happy to know that my mother is well and in good company. It eases the guilt of abandoning her.

*

The book is my solitary companion for the night.

There's not much to decipher. Up until now, the message has been quite clear. I open it where I had left off—following the instructions of the man at the bookshop. I see a man's hand holding a spoon with a dessert on it. It is a peach cut to look like a woman's bum with some cream over it. The word *pécher*, which in French means *to sin*, is engraved on the handle of the spoon.

I remember the story of a dessert called peach Melba, which we used to eat a lot at Grandma's house when we were children. From memory, the sweet was a chef's invention for an Australian opera singer. It was an act of love and passion. Is that what they want to say here, that we are only allowed to have pleasure if we are in love? Could they be saying gluttony is the sin? That doesn't seem right. Why do they depict having fun with the body as ugly and dirty in the previous image, but here, a man can use a woman's body as if she is food? Is that not a sin? Are the pleasures of the body only allowed to man? I will keep reading; I'm sure it will all make sense in the end.

Then I see seven little Russian dolls across both pages. Each one differs from the other. The dolls get progressively happier as they get smaller. Only the last one, the little one, which is inside all the others, seems to be happy. Do they represent the stages of life? Can only children be joyful? What happens that makes us so miserable as we grow? How many layers do we have to peel back before we find the happy one? How many lives live inside of me? How many *me* are in me?

The scene I delighted in at the bookshop, that of the woman who turns into a butterfly while crawling creatures try to pin her to the ground, appears now. I look at the man around her hips and wonder if he is helping or delaying her transformation. He may be doing both. He may be the one who is devoted to her freedom, the one who creates a safe place for her pleasure by keeping the pests away. But, while still on the ground, he won't be able to fully let her go. What if he allowed himself to join her? Can we grow together with someone? Can two people ever be set free at the same time? Who are the people who help us peel away the layers of worms and mud, and who are those who leave us stuck to them? How do we know which person in our lives helps us be free and which holds us like parasites?

Caio comes to mind. As a parasite. A thought I will never share with anyone. I'm embarrassed to even consider this. But what can I do? That must be how I feel. Is he holding me back? How can it be? I travelled the world because of him. Am I being ungrateful?

I must keep going. Two blank pages with the word *Liberty* written on them, followed by two more pages where, on the right-hand side, a woman seems to emerge from inside a snake, as if she were the snake itself shedding its skin. On the left-hand page, a lobster loses its shell, giving way to a man, as if the lobster had turned into the man or the man had taken off the carcass he was wearing. The only writing says *to all.* Freedom to all. Shedding our boundaries, our outer shells.

The next set of blank pages says *Equality*, moving on to an illustrated spread where a man, on the left page, gushes with pleasure while a faceless woman lies on the bottom corner of the right page. Her illustration is densely painted black, while he has a clear background with dense black outlines. Contrast. Equality. They are making it clear: equality between genders is also a problem in the realm of carnal pleasure. I wonder if women—me included—are ashamed and if men are blind to the problem. Maybe this image is about all women who were—and are—sexually abused. Can we be equal in sex?

I predict that when I turn the page, the drawing will be that of a woman with a partner reaching orgasm with the saying *to all.*

I'm right. Except that it's unclear who is the man and who is the woman. I suppose that is even more appropriate: *all* is hard to define. I think the fun is about to begin.

If the first subtitle was *Liberty*, the second *Equality*, I'm sure the next one will be *Fraternity* and an illustration saying *to all.* I'm right. What does the French Revolution have to do with desire? I remember classes from school, uni and the lengthy conversations my parents would engage in at home. Two things come to mind: the beginning of the revolution, when women marched to the palace to demand better prices for bread, and the fact that the revolution was not to free women. Despite having started the revolution, their role as mother figures was reinforced—considered to be a civic action by the philosophers of the time.

Fraternity to all shows a party where several people bow to each other, women bow to women, men bow to men, and men bow to women. Everyone is in the same position, naked but wearing masks that cover their entire heads. What does this mean? We can be civilised when we don't know who the other person is? It doesn't make sense, does it? Can a party like this exist? Maybe at a nudist community, where people are comfortable with their own—and others'—bodies. I can't imagine it working well at a normal nightclub, where I have been grinded, pushed, bumped, squeezed and otherwise intruded upon by strangers' hands and body parts.

A page that reads *The Key* comes up next.

I want to keep reading despite the time. It's 9:47 p.m. But I also need—and want—to say goodnight to Caio. I call him. He doesn't answer, so I just send a brief message: *Is everything OK? You haven't said good night yet. I missed you. I'm going to bed, xx.*

A new illustration shows several hanging bird cages with windows in the background stacked like a multistorey building. They give the impression that the cages are on the street, outside the buildings. The two closest and drawn in more detail have, in each one, a hybrid animal. Half human, half bird, one male and one female.

The male cage is open, and the animal is standing, with its very athletic body, on the wire of its door. Her cage, on the other hand, is locked, with a key hanging by a thin chain underneath, as well as several small objects: a magnet, a magnifying glass, a mirror and a clock that shows seven o'clock, among other objects that seem unimportant. She can't get the key, nor does she seem to know that there are these objects that can help her.

I have a familiar feeling that I have seen these cages somewhere before. Maybe in London?

The image of the couple in the alley comes next, together with a wish that my dream with the man from the bookshop had been true. I notice more detail in the illustration, looking at it a second time. She wears a watch marking seven o'clock, just like the one from the cage drawing. Are there others? I flick back the pages and find another one with the same design in the fraternity party illustration. Why is it repeating throughout the book? What happens at seven o'clock?

The building in the next illustration is named Portia. To the common eye, it could pass by as an artist's impression of a rich Victorian construction, but to the trained architect, it is a replica of the Strand Arcade, the shopping haven connecting George Street and Pitt Street Mall. A woman with wavy, long hair, wearing a tight, long dress on her curvy body, stilettos, a bag holding a feather and large sunglasses steps out through the arches of the façade. The street is water, and she seems to be able to walk on it. Two men walk behind her, one on either side, water up to their knees. The tip of a Venetian gondola appears on the right-hand page. There is a poster in the shop window with the writing: *Put on a mask to reveal your truth.* I can only imagine that this is a reference to Italian carnival masks and *The Merchant of Venice*—because of the name Portia.

From this mix of Shakespeare and Sydney, we are back to an undoubtably Aussie landscape: Harbour Bridge. A man reads a newspaper with the bridge and the Opera House behind him. He has a suitcase by his side, and the folded part of the newspaper that faces the reader has a large inverted number 2.

His watch marks seven o'clock. Another seven. His broad shoulders and upright posture while sitting on the bench make him look fit and strong. The wrinkles on his face clearly show he is a few decades older than me. He has a confident smile and is quite attractive, but no one around him seems to notice him. People with sculptural bodies exercise around him. They all look sad. I'm not quite sure what this image means. Maybe beauty is to be relaxed within yourself? What if you like running and having a defined body? As long as you are happy, I suppose?

Next, the spread has a poem with seven stanzas. Seven again. What's up with this number? And a faded pencil-drawn sketch underneath it. It's the Harbour Bridge again but seen from George Street, on the Rocks. It's very different from the rest of the book. Is this the start of a new chapter? The poem says:

White Petunias
Break on pillars like waves
Believing man to walk
Over the water as they crave

When the sea is pink
Those who scrape the sky
In the finite horizon bring
The hidden Paradise

A petal holds as many colours
As the garden in front of it
Where the birds and children
Are as botanical as it.

When the night sky glows purple near your feet
The best place is the Fort on the Lower Street
Celeste will shelter all those who
Fear to see

Remember to follow the path
To the mill
When yellow surrounds
All the joy around

The green leads you
To a secret place
Where across the cove you see
Only sails of concrete

And the day the colours are too many
Know there's nowhere to go
Just go it alone
The path that is yours to own.

The last illustration I cast my eyes on before falling asleep shows a stone-carved arch in the classic European style, but with a thematic difference. Usually, these buildings have erudite images of members of the clergy and royalty. Not here. Here, they are normal, ordinary people. The carving on the left side of the arch is of a couple lying with their backs bent, clearly in an intimate pose. Both watch what happens on the other side, where four children are innocently playing and laughing. Between the two sides of the arch, there is a winking face. Delightfully funny. I have seen something like this before, but I am so tired that I let myself fall asleep, after, of course, setting the alarm for five hours from now. I won't be able to wake up without an alarm.

5

I feel lazy. I take the bus to work. Lazy. Maybe I'm paying the price for staying up too late reading. Reading and trying to figure out what that book means. I photographed the entire book. Page by page. I won't be carrying it around until I need to pass it on. The very last page says *We are waiting for you* in cursive letters. The inside of the *o* in *you* has lines in bold, looking like the hands of a clock marking, again, seven o'clock. I create an album on my phone with all the images that have a time on them and realise the first one is the party, where everyone is naked, wearing a mask, unrecognisable. *We are waiting for you*: the last page. Waiting for me where? At the party, at the Strand Arcade, at a cage, under the bridge, at the opera house? In an alleyway? What am I missing?

The bright blue sky and the terrible traffic accompanies me until I get to the grey and stylish office just before 9:00 a.m. I promise to never take the bus again. What a waste of time. I feel flat and late.

As I stare at my computer, I allow my brain to parallel process and come to its own conclusions about the book and the man at the bookshop. Some people smile at me; others shout good morning to everyone. It's nice to have some time to be civil instead of pumping through a deadline and ignoring the world.

Despite not really knowing what to do next, I can't help but think this book is a treasure map. They are waiting for me somewhere; all I need to do is find the road that will take me there. Thank you, bookshop man!

My excitement is crushed at 10:00 a.m. when the real world knocks. *She* arrives, disrupting my morning by demanding last-minute changes to the project. She justifies to herself that the design needs to improve because she wants the client to be happy. The stress that last-minute changes cause is completely ignored. I won't have time to breathe until the meeting. My peace is gone. Worst of all, she continuously interrupts me to tell her weekend stories and the reason she is always late on Mondays. Honestly, I am not interested. Her reasons are always the same, with small variations on the theme. They are more excuses for her Sunday night drinking habit, which leads to her not being able to get up early the next day. I'm compelled to cut her monologue short, politely and in a very pragmatic way—with data.

'Sorry, but without wanting to interrupt you, I need to finish the perspectives with the modifications you asked for, and we only have a little over an hour before the clients arrive,' I state in the most emotionless way I can manage right now.

I have not seen this look on her face before. She's not angry, not embarrassed, not apologetic. Her million words per minute disappear. She smiles, keeping her lips together. I blink.

'Right. I will leave you alone to do what you know how to do best.' She speaks, and her anger is there in the tone. A passive-aggressive tone.

*

The meeting goes well, except for the *Tayeenah* overly emphasised, as if she has to prove to the clients that she is not xenophobic. I don't think she is. If anything, she is more afraid of me for being younger than her. She is just insecure. I don't even know if she is sexist, even though she treats men better than women. I think that is just how she was conditioned; it's a survival mechanism for someone working a male-dominated profession. I don't think she is doing herself any favours. I notice the clients' subtle body reactions when she pronounces my name: eyebrows lifting, deep inhales, forehead rubbing, leaning forward, leaning backwards . . . I'm sad for her. Annoyed, yes, as I am every time she pronounces my name. I want to leave the country. But I'm mostly sad for her. I don't even think she knows what she is doing.

At 1:05 pm, the woman who talked to me during the weekend bumps into us on our way out of the meeting and tells my boss to give me the afternoon off in recognition of my effort and dedication over the last few weekends working. Of course, the cow didn't like it one bit, but she doesn't seem to contest her suggestion. I imagine this woman is higher up in the chain, or why else would my boss agree?

'Tainá, remember to put our chat in my calendar,' she says with a perfect pronunciation of my name, exuberantly cheerful and energetic.

I answer yes, I will do it soon. Ashamed of not knowing her name to find her calendar and book the time, I ask Fleur, who is equally oblivious. She only knows that the woman is the new director of human resources—I hate this expression: *human resources*. Surely, we are more than resources. Fleur says they announced her name last Friday during Friday night drinks, which I missed because I was working, and she missed because she went home to her family. I think about asking Lynette, but she's already gone out to lunch. I'll have to schedule that meeting later.

A few people follow Fleur, Tommy, and I down to Martin Place but soon disperse as we get to the street. Gossip runs wild once we are out of the office, which is fun, but I can't help but be distracted by the GPO building as we wait for the traffic lights. By coincidence, luck or mere observation, I notice that the arches on the Pitt Street façade don't have classical motifs as they would if they were late-nineteenth-century buildings. Here, the sculptures in the arches are of ordinary people and contrast with those on the main façade on Martin Place, which do have the expected classical motifs. I google the building on my phone and *voilà!* The *website* tells me that this Pitt Street façade, carved by an Italian immigrant, caused a furore and much confusion at the time for putting the spotlight on a fishmonger, a bar attendant and a postman—banal professions that should never be celebrated in a work of architecture this important. I discover in my search that this façade is considered by many to be the beginning of art in Australia. A break from traditions, from paradigms. The illustration in the book is a reimagining of those arches! It makes perfect sense for the book! I also learn that the building went through some reforms and now, besides the post office, it also houses a hotel, some luxury shops—which are noticeable from Martin Place—and a food court.

'Guys, how about we eat at the GPO?' I ask.

'*Oooh!* A luxurious treat on a Monday?' says Tommy.

'I'm in! Who cares about saving money to buy baby stuff, right? I want to feast before the baby is here. I know that then, I'll barely have time to eat a grape!' Fleur always jokes about her maternal life.

The slow walk to keep pace with my friend on her third trimester doesn't take away the excitement and joy of celebrating our lunch and time together. My local friends always get ecstatic about marble floors, something normal for those of us who grew up in Brazil, as we see it there everywhere, even in footpaths. What impresses me more is how architects can manipulate people's feelings and beliefs about themselves: here, we feel small, inadequate, poor. This building's enormous height, the light coming from above, the wide spaces, and two grandiose semicircular staircases that converge down towards the basement as a focal point make it feel like a modern cathedral; at work here are the same design principles, to make us feel less valuable. Downstairs, at the bars, the prices confirm we don't belong and make us feel awkward, inadequate. I call the shots; I have plenty to treat my coworkers, since Caio's company pays the rent.

'Are you sure?' Tommy says with a genuine gratitude in his eyes.

'You can't pay, Tatá! You just started working here . . . don't be crazy.' Fleur tries to protect my money.

'Don't worry, I have enough. It's on me; just don't order lobsters and . . . champagne?' I am clueless when it comes to price of alcohol.

'Bless this woman!' He hugs me. 'Look, *Fleurie*, may your children not be architects. We better start telling them now to choose money over passion; they need to take their godfather—me—to eat in fancy places like this . . . Did you hear this, dude?' He talks to her belly, and we agree that there is not the slightest possibility of Fleur letting her children be architects.

'They can be engineers, earn twice as much and work half as hard,' I say, letting slip what nobody has the courage to say in front of other people.

We've barely chosen our food when my mind starts wandering through everything I've absorbed in the last few days and what I still have to do with this book. Tommy notices my long-distance gaze and interrupts it by asking who I am thinking of to be smiling like that. I didn't know I was smiling. After much insistence from his part and my commitment to not saying anything about the book, I find some precious moment I had with Caio in the past and tell him about it. I quickly change the focus to Tommy's life, playing the role of love counsellor—not that Fleur and I know much about the homosexual world, but love is love, and the dynamics of matters of the heart seem as universal across cultures as they do across genders. It's all the same. As soon as Tommy thanks us for being the best friends in the world, I feel I can leave for my afternoon off. I barely touch my food. I apologise for my tiredness and excuse myself—I lie; I'm not tired. I'm curious, impatient. I need to know where this book will lead me to. I can't leave it alone until I unveil the secrets that the book holds about this city.

Put on a mask to reveal your truth. The phrase in the illustration that camouflages the Strand as Portia starts a wave of excitement and worry. What will I discover with this quest? It can be joyful and pleasurable if my reading of the book is right, but it can also be painful. We all know the atrocious things one can do when it comes to the pleasures of the body. Imagination is a powerful tool.

In the absence of another solid clue, I decide to disguise myself to avoid any misunderstanding or embarrassment as I start this investigation. Who knows what or who I will find in the Strand? I withdraw some cash from my account. It's not some; it's a lot of money. I make my way to a costume shop near Wynyard and pick out the best wig I can find. It's still not convincing, but I have no other choice. I consider buying some cheap clothes, but I can't bring myself to throw money away on five-dollar outfits. I stop by my favourite activewear shop and spend a good sum of money on new leggings, a jacket, a cap, gloves, a scarf and a bag big enough to hold my work clothes. The last stop before I can continue to the book quest is to walk into a sports shop on the corner of King Street to get new running shoes, which I should have bought long ago. It's not a purchase exclusive to this endeavour, so I buy them on the credit card to make Caio happy. He complains often that I don't spend money on myself.

The adrenaline makes me stride, erect, spindly and smiling. I must have gained a couple of inches with the thrill. I feel as if I own the street, as if I've won the lottery. I go into the first pub that appears in front of me and immediately regret it. I should have chosen a department store like David Jones or Myer. The impregnating smell of old, dry beer on the carpet mixes with the guilt that I'm doing something wrong. Am I doing something wrong? Yes. If it were right, I wouldn't be disguising myself, would I? If it were right, maybe I should tell Caio. He would never support such an adventure. He would tell me to focus on my work and stop living in fantasy land. 'We could use this book as inspiration,' he would say, hinting at the erotic positions we could use in our quiet lives.

It's amazing how beer stinks anywhere in the world. It is not possible that those who design bars have not yet found a solution to this problem. Disgust invades me through my nostrils, preventing my interior design thoughts from coming to a conclusion. I walk around the place, looking for the toilets. I am doing something wrong for the first time in my life, and as much I am cursing myself, I am drawn to continue. I can't stop here; I know there is something incredible to be discovered. I will never have an opportunity like this again. I need to move on. I need to find out what this party is about—if it's a party. I hope it's not somewhere I need to be naked, wearing only a mask, like in the illustration. I'm not a nudist, nor a banquet to a bunch of freaks. I wonder what would happen at a party like that. Maybe there are no freaks. Maybe it would be just a nudist celebration party? It can't be. I can't imagine they would go through all the logistics and mystery for that. They have beaches and other places to go. I only hope that, at the end of this investigation, I don't find a vulgar, promiscuous, and disgusting place.

The toilet, unlike the rest of the pub, is very clean, spacious and well designed. The contemporary finishes push away the disgust I feel. I stare in the mirror. A shy smile and worried eyebrows. I'm going to do this. I look around. I'm alone. The silent toilet takes me to another world. I look into the mirror one more time. Who am I now? My blood pulses faster, like the waves in the middle of the ocean. They don't crash. They flow. An inspired smile and softened eyebrows. I go into the cubicle nearest me. The sole of my shoe skidding on the cold, polished floor adds a tone of comedy to this scene. What is this movie of my life? What am I doing? A light chuckle comes out of my throat. Who would believe me if I told them all this?

A good observer would appreciate my wonder at finding two hooks for bags behind the door. Anyone who has never had to go into a public toilet carrying more than one thing would be flabbergasted to find that I have an emotional response to such small items. The hooks behind the door of the cubicle are my marble floors. I could never get them back home. I put my bag on one, and the other gets my overcoat.

The bag with my new purchases lies on the floor near the door. I quickly sit down on the toilet, its lid sinking slightly with my weight, and I get a little fright. For a moment, I think I have broken the lid and will have to abort the whole operation to talk to the manager and pay for the seat. I'm relieved when I see that the top has not broken. I put my feet up. I take off my shoes and trousers. A creak makes me shiver. There is someone else in the bathroom.

I know the chances of it being someone from work are slim, but I need to protect my identity. I'm not that far from there, and it could be a colleague. How would I explain what I'm doing here? If I'm identified, it could put an end to this mysterious party. With my legs still raised against the cubicle door, I carefully pull the bag with the new clothes close to me, so as not to draw attention in case someone I know has entered the bathroom. I put on my leggings, socks and trainers, I carefully place my work clothes into the gym bag. I hear someone else flushing. Confident in being disguised from the knee down, I get up to finish changing Tainá from work into Tainá the sportswoman-ninja-journalist. The fear of what's to come and the exhilarating anticipation of the unknown keep me fuelled with adrenaline. I take off my cardigan and blouse and fold them carefully into my gym bag as my thoughts try to be a voice of reason: *You have a boyfriend! Who has been with you for seven years! Seven years living everywhere—so many things you've been through together. He saved your life! If it wasn't for him, a cheetah would have devoured you! Tainá . . . go home, run on the beach, do yoga on the sand, warm up in the sun and wait for him. Soon you will be together again!*

I consider with affection my judicious voice and decide to ignore it. I'd rather throw myself into the unknown in the hope of scaring away my boredom and collecting one more story to remember. Distance separates; if Caio were here, I wouldn't even have opened the book. Maybe I wouldn't have even seen it.

I continue getting ready, with my black long-sleeved top and my new hooded and zipped jacket, also black. A two-metre-long thick scarf in a shade between nude and pink twists around my neck; the ends fall forward just above my waist. I'm almost done. Now, all I need are the wig and the cap. I stop to listen to the noise of another person in the bathroom. There's no one here. I must be going crazy. I step out of my cubicle, and the mirror is right in front of me. I can't manage to place the wig properly. I need to step out of the cubicle. I need to lock the toilet. The door—very wisely—has no latch, but they forgot to make built-in bins, so I improvise a lock, dragging the full trashcan over and placing it behind the door. I wash my hands thoroughly and try to put on my wig as I read the instructions. This takes longer than I expected, until 2:20 p.m. It feels like I've been here for hours, but not even ten minutes have passed.

The wig is dreadful, a bunch of nylon threads stuck to my head. I doubt anyone will recognise me from afar, but I realise now the blonde wig seems like a bad idea. People look more at blonde women; maybe I should have chosen red hair, but I guess people still look at redheads more than blondes. I tie my fake hair into a low ponytail covering my ears. It looks less horrendous.

I push the trashcan back into place. I wash my hands, look in the mirror once more, and bump into her. A different person. Not me, inside or out. Divided inside, decided outside. Caio is there working, thinking about our future, and here I am disguising myself to start a treasure hunt that, as far as I know, will take me to a hedonistic party. Where I may become a cheater. I won't. I will find out all I can about the book and the party, then I'll decide what to do with it. I don't think the party is now, at the Strand. It's just a hint; it's just the beginning.

My watch is still on my wrist. I hide it under my long sleeve instead of taking it off. I wish I had bought some cheap glasses to wear, but mine have such a common aviator style that they would not be the thing that would make someone associate me with her—the woman in the mirror. There's no space in my new gym bag for my overcoat, a flaw in my planning, so I am forced to carry it to avoid any possible identification. Overcoats can easily give away your identity.

The few people who extend their lunch hour to 2:30 p.m. don't seem to care who goes in and out of the toilets, so I continue to walk to the front door and leave the bar without consuming anything or talking to anyone. I feel silly for thinking I needed to be so careful.

As it should be, my cover is put to the test as soon as I reach the corner of George and King Streets and bump shoulders with a man about my height. He looks at me and apologises. He's our client, the director of the fashion magazine, and he's with my boss! She looks right into my face, but I'm not surprised when she doesn't recognise me. Surely, she is more interested in herself and impressing him, so I carry on, relieved and energised.

If there's one thing my wandering years have taught me, it's to get lost in style. Every self-respecting immigrant and tourist knows that standing adrift on the street is a sure way to become a target for strange happenings. A decided, steady walk is sure to make you look like you belong somewhere, and that's how I explore the ground floor of the Strand, naively believing something would be right in front of the public eye. It wouldn't be so simple. I glance through the directory at the entrance, but there are no names that I can relate to the illustration or the book. I search for any and all signs that might lead me somewhere closer to where I have to go. *Put on a mask to reveal your truth* repeats endlessly in my head. The first floor seems more promising, but after paying attention to each shop, from the name to the logo design, to the details on the doorknobs to the clothes of the attendants, after circling the floor twice—once on each side of the mezzanine—and getting nothing, my hope starts to fade away. Nothing is connecting back to the book. I give way to a grey cloud hovering above my head. I must be delusional thinking this book translates into the real world.

It's not until the very last shop—as it ought to be—that the corner of my lips turns up in hope again. It is all true! The shop sign says *Portia* in cursive calligraphy. It's more like an art gallery than a store. I am greeted by the sound of bossa nova, and, to my delight, it is not 'Garota de Ipanema,' as the cliché would have it. It's 'Samba de um Nota Só,' by João Gilberto. Although I love the embrace the music gives me, bringing back great memories of my childhood afternoons, I also remember the day those afternoons stopped. Grief is a ghost, showing up at the most inconvenient times, when we least expect to revive the pain of when you lost part of yourself. Grief is a curse, reminding you happiness doesn't happen for those who loved. How can you not love though? Why don't they play something in Italian? Why Brazilian music? Is anyone following me? Am I being paranoid?

Everything is in shades of white, except the masks. Colourful, they are displayed on pedestals at eye level. Some are hung on the wall. It's like being in the middle of the clouds flying around birds.

Most of the masks cover a good part of the face; only a few leave your jaw fully exposed. The full-face ones look like they've been flown in from the traditional Venice carnival and remind me why I don't like masks. They look alive and dead at the same time. I much prefer the contemporary and geometric ones.

Why masks? What am I getting myself into?

There is no one else here, except a man behind the counter, sitting sideways against the door, looking down, and it seems he is reading a magazine. If it weren't for his thinning grey hair, I'd say he was young. His erect, slender posture tells me he could be a frequent swimmer. His skin has no deep wrinkles or sunspots, and I judge he prefers swimming in indoor pools rather than outside on the beach.

'Good afternoon.' Animated and happy, he greets me without looking at me. 'Make yourself at home.'

'Thank you.'

I decide that the clue from the book is to buy a mask to go to their secret party. So, I look through them with more care and purpose, searching for a simple one with as few feathers as possible, that covers most of my face but not all. I don't want to scare anyone by looking dead and alive at the same time. To my surprise—and I'm not sure why I would be surprised by this—there are more masks that cover the whole face, so I am down to a few options, which makes the choice easier.

'Can I help you?' The gentleman turns to me, rising from his chair, and I quickly realise that he is blind.

'Maybe, I'm looking for . . .' I pause to correct my gaffe. 'Browsing . . . I'm browsing for a mask. I've never had one.'

'A young voice, but no longer a girl. Thirty? Twenty-seven years old?'

'Spot on. How do you know my age just by hearing me?'

His gentle, vivid, playful smile enchants me.

'I don't see with my eyes. But nothing stops me from seeing with my ears.'

His serenity brings me so much comfort, yet I feel like an idiot for having asked this question. Of course he can identify someone's age by their voice.

He walks around the pedestals and says without the slightest ceremony: 'You're embarrassed; don't be.'

I put my hand on my glasses to take them off and he surprises me by holding my hand, guiding me to make a choice: 'Eyes don't lie. If you're going to buy a mask without wanting to be discovered, you'd better keep your sunglasses on. Look.' He shows me a camera in the corner between two walls and the ceiling. I leave my glasses where they are.

'What's it like to not rely on your eyes?' I ask.

'Can I touch your face? I promise not to take off your glasses.'

'Yes.'

He rubs his hands together to warm them up, but something tells me he doesn't need to; he seems to emanate warmth and does so only out of kindness, to prepare me. Gently, he touches me symmetrically, tracing every corner of my face. No one has ever touched me like this before. Probably not even myself.

'Is my identity safe? You have seen me now.'

'Yes, but I'll never know your name.' His charming, good-natured smile again makes me feel at peace. 'So, if someone asks if a Fiona came here, I can't say yes or no. But if someone asks me if a woman of a curious, adventurous spirit, with a long, stubby nose came here, I will have to say yes.'

I smile. He makes his way through the shop without bumping into anything, just grazing the pedestals.

'This one, I think it was made for you,' he says, stopping in front of a black mask.

I go to him and to it. I admire the detail of the very fine lace that covers it entirely, even passing over the eye hole. The braid is a beautiful and elegant tangle of twigs, branches and flowers, leaving only the mouth and part of the jaw exposed.

'It will fit you perfectly. Try it on,' he encourages. 'There's a mirror there.' He points at a wall with a mirror that goes from the floor past my head. The frame is detailed in wood painted gold.

I touch the mask apprehensively, as though I'm touching a crystal goblet. It feels so delicate. I stare at myself with the terrible wig, the cap, the scarf. Mirrors can lie. I breathe deeply, on the one hand hesitating about being one step closer to doing something I shouldn't be doing, and on the other hand thinking through the logistics of how to put it on while wearing glasses and avoid being caught on the security camera.

A person walking in the corridor outside interrupts my moment. Will I be able to hide who I am just by covering my face?

'Don't worry, just try it,' he says.

'Are they unique? I mean, do you have any other masks like that?'

'They're not unique. Otherwise, it would be easier to find out who's who, don't you think?'

'That's right.' Of course they can't be unique.

I breathe deeply again to gain courage; I take off my cap and hold it between my legs. I use my two hands to avoid the camera: one holds the mask right over my face and the other takes off my sunnies slowly from underneath the mask at the same time.

'What do you think? Was I right?'

I pause. It is alive. It is *a she*. And this is how we meet.

'I think you were . . . it doesn't cover the whole face though.'

'You have a lot to say. There's no point in covering your mouth.'

'My eyes, on the other hand . . . ,' I say, referring to the layer of lace that goes over the mask's hollow.

'Only for those who deserve it. Few or many, they are only for those you let in.'

'Thank you. It's elegant.' I should have said mesmerising, dazzling, but elegant is what came out.

Like the lattice in good Islamic architecture, the lace over the eyes of the mask allows me to see the world without anyone seeing me. It's a nice feeling, comforting again. The warm air I exhale releases all the anxiety that was trapped in my lungs.

I'm as light as the clouds.

The price tag takes the sublime moment away. It's $650! That's 65 percent of my weekly salary. I can't spend all that money on a mask. If it weren't for Caio paying rent, I'd never be able to afford it. I rationalise. I recall the arguments I have had with Caio over the rent: he doesn't let me pay. It's not his money, it's the company's money. The same company that made us move to Sydney and soon after sent him off to Singapore. If it wasn't for them, I wouldn't be here today. I breathe out the relief of my guilt. I had withdrawn the money anyway.

'I'll take it.'

I open my wallet and take out the money. I am still perplexed at the security of this city. I would never walk around with this amount of cash in any of the places I've lived before, but Sydney is very safe. I hand over the money. It hurts. I feel lighter indeed.

'Here you go—$650.'

That there's only $150 left over racks my stomach. That's a lot of money spent on something I'll only use once.

'You won't regret it. Do you know where to go from here? With the mask?'

'Not quite yet.'

'It's good to check the paper, even more so if you like to travel . . . And your accent gives away that you do . . .'

'Thanks, I will.'

Bloody accent. No matter how hard you try, it is a reality that every immigrant has to live with. You will never be a local, you will never fully fit in.

Still smiling, he delicately takes the money and slowly walks behind the counter. His nimble fingers count the notes, and it is the first time I notice the notes have different lengths, perhaps precisely so that the blind can know the value of each one. An incredible detail that most people have never realised, and sadly never will. Design is awesome when properly done. He uses a machine a little smaller than a toaster, and almost immediately, it announces the amount counted with the voice of an airport woman. As the gentleman exits through a narrow doorway at the back, I flick through the newspaper that sits on the counter. Before I can read anything properly, he reappears with a rectangular black box, lined in fabric, where the mask fits perfectly. On the lid is written a small name: *Illyria*.

'Look after her and you,' he says, cheerfully and enthusiastically.

The name Illyria is pretty. Maybe it could be my codename at the party in case I need it. We must have to have a fake name, right? How do you spend an entire evening with someone without knowing their name? Come to think of it, most lovers at normal parties these days can't remember the name of the person they just mashed up against the wall. Maybe *lover* is too strong of a word to define people who exchange kisses and caresses for a few hours. So maybe, in this context, it is possible to spend an entire night with someone without knowing their name. I am distracted by Illyria again. Do all the boxes have that same name? I don't know. I don't ask either.

'Here, take this newspaper. You'll need it.' He puts it into the bag with the box.

You'll need it sounds like a clue. Why would I need the newspaper? This first stop, the shop with this peaceful man, is encouraging. I think this party is safe.

Proud of my successful discovery between the book's illustration and real life, I walk like a madwoman. It is impossible to contain my excitement despite the horrible disguise I wear. I pick up the phone and pretend to tell someone the news so I can laugh without attracting suspicious attention.

My satisfaction is, however, short-lived, for I think of the shameful amount of money I have spent, and I still don't know where this party is, or when. What if I can't get there? I will have bought that mask for nothing.

There should be more hints in the other illustrations. On my phone, I open the album with the photos I took of them. It doesn't make sense to carry a heavy piece of luggage along the street—the book in this case—or I run the risk of looking like a technology-averse person, like my grandmother.

Perhaps it is because I'm on George Street, perhaps it is because it's the first photo I see on my phone, but I focus on the photo with the illustration of the couple in the alley, seen by a policeman. I can't figure out where it is. In my dream, the alley was an arm of George Street, and I could swear it was Temperance Lane, right near the Strand. But now that I'm here, I don't see much resemblance, especially as there's absolutely nothing to hint at a party. The small bar at the end of the alley isn't big enough to hold a large event, unless there's a secret door leading to a hall or something. I examine the closed door: its frame, the railing, nothing unusual . . . I may have to look elsewhere.

I decide to go to the Rocks as it is the only other part of Sydney that has lots of alleys and lanes. The illustration turns into a map, and I look for architectural similarities between the image on my phone and the three-dimensional reality in front of me. As I walk down George Street, I discover the location of another illustration: Angel Place, with its hanging cages. The plaque explains the permanent artwork and the sounds we hear coming out of them: birds that used to live here but were driven out or made extinct because of us. People, architects, urban planners, politicians, and entrepreneurs who build without thinking about our most valuable resource, nature. I look for the illustration of the cages on my phone. I search for something useful, something hanging, or a hybrid creature sculpture just like in the book. In the absence of a magnifying glass, I use the zoom on my phone's camera to look for a hint, but it doesn't get close enough for me to clearly see it. I breathe in confidence and breathe out shame, summoning the courage to ask a passing tourist who looks to be from Southeast Asia to lend me his semi-professional camera for a few moments.

Based on his nervous expression and stunned reaction, I think he has the impression that I am a thief.

Feuilleton. My French is very rusty, but from what I remember it's a type of serial novel that comes in a newspaper. I have no idea what the name is in English. Maybe I need to look at the newspaper the man at the mask shop gave me. Could there be a password in it? I hand the camera back to him and quickly set myself in motion to the Rocks.

Although I was searching for that alley with the couple, I found the cages, and now I'm sure I've found another confirmation the book is giving me clues. It is indeed a treasure hunt! The flower beds in front of the MCA contain evening petunias, purple with white polka dots, or, for those who see poetry: *When the night sky glows purple near your feet.* I don't quite remember the rest of the poem, but I do remember something concerning the word *fort.* There must be a street or a pub called

Fort somewhere. But I'll look into it later, because right now, I am where I wanted to be in the tangled laneways and alleys of the old part of Sydney, the Nurses Walk in the Rocks. I wonder if all this is just a joke being played by the tourism department.

My quick Google search tells me that Suez Canal is an old street connecting both sides of the Rocks—*den of prostitutes, danger, slavery* it says. It makes perfect sense to have a policeman there. Shifting my eyes between the illustration and the real buildings, I am astonished by how perfectly they overlap. Every window and every stone on the ground. Someone has gone to enormous trouble to put this book and all these tips together.

I put my gym bag and the bag with the mask on the floor, and using another great don't-look-lost-tourist-technique, I look for the clues while taking pictures. I step, jump and observe each stone block in the alley floor; I pull at the ones that seem a bit loose, avoiding the dozens of people who continually pass by.

There's nothing. Nothing . . . I want to cry! It has to be here. I contain the urgent need to sit on the floor and look like a beggar when tiredness and frustration begin to overwhelm me. I grope the bricks on the walls of the buildings, uselessly pushing and pulling at the ones that have some mark or are slightly broken, when I come across one that has a raised symbol. In the same colour as the brick, like a chameleon on the trunk of a tree, there is a snake eating its own tail. I have seen this somewhere before; I just can't remember where or when. My phone dies on me, so I can't even look for what it means. Frustrating. All I can do is to do what it's available to me: press and pull the snake. The brick is wobbly—it's loose!

Before I take it out, I scan my surroundings for a stalker. No one seems to be paying attention to what I'm doing, so I try to move the brick out of place. One more piece of the puzzle is solved, one more clue to unravel. Inside the hole left by the brick, there is a metal key that looks like it was made decades ago, full of twisted and symmetrical details and with an engraved number: *1790*. There is nothing else inside the void in the wall. What is this key for? Can I take it? I must be able to take it. Maybe I need to leave it here and come back once I have something to open. *What if there are other people doing what I am doing?* I think, as I put the brick back on the wall and the key in my pocket. It seems I'm taking the key.

Exhausted, I sit down at the first coffee shop I see in front of me. I have no idea what I'm going to order, I just know I need to sit and think about it all. The sun setting in the sky confirms I've been walking for a few hours, and the cold chair soon warms up thanks to the gas heater beside my table. The waitress brings the menu and tap water; I ask her if she can charge my phone for fifteen minutes. I explain that it is to call a taxi, and, to my surprise, she says okay. What kindness—it really is an incredible city. I take my sketchbook out of my bag—a line-free Moleskine that I gave myself as a present when I got this job, and my solid carbon pencil that I bought at La Sagrada Familia in Barcelona. I doodle and draw to remember the symbol I saw on the brick wall. Hunger speaks louder, and instead of just having a soda water or something to be able to sit down, I decide to eat half a portion of spaghetti carbonara. A small pleasure as a reward. I don't know what I'm rewarding myself for, because so far, all I have is a key, a mask, a newspaper and a lot less money. The key could even be stolen. How would I know? I don't know, but somehow I feel entitled to a nice, hot, greasy dish as a reward. I deny my attendant's wine suggestion and choose the odd combination of eating pasta with tea. While I wait for my phone and my food to arrive, I try to make sense of all the information I have, from the bookstore to this key. I know it's all connected; I just don't know exactly how.

Next to my poorly drawn snake, I write the number 1790 found in the key and *Feuilleton,* from the cage. I write, *GPO*, General Post Office Building, trying to understand why the arches of the building were drawn in the second part of the book. Could it be that the party is in the GPO? I doubt it. I've left the office around seven o'clock at night countless times, and I have never seen any masked people walking around at that time or any other time. Could the building be just to inspire the breaking of paradigms and a new beginning? Maybe, but I can't be sure yet. Without my phone to look for what the snake and the key mean, all I have left is the newspaper to explore.

When I open it, I see an insert called *Feuilleton—Sydney.* There's something here! A rush of excitement pumps my energy up, leaving the tiredness behind. The blind gentleman in the shop didn't put the paper in my bag for nothing! *It's good to check the paper, even more so if you like to travel . . . And your accent gives you away . . .* Travel! The illustration of the guy with a travel bag on the beach and the number two on his newspaper. I flick to the second page; the story is about a woman who travels. The details of the article seem useless, but there's a launch date for her debut book. It's tomorrow. There's no location. It seems like a long shot to relate the party to this date, but what else could it be? It's my only clue, so it'll have to do. All that remains is to find out what to do with this key.

At the end of my meal, with my phone charged and my energies renewed, I summarise what I know again. The petunias will send me to a place called Celeste, which is on Fort Street, or to a pub called Fort—I still need to look for it. It is at 7:00 p.m. Tomorrow, I must wear a mask, and I am certain that I will not be naked. Can this key be my way into the party? A form of invitation? That would be cool.

What I don't know is why the GPO would have been drawn in the second part of the book, as everything in that part belongs to the quest around the city; they are all clues. I also don't know what to do with the symbol of the snake, but this is an easy fix. A quick search on my phone tells me that it is an *ouroboros*, the serpent that devours its own tail. With no relation to cannibalism, the circle represents eternity, alluding to the continuous cycle of rebirth and death. Further research in an academic article I find on Google Scholar delves into its meaning across time. For the Egyptians, to whom its origin is attributed, the serpent eating its own tail symbolises a divine wrapping of protection, but it was the Renaissance Italians who contributed the idea of eternity. Renaissance again. There are also Nordic, Hindu, Greek, Incan and philosophical interpretations; it is fascinating how symbols and their meanings can travel the world for hundreds of years, surviving only through oral tradition and a few pieces of paper, parchment and books that have withstood the weather and the wars. The idea of being in a protected enclosure for all eternity makes me feel as though I am floating in the warmth of a calm tropical sea, hugged by Mum, Dad and Kadu. Flowing gently with the small ripples on the water.

*

It takes me exactly twelve minutes to walk back to the corner of Pitt Street and Martin Place—where the GPO is—and my body is one big goosebump. Not from cold, but from a mixture of fear and excitement. The thought that this key might open the door to a room or a hall with a despicable underworld of vulgar orgies filled with strangers haunts me. I should have gone home but not before exploring what this building can give me; maybe it is the link between the key and the snake symbol.

I judge the key must be related to the hotel and not to the post office; also, I am closer to the hotel entry than to the post office. By conviction or convenience, I head to the reception with wide, determined and undistracted steps, trying not to be discouraged by the opulent atmosphere judging my bad wig and sports clothing.

'Good evening,' I say elegantly, trying to compensate for the cheapness of my fake hair. 'May I ask you if this key is by any chance a key to a room . . . or a hall here?'

From the lack of a receptive smile and the distance he keeps from me, stretching his posture and taking a step backwards, I conclude that I've scared him. The receptionist. As I stare into his eyes without my sunglasses, I realise what a mistake I've just made. I am without a mask; if this key is to be used here, this guy will know that I am the newest participant of this secret thing.

'Excuse me, ma'am . . . ,' he says, causing me shock. This is the first time I've been called *ma'am* in my life. Am I getting old? *Let it go, Tainá. You don't even have wrinkles; he's been trained to call all women, ladies and all men, gentlemen.*

'All our doors open with a card and a password. We haven't used conventional keys for quite some time. Over a decade,' he answers, sneaky as a vegan chocolate cake made with beetroot—beautiful on the outside but unpalatable from so much arrogance, thinking he's better than every other cake. I stare at him in silence until he finally gets uncomfortable and suggests I go to the post office boxes: 'They still use keys. If you make your way over there, you will find them.' He points to the other side of the building, where the post office is.

'Thank you. Have a good night.'

'Good evening. Excuse me.'

He turns his back on me and goes to assist a couple with many bags and a room booked.

Here I go again. More walking. The wig is so itchy on my head. The post office will be my last stop, and then I'm going home. I arrive in less than a minute. As I should have known, it is closed. It's 7:34 p.m. No one's inside, not even a cleaning person. I look through the glass pane at the door again, trying to find the place for the PO boxes; it's not inside. I search outside for a sign to point me in the right direction. No sign of the boxes. I dread asking random people on the street, an art my generation has probably not mastered. But I have to do it as my phone is no help. The first passer-by is an impulsive choice, and I only get a hand wave and a 'I'm in a hurry' mumbled through his teeth. At the very least, he must have thought I looked like a health insurance saleswoman, or an activist asking for money to save someone who really needs help. The second person I approach is a lady with a more serene physiognomy and a calmer pace.

'Oh, dear, I don't know. I've never used those boxes. I don't trust them . . .' So she goes on to tell me her strong opinions about the post, the city hall, the federal government and how worried she is with Sydney. She complains the Council doesn't consult people about anything, and they end up doing whatever they want in the end to make the big companies make money. *Things are not how they used to be, you know? It's so dirty, expensive and violent now.*

I thank her and reply that when I become the council architect, I will make sure every decision will be made by public consultation. She says goodbye with a smile, saying she is late for dinner. Only the third passer-by, an elderly gentleman walking with his granddaughter, responds to me that the boxes are now at the Market Street post office. My phone wasn't wrong, I just couldn't believe they had moved a few blocks away.

Five minutes walking is not too far, but all these wanderings, even resting in the restaurant, make me aware of the pain in my feet. They are throbbing to get out of my shoes. It is 7:49 p.m., and I have been walking since lunchtime. How can I have spent so much time doing this?

The post is in the basement of a large corporate building. It feels like going into an underground train station. The boxes are right in front of the York Street entrance, in a brightly lit room, a type of hall right outside the office itself with the tellers and all the products. There are hundreds, maybe thousands of black boxes of different sizes built into the wall. I'm on the lookout for the snake symbol, and I catch myself also looking for thicker locks that would fit the key. It's a useless thought; the key has a number on it; it can only be that one. I sigh, not knowing whether to be proud to have gotten this far or disappointed by having a brief moment of brain fog.

Until I open the box. Box number 1790 is the winner. I'm proud. Definitely proud—and annoyed. Just like the little Russian dolls, inside one box, there is another box. And this time, it's a box without a lock.

This key no longer serves any purpose, I don't think. I quickly look at the countless carved details but don't find anything useful. The disappointment is equal to the dryness of my mouth. My motivation is gone; all I just want is to go home, but can I take the box with me? What do I do with this key? Maybe I should go back to the brick wall and put it back there. I sigh louder than I would like, a sign of tiredness. Walking back all the way to the Rocks just to leave the key inside the brick wall is an impossible mission right now. I will take everything home. Tomorrow, I can return things to their proper places.

I call my mother as soon as I surrender to the ride-share app and get into a complete stranger's car, nauseated by the smell of air freshener hanging from the rear-view mirror. My mother doesn't answer. I text her, asking her to call me. I call Caio who, obviously, is too busy to answer or stop working for ten minutes. Bibi is on the plane, so that leaves me with Fleur. The background noise in her house sounds like an apocalypse. Screams, cries, falls and lots of onomatopoeia prevent her from being able to complete a sentence, but at least she keeps me company until I get home alive. Very generously, she apologises to me for the lack of attention but is happy to have 'taken' me home. She was the only person with any real reason not to answer my phone, and yet, she answered.

I dismantle my outfit without care. I throw it all on my dinner table. A mess. An unusual mess. A tired mess. I'm left with only the first layer of clothes stuck to my body. My feet feel the chill of the floor. I turn on the heater on my way to the couch and the nostalgic darkness of the night sky and sea.

I am forced by my emotional needs to close the curtains. I don't want to be in that headspace tonight.

Sometimes, our brains need a break too. I can accept that mine did because it started working again with more clarity. After a few moments lying down with my feet up and my head settled on the cushions, I am grateful to remember my art classes at uni. My brain connected that the motifs carved into the wooden box are from the art nouveau era. I remember the knowledge gained by spending a lot of time in Europe and its museums that the artistic expressions of this period were geared towards the expression of female liberation. Another subtlety rich in meanings of this hunt. I turn the gears of the lock in the box, analysing what the password could be. There are seven cogwheels, like gears, and each one has twenty-six tiny letters of our alphabet. One word. Seven letters. I search for words in my head that can relate to the book, but nothing I can think of works.

It takes me some effort to get out of my comfy state on the couch, get up and get the book from my room, but I do it, convincing myself that my bed is even better. I search for words in my head that make some reference to the book and its story.

The vibration on the phone interrupts me. It's Caio. Three short messages: the first is an apology for not answering the phone. *Hi! I couldn't get to the phone. Busy busy, you know, work hours.* Then, he says that he will *try to* call me on video later to tell me goodnight, and the last message is a link to listen to a romantic song. This is how he says he loves me. Through lyrics that he himself cannot write. At least, he can feel.

I take a shower to gain energy, unravel this mystery and wait for Caio's call. I take my phone off vibration mode. The hot water hits the back of my neck, my forehead on the cold glass wall. My fingers count letters on the small tiles. I hear a song and take time to realise it's Caio calling. How long have I been in the shower? I come out dripping and, still in my towels, I talk to him on the speakerphone while I get ready for bed.

'Did you like the music?'

'I haven't heard it yet. I went to take a shower.'

'Ah, Tatá. Only you! I've never seen a woman receive music and not listen to it straight away. Let me play it for you.'

He puts it on loud enough for me to hear it and once again asks me what I think. He says that if the singer knew me, he would be sure that it was written for me.

'I doubt a guy like that would ever be interested in someone as normal as me.'

'What's up, Tatá? You're a hell of a woman!'

'Thanks, you too. I don't know anyone else who has a boyfriend sending them songs these days, particularly not someone bordering on his thirties . . .'

'Are you calling me old?'

I change the subject to cut through the self-pity, asking how his day is going, and in the sameness of his reply, him rushing and not asking how my day was, we wish each other goodnight and good afternoon, as we have done since February when he left here.

Lying in the dark, in that state between being awake and asleep, defeated by the password on the box, I have an intuitive—or neurological—moment of connecting the dots. Illyria. The name on the mask box. Illyria. Seven letters. That has to be it! Hastily, I turn on the bedside light, tuck the box in my lap and work on its lock. A click. Inside, there's an envelope.

Tailor-made, the cream envelope, on linen paper, sealed with hot wax shows the same symbol that was on the brick, the ouroboros, the serpent eating its own tail, representing the eternal cycles of life, of the protective wrapping that has intrigued people of the world for millennia. I need to open this envelope!

Dear guest 1262,
Welcome to the Secret Society of Illyria, where dreams, pleasure and truth thrive.

We are thrilled you unlocked the mysteries contained in the book and earned the right to attend our exclusive parties. You have been called by another member of our club and will now pass on this invitation.

At the bottom of the box is an adjustable 24k gold ring with your number inscribed on it. The ring is your invitation. You must wear it to every party and show it to our concierges when you enter.

In order for everyone to enjoy paramount security, certain rules are necessary. They are designed for the physical and mental safety of all members of the group and to protect our values.

We rely on four basic principles: anonymity, security, consent and elegance.

Principle One: Anonymity

1.1 You must wear an opaque mask that covers at least 75 percent of your face—lace and semitransparent coverings that allow more than 25 percent of your face to be seen will not be accepted, and you will be refused entry.

1.2 A simple mask may not be enough to ensure your anonymity. You should cover or modify your silhouette from your shoulders to the top of your head. Examples include, but are not limited to, hats, hairstyles and colour, clothing and scarves.

1.3 You must cover or disguise any feature of your body that makes it easy to recognise your identity such as, but not limited to, tattoos and scars.

1.4 You must make up one—or more—names that do not resemble your own and use them at will during the parties. You are not allowed to invent surnames because the combination of invented names may be someone else's real name.

1.5 You may not under any circumstances exchange phone numbers, emails, social media accounts, addresses or any other contact information with other members of the party.

1.6 You may under no circumstances show your face, even in photographs.

1.7 You may not comment to your family, colleagues, friends or people in the wider community about our parties. Doing so may result in your expulsion and the cancellation of the event. Be aware that your actions affect everyone. Remember that anyone might be part of this group, including your best friend.

1.8 You may not under any circumstances post about the party on social media. This includes showing your outfit, how it is made, how you feel about going to the party, and so on.

1.9 This invitation is individual and cannot be passed on to anyone you know personally. The invitation is only given to the person who receives the book. You must now pass the book on. You have one week to find someone, and that person must not know who you are. You may choose how to deliver the book. Choose wisely.

Principle Two: Safety

2.1 You should complete the attached form, seal it and send it with the sender and address described at the end of this letter. You must put the number on the ring after the sender's name. The envelope with the form will only be opened in case of complaints against you, as listed below in Principle Three.

2.2 On the day and date of the party, belongings that may have some form of identification, such as passport, driver's licence, bank cards and mobile phones, will be kept in a locked box by our concierges. They will not touch them. You will receive a box with a blank password like the one you have just opened. You must create a new password with the number that you received in this invitation. You may request to open the box at any time during the party.

2.3 Watches are not permitted due to the advanced technology in many models that threaten and undermine the safety and anonymity of other guests and the party.

2.4 Upon arrival, it is mandatory that all members pass through a metal detector.

2.5 Always check the ring number of your partner(s) and memorise it. You may write it down as soon as you make your decision to talk to a person. No guest may deny their ring number to another guest.

2.6 If you encounter someone who is not willing to show you their number or who is not wearing a ring, contact our team immediately. Any concierge or bar attendant will be able to take the case forward.

2.7 Your safety is our highest priority. If you believe you have been a victim of nonconsensual acts, you should contact the police and medical professionals immediately. At the end of this invitation, there are important telephone numbers so that you have the necessary support. Remember to keep your partner's number.

2.8 Code Red. If you hear that expression or see it at the door of the location of the party, it means that there has been a death in the group as a result of interactions during one of our parties. In this instance, the party in question and all other parties will be cancelled. The clues will no longer be placed in the media you discovered. Activities may or may not resume at a later date. There is no guarantee that you will be chosen to participate again. Code Red has never happened, and our group has been around for seventy years.

2.9 Hallucinogenic drugs and alcohol will not be permitted. Anonymity has been entertaining our guests for decades while sober. Be brave and come experience a different reality.

Principle Three: Consent

3.1 Any acts during the meetings must be consensual. Failure to adhere to this will result in legal action being taken against you. Your identity will be revealed to any media or institution necessary, according to current laws and regulations.

3.2 If you have been the victim of nonconsensual acts, you have the right to press charges against the individual who committed them. In order to do this, always check the number of your partner(s) and remember it. Memorise the security number written at the bottom of this letter. This is an internal reporting number where you will be helped. Alternatively, call the police as soon as possible.

3.3 All intimate relationships must take place in the same party venue, in the rooms reserved for this purpose. If those involved decide to leave the party together, the safety and identity of all involved will no longer be our responsibility.

3.4 Our security guards are on standby to remove anyone causing a disturbance, insulting another member, or removing their own or another group member's mask. The offender will be removed from the event and will not be allowed to return.

Principle Four: Elegance

4.1 We are a place of respect. There's nothing more elegant than respect. We are elegant when speaking, walking, talking and in any interaction with another human being. Respect is the highest principal we value.

4.2 The dress code for the party is gala.

4.3 You may be denied entrance if your costume is deemed to be of inferior quality.

4.4 Although we are not a fancy-dress party, we encourage sophisticated artistic creativity in the form of personal expression through fashion.

General and Final Notes

This club is free. Your expenses are paid by the cost of what you consume at the parties, the hotel room rentals for the night and the workshops, which vary each week, if you wish to attend.

To ensure your privacy and identity, any expenses must be paid in cash. Attached is a table with a suggested budget for food, drinks, hotel rooms and workshops. They are the same no matter where the party is held. Keep an eye on the flowers every week for a precise location.

Enjoy. This is a place of freedom and discovery of your desire. Your imagination and respect for others are the limits!

Welcome!

The stillness of my muscles is only broken by a smile, the broadest I've smiled in a long time. If my life were a movie, this would be the moment where I fall into a pillow in slow motion. Happy, astonished, comfortable.

When slow-mo becomes reality-mo, worry and guilt take over the plenitude I felt a minute ago. I can't go. What am I going to tell Caio? How can I lie to him? I read the last sentence of the invitation again—*'discovery of your desire.'* If I find out what I want, I think Caio only stands to gain.

Black dress. Beautiful. Caio. Kisses. Messages not answered. Dance. Cheetah. Snake. Planes. Book. Bookshop guy. Dad. Kadu. Itacoatiara. Spain. Illustrations. Walking. Dream. Kiss. Illustrations. Hands. Wig. Perfume. Bianca. Mum. Bookshop guy. Cages. Sydney. Timber box. Blind man. Masks. More masks. More illustrations. Invitation.

My head is about to explode, and I can't talk to anyone! The left side of my brain tries to make sense of it all, rationalising that I don't need to do anything that will break the pact I have with Caio. The monogamy pact.

I take out my notebook and write everything I know on the next blank page.

Location: Look for the colours of the flowers (petunias) in the flowerboxes on the streets . Each flower is a location from that poem. I need to discover where the parties are.

Day of the week: find out by the date of the party on page two of the newspaper insert. It only comes in the Saturday paper. I won't need it, as I will only go once.

Time: the only clue is the clocks on the drawings. I'll take a chance on 7:00 p.m. because *7* is what is always shown in the book. I doubt such a party would be in the morning at 7:00 a.m.

Costume: gala with mask. I have the mask and a couple of dresses but may need some help there. I won't. I'm likely to go only once.

No alcohol or drugs. How will these people here manage to have fun without it?

Entry: the golden snake ring. The design allows it to be adjustable. The tail continues to penetrate the head until it encircles the finger perfectly. I try to place it on the ring finger of my left hand and wonder if it's the kind of ring I would like Caio to give me. Will this be my last adventure before we get married?

I look at the empty flat, filled only by the memories evoked in the photos on the wall and in his almost idealised presence. Caio seems to belong to a category that is difficult to classify. Far away, absent, but still here, hopeful—the hope that tomorrow everything will be like before. Not quite tomorrow but in September, when he'll be back for good and we can pick up where we left off before he left. This business of long-distance relationships doesn't work for us. I must keep these worries in the part of me that needs to be patient and wait. Besides, I have a far more interesting subject to focus on now.

I have never felt this conflict before: I am calm and apprehensive at the same time. I oscillate between the repulsion toward extraordinarily vulgar people and the romantic attraction to a sophisticated place full of meaning. I read the invitation one more time, look at the illustrations in the book, remember the man from the bookshop and the fact that it is a party without drugs or alcohol. Everything leads me to believe that there is more refinement than banality at these parties. I breathe a sigh of relief. I read the last sentence of the invitation one more time: *Freedom and discovery of my desire.* My desire. Mine.

What do I desire? What do I want?

New climbing boots. New surfboard. Sailing again. Home. Caio. Spain. Bianca. The Book. Chocolate. Food. All of them. Bookshop guy. His scent. His eyes in mine. Dance. Kiss. Touch. Mum. Dad. Kadu. Skydiving. Scream. Pillow.

I lost track of time crying over what I can never have. What I want is a ghost. Two ghosts. They live in another plane of ether, imagination and faith. My true desire, the thing I most hope will happen, will never be fulfilled; they don't live in the material world.

I need to stop wanting the impossible and focus on what I can want. Just like Bianca, Bibi. She's not haunted by ideal futures or traumatic pasts. She is here in the only time that one can live. That's a skill, an art. Can I ever master it?

The photos and my memories point in one direction: marry Caio. I'm sure we will be married if we don't . . . break up. Do I *really* want to marry him? Do I want him here in my flat? Our flat. Or is it only the long and constant presence of our past that makes being together the natural progression of our lives? Does *he* want to be with *me*? I can't imagine myself with anyone else, we've been through so much together. I could never betray him, proper betray him with someone else, so I need to be patient. What about this party?

I pull the curtains open slightly, asking the sea whether I should go. I interpret the serene image of the waves slowly lapping at the cliff below me, the comforting smell of the sea air and the clouds passing in front of the almost new moon as a big yes. I am going. Until I touch someone or allow someone to touch me, it's not betrayal. The phone vibrates at this exact moment, and the pure thought of it being Caio tightens my stomach in a knot. A sign I shouldn't go. I was wrong, I can't go. It is betrayal. Why am I afraid of a lousy party breaking us up? If only I could stop thinking! I open my phone like someone taking off a bandage: quickly, to diminish the pain of an inevitable fact. The message is from Mum, who, like an angel, appears when she is needed and disappears when I can make decisions for myself. *Look what I saw today in one of your uni books.* And she continues with a quote from Luis Barragán, one of my favourite architects: *It is essential for an architect to know how to see in such a way that their vision is not dominated by rationality.* That's the answer I need. I don't need to overthink it; my vision tells me I should go. I want to go. I thank her, say I miss the two of us, and she immediately answers: *I miss you too, always! I love you, my daughter! I'm in a hurry, but I'll talk to you soon.*

I text Bibi, and I drift off to sleep wondering what I'm going to wear—perhaps the black dress.

*

I'm going to this party tonight as I would go to any work event where the main purpose is to celebrate the end of the year or meet people I'll never see again. At this masked party, I still have the benefit of not being obliged to exchange business cards, nor must I smile when I don't feel like it. After all, who cares if someone thinks I'm rude? I will go as an observer of human behaviour, a simple anthropological experience that only needs to happen once. One time, and I don't need to go again. Yes, that's what I have to do, to bring out the investigative reporter in me, kill this desire and move on. I'm sure that any woman who has ever spent carnival in Rio can take a party like this easily. The scary difference is that here, I'll be alone, and there, back home, with friends or boyfriends, there was always someone to protect me.

Taking time off work is like putting a rope around your own neck. Yesterday afternoon was important for me to say the least, but with so many unanswered emails and a need to leave today at 5:30 p.m. sharp to go to the party, I can't breathe. I am forced to make up time and condense everything I didn't work on yesterday into this morning. It's 2:00 p.m., and only now I can go to the bathroom; my water bottle is still full from this morning. Mentally exhausted, I debate with myself about the need to buy make-up and conclude that, at most, I'll pick up lipstick. My eyes are practically invisible under my mask, so no need for make-up there. Lipstick. Yes, just nude lipstick. Should I even bother if it's nude colour? I leave in search of a green juice, sushi and lipstick; it won't take more than thirty-five minutes. Bibi confirms, in reply to my message, that I can stay at her flat tonight. I don't answer all her questions. She sends me a kiss. It would be impossible to get to Bondi and back in time for that party. If I ever find out where it is.

I spent most of this morning's bus ride looking for Celeste and a combination of fort-related streets. Fort Street, Lower Fort Street, and countless others. The only one I found is a street in the Rocks called Lower Fort Street. I have no idea what Celeste is, but I imagine it's the name of the place. My shoes, my dress and my mask are in a small bag hidden under the desk, and I catch myself thinking about it several times during the day. I'm afraid someone will ask what's in there and why I'm carrying a suitcase on a Tuesday. Finally, at Myer, increasing my sensory load with so many lights, smells and options, I enter the first make-up stand that is familiar to me, because I know exactly which lipstick has worked before. I'm wrong. The kind woman hands me a lipstick that's similar to the one I had and warns me that the one I want is discontinued. She manages to convince me to also buy a highlighter, eyeshadows, several pencils for various things and an eyeliner. I leave in the direction of my lunch—the sushi and the green juice—annoyed at having let myself be talked into buying so much. The only sushi left is the bad kind, with *kani* or chicken and avocado, so I decide to have a smoothie instead of the juice and the sushi. Packed with protein, banana, mango and matcha, it should sustain me for the rest of the day. It might not. I feel dehydrated. I take a deep breath and buy some ibuprofen to have on hand in case a migraine tries to end my evening. Back at work, I learn that nothing is so bad that it can't get worse. Aside from the workload I've accumulated from taking yesterday afternoon off, my disappointing lunch and the money spent on make-up, my work computer decides not to work as it should. It crashes. Just like that. Switching it on and off doesn't make the slightest difference.

'Call Luke. He'll fix everything,' Tommy tells me.

'Who's Luke?' I ask, and he points to a guy who sits next to the urban design team.

Luke seems like a super calm guy. I explain what is going on with my machine, and he promptly gets up and goes to my desk to solve the problem. As we walk, he thanks me for not contributing to the *tec-tec* sound made by high heels. An observer. Sometimes I wonder if putting carpet in offices is meant to muffle the sound of high heels. I'd rather remove the heels from women's shoes, which clearly serve no purpose other than aesthetics, than cover a perfectly laid floor with glue, carpet and dust. Not to mention the unhealthy amount of dust that carpets accumulate. Carpets, just like any adornments, are a kind of armour, a way of covering up the ugliness underneath. Beautifully set materials, on the other hand, do not need cladding.

We spend the next ten or fifteen minutes in a pleasant conversation about the problems caused by huge files and impossible deadlines.

'There you go; you're now ready to fly, fly this machine. I've taken out all the worms and vermin for you,' he says, making some suspicious comparisons.

The reference to taking out worms to make me ready to fly reminds me of the image in the book. Paranoia perhaps, but I wonder if he has something to do with these parties. I can't ask.

I don't remember seeing any ring on his hands, but that's also not allowed. Maybe the way he said goodbye is common here.

*

Illyria, the soft black cardboard box, is lying on the bed, calling me. Calling me to do something I will have to keep a secret. Certain secrets are necessary, but this one might hurt someone I don't want to hurt or disappoint. Would Caio understand why I'm going? What would he do in my place? As long as I don't cross the line, as long as I don't run into the guy from the bookstore again, and as long as, even if I do see him, he doesn't get close, everything will be fine.

My dress was bought years ago when Caio took me as his date to a work party in Cape Town. I never got the chance to wear it again, but I could never get rid of it. I remember him telling me how beautiful I looked that night and that he regretted not having a ring to give me. *I should have planned it better! It would have been the perfect proposal*, he told me. He never mentioned marriage again; the closest was the song he sent me the other day. Maybe it's my fault; I must not be giving enough signals. Maybe I don't want to get married, but why not? We are . . . were once very much in love. Do I still love him? One thing is for sure, despite no paper or ring, we are committed to each other. And if I cross the line, I will be in the wrong.

I have trouble closing the dress with the zipper at the back. The turtleneck dress falls into long lacy sleeves and a solid torso, broken only by a discreet slit making the cleavage. The waist is marked by a satin band opening to several layers of the long, round skirt that falls on the floor.

The mask is protected by a cushion covered with a cream satin fabric. She is enchanting, like the voice of a siren who seduces men into the sea. The only difference is that this mask is hollow; there's no magical creature behind it.

Bianca's flat in Kirribilli is as cold as a fridge. The wooden floorboards are the ceiling of the flat below, and if it wasn't for the view of the Opera House, I'd say I was in a shack. Even the favelas in Rio have concrete floors which prevent one from hearing the sneeze of the person living above, or their broom sweeping the floor. Luxury compared to here.

I need to be at Bibi's. I wouldn't have time to leave work, go to Bondi and get back to the Rocks by 7:00 p.m. I had three options: get ready at work, in the bathroom of some bar, or go to a hotel. Work wouldn't really be an option because my identity would not be safe at all; someone would see me and ask a bunch of questions. If I got ready in a bar, I would have to go to the party with a suitcase carrying my work clothes. Not a chance. Going to a hotel would solve this problem, but it would create another—Caio snooping around my credit card life and putting unnecessary stress on us. So, I'm here at my friend's place.

I watch a few free make-up tutorials online and pull from my dusty memory the tips my friends have given me over the years. I don't give in to the suggested red lipstick *to highlight my skin colour as an indigenous person from the northern areas of the country*. No one who wants to go unnoticed would wear a red lipstick.

I open my flesh-coloured lipstick and take out the rollers from my hair. They were an impulse buy when I passed a hairdresser on the way here. My feet soon get used to the heels

I haven't worn for so long. I put on my necklace and the hooded cape. I'm surprised by what the mirror shows: a new me. My eyes glow, transparent in a watery blue green. I almost don't recognise myself. In a good way. I put on the mask. The tension in my shoulders disappears; sparks shoot up my spine; the air warms me with confidence; my legs, solid as the trunk of a tree, seem to have grown infinite roots. The migraine that was threatening to attack disappears without medication. I have never been more me.

Courage just isn't strong enough to put safety and responsibility aside. I write a small note explaining where I am and place it in the middle of the table on top of the book. The book. In case I disappear, someone will be able to discover what happened to me.

I grab my bag and a canvas bag to protect the mask; it's better not to take a chance leaving the house with it—what if my neighbour is going to this party too? The darkness of the night falls early, and in the middle of winter, it is fifteen degrees outside today. Only the appetite for the unknown gets me out of the house.

*

I come up a lot of things to talk about with the taxi driver, and he couldn't be more disinterested. The silence lets me watch the streets outside the car. The evening lights kick out the city's corporate atmosphere and, even on a Tuesday, Sydney manages to have a lively nightlife. Early, admittedly—it's 6:20 p.m.—but the bars, restaurants and streets are full of scarves, gloves, beanies and leather boots. The courage I had in front of the mirror at home alternates with shivers of fear and excitement, clearly seen in the shaking of my hands. I ask the taxi driver to drop me off on Argyle Street. The man doesn't even say goodnight to me; he spends the whole route talking on the phone and very quickly kicks me out of the car when I tell him he can stop. New York beats Sydney in that respect; I loved the stories from the taxi drivers there when we used to go on holidays.

In the shade of a fig tree, surrounded by the silver light of the moon, I am like a child who has just discovered the hiding place of her Christmas presents. On Lower Fort Street, there is a house with an old and discreet sign: Celeste. Do I really want to open this present? I may be deeply disappointed; after all, my imagination is sometimes much better than reality. Also, much scarier. I see a person walking towards the house. The broad build of his shoulders and slim build of his hips makes me think it is a man. He wears a mask and a very sophisticated outfit. A white scarf covers his neck, going down his front. The blue velvet jacket matches the trousers, and both are meticulously adorned with gold details. I wonder if he wants to hide his neck because there is a scar or mark that only he has, or is it just a matter of the cold of winter? Maybe it's just a matter of style and good taste. It matches the rest of his outfit. The door of the house opens, and I see a person dressed in character with a smiling mask covering his entire face, a feathered wig framing him, a burgundy red suit, black trousers and white gloves, assuming the position of night porter outside the house. This person who has just entered might be the first guest.

Soon after, two more people appear, also on foot. Dragging on the ground, the woman's dress is very elegant, the only skin you see is her back, in a deep V, and her lips, which pop with a deep brownish-red lipstick. He wears a more detailed outfit, looking as if he has stepped out of Venice in the middle of a carnival. A red suit frames a perfectly white shirt underneath. His hat, in the same shade of red, sits atop a curly white wig, and a golden sceptre completes his outfit. The two cross paths on the street before reaching the house; he extends his left arm very courteously, and after a small bow she hooks her elbow into his. That is the only part of their bodies that touches. They talk, smiling. The man doesn't try any 'funny' moves. Do they already know each other? I imagine not. How would you recognise the same person twice at a masquerade ball? Maybe they wear the same masks or clothes every time—a very likely possibility, since it would cost a lot to buy masks and keep clothes that you will only ever use to this party. They look so polished, so refined.

As soon as the couple enters the house, the street buzzes. More people arrive, and I notice I'm driven by an excitement that runs through my body, wanting to shout out: I did it! I got this riddle right. For obvious reasons, I don't do that. I just smile and approach the house with confident steps, as if I've been here countless times before. The best feeling is self-satisfaction. The doorman greets me with a 'Good evening, miss.'

The white marble threshold contrasting with my black shoes reminds me of what I felt when I went out for the first time to travel alone. It was in that moment, in the house where I grew up, when my black trainers contrasted with the white marble threshold that I was able to define courage. Just like the French Revolution, the bombing of Hiroshima and Nagasaki, the birth of a mother when her baby arrives, this moment is, for me, crucial: I can never go back to who I was before. This is the gateway to another world; it is the milestone between the Tainá who existed yesterday and the Tainá who will exist at the end of this night. Courage is exactly this, accepting that your world will change, and despite apprehension, fear and doubts, you keep walking.

6

People make their way to a large counter with five receptionists who place their belongings in wooden boxes. I do the same. I notice that everyone follows the rules, and that makes me feels safe. Everything seems to flow in a relaxed way; these people have been here before.

The receptionists who guard our objects don't wear masks. Just headpieces, giant coloured hair, flamboyant clothes and lots of make-up. They all seem to be dressed as birds, the quality is so good that I could swear they came out of a musical or Cirque du Soleil. They are all beautiful and unrecognisable. I would never be able to identify them on the street.

Standing with a smile, one hand over the other on the counter, a white male cockatoo patiently waits for me to unbutton my cape and hand it over to be put away. His politeness is impeccable, as is his attire. The white outfit full of textures of the same colour contours his body and blends with the make-up that goes up his neck, face and hair, an honourable impression of the bird. The crystals that go around his eyes reflect a shine that seems to be coming from inside him, but the reality is that it can only be from the chandeliers in the house. Apart from the receptionists, the other people who work here are all dressed like the guy who opened the door, with masks, gloves and suits, including the women. It's quite hard to be sure of anyone's gender here. The only two similarities between them are that both the receptionists and the circulating staff wear gloves, and they are dressed up in an unrecognisable way. I imagine the gloves are to protect their fingerprints.

My belongings were nimbly and securely placed in a wooden box locked with a code like a suitcase. I need to show my number on the ring, and the box is locked with this code. My receptionist raises his left hand and indicates the location of the lounge with a curtsy. 'Enjoy, miss,' he says. I wonder if it is my long, wrinkle-free neck that allows me to be called miss, as the rest of me is covered. I prefer *miss* to *madam*, like the guy called me yesterday.

The three floors that descend from the entrance hall are beautifully designed. Like a jewellery box buried in sand, this house is on the inside the opposite of what it is on the outside. Its façade has a small, simple and hidden—and ugly—entrance, but as I enter, I see a masterly combination of the pre-loved building charm with the new purpose of what it serves. Everything is carefully designed. I walk in and stretch my view, realising that it is not just one but four houses united by bridges, lifts and mezzanines. From the hall, as soon as we pass the reception, it is already possible to see the window that lets the Harbour Bridge and the lights of the lives of North Sydney enter the party.

Winter doesn't seem to exist in here despite the large spaces and full-height glass walls. Many of the jackets and overcoats stay in the reception area, while others remain with the characters they've helped invent tonight. The half-light of the lamps on the old red brick walls joins the candles that are spread around a quartet playing classical music, and the intimate atmosphere they create welcomes me; they hug me, calming or inhibiting the overdose of adrenaline that I pretended not to have accumulated in the last few days, especially today. My breathing, now less arrhythmic, allows me to move forward with more fluidity and less resistance.

The idea of anonymity that used to scare me now pleases me with every exhalation. I don't need to say anything true at all. How much could I lie or omit about myself? I wonder what people do or want to do when no one knows who they are. Who would I be if nobody knew who I am?

I avoid the queue at the lift—definitely too small and slow for the demand—and using a camouflage tactic I've honed as an experienced immigrant, to avoid looking lost, I keep walking towards the stairs, not knowing where they will lead.

The combination of the high heels I haven't worn in so long and my long, flowing dress will be a disaster if I'm not careful on these stairs. I lightly hold the handrail, lift my dress with my right hand and keep my head up, observing clothes, masks, hair, make-up, postures and bodies. I imagine the hall I see at the end and to the side of the stairs is the main one. People who made their way there before me are talking and dancing in groups of two to seven. There is no one alone. I cannot help thinking that this place seems to be the ideal remedy for the shy.

The letter with the rules, people's cordiality and the sophistication of the environment transform my hope into a sense of certainty that I am in a safe place. My apprehension about the possibility of a disgusting party disappears. Everything is completely opposite to the gloomy place I imagined, and I conclude that it was the right decision to come. Despite that, I don't want to give away that it is my first time here. I walk with calm but firm steps, avoiding looking dazzled. People approach each other, exchanging glances and cordialities worthy of a renaissance ball. Few guests seem to come down the stairs or lifts now; everyone has already entered. People walk erect, with that proud posture, confident of an excellent evening to come.

The large glass wall reminds me of a giant LED screen, like those we see in epic concerts. The view is of a garden with tiny lights and fire torches, evoking an enchanted fairy world that joins with the lights across the bay. This magical and real Kingdom of Sydney stretches as far as the eye can see. I feel as much a part of it as anyone else here.

I soon reach the bar and order a passion fruit mocktail, which is served to me in a martini glass. In fact, even soda is served in glasses, perhaps to recall the aesthetic of a bar serving alcohol.

A woman calls to me, asking if I want a drink. Unobservant to say the least. I am agitated to see her mask covering her entire face. The big painted smile may hide her anger or disappointment, and I try to control my insecurity with two deep breaths. I think about how many times I didn't know if someone was really feeling what they were saying and conclude that most of us hide tears behind a drawn smile.

'A *drink* for your thoughts,' she says.

'I've already got one, thank you.' I point to my glass. Having your own drink is an excellent way to avoid being drugged and raped.

'Even better! I don't have to spend money!' she says, and I take great pleasure in hearing that. It's the mask already speaking the truth. 'Who are you today?'

'Maitê.'

'Mai who? Very difficult. Choose another one, a bolder name, something that has more to do with you.'

'Lina', I say, in honour of my favourite architect.

'Lina? Different, but very girly girl. Come on, who's the burning beast inside you?'

While I respect her good intentions, I don't know if it's worth spending my neurons and time on her.

'What about yours? Let me guess—Sarah Smith.'

'You got it! If that's what you want me to be, that's who I want to be! Come on, let's dance. I think we can have a great time! How about it? We can try on some props together!'

'Thanks for the invitation, but not now.'

She seems offended, changing her tone of voice from normal to shrill, telling me that I don't need to be polite here, that she could be my work colleague and will never know who I am. In short, if I don't like a woman, I should just say so. I reply that, mask or no mask, I will always be polite. I excuse myself and go off to find a place away from her, hoping that I'm not wrong about the guests' good manners, fingers crossed this party won't become vulgar, as my imagination feared.

Just like the tourist on the street looking for where to go, standing still is a magnet for strangers at nightclubs, conferences or dinner parties. So, I decide to walk around, and even though I don't initiate any interaction with people, I don't go unnoticed. People greet me. One of them even says, 'I'd like to kiss you on the lips.' But that's it. She doesn't even come close.

I notice that some don't wear masks, just extremely elaborate make-up, as do the receptionists. One woman looks like a lioness, wearing an orange wig with a bright green hat; another has outlined her eyes with a design, making a gradient for a metal veil intertwined between her nose and mouth and a huge blue wig. It would be impossible to know who these people are on the street. They are, in fact, masked.

One of the people disguised behind the make-up passes very close to me, staring into my eyes and making their natural features more visible, although still unrecognisable. It's a he, and I can see his eyes are orange. Contact lenses, for sure.

'Why do you hide your eyes, beauty of the night?' he asks me.

I repeat what I learned from the blind gentleman:'Because they are for only a few.'

The smile I get back confirms the wisdom of what the blind man told me. He bows and goes on his way.

I realise that nobody touches you if you don't let them. Very different from the nightclubs, shows and bars I've been to in the past. Although in the minority, the people who look like they came out of a film with their dazzling make-up are fascinating. I could spend the night observing their behaviour, which walks the line between animal and human. Here, protected by the black, the lace, the make-up around my eyes, I feel trapped when I compare myself to the freedom I see radiating from these creatures. Something that changes their faces, their hair and their necks is enough for them to take off the masks of their daily life. Without fear of doing what they want, without fear of being judged for showing off, for experimenting with their own bodies and those of others too—so far, it seems.

At this point, certain guests intertwine, kissing, squeezing and kneading each other. The armchairs are occupied very quickly; the people with harder and less malleable clothes, like heavy skirts and twirls, remain standing, some leaning on the high benches near the tables, where they try to eat peanuts and drink in the way their masks allow. The vast majority warm up the temperature of the place with a great synchronised dance in the hall, which I observe keenly so that I can join in when I finally understand that nobody here knows or has any way of knowing who I am.

I look for the guy from the bookshop. I know I shouldn't. I walk among people, mentally calculating if anyone has the same difference in height to me. Considering that my height comes from my European genes, my sample is limited. There aren't many people much taller than me. The food that passes on white trays is prepared by a chef and his team, whom we can see through a window. They are not masked; I imagine for good and hygienic reasons. Who would be ashamed to be a chef, to make beautiful dishes like that? Why should we be ashamed of doing anything we do? Behind what mask do we hide? What are we afraid of? On my exploratory walk, as I'm getting the lay of the land, I notice a door half open. A light as bright as daylight escapes the gap and incites me to peek inside the room. Hanging from a rough rope, a sign says *Knot.* I can tell there is a body hanging from a tangle of ropes with another person around it, when I am interrupted by a gentle but large and intimidating security guard.

'It's at full capacity; please come back in about an hour.'

I thank him with a small nod that must have looked more like an apology and return to the dance hall.

The side effects of wearing such closed, dense masks are having one's field of vision reduced and the heat increased. But the heat still doesn't bother me. The field of vision does. I wonder if I have a bit of claustrophobia, but I don't give wings to this thought because it would be a slope to despair and the night would be over. I quickly realise that I need to move my head sideways to see what before I didn't even need to make an effort to see. Peripheral view. But reduced is not eliminated, and as I continue to look at the dance hall, I see a golden tip that intrigues me out of the corner of my left eye. I turn my neck and see someone I believe to be a man. He wears an unmistakable, huge nose mask. Golden.

This guy won't get far with this nose. How will he dance? Or kiss? I pause my thoughts and smile. It was worth coming. I've seen enough. I can go home and rest my head on the pillow peacefully after I call Caio. No big deal. I created a much bigger problem in my head than I needed to.

I turn to put my drink back on the counter and, by a coincidence of fate, one that only foolish romantic souls choose to see, my big-nosed friend turns around at the same moment and, of course, a collision between his protuberant mask and my arm is inevitable.

'Oops! Excuse me, miss. My deepest apologies. You know, noses never stop growing, and if you use your smarts, you'll know how old I am,' he says with a joyful sense of humour.

'About 150,' I reply laughing. It's obviously a joke.

I calculate from his height, broad shoulders and upright posture that he might be a little older than me, maybe the same age. Without access to the wrinkles on his face, neck and hands, it's hard to guess someone's age.

'You got it right, shorty. I'm a turtle,' he says, oozing a charming and enchanting smile. I notice I smile back. Am I flirting? What am I doing? Nothing. I'm not doing anything, just talking. Is he calling me shorty because he is so much taller than me?

Meanwhile, a bar attendant cleans up the spilled drink and the big-nosed man gives me the handkerchief from his jacket pocket to clean myself. Either he is very polite, or he is gay. He didn't even try to get close to me to dry me off, as most men would. I expected a typical, 'Your dress is wet. I'd better help you dry it.' But not this guy, he just hands me a tissue.

'Thank you. I haven't seen handkerchiefs since . . .'

'Your grandfather's time, I imagine. This was a wedding present . . .'

A married guy? Could it be possible the world is full of disgusting idiots?

'What did you say? I couldn't hear properly.' I sort of lie; I think I heard *wedding* just fine 'The music, the nose in front of your face . . .'

He comes closer and, instead of facing me, he turns a little sideways so that his golden beak is over my shoulder, and with his mouth closer to my ear, I can hear him better. As I notice the involuntary shiver on my skin running through my entire body, the urge to not want to leave his side, and the heat we exchange in the space between his chin and my shoulder, I conclude that my trepidation towards the guy from the bookstore was not exclusive. It's been a long time since another man has come close to me—this close.

'Is this better? Can you hear me? This nose . . . I'll tell you, it's a problem!' he says playfully.

I nod, and he explains to me that he got the handkerchief when he was the bridesmaid—yes, *bridesmaid*—at his sister's wedding. The only purpose for telling me this would be to clarify that he is not married, or to say that he has a sister and is very affectionate towards her. Maybe both.

'She said a bridesmaid should be your best friend, someone you'll be sure will be by your side in twenty years, and she only had this certainty with me. She had other bridesmaids, but I was the main one,' he says proudly and continues. 'I thought it was fitting to wear today; it matched the outfit.' You can feel the lightness in his voice. 'What are you drinking? I'll get you another one,' he offers.

'You don't have to. I'm not thirsty. Better avoid the drinks, you know—peeing in this dress would be terribly tricky.'

He laughs and holds out his hand to me. I notice the golden cufflinks matching the mask on a navy-blue jacket-blazer. Considerate. Attentive to detail.

'Dance with me?'

He looks into my eyes so fixedly. I presume there's nowhere else to look when you have no peripheral vision and no face to see, no expression to analyse except the eyes and a corner of the mouth. Can he see through my lace? Can he see my eyes? I hesitate against my will, but the accelerated heartbeat and the image of Caio in my head indicate a warning, so I delay saying yes. My rational side convinces me that it's just a dance, a group dance. Nothing more. I notice that there are more musicians in the orchestra and the music is faster. Caio would not have a problem if I were to dance with a woman; he would probably even like it. So, why should I worry so much now?

We soon join the rest of the guests around the hall, and thanks to my powers of observation and motor coordination and his conducting, we dance to everyone's rhythm. A daze of happiness arises in my feet, rising just like the violent waves created when they meet barriers on the shores, and as soon as it reaches my hips, it spreads to my upper body, my brain, my hair, my soul. I hover on the ground. Everyone is dancing, everyone is happy. I move from hand to hand, following the choreography that I soon master with ease. Those who are in this arena don't even try to kiss, touch, pull, rub or grope. It's all one big, respectful play. The laughter, the exchanges of glances, the hands on hands, the hands on waists, the whirls and the clapping transport me to a world I haven't seen in a long time. Maybe too long; maybe I have never been somewhere like this. I can't remember the last time I felt myself floating. It's impossible to contain the smile, the giggles and the laughter. It's reciprocity, it's freedom. I make their night—as they make mine—unforgettable. It's like being two years old again in a playground with a bunch of other kids you'll never meet again.

In the silence of the music and the music of the clapping, the orchestra stands up after the last piece is played and invites a DJ to share the stage. He is received with a great commotion by the audience. The lights of the candles, which have already lost their strength because they have finished burning, give way to new lanterns with lamps hanging from the ceiling. The intimate and familiar atmosphere doesn't end with the DJ and the electronic music. I've lost sight of my big-nosed-guy during the dance, but I don't feel alone. I feel welcomed by this new family. I belong here, and this place belongs to me now.

'I love you guys! All of you!' someone shouts.

'I love you too!' shouts another voice.

'Me too!' shouts a third, soon followed by most of the guests.

The golden-nosed man appears between a few heads; he lands his gaze on the black lace covering my eyes and seems to penetrate it as he walks towards me.

'Come, I want to show you something,' he says close to my ear, holding one of my hands.

We climb a circular staircase leading up to the mezzanine. I'm behind him. He stops scanning the place. He turns to me and jokingly says, 'It's okay, you can come up. There's no food fight here.'

We exchange a quick laugh; soon he shows me the people dancing in the great hall below us. 'See? We were part of the picture, of the previous sea.'

'Yes, we were.' I like how he called it a sea, a sea of happiness.

We hover side by side in a delicious silence. Something you don't find everywhere. He must be an artist. Maybe a musician, maybe a painter. Caio would never say something with so much sensitivity. In fact, Caio would never agree to be here. I force myself to stop making unhealthy comparisons.

'So, lady in black.' He breaks the silence. 'Apart from wearing black and dancing, who are you?'

'A rather philosophical question, no?'

'Absolutely! I don't even know if there's an answer.'

Light, open and creative as music and sweat leave us, I reply: 'Let's try. We are something, right? I am a friend, a daughter, a *sis* . . .' The word *sister* sticks in my throat and comes out through silent tears. Tears that make perfect sense for me, the lady in black, grieving. I see my entire wardrobe in front of me at breakneck speed: black, charcoal and hints of white. The memory of my printed, vibrant dresses from my childhood invades my thoughts, and I realise that I like monochrome for the wrong reasons. I have always attributed this preference to getting older and not wanting to look like a child. In adulthood, I've been embodying the stereotype of the architect.

'Sis . . .' he repeats, calling me back to where I left off.

'You know,' I stutter and swallow the tears that have not come down yet. 'I can say what I studied, what I work with, but who am I? I don't know.' I switch my role from interviewee to interviewer. 'Who are *you*?'

'I am a turtle, as you already know . . .'

He notices my smile but not the tears. He would have no way of knowing about them or that the past scared me a few seconds ago. There are other people in the mezzanine eating, dancing, drinking and, yes, some are kissing and intertwined on columns and armchairs, as far as their costumes and masks allow. They explore themselves, massaging their hands, hair, shoulders and other parts of their bodies.

'Sorry, I got distracted,' I say when I can't pay attention to what he's talking about.

'I just said I'm a turtle. What is distracting you? What holds your attention?'

I discreetly point to the people snuggling up to each other.

'That's what I call a talent. It's cool they aren't just doing the traditional grabbing sequence of mouth-ass-breast,' he says laughing, making funny hand gestures.

'I know one thing you are: fun . . . light-hearted.'

I am surprised by the compliment I give. I'm not known for celebrating the best in others, at least not in front of them. I'm one of those who doesn't criticise, but I won't praise obvious characteristics either. This time, it came out without thinking. Maybe it's the certainty that I'll never see him again and that he has no idea who I am that leaves me free to praise him more and tone down on what is left unsaid.

'Good to know . . . Did you enjoy dancing?'

'I don't think I've had this much fun in decades!'

'You seem to have had a childhood like every childhood should be.'

'I did.'

I answer without hesitation. I was a very happy child. What can't come out, and now not even through tears, is that my childhood ended at fourteen. Not by the arrival of my adolescence or the cycles that made me a woman, but by the abrupt rupture, like an infinite train line that cuts through a forest, leaving you unable to cross the tracks. I stay on this side, trying to see him on the other and, despite his spirit that comes to calm me in my dreams, during the day, it is like hearing his call for help. When I'm awake, he's more like a ghost.

'I'll leave you alone. If you want to dance, you can find me.'

'No, sorry, I've totally gone somewhere. In my head. My body was here, my mind somewhere else.' I point to my head. 'I'm here now, so tell me then, who would you like to be today?'

'I think that one is harder than trying to figure out who I am. 'What should I call you? What's your . . . name?' he asks.

'I don't know. The name I made up was crucified by someone else. She told me it wasn't . . . I forget the word . . . bold enough?'

His jaw wriggles; he must be smiling.

'I think it was. She said my name wasn't that of a burning beast. And yours, what name did you come up with?' I ask him.

'I haven't decided. In fact, I haven't even thought about it.'

'Okay, so we're Don't Know and Haven't Thought,' I say, and he laughs.

'How about I name you at midnight and you name me at midnight?' he suggests.

I don't remember reading that the party ends at midnight, but trying not to give away that this is my first time here, I just agree.

'Do we have so much to talk about until the carriage turns into a pumpkin?' I seem to have no brakes on my tongue today! What is wrong with me?

'We do! We need to work out who we are and who we want to be! There's plenty of talking to do.'

We walk around the mezzanine and, at some point in the evening, we see ourselves out in the garden, we laugh wildly, we philosophise about the lives of people from across the bay, making up fictional stories for them. We don't stick to knowing our names, where we came from, where we're going, what we studied, where we work and all the questions that, to me now, seem like a relationship shopping list. Why should I care about your professional aspirations if after today I will never see you again? We are just having fun, telling jokes, sharing stories and, little by little, getting to know what we'll allow the other to know. He asks permission, offering to get me a drink, and I accept a lemon water. He insists on something more elaborate, like a lychee mocktail, and faced with my refusal, he smiles. He seems enchanted by our time together. In the few minutes I'm alone while he goes to the bar, I become disappointed in myself for not knowing how to behave without my phone. My fingers poke at my fingernails in a nervous tic; my mind shoots into guilt, I'm getting cold and the excitement of the night is not enough to keep me warm.

He returns with the drinks, notices I'm cold and immediately asks if he can give me his blazer, I try to refuse by saying he will be cold. He says it's nonsense, takes it off and asks again if he can put over my shoulders. I thank him.

'Back to names . . . How come you don't have a name to use at the party?' I ask, 'Is this your first time, or do you come up with a new name every time?'

If he's observant, as he seems to be, he'll connect the first part of the name conversation to this one and may conclude that it's the first time I'm here. I don't have a 'party' name.

Would it be so tragic for him to know it's my first time coming to the party? Except for the bookstore guy, no one knows my face. He doesn't seem to be the guy.

'Second time. But the first time, I didn't talk to anyone, so I didn't have to make one up.'

'Why didn't you talk to anyone?'

Wait. Second time? He could be the guy from the bookstore, he was the last invitee, I got the book from him. Unless there's more than one book.

'I'm shy.'

'Shy? With that golden nose? How can you be shy?' I say, incredulous.

'You see, I didn't come with a golden nose the first time . . .'

'So, it only takes one time here to have the courage to wear a gold mask with that huge nose?'

'Yes! Are you going to tell me that after dancing like that and being immersed in all of this that you're not a little *lighter?* Free of what's stopping you from wearing a gigantic gold nose?'

'I don't know if I would have the courage to have that much gold on my face. I don't even know if I would want to look like a bird,' I touch the tip of his mask with my index finger, which trembles a little.

He raises his arm, stretching out his left hand, and calls me to dance again.

'How about you come fly with me?'

And back to the salon we are.

That's it! I've solved the mystery of the book! I need to find someone to pass it on to. The piercing voice of the bookshop guy doesn't seem to torment me anymore; the voice of the masked man is not that of the bookshop guy. There must be other copies of the book being passed around. Am I starting a series of short stories where, each week, I will fall in love with some mysterious stranger I will never see again? Is this the replacement for the travels I love so much? Is this the new adventure of my life? Staying on this tightrope between the right and the not-so-right? Caio would not like to see me dancing with a man, much less to know that I find him funny, that there is an acceleration of my heart every time he looks at me. He would not be able to bear knowing there's an interest on my part in feeding this tension between him—this guy—and me. Careful. I need to be careful.

At the end of the song, back at the bar, looking for some mocktails and lemon water, I ask how he passed the book on. Something in me still thinks he might be the guy from the bookshop.

'Good question. I found someone interested. What about you?'

If I say I'm still about to pass the book on, he will know I am the last one. And in case, there's only one book; he will know how to recognise me on the street. I generalise, not to lie but to not say too much.

'Bookstore.'

'Bookshop? What a coincidence'

'You too?'

'Yes.'

I stare at him, doubting that he is not the guy from the bookshop. I can't overlap their gazes. They don't seem to be the same person. More than two people could have chosen their new guests in bookshops. Maybe this is his second party, but the first wasn't last week, or he could have taken some time to come to his first party. Quiet, with his eyes fixed on mine, he lets me observe him. I wonder what he is thinking. I like it when he looks at me like that, but I think he's hiding something. Is he hiding something? Does he recognise me?

'Do you know if you found the person you chose?' I ask.

'I don't think so. I didn't look for . . . them either,' he says.

'Them?'

'Oh, I just don't want to say if it was a woman or man. That could violate their privacy. That sounds stupid, actually. It was a *he*; I gave it to a man. I thought it would be good to have more men learning to respect women's freedom. Too idealistic, perhaps.'

'It's quite honourable. Surprising.'

Despite the similarities in height, elegance and jawline, I don't think they are the same person. The voice doesn't match, and neither does the personality.

Shortly afterwards, as we engage in books recommendations and why some of them should never have become films, the stroke of midnight knocks on our door. The lights gradually get brighter, the music softer, some people head towards the exit, while other pairs, trios and even quartets go somewhere else. I imagine it to be where they can continue the night, in the privacy of the house rooms. It feels like a quiet reverse migration, in which we leave summer for the winter outside.

'Looks like it's our time,' he says, and we make our way towards the end of our evening. Between jokes about carriages, pumpkins and crystal shoes, he hands me a piece of paper just before putting me in a taxi. A tightness in my stomach confirms that I'm sorry I won't be able to see him again.

'Read it at home,' he says. I nod.

'Eva,' he says.

'What?' I don't understand.

'I will remember you as Eva.'

'I hope it's a compliment!' The tone of my voice shows a certain scepticism and distrust.

His extraordinary gaze pierces the lace that covers my eyes, and I wish he could see my desire for this night not to end. He puts his golden nose over my left shoulder and whispers in my ear without touching me: 'Do you have any doubts?'

I suck in the icy air and the warmth of his aura emanating through his neck. The heat inside my body contrasts with my cold shell, my skin. If he knows this is the only time we'll see each other, why hasn't he tried to kiss me? Why doesn't he try now? I give desire a chance and turn my face towards his. A kiss would be impractical with his mask. He pulls away, making the decision for me. He must know I shouldn't be talking to him, or that he shouldn't have spent the night with me. I don't cheat on my boyfriend—but just barely. I breathe out relief and frustration at the same time. I wonder what my masked man has figured out.

I get in the car and wave goodbye. A regretful yet relieved goodbye.

A new portal opens as I enter Kirribilli's flat, transporting myself to a world filled with exuberance and marked by the end of tonight. I bask in a blanket of flattery from the flirtation with my masked man, the true atmosphere of the party, and most of all, the pride I feel in myself for knowing how far I can go if no one knows who I am.

7

I want to shout to the world, spread to the open windows the happiness that embarrasses and bewitches me, for the same reason. But since I can't, I scream into my pillow. *In love. Ashamed. Satisfied.*

Winter sun, old buildings, books, illustrations, charming man, his eyes stripping me bare, his perfume, work, Caio, more old buildings, symbols, more illustrations, key, snake, post office, wooden boxes, bicycle, bus, masks, costumes. Him. The golden-beaked man that I have not named yet. The moments that led me to find this city a little more interesting last night scramble in my memory. Sydney has just become much more interesting.

Anonymity seems to recover what we have already lost: our privacy, our freedom. I open, for the thousandth time, the handkerchief the masked man gave me as a present. I can't refrain from being slightly narcissistic.

The thin paper has a blue ball-point pen drawing of me, waiting for him on the balcony. He must have done it when he went to get drinks for us. The moon is the symbol of my necklace—how he paid attention! Next to the drawing, a little poem—a poem!—written in excessively small letters.

What if I never see you again?
I can't miss the chance to tell you
If nothing else is of me and you
After today has passed
know that I will always remember you

See me again? Interesting choice of words.

Secret-keeping is an art; you must be very confident in your ability to not tell the world how good a secret-keeper you are. Would it be possible for a child to fully hide that they managed to find their hidden presents? Would it be possible not to mention, not to giggle, not to whisper to their best friend they have just found treasure? Would it be possible to keep a secret without letting anything change in you? Would I be capable of never mentioning anything to Caio about this party and the reasons I sought the clues for it? Would a *I was bored* excuse be plausible enough? Could I put the blame on his absence? How severe must a punishment be to prevent you from following your heart, your curiosity, your desire?

I type and erase three messages to him. What should I say? I record a voice memo saying I miss him and can't wait to see him on Friday, but I bin it before sending. The tone of my voice is too suspicious: it's too happy, too cheerful compared to our last few phone calls. I'm not *that* excited about him coming. Reflectively, I regret not feeling the nice rush and goosebumps to prepare myself and our home for us as I used to. I am far more thrilled about yesterday's party.

I will never forget the 'treasure hunt,' the ideal behind Illyria, how the book was given to me and the golden-beaked mysterious man. I will keep his gift as a pinch to remind me it was all true when I grow old.

My final message to Caio says: *I can't wait to see you on Friday* and has an airport emoji with a question mark. A few hours later, he replies with a simple message that I don't need to pick him up.

The next day, I wake up with my phone beeping a few times. It's a bunch of his messages with one or two words each. Does he want to wake me up? It must be serious; it's too early in Singapore. The messages are not important. I don't know why he is making a fuss about it. All he wants to know is why I'm not spending money—*I can see there's not much spent, look after yourself, babe*—and if the company is paying me properly, as he hasn't seen any salary deposits on our account for the past couple of months. *We are a family; we don't need to separate our finances. We get wealthier together. Whatever you need, just ask me. I will give it to you.* I only reply that I have enough, I don't need to spend money. I don't want to explain why I have a separate account; I don't even know why I have it. What I do know is that I opened it before the book, the party and the masked man.

Tommy makes use of my relatively quiet day to catch me up on gossip. The day is blissful for a few reasons: first because my cow of a boss isn't here to mess up my workflow, and second because I'm in that state of consciousness where we rarely are. I'm connected with a new part of myself, a part that I recognise as being *me*. I feel I'm someone other than who everyone else sees. I am more than a lonely girl with a nomadic life.

The good thing about moving so frequently is the ability to retell your life with as few or as many details as you would like. For too long, I've lived with people feeling sorry for me, and I've learned that a tragic story interests others because it makes their lives better. It's not compassion, it's selfishness. It's that obscene pleasure people feel when a beautiful woman is sick or gets dumped by her boyfriend. No one admits it, of course, but the first thing they think is, *beautiful, but dumb and boring . . . she can't have it all.* Other people's happiness bothers us, other people's suffering validates us. A sad reality. That's why only a few know of my bereavements since I left home.

Misfortune also makes you feel less guilty about your accomplishments: it makes you deserve the good things you have. You can't be called greedy; it's only good karma making up for the bad that has happened.

It's like Gaudí, a genius with a miserable life, full of suffering. Of all the architects I know, none would exchange their life for Gaudí's professional success if that success had to come with his personal life. Real sadness is seeing those who spend their lives in misery, unable to achieve any form of success. They vanish. Their lives pass away, their names will never be remembered, and they have no one to tell their miserable—yet valuable—story.

Well, at last Tommy got tired of his so-so love life and decided to use a dating app a few weeks ago, and now he wants to update me on his new passion. His excitement and courage deserve attention, and I respond with the same interest he has in sharing his life with me.

'Wow, T! He's hot. Have you ever seen him in in real life?'

'No! Are you mad? Not yet. I need to marinade him a bit!'

'Sure. Foreplay. Online? Does that work?

'How old are you, *creature*? It just works! Are you going to say you've never . . . you know . . . *had sex*,' he whispers, 'from a distance?'

Reality hits me; I have been dating long-distance since February! I don't think we are doing a good job.

'I've never had to win anyone over from a distance, no.'

'Never? That's lucky! But then again, men . . . You're straight, right, not bi?'

'I'm straight, yes.'

'Men must be drooling over you, drooling like dogs in a butcher's shop.

'Not so much. Aren't you afraid?' I change the focus back to him

'Afraid of what?'

'I don't know, a *serial killer*, a pervert making films of you and selling them on the internet? How are you sure it's not some bizarre, disgusting person?'

'Do you think meeting someone face to face is a guarantee of safety? Of true love?'

'Yes, I think so. At least you can look them in the eye, know if they're telling the truth or not . . . if they're lying.'

'And who guarantees it? The guy who comes home and catches his wife *in the act* with the gardener?'

'You're watching too much porn . . . ,' I say, and we laugh a little.

But he is right. How do we know if the people we meet are telling the truth?

'Look around. Who do you really know? No one is an open book. It's all a game, a shitty-ass game, if you ask me . . . ,' he says.

'I think you're absolutely right! It's all rubbish!'

We laugh, he compliments me, asking where I've been all these years, because I'm everything this office needs to liven things up. I say the same to him. Another compliment I honestly give. It's a strange and decent feeling.

We end the morning chat with my question: 'Hey, Tommy, what would you do if no one knew your name or your face?'

'Um . . . I'd rob a bank! I can't stand working anymore!'

'Seriously, what would be the first thing you would do?'

Realising that my question is genuine, he shifts to a more reflective state: 'If no one had any way of finding out who I am?'

'Yup.'

'Interesting, my dear Tainá . . .' We exchange philosophical glances. 'I'll have to think about it.'

I wink. Not flirting, just agreement. Nothing more interesting happens, except that I'm glad to be getting to that point every immigrant loves, when their friendships begin to solidify while new ones emerge. It's a beautiful balance between having someone to confide in and having newness to explore.

Making the best of Thursday night shopping, I meet Fleur in front of the escalator at Myer. We are going to create a baby shower wish list. Who knows why she wants new things for the third baby? Besides a few basic pieces that have been destroyed by vomit, poo and blended food, what else can a baby possibly need? But who am I to say? I understand nothing when it comes to babies. Nothing. Ten minutes of browsing and chatting, and I discover this amazing idea: nursing shirts. I add some to the list. Her eyes fill with tears, and she hides her crying but not her emotion, with a tight, lingering hug that I gladly return. I don't think she's felt hugged for a long time, and this little gesture opens a floodgate of self-care. Bras, teas, anti-stretch-mark oils and bath salts enter the list. I insist on a new coffee cup and a book so she'll give herself twenty minutes of quiet a day.

'What would I do without you?' she tells me gratefully, squeezing me in her arms once more.

She stops me from putting candles on the list. Candles are forbidden in homes with babies, apparently. After the very efficient assembly of the list, she asks me for the best present I can give: stories. Stories about twentysomething singles. I'm not single, and I have to keep a secret about the only exciting thing that has happened to me in Sydney so far, so I have my reservations about saying anything about the drawing and poem the masked man gave me. It would be difficult not to tell her how I found out about the club, and if I tell her, who knows what will happen—maybe they will kick me out. Maybe she is also a member of the club. Although I saw some pregnant women there, I don't think Fleur would have time to go to parties, as she has two other children at home to look after. We don't talk about work during Thursday night shopping, so I tell her about what's inside the bag I'm carrying: a dress I received from the magazine's fashion producer when I went to deliver the material board this afternoon to their office. Fleur's eyes sparkle as I open the bag and show her the fluttery green fabric. Her enthusiasm for wanting to see me in it is so refreshing that I give in, and we go to the fitting rooms. I refrain from saying that I think these expensive pieces are trivialities, made to prepare women to seduce and pretend to be someone they are not. I don't say it for a good reason: since the party, I doubt this belief.

The only skin you can see is my chest, shoulders and hands. I'm intrigued by its construction as it attaches a long, ballooning, semitransparent sleeve to the tight upper body part. The fitted waist opens to a flowy skirt of many layers all the way to the floor. The ambient song playing through the PA system in the fitting room is appropriate for a dance, and Fleur doesn't let that escape from me by guiding our little waltz of a few seconds. Besides feeling sublime, I am with someone who has not the slightest reason to tell me some lie, and she puts me on a pedestal. She sees me as I have long—if ever—seen myself.

'You're like my sister—tall, beautiful, thin and childless!' she tells me. 'Who made this dress?'

'I have no idea!' I reply, embarrassingly giggling.

Although the promising designer's name was repeated over and over again as the magazine interns bellowed about how lucky I was to get such a dress for free, I don't remember it. I, concerned with ethical and mundane issues, ask Fleur for help on whether I should report it to the office, as I have no idea if there is any policy on receiving gifts from clients. I explain that it was an unexpected gift, that I was at the right time in the right place with the right person.

'If it wasn't harassment or asking for favours, I wouldn't say anything. You run the risk of losing your dress for nothing!'

She looks like a child in an ice cream shop. And there she goes telling me I should wear the dress on a romantic evening with Caio this weekend. Certain that I need new lingerie for the occasion because I am still too young to only have big panties and sports bras, she promptly gets me a set of panties and a bra that would puff up what has to be puffed up and will excite who should be excited. A few hundred dollars later, and I'm ready for my weekend with my boyfriend.

'Not that Caio needs special lingerie, does he? Unless he's with a mistress there, just one look at you at the airport and he'll want to take your clothes off right there!' She laughs, holding her belly that, being so big already, barely lets her go through the racks without touching the clothes.

The idea of sexually active people amuses Fleur, which seems to me to be a contradiction, since she has three children, and they are not beans sprouted in cotton.

Her comment creates a seed of doubt in my mind: Would Caio have a mistress? Can he manage to stay so long without anyone by his side?

The day ends with pleasant surprises evoking the smell of home and a mother's hug. My phone is the one who ends up hugging me, with a message from my mum saying she will be coming to see me, as she has been invited to take part in a research project at Auckland University about her work with neuroscience and psychoanalysis. She's asked them to buy a ticket to Sydney, and she'll pay for the leg to Auckland. She'll be here for a week. It's short, we know, but it's better than nothing.

She assures me that the tickets have been bought, but she can't remember the day she arrives; she'll check and tell me. A virtual hug that sometimes is enough for those who are far away. I send a voice memo overflowing with joy in response. I thank her for making the effort to come see me. Mentally, I thank her hippie-spiritual retreat, which must have given her unlimited access to my anguished vibrations—some of which I'm not sure I am aware of. She knows though. She always knows.

Caio sends a very simple message: *good night, see you tomorrow.*

*

Friday promises to be a curious day, to say the least. One hundred and twenty people who claim to work together but would barely recognise each other on the street will be mixing into groups for a team-building activity—whatever that means. We are all slowly coming together, and it's clear that people would rather talk to those they already know than take a chance by sitting next to someone insufferable for the rest of the day. The word going around the corridors this week was that today will be the first time the company has done this workshop with everyone. Apparently, in the past only project leaders, human resources and directors have done this kind of training, while the plebs—me, Fleur, Tommy and the vast majority—did computer programme training. To work more efficiently, of course. I am happy to be part of such a new event. I have always been a bit envious of these corporate activities that Caio has done and talked so much about.

Although I don't attach much importance to uniforms—in fact, I despise them—I think the dress code should be enforced and clearly stated. The normal casual Friday—which already has its problems, with ripped jeans and dirty trainers—is transformed today. For some, it looks more like a day to go to the local market; for others, especially for Martha, a lady who works in admin, it looks like a day to go to a wedding. I have never seen her with so much make-up, walking with such a posture in huge high heels, her hair professionally done—waved. I bet she has just ended a relationship—a woman who dresses like a peacock to attract others can only be trying to fill a void. I hope she's happy. To be fair to her and the women I may have offended now, some men appear to be equally desperate for social interaction beyond work relationships. Between those two extreme groups, there's me and most of the people who have taken the trouble to come in nice jeans and buttonless blouses, complying with the request to be in comfortable clothes, low shoes, and well groomed.

The noise in the conference room sounds like that of a restaurant; there is a large table with free tea, coffees and biscuits, apples and bananas. The fruit reminds me of the luscious breakfasts we had when I was little back in Brazil. Some people take a banana to their table, but not many people go for them here; coffee and biscuits clogging the plates seems to be the thing. I think people have an incredibly hard time not having anything to hold in their hands. We are so addicted to phones that I wonder if it is nicotine that makes cigarettes so addictive or the simple fact of having something in your hands. I am very judgemental today. These negative thoughts are the fruit of my irritation at waking up to the message—text—from Caio this morning, saying he's not coming to Sydney tonight.

I tried to call to find out why; he replied with an audio message: *I'm trying to finish something here at work. I had to cancel my travel because we're having a party for this mega-important guy, they told me today. I'll call you later.* I snort with rage as I listen to the message again. I wonder if he'll rebook or act like a rich businessman and just cancel. I think he'd better call me instead of texting.

I decide to have a good day, fighting against my irritability. Today is just like any workday. We are all stuck in the same room until 5:00 p.m.

The lively facilitators start the day with some embarrassing activities. What adjective would you give yourself with the first letter of your last name? *D.* The first word that crosses my mind—and I don't even know if it is to my surprise—is *depressed.* I preferred not to start introducing myself to a hundred and nineteen other people like that. Not that I'm really depressed, I've just been very lonely. I am probably belittling people who are truly depressed. It's unintentional and ignorant of my part. The second word that comes to mind is *desired,* and that one amazes me. When was the last time I felt wanted? It certainly isn't today. I've been internationally ditched by someone attending a *mega-important man* party. My mum would have some explanation for these words coming up from my subconscious mind. Scientific explanations. Maybe I should ask her. Maybe not. After rejecting the adjectives *divine*—my mother's influence—*dependent* and *decent,* I decided to stick with *dancing.* Tuesday's party reminded me how much I love to dance.

They divided the large group into two, then two more, and so on until we reached groups of six people. In mine, the only person I've ever spoken to was Luke, the guy who fixed my computer this week; I've only seen the other four *en passant*, exchanging kind and polite gestures of *good morning* and *see you tomorrow*. In our first task, we must look into each other's eyes for twenty seconds—this seems to be the theme of my week since the bookshop guy turned up. Twenty seconds seems too short a time to get any results, but no, we all have quite a few laughs, and something changes between the people in this small group. We seem more connected. We are four men and two women. Michael is a structural engineer, a fortyish cool grandfather and, as it turns out, funny. Jack and Greg are the babies, in the last year of their bachelor's programmes, working madly to save enough money to start their master's programmes next year. Bec is my age but has a much more advanced career than mine and works in urban planning. She's a local, never lived overseas. Perhaps this stability is what has allowed her to become a project lead already.

We manage to complete the first stage: making a square with a rope while blindfolded by one of those little sleeping pillows. It is quite interesting to see how we depend on our eyes to solve problems, and when we take vision away, we are forced to use clearer speech to communicate. We have to be more careful with the words we choose; there's also more touching of hands and accidental bumping of bodies. We congratulate each other, and although I control my Latin urge to hug everyone, Michael starts our group celebration by giving us all a high five. It is fun.

After we loosen up with a few simpler activities and a morning tea break, when once again, people fill up on saturated fat and caffeine, we pair up. Coincidentally, I'm paired with

Luke until lunchtime. We need to choose one of us to be blindfolded again.

'What would you prefer? Would you like to try being blind for a few minutes?' I ask.

'Do you know what we're supposed to do?' He proves that he was not paying attention to what has just been explained.

Someone asks the same question out loud, and the answer from the facilitator is clear: 'For now, just pick one person to put on the soft, seductive eye mask. Don't be shy—it's silk!'

I wonder where these entertainers get so much energy from.

'Do you want to put the eye mask on? I promise to be a good guide dog.' He smiles and, as there is no reason to disagree, I accept.

What I feel now is the extreme opposite of the safety I felt on Tuesday. With the eye mask in place, everyone can see me, but I can't see anyone; there is a hole—a metaphorical one—under my feet, and I hope that the trembling in my legs is only perceived by me. It's a fearful circumstance. After all, how many times have we gone through the experience of being blind? I remember the old man at the mask shop.

Luke holds my hand and, noticing my nervousness, tells me: 'Trust me, you won't fall or hit anything. I promise.' He puts my hands on the rope. 'The rope isn't very long, but it's thin and long enough for me to fasten around my waist, and you can hold on to the end of it. I haven't seen the obstacles yet, but I think it might work. Do you want to try?'

'Good idea, let's go.'

'How long is the rope?' I ask. He touches my hand, placing it on one extreme of the rope. I find the other end.

'See, it's not very long,' he says.

He is not allowed to do anything with the rope, so I loop it around like a belt, put it on the floor and ask him to step inside the circle. I lift it to where I think his waist is and tighten the adjustable knot I just made.

'Impressive! Making knots is not a skill everyone masters, particularly when you can't see.' He compliments me and asks if I was a Girl Scout as a child.

'No, I just learned to untie them in case I was kidnapped . . .' From his prolonged silence, I understand he didn't get the joke. 'I'm joking . . .'

'Phew! That's a relief, I was wondering where you grew up!' he sighs. 'I'm going to pace us, okay? My arm is in front of you.'

His elbow is bent. I hook my arm around his, and I feel we are about to enter a dance floor. It is not one. Another man's arm. Another encounter with the temptation gender. I am okay. I have done nothing. Caio would be infuriated if he saw this. I don't know why though; I don't believe I have ever done anything to make him jealous, but he often is. I'm not the only committed woman here being paired with a man who is not her partner.

'I'll start with my right foot, left foot, right foot . . .' He does so and guides me until we reach the beginning of the obstacle course. 'Take a deep breath; we're first.'

'Are there a lot of people watching?'

'Half the people.'

'Funny guy,' I say, showing I understand his joke.

'Don't worry, I promise to tell you what's coming in front of you with enough time, okay?'

'Okay.'

'Well, the circuit is all padded. It's one of those giant inflatable bouncy things; you can't get hurt by hitting anything hard or sharp, but you can fall off. Some pairs are also strapped themselves in by the waist like us.'

'Good ideas have to be copied, right?' I say, trying to ease my tension with a mediocre joke— all my attempts to be funny are mediocre.

'I smiled a bit, but you didn't see it.' Sensitively, he describes to me what he's doing.

'Thanks, Luke. You don't have to tell me what other people are doing, okay? Let's just focus on what I have to do.'

'Sure.'

Finally, the start is sounded by a shrill horn, making my ears ring. Luke narrates everything exactly as he promised, and, after some initial falls and stumbles, we find our rhythm. After the second slide over the hump of a steep climb, I trust he wants only to guide me; he doesn't take advantage of my vulnerable condition, and I overcome the unsettling sensation of being under his will. Other obstacles, such as navigating through small tunnels, swinging on ropes, alternating feet on tyres and many new tasks occupy the next minutes of our lives. Maybe fifteen minutes. I'm not sure. We complete the race feeling accomplished, with that excitement in our nerves that lifts us to a higher plane, an innocent transcendence, an experience shared and achieved in trust. I begin to give these adult party entertainers my respect. Facilitators, not party entertainers. Luke hugs me as I take off my eye mask, and we jump up and down in celebration that we're done. Knowing our time or whether we will beat the rest of the group is unimportant.

'High five, partner!' he says, and we walk to the area where we will wait for the other fifty-nine pairs. 'Thanks for trusting me.'

'Thanks for guiding me so well, after that horn; it kind of worked. Before we started, I thought I was going to take this thing off in two seconds,' I say, pointing to the eye mask, and laugh proudly that I didn't take it off.

Partner. He called me *partner.* I supposed we partnered. I wonder if replacing the word *boyfriend* or *girlfriend* for *partner* is a good thing. We can and we should have many partners in life at the same time. Not necessarily only romantic ones.

'What's next?' he asks while we wait others to finish the circuit.

'I don't know, maybe we have to swap. Do you wear the eye mask and I guide you?'

'I hope not. I won't do nearly as well as you. But if I must, I'll swap, of course. I trust you won't let me embarrass myself. Please don't let me embarrass myself!' he laughs, and so do I.

The activity takes a long time; we wait for almost an hour for the last team to finish. Some will curse their partners as a joke, some will openly admit they hated being blindfolded, but regardless of how many falls, tumbles and mistakes they've made, the outcome is always light-hearted.

The following activities are not nearly as impactful as this one; Luke doesn't need to cover his eyes, and I feel slightly disappointed. Could I guide him as well as he guided me?

At the end of the day, some of us, elated by the shared fun times, decide to go see the light show in the city, an annual event that gets people off the couch, out of their beds and into the streets to spend money and marvel at the wonders of technology. A speck of wonderment.

We spread out around the food stalls and vans on the street to choose our preferred dinner—given the options. I am convinced to try a Mexican burrito, and the taste of black beans makes me feel nourished like I haven't in a long time. How much I miss my childhood food! Thanks to our phones, we gather back on the lawn in front of the MCA for an evening picnic. A relaxed and easy-going picnic.

The magical evening walking around Circular Quay, indulging in the lights, discussing architectural, technological, social and cultural issues, ends when we see ourselves in front of a nightclub. I don't know how we got here, but here we are. I try to get out of it the best I can, but Tommy and Bec insist, and I run out of empty excuses. Fleur is the only one who escaped, but she also missed most of the night up until now because she couldn't walk as much or as fast as we do, so she left much earlier.

The mood—of people and of the city—changes a little after 9:00 p.m. I should be getting ready to sleep by now. Families, the elderly and couples make way for a darker place where people dress to show how much money they have and how high their tolerance to alcohol is. It's a competition; it all seems like a self-proclaimed win. Except for us. We are all wearing the clothes we spent the day in, some even wearing trainers we've bought on sale. Bec is the one who drinks the most, but it's still not nearly as much as some of the strangers around us drink.

The nightclub is an excellent example of a well-restored old building: the old was kept old, the bricks, for example, while the new is clearly new—the glass-and-steel lift. It is dark, except when the rays of the revolving neon lights strike a surface or a face. It stinks, with the dense smell of beer mixed with vomit and odours of other various fluids. It is inhospitable; the lack of smiles from the bouncers and bar attendants indicates that they are tired of the drunks and junkies. It is all that the masked party wasn't. Would I be able to recognise him if I saw him here with a naked face?

'Hello! A penny for your thoughts,' says Tommy. 'Who's the guy?'

'What guy? I'm not thinking about any guy,' I lie. 'I'm just happy to finally go out with you!' That is true.

We have been trying to go out for ages, and I always end up working late or being too tired. I try not to compare this party to my party last Tuesday, but it's almost inevitable. I want to go back to the other one. Should I? It's better not to; I was so close to doing something I shouldn't. Will I be able to control myself next time?

At a certain point, when everyone is sedated enough to leave their shame aside and say things they might regret the next day—or laugh at today's little gaffes—someone suggests a game of truth or lie. Each person must say three statements, two true and one false; the others need to guess which is which.

We find out that Bec was a chef before she became an architect, that Jack has just come out of the closet to his mother and has never been happier. Luke enjoys sailing—like me. Tommy learned to speak Spanish to backpack through Latin America but discovered that we speak Portuguese in Brazil after arriving there, which caused some memorable times. Martha and Michael discovered they have a lot in common and disappear into the shadows of the nightclub or perhaps the night outside.

'Your turn, Tainá.' Jack puts me in the spotlight I was trying to avoid by being the last one, hoping they would forget about me. They didn't.

'Me? Okay, here it goes: 'I've been attacked by a cheetah. I've had a boyfriend for seven years. I am an Olympian in sailing—laser category.'

'Easy!' bawls Tommy. 'Dating! Nobody dates someone for seven years!' A chorus of the others agree with him.

'What? I am shocked!' I have that nervous, disbelieving giggle in my voice. 'Do you think it's more credible that I was attacked by a cheetah or that I am an Olympic athlete, then?'

Everyone agrees, laughing. The lie is—obviously—the Olympic athlete. I was almost an Olympic athlete. Almost. Maybe it's the one *caipiroska* I've had, maybe it's the company, but when I finally manage to throw out my comparison to Tuesday's party and let myself get carried away with everyone's silliness, I have a wonderful time.

Caio calls very late and, amid music, talk, noise and glasses toasting, it's hard to hear what he has to say. I tell him I'm out with the people from work and I'll call when I get home. Not knowing if he can hear, I send a message repeating what I just said and, thinking he must be as surprised as I am to see me in a nightclub, I add he has nothing to worry. I'm fine. More than fine.

I'm at the bar on my own buying my round when someone crosses a very clear boundary: my body. A small, skinny guy kisses my face. I push him away, and Luke appears out of nowhere and places himself between the guy and me.

'I didn't know you had an owner!' The guy goes away, mumbling and gesturing apologetically to Luke. To Luke, not to me. 'Sorry, mate! No hard feelings, yeah?'

'I don't understand how there are so many disgusting guys out there,' he says. Disgusting, just like the worms from the illustration in the book. 'Are you okay?'

'Yeah, thanks.' I'm perplexed. 'It was nothing.' I had forgotten what these nightclubs are like and why I don't make an effort to go anymore. I think that's enough. It's time to go home.

'Of course it was. He might have not hurt you, but he didn't ask . . . Did he?'

'No, definitely not.' I don't know how long it takes me to continue 'He apologised to you . . . I could have beat him up myself . . .'

'I'm sure you could have. I'm sorry, I didn't mean to say you couldn't . . .'

'Oh no, thank you. Really, thank you. I haven't been out in a long time, I didn't think these things would still happen . . . I'm noy seventeen anymore.'

'A guy like that can't ruin your night. Let's dance! Where's Tainá *Dancing* Drummond?' Bec takes her drink from the counter, pulls my hand and we are off to the dance floor.

It doesn't take long for the worms to approach over and over again. It is tiring to continuously protect our own space. The fun is over, so I go home, without letting it be obvious to anyone that I have already passed my limits. As I wait on the street for a licensed cab, I sense someone getting closer from behind. I wish we never had to fear for the integrity of our bodies; I have no weapon with me—and would I do anything with it if someone attacked me? I walk towards a restaurant that is expelling their last customers; it's a mix of women and men. It's safer to wait for the taxi there. I take the phone from my pocket to call the first name on the list. Anyone. The steps are closer. Should I turn?

'Tainá!'

The relief resets my body. It's Luke. I hang up the phone.

'Can I take you home? I want to know if you're going to be okay . . .'

'No need. Don't you live around here?'

'I'm going to Tamarama. It would be nice to share the cab and a chat on the way.' He looks at me and waits for an answer. I'm thinking very slowly. 'Don't worry, I'm not like these guys . . .' He points to his wedding ring. Have I noticed his ring before? Is he married?

Out of fear, more than to save money, I say yes.

I get into the taxi with him, and we sit in the back seat at opposing windows. Luke talks almost in a monologue about everything that is wrong in Sydney and in the world, and how he would fix it. He talks about his kids and says I shouldn't date for so long, because when you know who your life partner is, there is nothing better than creating experiences together and, if possible, proliferating more life. I think he is a good father, in love with his children and his wife. As promised, he drops me off at the door of the building, and, like a true gentleman, he waves goodnight twice, as soon as I get out of the car and then again as I stand behind the glass door when I enter the building.

*

Winter in Sydney would be reason enough to be happy here. Little do those who live here know that the blue skies and that ever-warm sunshine make the city so famous. Very promptly the next morning, I get up to run and kick that headache caused by the generic caipirinha, the caipiroska, I had last night. I can hardly believe that a small drink has left me with such a horrible migraine. As bad as the headaches I used to have before I moved to Spain. Next thing I know, I remember that I didn't call Caio, and my phone has twenty-seven missed calls, all from the same person. The boyfriend himself. I call back, and he is still awake, waiting for me to call, according to him. I don't even know how many days it's been since we've spoken properly, but this is unusual.

'What a night, huh? You've only just woken up? Did you have fun?' he says without me being able to tell if it's sarcasm or if he is happy for me. Could this be joy? 'I was worried with you running loose at night.' Sarcasm, definitely sarcasm.

'There's nothing to worry about. It was just work. A drink after a pretty long day.'

'What did you do? Who was there?'

'Everybody from work.'

'Everyone?' I notice suspicion in his voice; I don't like it at all.

'Yes, everyone went to the event during the day, and gradually people went home. Not everyone stayed for the whole night.'

'And who was there at night?'

'Caio, are you jealous?' I throw a little bait to see if this interrogation is due to him feeling insecure.

'Jealous? Of course not. Why would I be jealous? Do I have reason to be jealous?' he replies with a certain aggressiveness and a dismissive tone. I am confused as to whether he is implying that no one else would have any interest in me or whether I would have the ability to betray him.

'No, of course not.'

I tell him the truth about yesterday; there's no reason to be jealous, but our conversation is not the best. Caio doesn't try to turn on the video to see me. I don't try either, but in my defence, I never try. I attribute our friction to our distance, and in an attempt to see if things will resolve on their own, I change the direction of our conversation to more tangible and objective matters.

'Do you know when you're coming to visit?'

'No,' he replies dryly.

I sense a hostility in that 'no' and insist on a real answer, the kind you can do something with. 'Are you upset with me?'

'Not at all,' says Caio, pretending not to be bitter and angry.

'Are you jealous because I went out yesterday?' I make one last attempt to have a productive interaction. He doesn't respond; he remains silent until he changes the subject, asking what I'm going to do today. My impulse is to respond in the same ironic, passive-aggressive tone, but I decide to reset things by saying I didn't make any plans for today because I thought we'd be enjoying the winter sun on the beach together.

'Tainá, you know how we met.' He throws that in the air, not mentioning anything about why we are not on the beach together. He was supposed to be here today. What he is implying is that we became interested in each other while I was with Miguel, when I lived in Spain. What he doesn't say, although he knows, is that my Spaniard and I were in an open relationship. Both Miguel and I knew very well that we would last two seasons: the six months I had left before I finished my year in Barcelona. A fleeting, intense and short-lived romance. It is understandable that Caio is insecure now, but I have never cheated on anyone.

'Caio, I don't know what you are trying to say. If I wanted to cheat, I would break up with you first. How can you compare what I had with Miguel with what we have? I just went to a nightclub with I don't know how many men—very hot by the way—and I wasn't interested in any of them. Don't be silly. But you, on the other hand . . .'

'What about me? What are you implying?

'We know that a successful man alone is a magnet for attractive, opportunistic women.'

'Tainá Drummond, are you jealous?'

Am I? I'm more irritated than anything; he is being so patronising, as if he is talking to a child.

'No, definitely not. I'm only jealous of your work. As for these other women, I . . . trust *you*.' I emphasise the *you*. Not them.

I am jealous and envious of his work. Being an immigrant doesn't seem to stop him from progressing; he has decision-making power, he is valued, he earns much more than me, he has me, who follows him around the world . . . It keeps him so busy that he forgets there is a life outside of work. He forgets that I exist. I am often alone whenever we live in the same place. I do hate his work. As for being jealous of him, romantically, I feel a lie has just come out of my mouth. I had never thought about whether I trust him or not, I always simply did. Now, I have a flea whispering doubts into my ear. What would be the signs he is cheating? I could have kissed the masked man; it would have been so simple. I imagine that for Caio it would be even easier to find another pair of legs to satisfy his needs.

'Yeah, I know, my work really consumes a lot of our lives,' he says gently, calmly, caringly.

And so, in a single word, *our*, I can tell that he is still with me, that we are still us, a couple. That there is still a chance to be what we were before he left. A word can fill a hole that not even I knew was so deep. He once more promises to be more present. I let the hope overtake my doubt.

We end the conversation without him mentioning or apologising for cancelling his flight or giving me details of what he did last night, but it doesn't matter. Caio has a unique ability to dodge difficult answers.

I finally get out for a run but don't get halfway to Coogee. I stop at the cemetery, exhausted. My legs are cramping, and I'm short of breath. I could be hungover, but I reckon it's the suffocating doubts stopping the air from going into my lungs. Doubt never really leaves you, does it? Why did he really need to go to that party? Who is this guy? Why is everything from work more important than me? More important than us? Could he be cheating on me? I need to let it go until he is back.

I walk back home, listening to the ocean and the chatter of people passing me. I go to a pharmacy to get an anti-inflammatory. As I pay for it, from the corner of my left eye, I see a stand with a stack of newspapers. The date of the next party is there, right in front of me. I know the chances of seeing the masked big nose again are infinitesimal. There's no danger of meeting him again. He was . . . He was that paper, that drawing, that poem, that night. I will remember him forever; he will remember her, Eva. He will remember me. Just as I remember Miguel and Miguel must remember me. The taste of Spain, of our skin awaking to our passionate mornings, comes back to me as if it was happening right now. I can smell his neck. I feel his hands around the curves near the bottom of my spine, slightly above my hips. I'm sure it's just my brain activating parts of itself to trick me, convincing me that I'm there with Miguel now. I look to the side and, obviously, he is not here. But I do see a *Sì* perfume. It is not our smell, but it is one of those signs that we choose to notice because believing in them brings a special taste to life.

'Excuse me.' The attendant asks me if I want anything else.

All this happens in a fraction of a second. I put the newspaper on the counter and pay with the cash I tucked in the small pocket in the back of my leggings.

I spend the rest of the weekend reading, walking, drinking juice and coconut water and feeding myself contradictory, nostalgic and hopeful thoughts. While Miguel, the bookshop guy and the masked man disturb my morals in burning, uncontrollable memories and illusions of love and passion, Caio's love brings me comfort and hope that we can go back to the night he loved me as if there's no one else in the world that matters.

It wasn't love at first sight; it wasn't a desire that stripped us off any values of good behaviour and naturally made us experienced lovers. There was nothing memorable about the first night we were together except that it was the first night. We were rushed, full of expectations and out of rhythm. Our love grew with experiences and time—the way any long-lasting relationship should. There is *the* night however, the night we sealed the depths of our trust in one another, the night my skin recalls and the one my body reacts to as if I was there, simply by thinking of it. On that night, we wove our bodies together and merged into each other. We didn't limit our bodies to what is appropriate, what is beautiful or conventional. We loved each other intensely and free. He desired me with the thirst of a man lost in the desert who had just found fresh water, and with the transcendence of someone who almost lost his life. That day, Caio elevated my existence without saying a single word. Like a fight worthy of a movie, he put his own life in danger so that I could live. Few things will change someone as much as going through such a moment. We were grateful for each other's lives, verbally and physically demonstrating it day after day, loving each other like fused souls until . . . Nothing new happened. Until, progressively, everyday life tried to drown out the magic of that night when we were born again. Today and for a couple of years now, I thank him for coming out from under the cheetah unharmed.

The weekend ends with a practical conversation with Mum on the phone. All set for her arrival in a few weeks.

*

The way Caio chooses to be more present is to clog me up with flowers. Every day, a different arrangement arrives, and they get bigger and bigger. No cards, no messages, no phone calls; he just sends the flowers, and they always arrive between 8:00 p.m. and 9:00 p.m. Maybe because he knows I'll be home. I send a photo every night saying, *They've arrived!* Maybe I should remove the exclamation mark. I think Singapore has changed him. I don't know how, but he would never have sent me flowers before. Caio knows I can't stand flowers that will wilt and die in a few days.

Singapore has changed me too; maybe not Singapore, maybe it's everything else. Will it be possible for us to last?

8

It's June 21, Winter Solstice, a perfect day for the masked party. A reminder of the eternal cycles of birth and death, a day to be hopeful that spring will rise again. Soon. Now that everyone seems to know each other, work has become increasingly lighter, less pressurised somehow; even the miserable rainy day outside doesn't seem to bother anyone in here. The atmosphere has changed, and I wonder which deadline will come along and destroy this delicate balance.

Even my boss, whom I will call Joanne, her real name, seems more human to me. I have discovered that the real reason she is late every Monday is her mother-in-law's illness. She has dementia, and Joanne's ex-husband, the old lady's only son, has disappeared by choice. In the beginning, he convinced Joanne that children only spoil romance, finances and sanity. He then made a pact: he promised her they would look after each other until they *perished in old age*—his words. Joanne, in love and grateful to have a good man by her side, believed him. All it took was her wrinkles and his fear of finitude to emerge, and he dumped her to live in Hawaii with a twenty-something year old bimbo—her words. He now has two young children. He, heartless as he is, still sends pictures of his beautiful family to Joanne. He believes she is happy for him. If that wasn't enough, he abandoned not only the woman who saw him rise out of poverty and into wealth, but also the one who birthed him into this world. Joanne now takes care of her former mother-in-law because she is a good woman, who joins her in her hatred of her *new* son, because the one from before, the one she raised, would not have left her to her fate. She tells Joanne that if a life was meant to be lived solely on wishes and happiness, we would only indulge in sweets, fat, drinks, drugs, sex and everything else that makes us less healthy. Maybe that's why Joanne is so angry at me, or so angry at life. I don't blame her. I want to see if anyone would be different in her place. Since Friday, I have not cussed her again, and this week I have come to a compassionate peace with her aggressions. I think, but I could be wrong, that she respects me now. The other good things to come out of Friday are Martha and Michael, who seem to find each other down the corridors, and Jack and Tommy, who are inseparable lunch companions. I conclude that love is in the air.

I take advantage of this expansive air and embark on my second party to disconnect and forget the countless insinuations of infidelity from Caio's jealousy. He won't admit it, but I know he wants to know what I'm doing every second. I know that as soon as I leave the party, there will be a message from him wishing me good night. Maybe even more than one. Bibi is having trouble renting the flat, and I, once again, asked to stick around to ease my way to and from the party.

Bibi's house is far less equipped than mine, but I feel at peace here. The trees right outside the living room and kitchen windows nourish me; they make believe I am in a forest. The view of the water and the city across the bay brings me great peace by holding my thoughts that so easily fly away when I see vast horizon of the Ocean. I have far less hesitation than at the first party, but I am too cautious to be able to call myself brave. It is easy to have strengths and ideals in my imagination, but what will I do if he finds me? What if I find him? If he opts for the same mask, it will be hard not to . . . What am I going to do?

To avoid obvious recognition and tread the fine line of temptation, I bought a new mask during a lunch break this week. But since life seems to be an eternal dichotomy to me, I wear the same necklace, in the remote—and guilty—hope that he will be able to find me.

I get ready much quicker. My make-up needs to be a little more elaborate, as this mask has no lace over my eyes. I wear the green dress I was gifted by the magazine, and just by thinking about Fleur's face seeing me try it on at the shop, I smile calmly about our friendship. I'm getting to the sweet spot of immigration. The chest and shoulders sticking out are perhaps a little too daring; the bodice squeezes my breasts, revealing a curvature I've never seen before. My cape will cover them on the street, but not during the party. I have a vague guess where I should go today, but I'm not sure yet. This morning, I took the longest route to the office, the one that runs through the middle of the Rocks, so I could see that the flowers are white. I spent my spare time today rereading the poetry on my phone to the point of distracting myself from what I was meant to be doing: working. I delayed emails, I searched the internet, I made notes in my notebook, I took a longer lunchtime and I nagged people to help me translate the poem without giving away anything about the party.

White Petunias
Break on pillars like waves
Believing man to walk
Over the water as they crave

As I tidy up my bed before leaving for the party, it seems pretty obvious that the answer is a pier. Columns that make man believe he can walk on water can only be those of a pier. I thought about an art installation, something like a glass floor, but I couldn't find anything that was happening in Sydney as such. The only other way to walk on water is during a flood, when you have to walk on the road, or take a boat. But boats and roads generally don't have columns.

I ask the taxi driver to leave me on the west side of the Rocks at Walsh Bay, where there are several piers and decks. Truth be told, this is a long shot. There are so many more piers around Sydney.

I stand by the column of one of the bridges that pass over on Hickson Road, waiting to see other masked people around. Fifteen minutes of waiting in the shadows can quickly become a problem. A police car parks close by, and I see myself walking away towards the theatres and restaurants. It's only when I get to the roundabout that I find another person like me, and I follow her at a decent distance.

Despite a far more imposing entrance, compared to Celeste House, the initial formalities are the same. There is a masked man welcoming people and guiding them through the large, heavy, old wooden sliding door, in contrast to the hotel's marble lobby and contemporary finishes. The ambience is similar to that of the first party, elegant and intimate, in what appears to be a converted warehouse. The rhythm of the building's structure is emphasised by the lighting. This warehouse is about 170–180 metres long.

Stone walls and bricks fill the spaces between the gaps in the structure. Where the original material could not withstand the weather, walls, beams and columns of exposed concrete fill the void. The floor is made of wooden planks worn down by use; the ceiling invites the sky in with a triangular skylight in the centre of the roof. I admire the ethereal sensation that looking up gives me. The sofas, tables, bar and bathrooms are of the highest quality and super new. An exquisite conversion of a large warehouse to a much more pleasurable space. I observe the place as much as I observe the details of the guests; my heart skips every time I believe I see a golden, huge-beaked mask. They are all false alarms, and I try to pull myself together by taking a deep breath with each moment of frustration. *It's better, Tainá. You'd better not see him.*

I force myself to look at other parts of the party and realise I'm in front of a closed room with a handwritten sign—*Free Body Culture*—and underneath in small letters, *based on the Germanic FKK movement.* Another sign with the rules explains in more detail what the FKK is and how it was adapted for this group. In short, we must keep our masks on, but clothes are removed and placed in a wardrobe within the room itself. It is a space of nudism for non-nudists and, as they say, *a place for experiencing the freedom of the body during everyday life*. The activities listed include cooking, playing table tennis, eating, watching TV, playing video games, bathing in a jacuzzi, doing yoga, meditating, riding a bicycle—stationary—and running on a treadmill. What strikes me the most is the fact that it's communal. You don't do it alone; you share the experience with a group of people. There's an electronic number on the door saying that the capacity of twenty-five people has not been reached and that there are two spaces left. Should I go in? What have I got to lose?

My dress is particularly difficult to take off by myself, but I manage after a little contortion. So far, so good. My new lingerie that Fleur made sure I bought stayed at home because the outlines of the underwear show through, and I have my doubts as to why I should wear it on a day like today—no one will see it. I tamp down my reflexive inhibition by reminding myself that what the lingerie covers more of me than my bikini. No different than going to a beach. *It's okay, Tainá, you can slowly get naked.* The touch of my feet on the warm floor gives me the nourishment—and therefore the courage—I need to continue undressing. Taking off my bra makes me a little afraid, and I imagine that everyone looking at me must know I'm a newbie. I seem to be doing things in slow motion. When I look around, no one is looking at me. I don't cause a fuss, taking off my clothes here is normal, as it should be everywhere. So, I gain the strength to take off my underwear, and with a deep breath I see myself completely naked in the middle of strangers. Gradually, with each step, the fear of humiliation fades away, and I can see my shoulders open and my back elongating. While we wear our masks, while our identity is secure, there is no way to carry what happens here to the world outside.

I'm not sure if I look like how I feel—a lost tourist—but nobody offers help, nobody calls out to me. Just very polite, simple greetings from a nice, comfortable distance. And that's how it is with everyone else. An instant, unjudged welcome. You don't have to do anything to be accepted; on the contrary, you get kicked out if you do something disrespectful. I join the two cooks, who decide to make a pizza to be shared by everyone. We end up making fifteen pizzas with a huge variety of flavours. We leave the pizzas on the counter, cut into small squares—my idea—with bamboo skewers for each person to serve themselves. After that, I join a very short yoga class. I lose count of how many people I chat to. The mask is starting to make me itchy, and someone tells me that there are other nudist clubs where you don't wear a mask. Maybe I should look for them too, but I don't know if I have the courage to be completely exposed. I could run into a client or a colleague; the idea of someone from the real world thinking of me naked and free causes me to shiver, a bad shiver, a disgusted shiver.

Almost an hour later—the maximum time we can stay—I leave the nude room and, fully clothed, join the main party. My serenity from when I was naked disappears as soon as I find myself looking for my masked man and remember the drawing with my pendant as the moon.

I hold it. I feel a tight reminder in my heart—not the organ that can be cured with medicines—but the other heart, the one that holds the emotions. The one without a simple solution sold in a pharmacy to ward off the cuts of suffering. My anguish comes from the memory of the trip to New Zealand when my brother turned fifteen and where we vowed, with this necklace, that even during life's turbulence, we would always be together. *How I miss you, brother.* His voice seems to whisper as if he were here; my hand absorbs a warmth that emanates from the moment of life that was sealed inside this pendant. I am a soup of contradiction; my legs, which were just now freeing themselves to nakedness, are now stiff as two century-old trees, but with spongy cores. A little squeeze would be enough to cause them to collapse.

I distract myself from the past with the guilt of looking for the masked man. Why do I want to see him? Being here should be enough; that room I was just in should be enough entertainment. Today, despite the similarities to last week, is all quite different. A remarkable woman, who judging by the lines on her chest and neck has been around this world for more decades than I have, approaches me. Her exposed skin, squeezed by her ample breasts, shows signs of sunspots and lost elasticity. Unimportant details; they don't stop her from glowing.

'You look like you would be just as happy without that mask,' I say, admiring her energetic exuberance.

'Equally? Impossible, missy! This here'—she brings her index finger to her mask—'gives me incredible freedom. That guy over there could be someone from work. I wouldn't be able to shake those beauties like that!'

Needless to say, *the beauties* are the two melons protruding from her body.

'Try it!' she says.

'Mine don't swing like that . . . They're more like grapes than melons.' I fall into laughter, disbelieving that I've just said these words.

'Grapes are the fruit of the gods, girl! Enjoy!' She picks up her glass and makes a toast to me—or to my grapes and her melons—suggesting I drink it too. We laugh together, and as soon as she goes back to rattling her skills around people, I am surprised by a whisper in my left ear. A familiar whisper.

'Your laugh is remarkable.'

It's him! My smile expands, clearly proving that I rather that he showed up than now. The voluptuous woman looks at me from a distance, in the middle of the crowd, raises her glass once more and says: 'Enjoy!'

'Enjoy what?' he asks me.

'Grapes.'

'Grapes?' he repeats, confused.

'You don't want to know.' I turn to face him, and he also has a new mask. The golden beak is much smaller than last time; now it's the shape of an owl's. From the front, the beak covers his mouth to the end of the chin, the sides are open, and his jaws are strongly marked by stubble. With bronze detailing, the mostly wine-and-black mask has rounded ear tips pulled upwards, and the cut-outs for the eyes are surrounded by small indentations that look like feathers. The part that covers the rest of his head is moulded with lines as if his hair were combed back. His mask is actually a helmet. I'm not sure what it is made of; it is all opaque, and the sewing lines I see make me think it's thick leather. I don't look down at his clothes, as my eyes are attached to his and his to mine. All I can see beyond the mask are the black jacket and his black shirt with frills in the centre.

'What happened to the beak? Did it break?' My hands draw a curve, exaggerating the size of the nose of the old mask.

'It was hard going through that surgery. What if the big nose was all you saw in me?'

His good humour is like the emergence of a rare beauty: it invites, arrests and hypnotises. In that order.

'I risked you not recognising me,' he continues, 'but I had to get rid of it. It's hard to hear you in all this racket, having to stand a metre away.'

'Your nose wasn't a metre long! And how will you listen to me if your ears are covered now?' I speak loudly and smile because he found me and there's this comfortable pause between us. Inside, I'm torn in two. One part of me is not at peace; it is gathering guilt around itself in a grey, cold corner, feeling miserable, like the scum of the world.

'I can hear you perfectly; there are some little holes here.' He points to his ears. He wears wine-coloured gloves, just like the helmet, only made of a softer leather. He is very thoughtful about how he dresses. His shirt has longer sleeves than his blazer, and they're voluminous and elegant.

'Thank you for the drawing,' I say honestly, without revealing that I've lost count of how many times I've read the poem and unintentionally memorised it.

'Thanks for the company,' he says enchantingly. 'I like your hat. You changed from lady in black to puss in . . . are you wearing boots?'

I lift the dress slightly to show that yes, I am wearing new brown boots I bought on a childish impulse when I was with Fleur putting together her baby shower.

'Puss in boots . . . Musketeer, you didn't make it very easy to find you.'

'I didn't think I'd find you again.'

'Despite my hopes, I didn't expect to find you either. I thought it would be impossible to cross paths with the same person twice at one of these parties. And this new mask, new hair . . . difficult.'

'I put the same necklace on, since you seem to have noticed it.' I refer to the moon in the drawing; I know he understands.

'A little clue to test me. I like it, but I found you by your smile, your laughter.'

I can't hide my embarrassment at his flirtation; it's hard to imagine he could be interested in me. He doesn't even know who I am. Or is what he knows enough?

'Why were you looking for me? So many people to engage with . . .'

'I don't know. There are things we can't explain.'

'Have you been there?' I point to the nudist hall.

'No. I'm not ready for that yet. You?'

'Yes,' I reply shyly, and he becomes silent. I can't see his face, so I don't know what he is thinking. 'A penny for your thoughts.'

'I think the cat has my tongue.'

He makes me feel as if I am more progressive than him, but I don't think that is possible. I like the idea though, so I avoid saying that I only entered the room once. I let him imagine whatever he wants. I wish I could see his eyebrows and complete the shape of his eyes. Damned masks. Blessed masks. With just a charming smile and a light touch on my back, he leads me to the dance floor.

The euphoria of these moments is priceless. I levitate to another plane of existence—the laughter, the music, the smiles, the looks, the instruments, the touches, the synchrony of strangers transform my transcendent life. I'm alive somewhere else without responsibilities or worries; we simply follow the rhythm; we follow the other's cues, improvising every second. The safety gives me an incredible freedom. I am free.

Suddenly, everything stops. Not for the others, but for me. After we've circled the hall a few times, I realise we are entwined, his arms around my waist and his gaze fixed on mine. It is the line, the line I cannot cross. The disturbing line of respect I've not crossed for the last seven years of my life.

'I like to see your eyes without the lace. They are beautiful.'

I am frozen. Speechless. The cat has my tongue now.

The world around us continues to move, but we enter another dance, one that belongs only to the two of us and to another, who is not here to be consulted. By his hypnotic look into my eyes, reaching my soul, I am sure that his world has also stopped. What I don't know is if there is a fourth person in this dance, someone from his side. The silence between us is loud with meaning. This intense reciprocity transforms us into one. I know he feels what I feel. A mere illusion. Countless are the mysteries that surround us! What is clear between us is the synchronicity. How could he find me again? This attraction is difficult to explain. I have never been so close to someone who causes me this contradictory stir of shyness and power. Even in the midst of all this noise, I am sure that he hears and feels the uncontrollable sigh that comes out of my ajar lips. A physical reaction to everything that has happened in the past—not even two—weeks. In my imagination, I can taste him, the wetness of his mouth, the texture of his skin. I'm thankful for the masks since, if it weren't for them creating real distance between us, I would make a big mistake. A mistake with no turning back. A mistake that could cost my future with Caio. I need to leave before it's too late. Reluctantly, I break the spell, let myself loose and leave the dance floor. I feel his doubts following me. Is he coming after me? I don't look back; I only hear him reaching for me through my ears. 'Wait! Eva, wait!' I bump into people on my way out; my hat almost falls several times. He reaches me when I get to the entrance hall. The marble floor echoes.

'Is everything okay?' Of course *he* is going to ask; of course *he* is going to care how I feel.

'It's okay, I just got a bit . . . dizzy.' I look away, avoiding facing him and admitting to myself that I'm lying. I should be clear and say that *dizzy* is a euphemism for the war going on between my values and what my body craves. 'I need to go . . .' I say as I stare down to the floor, trying to hide my eyes below the hat. I don't move. Maybe I'm waiting for a sign that I'm not all that bad and, like Bibi said, I'm only human.

He stands mute, immobile. Is he waiting for me to move? Does he buy that I'm dizzy? What feels like a long silence is broken by his words.

'Let's get some fresh air and some water. You'll feel better . . .' He shows me the way to the small balcony off the lobby; I walk in front of him.

I couldn't open my mouth to explain that me leaving had nothing to do with lack of air or water. He magically appears with a martini glass—with water—and shows me that he knows more than I need to explain with words.

'You are free to choose what makes you the happiest.'

I stay still, looking at the endless ocean of lights across the bay. What makes me happy? Not cheating. Not cheating makes me happy. Does it? Not really. It makes me respectful. Dignified. Not happy. Can I have this life right here and the other one with all the rubbish that gets thrown at me? Some people can. Some people have two families—one secret and one open—which is totally wrong.

There is a polite and respectful distance between us, and just like me, he looks across the water. We stare in parallel. What is he thinking of? I take a deep breath and pluck up the courage to say that I have someone else waiting for me.

'I don't want to delude you.' There it is; it's done. Can he understand what I just said?

'Don't worry. I make my own decisions too. If I'm here, it's because I want to be the way you let me be. If that makes any sense.' He smiles, looking at me as if this is not the last time we will see each other.

'It makes perfect sense.' I nod in agreement, and the distance between us shrinks further. Not physical distance—as that remains the same—but soul distance.

'At the risk of sounding cheesy . . . ,' he continues seriously, 'the moon orbits the Earth, not Mars. Why? Maybe the moon doesn't know of the existence of Mars, but it only knows that it is so happy to see Earth spinning alongside it.'

'You are a philosopher . . .'

'Shouldn't we all be?' He speaks firmly, convinced, truthfully.

Why, even with the mask, even without him being able to know who I am, can't I speak openly? I could be more direct and say I have a boyfriend, that he is far away and I can't break up with him from here. He, the masked man, would understand. Maybe he would even wait for me. I can just say it, but why don't I?

'Do you have to go?' He breaks my thoughts.

'Not quite. Do you want me to go?' Why did I ask this? I know the answer, don't I?

'Definitely not.'

'Will I get it right one day?' I change the focus to him.

'Get what right?'

'What you do, your profession.'

'Who knows? Maybe I will tell you.'

'Really?!' I exclaim, only to wilt immediately afterwards with his answer.

'But not yet,' he says and takes his turn at putting me on the spotlight. 'Where's your accent from?'

What is usually the one of the first questions I am asked wherever I go he surprisingly didn't ask on the first date. Party. The first party.

'It's a mix. Several places . . .'

'London?'

'Yes.'

'Spain?'

'Officially, yes.'

'Amsterdam?'

'You've hit one more! You're missing two, maybe three . . .'

'And you're not going to tell me?'

'No . . . How many people do you know with such a mingling of accents?

'Mingling works—you can say that.'

'Oh good! So, you see, with my mingling accents, I can't take a chance; it might give away who I . . .' Somehow completing the sentence with *am* doesn't seem suitable; it's awkward. 'You know, the person who lives without this mask. What if you work with me and I don't know?'

'What do you do?' he asks.

'Photographer,' I say too quickly.

'You are charismatic; people must trust you. You must be a good photographer. Are you?'

'I take pictures of buildings. The people who happen to pass by at the time I click the button are there randomly, just to show that the building exists.' I am not at all wrong, nor am I lying, just omitting that photography is a hobby. I could have said I'm an architect. I don't know why I didn't—there are thousands of architects who have lived in many places around the world. It wouldn't give away my real name or anything.

'The moon exists even if we don't see it . . .'

'Einstein?'

'I guess so. Who can trust anything found on the internet these days?' His good humour delivered to me in that warm and friendly voice accompanies a smile and a simple gesture with his head. Endearing.

'We are the ones who give buildings a reason to exist. You can only call architecture a building that was made for people to experience. It has to be more than just a bunch of materials organised in an engineered, almost puzzle like way.'

'Without us humans, the moon would just be a pile of rocks, a satellite orbiting the Earth endlessly, never even knowing its full potential to charm . . .' He interrupts me. I don't mind; it's complementary.

'The moon doesn't feel, with or without us humans; it is still not aware of its power.'

The moon shines over in the sky. I can see he smiles, intrigued. He is thinking about what to say next. Am I too challenging?

'Just like buildings, they serve to touch something beyond matter, something within us humans,' he answers with bewildering sensitivity. I can't hold back my smile. It's so nice to be here.

We haven't broken eye contact since I said I take photos of buildings. The intensity is enigmatic; I can't remember the last time I did that with someone else.

'I'd ask to see some of your photos, but since we can't have our phones or . . . names to look it up on Google . . .' He diverts our conversation.

'Who knows? One day I may show you.'

'I don't think you can,' he says, and I'm left wondering if he doesn't want to meet outside the party. I don't know if I want that either.

'What about you? Tell me what you do?'

'IT.'

'IT? Information Technology? You can be ANYONE here, and you choose to be an IT guy?! Please, just say I'm boring and I'll leave.'

He laughs, tilting his head slightly backwards. An unusually large gesture for him.

'I don't need to pretend that I do something else. I like what I do. And tell me, how many data guys will you find in the world? Millions! I don't need to worry about you discovering what I do for a living,' he says confidently. 'There are no photographers in our building, but thanks for thinking I might be your coworker.'

'Thanks for being honest, then. I find technology fascinating. I'm quite good at it, but the backstage stuff, the behind the scenes of computer science, IT and all that . . . so boring. Sorry.' I smile.

'Backstage, behind the scenes . . . A photographer and an actress?'

'Definitely not an actress. I like theatre, but I haven't been to one in years! Maybe I just like buildings, and you know . . . theatre happens in a building. Or I just like to see how things are done, but not IT stuff.'

I seem to entertain him; I like that. Being here is comforting and torturous at the same time. Who would guess this is possible? A silence fills the emptiness my thoughts create. I martyr myself for being here, but I also stopped making an effort to leave. I don't want to leave. It's wrong to stay, to give wings to this exchange of delightful moments between us and be a step closer to turning myself into a traitor. An adjective I don't want beside my name.

'So, you're the boss. What happens now?' he asks. 'Should we go back to the dance floor? Do you want a drink?' He leaves some space for me to answer.

Faced with my hesitation to say anything, he shows me he listens. He listens to what I say between the lines of my silence, that place where what I would have already revealed the first time we saw each other lives: *I have a boyfriend, and yes, we are meant to be monogamous.*

'Do you want to go home?' he asks perceptively.

'I think I *need* to go home.'

My feet sink into the pavement; the concrete seems to be taking over my shoes, my lower legs . . . I can't move. Not literally, of course. The pride I had in living my values and going home last week now confuses me. By deciding not to hurt Caio, I'm betraying me. I am denying me. What would hurt me more? Going back to the dance floor with my masked man and letting myself be me or going home? I can't break a promise; I can't be a cheater. We, the mystery man and I, will have to wait. If we found each other tonight, we can find each other again.

He searches for my eyes, moving his head until he meets mine.

'Hey, I don't need to know about your *behind the scenes*; it's fine. Take your time.'

Can such a kind and wise man exist?

'Thank you. I'll come back next week.' Will I? 'It's just that today . . .'

'I will be here. Waiting. I'll be waiting,' he says gently. 'Come, I will walk with you. Can I?'

He gestures for me to follow him to the exit. He walks next to me, not touching me, not asking for anything. He gently guides me around one or two people in front of us. The air is a mix of disappointment, frustration and admiration. Admiration for him respecting me. He says he'll be waiting for me.

Arriving at the reception desk, I signal goodbye. He advances to the counter to get his things, but I interrupt, touching his arm: 'You don't have to go.'

He doesn't answer, only touches my hand on his arm. The receptionists ask us to move away from each other because they cannot deliver the boxes if we are too close, to avoid the possibility of us discovering each other's identities.

I want to ask why he doesn't go back, chase another pair of legs, happier, freer and uncomplicated ones. I imagine he could get several women a night if he wished to, women who would be up for a lot, much more than me.

'I was going to offer you some food, but I think it's going to be difficult to get anything other than chips with these masks on,' he says as he organises his wallet and phone on the inside pocket of his jacket. 'And we'd run the risk of getting arrested walking down the street with them on. Some madmen would call the police, and you'd find out I'm really an IT guy. Disaster! You'd never want to see me again.'

'If you are really IT, you must be a big success . . .' When you don't know what to say, it's better to not say anything at all.

'And you need to go home . . .'

'Sorting some things out . . .'

'I'll be here when you get back, waiting to finish our dance.'

'Don't leave because of me. Stay and enjoy yourself! Enjoy. It's early.' I get another smile out of him. I wanted to feel his hands on my waist like when we were dancing one more time, but he doesn't try to get closer.

'Other parties will come. I'm hungry. I came straight from work, and—'

'You can eat here; the food looks amazing tonight.' I interrupt him.

'I *want* to leave.' He implies—or clarifies—that I am the reason for him to stay. He takes my cape from my arms as we approach the exit doors and dresses me slowly. If I didn't have to answer to my conscience, I would let this space I've created between us disappear.

We walk slowly in the cold, past the first taxi drivers, delaying parting from each other, chatting about the details around us: bricks, bridges, lives. He sees a coin on the ground; he kneels for it.

'Luck,' he says, coming back up slowly. When he does, he looks deeply into my eyes, as if trying to penetrate my thoughts through them. 'What would you say to me now if you could tell me anything?' He holds the coin in his hands in front of our chests.

This time, the moment of vulnerability is his; he wants to know how I truly feel.

'You would never have come this close if it wasn't for the masks.' As I say it, I realise that's not true. I let the guy from the bookshop come as close as him.

I scrunch my hat on his forehead, making our masks touch. I keep looking into his eyes. Now that I'm being honest, he is closer.

'I don't think I'm talking to the Hunchback of Notre Dame, although even though he was hideous, he was quite nice.' He understands that I think I'm ugly and that he wouldn't be interested in me. A misunderstanding.

'Not by beauty or ugliness, but by my . . . my limits.'

'I'm a lucky guy, then; those masks have paid off.'

'I also hate bad karma, so limits plus bad karma . . . equals us now.'

'I admire you. Why didn't we finish our dance?' He smiles, strengthening the bond we have slowly and so intensely created.

I know I will come back. I hope I can resolve things with Caio.

I attempt to take the last taxi in the line parked in front of us, but we are sent to the front of the line. A break in our enchanted moment, slightly more time to be together. He thanks me for today, and I feel I have been treated very well; he seems like such a gentleman, very different from other guys our age—not that I am a teenager. I wonder how old he is. He must be older, right? Why wouldn't he be married? So many questions without answers.

I get into the back seat, the door closes, and I lower the window at his request.

'Don't let this be the last time I see you.' After a slight pause, I can feel his desire to see me again: 'Please. Take a good picture of me with your retina.' I can see he smiles, but I can't figure out his expression; it seems hopeful, but it could be nostalgic.

The light is terrible here. The driver gives us the look to get moving.

'Don't worry, I don't break promises,' I say.

He gives that little tap on the car window, smiles lightly with a sigh, walks away and waves one hand. I turn back, and he walks away from the hotel. I see he takes off his mask, but he has his back to me. I think about asking the taxi to change direction so I can see his face, but I don't . . . Some mysteries are better left unresolved. For now. Don't let my two worlds weave together. For now.

All I think about on the way home is how to break up with Caio, and how stupid the idea seems to be. Honestly, five years from now, I won't be attending these parties. Or will I? Would it be possible to sustain a relationship with someone who can't know my real name? Definitely not. The questions that remain unanswered, then, are: How long would it be possible and is it worth it?

The images of a future with Caio contradict what I want now, what I wanted tonight. If he were in Sydney, we'd be at home watching movies or going out to a work party. His work. A pain in the ass. What I feel when I'm around the masked man can't be compared; it's like an exchange of souls, a connection that reminds me of when Caio saved me from death. It's more than simply living. If what I feel for the masked man is so strong, have I already crossed the threshold of betrayal? Am I adrift, waiting for Caio to come back from his corporate adventure so we can try to get out of this inertia?

As I get ready for bed—undressing, removing my make-up, taking a shower and brewing some tea—my mind and my emotions transfer energy back and forth, striking the rest of me that lies in the middle, like a good old-fashioned Newton's cradle pendulum. Gratifying smiles and shivers at the gallantry of the little time we spent together tonight, and the grey cloud of guilt and doubt about Caio and I are the balls hitting everything else in my existence at the moment. I am lucky that insomnia has never shaken me, even in the most tragic moments of my life, and now is no different. I wish to dream with my masked man, but I know I will wake up in the morning without remembering any of my dreams.

It has been two weeks since I set foot in a bookshop, which makes sense, given the mess I got into the last time I went into one. I finally manage to keep my promise to take Fleur to lunch.

'Catch me up!' she says enthusiastically. 'I can't believe it, just the two of us having lunch!'

'I don't have much to catch you up on.'

'I doubt it! I love gossip and single people problems!'

'I'm not—'

'Single. I know, I know but you are not married. I get stuck at home, with children and family things or at work, with problems that are well . . . work. No passion, no adventure. Come on, feed me some excitement!'

'Caio cancelled his flight last Friday, and that's why I went to the club with everyone.'

'Yeah, yeah, and I heard that you and Luke got in a car together . . . ,' she says suggestively.

'What do you mean you heard? Nothing happened between us. We just shared a cab. He dropped me off at my door; he didn't even get out of the car. I have a boyfriend, many miles away from here, but I do.'

'Oh, really? I thought Luke was in love with you. He didn't try anything? Nothing?'

'No! Nothing! Thank goodness!'

'Luke's a real piece of work. All right, he's got kids and he seems to get on well with his ex-wife, but other than that . . . I wouldn't say no. If I wasn't married, that is!' Fleur runs a hand over her belly with exuberant happiness on her face.

'I thought he was married.' I remember him pointing his ring to me.

'I don't know details, but I think he was the one who dumped his wife. It takes a long time to get a divorce here; maybe they're not even officially divorced, but she seemed like a very difficult person. He was always leaving work when she called, always stressed out! He seems much calmer now.' She explains what she thinks, but it doesn't clarify what Luke's situation is. 'Now, what about that boyfriend of yours? Tell me about him; it's a shame he didn't show up and you couldn't wear your new lingerie . . . He is your fiancé, right? I love fiancé dramas because they are make it or break it! There's no middle ground. You're either in love or it's over. Wedding is off.'

'There's no wedding scheduled! He's in Singapore until September.'

'Hmm . . . *Sexting*!'

'No way! I'm ashamed to death!'

'Then how do you kill the urge? Have you been in an open relationship all this time? When Will and I took a year off to live apart, just before we got married, we agreed to meet as many people as possible, follow our instincts, our desires, our wishes, be super crazy! If we were meant to stay together, we would run into each other's arms at the end of that year. It worked out, and here we are, happy and full of banana stains on our clothes!'

If Fleur were an animal, she would be one of those birds that sings all day long, bringing happiness wherever it goes.

'We didn't organise or agree on anything. We didn't even talk about it. He went and . . .' I explain Caio's and my arrangement

'Did you think that you, beautiful as you are, all exotic with your earthy skin, those aquamarine eyes and this body of a Greek goddess, were going to stay at home? Either you have locked yourself up indoors, or you don't see men drooling over you. Maybe even some women. I have some friends who would love you, if you know what I mean. Girl, you need to fix that right now. There are two things that destroy a relationship: distance and excessive proximity.' Her monologue is wise.

She gives me that look: *It's about time, right?*

On my way home later that day, I spend every minute researching ways to talk to him. Not about breaking up; instead, unbelievably and shamefully, I find myself searching the internet: *Do long-distance relationships work?* As expected, the answers are obvious: *Of course they can work, but it depends on the couple. How important is physical and sexual contact to you and your better half? How long will the long-distance relationship last?* Miguel comes to mind. What an incredible six months. Light. Without the promise of a future. And then Caio came along. *Does the relationship have an expiration date? What kind of commitments did you make before the long-distance relationship began? Loyalty in a long-distance monogamous relationship should apply to both sides. How much will you talk about your social life to each other?* As I read through the questions, I realise how unprepared we were for this. We didn't arrange anything; everything was left to our own understanding and expectations. I need to admit to myself that we were naïve—or maybe just I was. This superficial research opens a box of questions I didn't consider before. What I can remember is Caio saying goodbye to me at the airport—*Wait for me*—and me nodding in agreement. At no point did I ask or think if *he* would be waiting for *me*.

I try to convince myself that he is as monogamous as I am, but how can I be sure? He doesn't talk much about his life there, except for work. I don't ask much either; I shouldn't complain.

*

Saturday comes slowly. I sleep late and lie in bed, reading one of the books on my reading list. The other book, which I should have already passed on, still sits on my bedside table. No longer needing it, I think about handing it over the same way I received it. I pedal to Gertrude & Alice, a small, historic bookshop on Hall Street, one of my favourite corners here, where the walls are made of books and the air is a perfume of their smells mixed with wines, cheeses, coffees and teas. My goal is to be unselfish; I need to deliver the book to someone who might be an appreciative partygoer. Secretly, I place the book on the large shared table and sit at a comfortable distance from it. I give it the necessary space, so that those curious enough will open the book believing it is there for anyone to see, but I'm close enough that those who are more embarrassed than interested will think the book is mine and walk by. I have a notebook in hand, a chai latte that cools as time flies and a book that I pretend to read while watching the reaction of those who get close to the book. All six people who stop to open it, each in their own way and in their own time, giggle and make obscene gestures. Despicably immature. None of them wins the book. I get up and leave.

*

I try to return to a certain normality, and today, Monday, I go back to my bookshop habit at lunchtime. The same place and time where it all started. The distraction is a hindrance. My corner, the sun on my sofa, everything is still there, the same books, the same background music, all very peaceful and calm. I look as serene as the scene, but those who see me from the outside cannot, however, imagine the sounds, words and memories creating a turmoil inside me. Guilt and doubts make peace disappear. It flies away like white doves ought to do.

On my way back to work, I go into Westfield to get a juice and come across a gorgeous lingerie shop. I enter out of curiosity and stay out of interest. I browse the racks, looking for a piece with more cloth and less lace than the lingerie Fleur made me buy. Something between my practical pieces, which I wear daily, and something as seductive and revealing as the new set I haven't worn yet. Still tied up with my own doubts, I stay mute until the assistant comes to offer me help and shows me some items that she believes will make me look super hot—not that this is what I want. One of them fits perfectly, and, without knowing how, when or with whom I will wear it, I feel it was made for me.

Maybe it's the guilt that makes me spend a fortune on my next consumerist splurge: one more mask. It would be easier to wear the same one as before.

The night comes, and I think of cautious ways to talk about our relationship status so as not to open the door to jealousy. I don't want to have a house full of half-dead flowers again. I write in my journal, intending to read it to him, but it only serves to get what torments me out of me and onto paper. *It would be easier if you broke up with me, if you saw my mistakes. It would be easier if you weren't so perfect. It would be easier if you didn't exist, if you discovered me; it would be easier if I stopped imagining you existing in the present, when in fact, you are there in the past, on a day that only exists because my memory still works. It would be easier if I stopped making you exist in a future that I'm unsure will happen.*

I call him, and as soon as I summon the courage after our initial small talk, I try to say what I wrote, but in less striking, less traumatising words.

'Caio, I . . . I'm very confused. I'd like to propose that we try to . . .'

'See each other more, I know. I know I cancelled last week, but I'll organise something. I will fix it.'

Words fail me. I stammer between syllables and sounds until I can speak again. I guess I was ready for our conversation to lead us to a breakup. Maybe that is what I wanted. Was it?

'That's nice to hear, but also'—I pause—'I guess while we don't see each other, I wanted to . . . I guess . . . I want to . . . be free.' I can't believe it, it came out! 'I want us to work something out, an arrangement, so we're not jealous of each other, or asking each other what's going on . . .'

He's mute; I think I said too much. I look at the clock. It's been already a minute. 'Caio . . .'

'I'm here. Tainá, I don't know what to say.' He sounds okayish, maybe angry.

'We're still together, but while you're there . . .' Why am I saying this? How did Fleur and Bianca do this!? How upsetting, I'm so shaky!

'I don't want to see anyone else . . . Do you?'

'I'm not happy, not knowing what you're doing there.'

'Tatá! Ah, you're so cute, don't be like that!'

Cute?

'And the flowers, Caio. You're . . . jealous.'

'I'm not jealous! The flowers were not a jealousy thing. Why would I be jealous?' He gets so defensive every time I suggest he's possessive.

'Well, I didn't do anything, I went to work and then out with everyone else, and nothing happened with anyone. And you don't believe me, and you smother me with flowers—very beautiful ones that I have to throw away now. They're all dead.'

'Tá, my bad! I promise, I won't do that anymore.'

'Okay. Thanks.'

We ended the evening with our normal conversations about weather, our mothers, food, exercise and work. Has anything changed?

9

I arrive at the magazine after spending the day preparing a presentation showing what the office will look like after the renovation. I've been here so many times, interviewing and talking to people to make sure we have a solid brief to work with, that I am proud of the great relationships, the trust and respect I've developed with them—most of them. Every time I'm here, I feel welcomed and cared for. As if the hugs, compliments, conversations and—how could I forget—the dresses I got from the fashion producer weren't enough, today, the make-up artist decides that I need to put more colour on my face. I haven't spoken to him that much before, but he is always so friendly that it feels like we've known each other for a decade. Confronted with my refusal, he changes his negotiating techniques and asks me to help him. He is experimenting with colours for a fashion editorial featuring different ethnicities, and he would love to test on my skin *half red, half white, half forest,* in his own words.

'So unique!' he repeats several times.

As always, the question that follows is where I came from and how I can have this reddish skin with such blue eyes. I say it is only the result of violence and colonisation. My parents and grandparents married for love, but my great-grandmother, to the amazement of many, was lassoed by my great-grandfather in the middle of the Amazon forest and never saw her family again. It was not four hundred years ago, but less than a hundred, in the twenty-first century. She was forced to leave her tribe and live between the farm and the city. Everything I know she told me on her deathbed when I still didn't know how to write. She told me that when I was born, she heard a message from the heavens through the singing of the *sabiá*—the rufous-bellied thrush—and the bird told her she would only live until the day I was old enough to remember her. I remember, but I wish she had lived longer.

Tears appear in everyone's eyes and are quickly wiped away so as not to destroy their make-up. I cry too, a little. I want to cry more, not only because I miss her but for all the violence she had to endure. It's all blocked up in my throat. What gives anyone the right to invade someone else's life?

During this campfire-story bonding moment, I receive the most beautiful make-up of my life. He made a red stripe across my eyes. It reminded me of the picture of my great-grand in our living room with a very similar tribal painting. I see her in myself. I feel her courage and her pain take over my veins. I am grateful that I said yes to the make-up artist and have an enlightening moment: there is no better place to leave the book. Most—not all—of the people I've met here need to free themselves from their self-image and the need for external approval. I leave the book among the clothes, on a small table with a pile of textile samples. I don't know who will pick it up, but I know that whoever it is will find their way to the party.

She, my great-grandmother, whispers in my ears that the only knot that should exist between two people is the knot of the word *we*. I'm going to the party, to get rid of this rope Caio has tied around us for so many years.

*

When the sea is pink
Those who scrape the sky
In the finite horizon bring
The hidden Paradise

I read the verses for tonight's party as I get dressed. Paradise is nothing more than a utopian and imaginary place where everyone is happy, healthy and without problems or discord. I think about the finite horizon. Horizons are infinite; I know them well. We never arrive, never catch up, never reach. The horizon is the line between the sky and the sea. It is visible and immaterial at the same time. To look at the horizon is to expand the mind, to think how small we are, how things are not what they seem to be. Like masks. The horizon is like desire; when we manage to get there, we discover that we want something else, we want more. An unattainable goal.

A finite horizon is only possible if we have two planes meeting each other, like a wall and a floor, forming an edge. The edge is an encounter with a beginning and an end, because either we touch the wall or we touch the floor. The edge is the finite horizon.

An internet search leads me to discover the address of a restaurant in one of the skyscrapers in the CBD, called the Horizon's Edge. I call, trying to make a reservation, but I get an electronic message saying that they only take guests by invitation. Something tells me that it is not just a restaurant but a large ballroom.

I stare in the mirror after putting my ring on. The key ring. The snake ring. The life ring. My dress, which I haven't worn in a long time, could not be considered gala appropriate, so I hope they let me in. I hope the rest of me makes up for its simplicity. I bought this dress on a trip through Spain I took with Miguel and some other people from uni, in a second-hand store in the middle of nowhere. It evokes the colours of the earth, light and dark blending with my own skin. Flowy. The thin, semitransparent fabric covers my arms and my legs all the way to the floor, moving with the slight breath of air. I open just two of the buttons that run down from the neck towards the waist. The thin cord around the neckline prevents it from hanging loose down the front of my body. It fits perfectly, with my great-grandmother's spirit, and mine now. I wear a body shaper thing that is made to work as a thermal layer and transparent stockings. I don't think it will be enough for this winter; I will need a proper coat.

The juxtaposition of my plebian dress with my noble make-up and mask seems to be the perfect declaration of who I am. The red stripe around my eyes is partially covered by the feathery mask that leaves only part of my lips and chin exposed.

The feathers go back along and up the sides of my head. I am something like a bird.

My lapis lazuli bracelet, which I got from Mum when we were on holiday in Chile as a child, still fits on my wrist. I wear my necklace.

*

The courage that made me come again tonight and dress so openly to the world, expanding my energy, calling those who identify with it, disappears as soon as I see my masked man. I recognise him by his mask, the same one from last week. The owl. I could go straight to him, but I don't. I observe from a distance. Can I? Should I go?

I wonder what I will say to him, the masked man. Wearing masks forces us to put words to feelings, because we can't rely on reading and deciphering someone's facial expressions. Not that we are aware our face is a painting of our nerves, but I know our bodies don't lie. It hurts more when we name what we have inside, but is it true for the *good* feelings? Can we love more when we say it? It's a relief to be able to find him again. As I walk, circumnavigating him for as long as I need to, my thoughts fade, and I finally arrive. Doubt free. In front of him.

We stand still, staring at each other, in the middle of the crowd. He recognises me by the look in my eyes, and by the necklace.

'You got me tonight; it was hard to find you.' He smiles.

'I don't know why. I put the same necklace on,' I tease.

Transfixed by my eyes, he goes mute. I sense words want to come out, but his lips remain frozen.

'Cat got your tongue?' I ask.

'Almost. Are you a cat or a bird?'

I smile, and he asks me about my make-up. I tell him the story of my great gran and soon afterwards regret it because this is a story that can't be made up. If he hears it somewhere else, he will know who I am.

'I think you'll be able to recognise me elsewhere now.' I express my fear.

'Yeah, I have to agree. That story is unusual.'

'Definitely.' I breathe deeply. He seems a bit off. 'What's up?'

'Nothing.'

'I know you want to say, maybe ask, something.'

'Perceptive.' He sighs. 'I'm trying to find out if you can continue our dance. Can you dance with me? No pressure. I said I will wait.'

My doubts return against my will, I feel evasive, thoughtful and . . . fearful. I go over the conversation with Caio in my head, and I think yes, we are free. We don't need to be jealous of each other, he doesn't need to know what I do. I don't need to know what he does. Right? What to do? I can't play with this guy anymore. He deserves better, and so do I. I do. I think I do. Dancing is too risky, we are too close, his hands on my back, the way he moves me . . .

'How about something different?' My head and my eyes point to the knot room I saw as I walked in earlier.

'What's in there?'

'Ropes, I guess . . . I'm not quite sure.'

'I wouldn't know what to do.'

'Neither do I.' I shrug, breathe in, and ask, 'Do you want to find out with me . . . now?'

He turns to face the room, moving his pressed lips side to side, his shoulders raised. He is going to say no. He has to say yes. Please say yes. With a small gesture, he returns to me, flexible, inclining his torso forward, folding his right arm behind his body, and with his left, he accepts the invitation: 'I'll be right behind you.'

When we reach the thick timber door, some inhibition fills the air around us, a hesitation perhaps. We stand in front of the door without touching the knob, without saying a word, without looking at each other. We are as stiff as two skyscrapers waiting for the ground to give way before they tumble into each other.

'What happens in there, sir?' he asks the security guard.

'Whatever you want to happen,' the big and gentle man answers him.

'Okay, that was not conclusive,' my masked man mumbles to me.

'I only had a glimpse on the first night . . . on the night we met.' I realise I've almost said when my first party was, and I think I've given too many hints of who I am tonight. Better to hold back the words. I will keep them for my diary. 'There are ropes and people hanging.'

'People hanging. So, that instead of dancing?'

I can feel his apprehension, like someone who is about to jump out of a plane for the first time, when the fear of danger and the excitement of discovering the unknown tears you apart. One more door that opens, one more experience in life that only dementia can steal one day.

The door opens from the inside; he makes way for a departing couple. They tell us that nothing will be better than entering that room: 'It's from another world, mate!' one of them says.

'You will never be the same again,' says the other.

We exchange smiles through our eyes, and we walk in together. Inside, we are greeted by a man, a yoga teacher type of man, wearing some shorts and a sleeveless top. Both are white. The room is well heated, as warm as noon of a sunny spring day and as bright as a summer dawn. The atmosphere is intimate and intense. The instructor asks if it is our first time, and whether we're embarking on this together or separately.

We answer 'together' at the same time. We laugh at our synchronicity.

The instructor leads us to an area big enough for three yoga mats side by side. In the middle, red ropes are attached by a circular hoop to the ceiling. He shows three more empty hoops next to them and extra ropes on a shelf and hands us two towels. With a calm and serene voice, he teaches us the pressure of the ropes, including how I can tie the masked man, the points on the body we must avoid and the ones that people report feeling good, the types of knots. He asks if we have any medical problems and assures us that we can call him if we want to and that we have all the time we need. He explains that each person feels different emotions and that there is no right or wrong, asks us to let it flow and really seems to treat us like a couple. At first, we really do seem like one. His final request is for us to take it slow and lie down on the yoga mat to settle the sensations and transformations in the neurological system once we finish. As he explains all this, he asks us to come up with two security codes, a verbal code, like a word or a sound, and a bodily one, such as blinking your eyes three times. Most people wear their underwear; some must have been here before as they are wearing bras and shorts; the freest ones are as naked as they can be while wearing a mask. This latter group also has the most elaborate suspension bindings, with a huge number of ropes and knots that stop their movements. Their bodies are hanging, tied up; there is a silence in the air, broken by moans of pain or pleasure. Hard to tell. The instructor asks us to get ready in an area with lockers inside the same room.

'What word do you want?' I ask.

'Coffee?' he suggests.

'What did you say?'

He takes off his gloves one finger at a time, carefully places them in his jacket pocket to reach for my hands, moving closer to my left ear and whispering slowly: 'Coffee.'

It tickles. I giggle. Every cell of my body reacts, perhaps release some of the tension in me.

'Is it funny? We can choose another one.' He holds my hand.

'Coffee. Coffee is perfect,' I repeat, finding the chosen word amusing, and for that very reason it must be our safety code. I'm frozen, transfixed by his hands on mine. 'What about a gesture?'

My masked man blinks three times, and I agree, nodding.

I turn my side to him, facing the wooden lockers where we are meant to put our belongings. I undo the cord on my dress. I let it fall to the floor. I don't look at him. It feels oddly harder today than the last time, when I went in the nudist room. I admit that the taking off my dress causes good and bad stirrings inside me.

The good ones I credit to this environment and the anticipation of the unknown. I am content to be wearing my comfortable shaper, glued to my body, shaping every curve. I don't feel exposed or vulgar; he is seeing nothing more than my swimming teacher used to see. The bad feelings are on Caio's account. I doubt—again—if our talk about an open relationship was an agreement. Maybe he thought I was cheating on him, and I'd hate to hurt him.

My masked man takes much longer to get all the parts of his clothes off; his outfit is much more detailed than mine. I observe the teacher-instructor; he moves effortlessly, assisting his students as they need him. He is comfortable where he is. It's so natural.

We are ready. I can't help but notice that my partner for the night—the masked man—is wearing boxers; they look brand-new. I can't tell if he's analysing my body, but I don't feel overly uncomfortable.

'This instead of dancing?' he asks one more time to confirm.

'Yes.'

He touches my back, and off we go to the middle of our mat.

We exchange glances that say, *I trust you*, and I am dazzled, amazed at how I give so much of myself to a stranger. It's the third time I've seen him. It's the third time I've spoken to him. I don't know his name; I don't know his face. I could never recognise him on the street, or at the police station, if he were to hurt me.

Red ropes hang between us; we kneel facing each other. He asks, gently, if I want him to tie me up or the other way around. Sailing and Luke come to my head briefly; I don't want to make any unnecessary knots. It might open a portal to feelings I don't want to bring in here. I hand over one rope to him; he understands what I want. He asks if there are any areas or scars I don't want him to touch. I say no. What happens from here is almost a hallucination, an altered state of consciousness.

Every pull holds me still: the material part of me slowly becomes immobile; yet my soul moves around him, intertwined. The trust soon elevates to a transcendental exchange. Love. The tightness on my skin begins to burn in some parts as he suspends me; the movement is uncomfortable, but soon I feel his hand—or maybe the instructor's—touching my head very gently, guiding it down. My neck hangs. Relaxing. Almost like a nurturing hammock swing. His breath wakes my skin where it passes, and eventually our lips find each other, naturally and gently touching. We remain in this stillness until . . . until I abandon my prejudices and my fears. Surrender. Loss, beach, waves, boat, rock, Kadu, Olympics, Miguel, blindfold, Luke, Mum, Bibi, uni, photos, buildings, waves, planes, cheetahs, dirt, camera, sailing, Dad, guilt, Caio, desire, me, him, masks, swimming, cliff, ocean, running, horizon. Tears exorcising my past stain my make-up beneath the mask, falling however gravity makes them and away from the bottom of my face. His lips are warm, full, edible. Our hanging, upside-down kiss is glorious. Pain, trust, pleasure. Timeless. Endless.

Spinning gradually around and downwards, my body meets the floor, his body over mine, embracing me in a gentle hug. We rest with the ropes still restricting my movements.

'Thank you,' he whispers, kissing my forehead over the mask.

A sign of respect. He presses his lips over mine again; I respond equally. We stay like that. Calm and at peace. He begins to undo the knots, one by one. The friction of ropes—ours and others'—is kind of music. A music called reciprocity.

At the end of our experience, lying facing up on the yoga mat, he reaches out his hand to hold mine. A gesture to close this unforgettable experience. Our nervous systems are rewiring. The instructor approaches me after a few minutes, when my body temperature begins to cool down, asks how we feel and offers us each a blanket. We sit to listen to him. He states that we will remember each other forever, that this relationship has been blessed with absolute trust, deep bonding and connection.

As soon as the instructor leaves, our foreheads, hands and knees meet. We rest; we let it sink in.

'Do I need to ask what you are thinking about?' I say.

He shakes his head in denial, kisses me, holding my face by my jaw, and speaks while still gluing his mouth against mine: 'Don't you know already? You've already given me more than I could ever imagine.' He smiles and asks me to wait for him outside the room. His clothes take considerably longer to put on than mine.

It's surreal to come out of an experience like this and return to the normal world. I float, but I'm sure my feet are on the ground.

It's my turn to say to the next people, just outside the door, that they will never be the same after going in. I ask the security guard to tell the owl that I will be back. I need to try fix my make-up in the bathroom. The tears must have smudged it.

There's someone in the mirror I know, but I don't entirely recognise her. I don't want to analyse her. For tonight, I will let her be. It's me, but it's not the me that everyone knows. Maybe I still need to meet her properly. I blend my make-up as much as possible by patting my fingers over the red band with the mask on, of course. It's tricky.

When I return to the dance floor, I see him waiting by the room, standing tall, in silhouette. There's a silence, a good silence when we meet; he looks at me with a fond and, dare I say, grateful look.

'Did I hurt you?' he says, passing his fingers over the rope mark on my wrist, just under my sleeve.

I reply that he didn't. Although it feels as though a lifetime passed while we were in there, the party isn't over yet; I have no idea what the time is, but I see that a band is getting ready to play. I could go home now and sleep, spellbound with the beauty of the synchronicities of the universe, but to leave is to say goodbye to this magic and to him for another week. So, without arrangements, plans, preparations or guilt, we embark on the remainder of the evening together, intertwined.

'I wish I could take you home,' he says as we say goodbye.

'I will find you next week.' I smile, touching his jaw with one hand. As the taxi drives away, I know every second will be a conscious decision to keep this feeling of aliveness alive.

When I get home—Bibi's home—I find a piece of paper, about A5 size in one of my coat pockets, with a pencil drawing. In it, I am climbing a staircase towards a dark world; people don't laugh; it's very dense. Behind me, where my disproportionately long and fluttering dress has passed, everything is happy and has various shades, shapes and patterns. I interpret these variations as the way he represents colour with pencil. You can't see my face; the mask covering it is today's mask. He's drawn it tonight. He had a pencil with him? In the bottom right corner, on a white spot on the paper, it says:

You are the breath of wind that carries colour
Left to the world in the wake of your scent
A walk of the brave
Who, despite fear, follows magic into the unknown

*

A nod and a wave call me from a shadowy part of the office; it's the HR woman. I must be in trouble. What could I have done wrong? Large rooms with few people are always intimidating and cold. I'm not sure if I'm cold because I'm intimidated or intimidated because I'm cold. She has a smile that I'm sure sees the dentist regularly, impeccable posture and beautiful, flowing, shiny, naturally silver hair. Like me, she also seems not to treat the office like a fashion show by dressing professionally, discreetly, neat and clean. The *clean* comes from Fleur, who constantly turns up to work with stains on her clothes and is forced to disguise them with scarves, blazers and cardigans that she leaves here so they don't get *infected at home*. Her words. I'm hoping the HR woman will introduce herself again because I can't remember her name; I thought about looking it up before our meeting, but in view of last week's confusion and news, it ended up passing unticked on my to-do list. She invites me to sit by pulling out a chair; she opens a notebook and holds her pen with both hands. She likes pen and paper too.

'We never really introduced ourselves properly, so allow me to introduce myself. I'm Stephanie, but most people call me Steph. I'm the HR manager, and I was wondering how things are going with you.'

'I'm fine, actually. Very happy,' I respond.

'What project you would like to work on next? Do you have a preference? We know that working with Joanne is not the easiest. Also, I looked at your portfolio, and you don't seem to be very keen on interiors. Am I right?'

I nod.

'Perfect. So, I want to make sure you are well looked after on your next project. That you can work on something you really like.'

I'm surprised and relieved, as I never imagined hearing something like this. I came in here thinking I would have some visa or performance problem, and she wants to know what I *want to* do? I don't know what I really want to work on, not so specifically. Of course, that's not a very useful answer. So, I tell her I'd like to work on bigger projects, like schools, museums and skyscrapers. Complex projects. She congratulates me on being so determined—I never realised I was—and promises me a new project soon. I just need to hang in there for a little while longer.

The cold disappears completely. The day is dazzling! But as joy is not a permanent state, it will always be chased by doubts. Late at night, before going to bed, at that time when loneliness, anguish and fears ravage our minds, mixing up with dreams and romantic imaginings, I call Bianca.

'Can you talk?'

She's the only one who will handle my monsters with respect and the necessary secrecy. She, in the middle of her day, happy and content with her continuing legion of loyal followers and her many new culinary friends, takes the time out of a crowded kitchen to talk to me. I just tell her I met a guy at a costume party; I don't mention books or secret events. My doubt lies in how to resolve this dilemma within myself and with Caio. Her advice is the best possible; without blinking or judging me, she goes off at once, saying that even we—who grew up free—suffer from society's prudish, sexist precepts.

'Sister I never had, since when do you have to deny a feeling? You don't have to blame yourself for finding the guy handsome, hot, charming, poetic or whatever! I'm not telling you to betray Caio, though it seems you agreed to be free for a little while. I'm just saying that we can't control what we feel. Not to mention that your relationship has turned into a flirtation, right? You've been with him for five hundred years, and he's been running the world at will, thinking you'll follow him like a lamb. Wake up, flower! It's time for you to do the things you like, and if Caio doesn't get on board . . . well . . . his loss. Not yours.'

She is so protective of me. She suggests I talk to Caio again about what to do while he is living his life in Singapore. She also offers her apartment in Kirribilli in case I want to leave Bondi.

'Take it for as long as you need it. Let me know, and I will take off the rental thingy.'

She adds that she won't charge me; I'll have just the mundane bills like electricity, water, that sort of thing. Only friends do that. Only family.

'You are the best. Thank you.'

'Nonsense! I have to go, but call me more, please?!'

I wish I could tell her every detail about the masked man, what we did last night, but I suppose we don't always need to reveal all our details for someone to help get us back on track. When we lose control, we need others to remind us of who we are. That's what a good friend is for.

*

I spend the weekend trying to agree with Caio about what we are going to do about our relationship while we are apart. I overthink what to say, and I'm not sure how clear I am; I need him here so we can talk face to face. I ask if he's still coming to Sydney and if he has any idea when. His answer is as dry as both of us have been since he left: 'Yes. No.' After being ignored a few times, I give up insisting.

Mum's arrival next Friday, for just one week, encourages me to take a holiday, so I get very busy at work to finish everything that needs to be done before she arrives. It's a busy week. Very busy. I didn't even have time to run, but I was able to figure out how to still make the party—also on Friday.

10

Nobody is an immigrant because they want to be. Some embodied angels migrate or spend their lives travelling for a cause, like saving a forest or an entire population of animals, defending a country, or something else. Others, more foolish, move for love. Without knowing that if love and passion do not end, they are transformed into small gestures on special dates. The more mundane migrants, selfish as they are, leave in search of the job of their dreams. But these are few, very few. Most expats move out of fear. Immigration is a salty dessert. It is a pact with the beings of the underworld; you must sign a contract in which your soul will forever wander between the memories of the past and that beautiful future of the next trip back to your homeland. A peaceful and abundant place. An immigrant is an immigrant by necessity or ignorance. I fit into all these categories. When one migrates or immigrates, there is no present, except at the airport.

The airport is a kind of church for wandering souls. Here, even without going anywhere, I am waiting for the comfort and turbulence of my soul. Where guilt and redemption meet. My mother. While I wait through the delays caused by opposing winds on the plane, the goodwill of the employees at customs and Mum's luck in picking up her suitcase from the crowded carousel, I confront my mistakes, my anguish, and my poor life decisions. The wait is worthwhile as, inevitably, I get a smile, a broad welcoming smile, a run and a wonderful hug, showing me I am forgiven. Holy mother. Already experienced in this process, I look forward to the emotional purge that only the airport gives me when she arrives. I thought today would be no different. But it is. It is because my phone rings with a message from Caio.

He says he'll arrive today and take me to lunch. Is he for real? I call back and, as usual, he doesn't answer. Annoyed by his interruption but grateful for his efforts in getting on a plane, I ask him to call me back. I remind him that I'm at the airport, that I'll be working until 4:00 p.m. and taking my mother out to early dinner. He replies, by text, saying it's okay, that he'll stop by my work to give me a kiss. At lunchtime. Maybe I wasn't clear.

Having to replan the whole weekend—I imagine Caio will only be here for the weekend—I text Fleur, asking if I can bring Caio to her baby shower, then I try to get an extra ticket to the opera house tomorrow, but it's impossible, since it's less than forty-eight hours until the performance. I need to find someone to give these tickets to. And then there's the masquerade tonight. How am I going to solve this? *Love you! I can't wait to see you!* It's his last message. He doesn't even seem to know me: showing up out of the blue, without asking, without agreeing on a plan!

Mum, on the other hand, defies all my expectations: glamorous like a sexagenarian Amazon, running towards me as if she had not just spent more than thirty hours in transit between her home and here. Her hug speaks for itself, but we don't restrain ourselves: she tells me repeatedly how much she loves me and how much she misses me.

'I love you too, Mum,' I cry over her shoulders. Her hug gets tighter, I try to pick up her suitcase, and she holds my face as if it were the last time she was going to see me. *It's not going to be, Mum. It's okay,* I say in my head.

With the same energy and courage that has always driven her to do everything in life, she promptly walks to the phone company counter to resolve her communication situation.

'I'm going to need just one chip; I brought my old phone unlocked, and I think it'll work.'

She doesn't follow my suggestion of using one phone with two numbers. Too confusing. She'd rather have two separate phones while she's here.

'Are you afraid of technology now, Mum?'

'No, but it makes it easier to have two.'

I notice that despite her spark, something has aged; it wouldn't have been like this in the past. She is still fascinating; I admire her while she turns around and says in her broken English: 'I want all internet, infinite internet. Yes, I do email, music, maps . . .' The kiosk guy understands, and Mum leaves with two phones working: a Brazilian phone in roaming and a local one working perfectly well. *You're incredible, Mum!* Her phone rings with her first Australian message, a generic welcome from the phone company.

In the taxi, I drop the bomb that Caio is arriving today, in a little while. She promptly gives me the *When did he tell you that?* and *Doesn't he know you like to plan everything?* and offers to go to a hotel.

'No way!' I offer Bianca's house for the weekend, and then on Monday she can go to Bondi, where we can stay together. Or I will join her at Bibi's.

I arrive at work late, as I had arranged with Joanne, and after a couple of frantic hours working, Caio turns up at 1:00 p.m., smelling like a plane, to take me to lunch. Lynnette startles me from behind, surprised by how good looking he is.

'You know what we would say in my days? What a piece of meat!' she confesses, whispering.

Yes, I agree that Caio is gorgeous, and in person even more so. My heart palpitates strongly; it seems that seeing him in the flesh makes me fall in love with him all over again. The emptiness of our virtual life disappears.

'Who is he?' asks Joanne, making a point of staring at him.

'My lunch, it seems,' I reply, smiling.

Very charming as always, he convinces Joanne that she doesn't need me, so he gets her to release me for an extended lunch with him. She invites him for drinks at the end of the day.

'Joanne, I'm taking my mum out for an early dinner, remember?' I say irritated.

'Sure, bring her and the hubby too!' she replies excitedly.

'Boyfriend—he's a boyfriend!' I answer hurriedly.

I excuse both of them, go to my desk to save my files, lock the computer and get my bag. I think about my masked man. My plan was perfect. I was going to take Mum to an early dinner and meet him at the party. Now what do I do? Looking at Caio from a distance, I feel like scum. He's so real now. What have I done? I do love him.

He takes me for lunch at Customs House, a wonderful place, delicious food. What did I expect from the first time we've seen each other in how many months? I've lost track. He talks about how stressful his job is and says he can't wait to come to Sydney for good.

'I have to go, Caio. It's already super late. I'm late. I'm leaving early to take Mum out for dinner. I'll see you tonight in Bondi.'

'Tatá, I'm also missing a day at the office. I took time off to come here and be with you. I thought that's what you wanted.'

'Yeah, but the difference is that you chose to leave your work today, I didn't. It's a really busy day for me. I'm going on holiday with Mum. You could have given me some warning beforehand or, if you'd listened to me, you would have come next week. I told you she was coming.'

'Okay, I got it. There's no need for you to go on a monologue. I'll drive you back to work.

'No need, too much traffic. I will walk.'

'Tell you what, your mum is sleeping now, you work all afternoon, I'll meet you there at 5:30 for drinks with your people, we'll take your mum to dinner at 6:30, 7:00 p.m. By then, she'll be rested from the trip, and you'll have managed to finish your work.'

Reluctantly, I accept his proposal. Mum is asleep, but if I know her, she's set her alarm clock for 3:30 p.m. so she can meet me at 4:00 p.m.

Her message at 3:35 p.m. confirms this. She is okay with the change of plan and as always, in good spirits, goes for a walk to see the neighbourhood.

Accepting this proposal also means I can't see my masked man today. I should at least let him know I can't make it. Somehow.

Caio comes back all primed for Friday drinks and wins over everyone at work, including our array of directors, who wanted to meet my 'fiancé,' the man who managed to soften my heart. Little do they know how shattered my heart is, held together by glue, ribbons and seams. I'm forced to interrupt a lively chat between the directors and Caio about corporate matters—because that's what socialising at work is for—as I do not want to be late for dinner with Mum.

But I am. I arrive five minutes late, and it breaks my heart to see Mum at a table alone. I thank her for being so independent and not waiting in the cold outside. The Indian restaurant in Lavender Bay has been on my list of places to go since I slept over at Bibi's house for the first time and ran down all these streets. Today, I finally get to take my mum—and Caio—to eat here.

He and Mum haven't seen each other since we came to Sydney last December, a few months after Dad left. There is no awkwardness between them; it is as if they saw each other yesterday. Familiar. Caio kindly brought her a box of chocolates and a bookmark from Singapore. He said he's dying to take us to Asia. He seems genuinely interested in Mum's yoga retreat, and throughout dinner he makes a point of telling her she's better than ever. My family. Me, her and him. It's all I have left.

At 7:00 p.m., the city lights call, distracting me from real life, taking me to a place I can't go today and may never be able to go again. The partying, the dancing, and the unpretentious nudity seem irrelevant when I'm with my family here. My spellbound state of Caio's affection for and attention to my mum grows bigger as I admire him for not being like his dad.

What I felt and experienced with him—the other one, the masked man—is not irrelevant; our time together has become memory already, but maybe they are fleeting as quickly as they came. Maybe it's only possible to feel that way once. That surrender with no expectations. How long does a couple experience that sense of novelty? How long will I be able to go to that party and find the same magic? At what cost? I force myself to change seats and sit with my back to the view, to be able to pay attention to the people who really matter. Caio suggests that Mum sleep in Bondi with us. He will sleep in the living room. Mum, wisely, decides to stay at Bibi's to give us privacy, as she herself puts it.

I look forward to Caio and I being able to salvage the broken connection between us. The only difference in the flat is his small travel bag, open by the bed. I am relieved my masks are in Kirribilli. What if Mum finds them? Will that be a problem?

Caio has barely taken off his shoes before he quenches the thirst that distance has given him. His hands behind my hips soon make their way into my skirt, smoothing my underwear. He tells me how much he loves me and how much he missed me. His vocabulary, as well as his hand, leg, mouth, tongue and body movements, contradict the gentle man I just had dinner with. I guide him into the bedroom in an attempt to caress and round his edges with the soft mattress. His inelegant, self-centred haste is a product of longing, according to him, and he says he will reward me tomorrow night with—and at—a romantic dinner.

The light of the world enters through the gap in the curtain, leaving him half in shadow and half in light. While he sleeps, I take off the rest of my clothes and put them in the wash. My body hurts slightly where he touched me. I take a shower, not knowing if some of the lines running down my face are tears or just water. The rope marks are gone now, but I lather my body where they were, trying to remember how I felt the last time I saw my masked man. I want to be reminded of the feeling of being free and light. I get under the covers in my warm, full-body pyjamas, hoping for a dream that will erase this abyss between Caio and me.

*

Saturday dawns with a message from Mum saying she's hooked up a group of other mums of Brazilians in Sydney and is going with them to Hunter Valley on a two-day excursion. She'll be back tomorrow afternoon, and I don't have to worry about her this weekend. Only my Mum, bless her. She's going to send me photos tonight.

Caio wakes up at 10:00 a.m. after I've run my 11 km, when I'm back on our balcony drinking my green juice.

'Am I the luckiest guy or what?' he says, putting on boxer shorts and sitting down next to me.

I smile shyly in response, waiting for him to say something about last night. My eyes are fixed on the sea, the horizon, the surfers and especially the cliff. In that place where the waves break, in the place between the calmness of the waters and the strength of the rocks.

'It looks like Itacoa, doesn't it?' he says, remembering my house, the one where the most important event of my life happened. Where I lost everything. I have lived like a zombie ever since. I agree in silence, and a gentle Caio reappears, 'Is it sad for you?'

I agree in silence again. I didn't want to cry in front of him, but he knows. He notices.

'I'm getting used to it,' I say, swallowing my tears, doubting myself. I don't think I will ever get used to it.

He kisses and hugs me gently, and we stay still like that for a few seconds—maybe minutes—on the lounger. A small gesture of hope for us.

'I don't have to stay here. I can find somewhere else,' he says.

I like it when he protects me, when he shows me that there are things in my past that I can't overcome on my own.

'No, it's okay,' I respond.

We get ready and head to the beach without any major incidents.

'I can't wait to be on the beach all day!' he says as we pick a place to sit.

'It's winter, Caio.'

'It doesn't feel like it. Over there, even those kids are in the water.'

'Up to their knees.'

'And the surfers? Where's the surfer in you, huh? I still want to see you in the wetsuit I got you.' He puts his arms over my shoulders and kisses the top of my head.

'I need to see if I can get someone to pick up the opera house tickets. No one got back to me yesterday.' I change the subject and stretch out my towel.

'How many tickets? Can we go just the two of us?

'Yeah, we can. If you want to and are in the mood to see opera. I was going to go just for Mum's sake, because she's never seen one.'

'If you're up for it, let's go, then. How about we go for dinner first?'

'The only reason to go is so I won't waste the money I've already spent on the tickets. I think it's better to stay at home . . .' I gently scratch his back, from his shoulders down, insinuating what I mean by discreetly grazing his shorts. I feel his hand stop mine. What's wrong with him?

'What are you doing? Leave this to a more appropriate place,' he says in a tone that is both seductive and reproachful. 'Let's have dinner, then we'll decide what to do . . .'

I wither like all plants that need to be watered to live. I wish I were on quicksand, sucked to the other side of the world, crossing a fantastical and magical centre of the earth, which would work like a time machine, taking me back to fourteen years ago. The accursed silence, with so many unspoken subjects, goes from uncomfortable to unbearable. Out of my mouth comes a request, or a criticism. It depends on whom you ask.

'Do you think we have become too complacent? Have we fallen into sameness? Are we more friends than . . . lovers?'

His response comes so quickly that I doubt he gave a drop of thought.

'After last night? Are you crazy, woman?'

He continues to praise my flexibility and ability to take him to the clouds. Sexually, of course. The other parts of my life do not inspire him.

There are few things that perplex me, and this attitude of his is one. The way he lies in the sand, lost in his own world as if I were miles away—come to think of it, just as he treated me last night—irritates me, but the irritation remains within me, and only confusion comes out in what I say: 'I didn't do . . . much . . . last night . . . I didn't . . . I didn't do much . . .'

I didn't even like it. Who would? But I omit that part. I know we can get better; it was a bad night, a clumsy one.

'All right,' he says. 'Just by working out like this and getting this body . . . you've done your job.' He steals a kiss from me, smoothing my legs.

The sand seems less bright and the sky less blue. My body shrinks. I wonder why I feel offended. Has it always been like this? Which Caio is this?

'Caio . . .'

'Yeah?' he says.

'Nothing, never mind.'

'What's up? Say it. Look, I know last night wasn't the best night of your life, but I'll make it better, you'll see. Too many months without seeing you . . . I couldn't control it.'

I'm grateful he at least acknowledges this. Not that he's apologised, but it's better than nothing.

There is a certain familiarity between us; that silence that is not so abysmal now. I know we'll get better; he's already accepted and recognised it. This long-distance relationship thing is complicated.

We are lying on our beach towels when he abruptly gets up and says he has to sort some things out. He needs to leave and will come back right at lunchtime. I imagine that this is his way of discreetly surprising me. Not discreetly at all.

*

As I imagined, Caio takes a few hours to go to Bondi Junction and buy me a dress, shoes and, yes, lingerie. I know I should be feeling flattered by the pampering, but something makes me feel uncomfortable. Does he not like my clothes? Does he want to see me different? Since I started working on the project for the fashion magazine, my knowledge of textile and designers has increased exponentially. Something I never had an interest in now seems to come naturally. The formal chiffon dress, long and with a V-shaped neckline, fits me very well; he got the size and shape right, but the colour . . . If I could give one tip to anyone planning to buy a gift for an architect, designer or artist, please understand about colour, or make sure it's black. Black. Not even white, as there are many varieties of this colour, and we all have our preference. The navy blue he chose may look great on him, but on me, it looks awful. It leaves my eyes grey and my skin dull.

I don't know where he got the idea I like navy blue. I've never owned a single navy-blue anything. To his credit, he also got right how cold I feel and brought me a long-sleeved dress, a new coat with a fitted waist and a red scarf. This one does match my skin, but it doesn't match my personality. Or does it? I see the me of the last party. She chose red. Intense red. The lipstick—Caio also bought lipstick—is also red, and although I thank him, I firmly refuse to wear it. He insists, telling me to wear it later. Just for him. There are things in these men's heads that one cannot understand. It's just a red lipstick. He also manages to get the shoe size right, although they are uncomfortable, as all heels are. It was a nice gesture. I think.

During our dinner at the Opera Bar, we bump into Luke, his children—two boys—and a woman, clearly the mother of his children. I'm confused. Isn't he divorced? They spent the day sailing. I see some grief in Luke, hidden behind the joy of being with his family.

'The kids love it,' he and his wife say, exchanging kind looks.

Caio chats like a salesman, exposing my past, revealing I used to sail competitively and that I didn't make the Olympics because I got nervous.

'Oh! You said when we were playing that game that the Olympic athlete thing was the lie,' Luke remembers.

'What game?' Caio asks.

'Yes, it was the lie, because I said I was an Olympic athlete. I was not. I am not. I did not make it to the Olympics.'

'What game was that?' Caio asks again.

'A Friday night drinks one,' I answer, irritated. What right does he have to go telling people things about me?

'It's so good you can sail! Maybe we can all go together one day,' his bubbly wife or ex-wife says to me.

'I haven't sailed in a while.' I know this will quickly spread around the office, and I'll have to explain why I no longer sail. I really, really don't want to have to dredge up this part of my life. Thanks, Caio.

'So, kids, what will you eat?' I focus on the kids; children are a great distraction from uncomfortable moments. Pizza and fish and chips, they tell me.

Luke asks me if we are meeting the guys from work at the Rocks later. Although I was aware they organised an outing tonight, I had my weekend planned around Mum. This is really not going where I wanted it to go.

'Oh, no, we are going to the ope—'

Caio interrupts, disagreeing.

'What about our tickets?'

'Not a problem. It's better to go out with your friends.'

'Caio, I really don't want to go to a nightclub. It'll ruin my dress, and we can't talk . . .'

'We can talk at home. Let's have some fun, do what we used to do before . . .'

'Before?' I ask. 'Before when?' I refer to when we met seven years ago in Spain, going to incredible parties. Still trying to understand the hormones of youth, we were like animals in heat. All the time, everywhere, with a quality that met our needs. 'Caio, we have a flat with a balcony facing the ocean. Why bother going to a nightclub? It's dirty, noisy, smelly—'

'Don't worry,' he interrupts again, 'we can do everything again at home. I want to be on that dance floor with you. It's been a long time.'

We make our way to a nightclub before we can even finish dinner.

Luke's wife or ex-wife tells him to join us, but he continues to the car park with them. I don't know if they get into the same car or not. It would be a shame if they are splitting; the kids seem very happy with them.

Once at the nightclub, my feet are already throbbing from walking all the way from the opera house. Caio goes to the bar to get a drink, and I stay with Bec, who is very excited by our *surprising* arrival. No one dances; we stand at the edge of the dance floor, waiting for those who went to the bar to return—mostly men—and we talk about work, mostly gossip. Someone calls out to me in the crowd. He doesn't say my name, but I know he's calling to me. I've seen him before, I've heard him before, I've even smelled his perfume. He's given me a present. The guy from the bookshop! I follow him; it's the only thing to do, and I hope no one is following me. I walk down the stairs without losing sight of him, and when I finally manage to lean on his arm, he turns around, smiling.

'Have you been enjoying the parties?'

'Yeah, this one sucks.'

'Free yourself.'

'Of what?'

'From your past. From who you thought you are. From where you thought you should be.' And, reaching that dangerous distance from my ear where I can smell his scent in the middle of this beer stink, he whispers: 'Where are your wings?' He looks at me longingly and starts to walk away. 'It would be nice to see you next week . . . Wednesday . . . Flapping wings.'

I watch him walk away, determined and calm, slender and alone, when I am interrupted by Caio:

'Who is that?' he asks aggressively, and I deflect, saying it was a supplier from the office. 'Too cocky for my taste.'

He rightly disapproves.

'You don't have to be jealous. He's just a coworker.'

'Come on, let's do something amazing like in the old days!'

Caio leads me by the hand out of the nightclub, agitated and walking fast. I feel the testosterone, anger and fear coming out through his nostrils. In a dark corner, he puts me against the wall. It all feels very passionate; he's in that nice state of jealousy where I can feel he wants me; he's afraid to lose me. His hands drive through my thighs, my back, my neck, and what felt nice suddenly becomes a tight grip on my face, and the passionate kiss becomes the kiss of a drunk, of a mindless, selfish man. I try to push him away, but he is much stronger than me. I ask him to stop.

'Stop! What are you doing?' I've never seen him like this, but it feels like it's part of who he's become since last night. I have to push him harder; it takes another couple walking by for him to stop. Intimidating a man takes more than a request; it takes someone stronger or more important than him.

'What's your problem?! I'm not going to have sex with you, drunk in the middle of the street! What do you think I am?' He comes after me, apologising, saying that he thought I would like it, to remember the times when he loved me the way he used to. He wants to make me happy. I don't understand. I'm shaky. I feel the tears building up.

'Tainá, don't make a scene.'

'You! You made the scene, Caio! What did Singapore do to you? We are over. Go away. Forget me.'

I get into the first taxi, and the tears flow on the way to my refuge in Kirribilli. Silent tears, hidden from the driver by my hair. I open the door, relieved I had my wallet and the key so that I don't have to go to Bondi with Caio.

Once my nerves are less reactive, I feel I overreacted. It's Caio, for goodness's sake. I have no reason to feel unsafe with him. What I said was a bit strong. *Go away. Forget me.*

Is that really what I want? Of course I don't want him to forget me, only age and dementia can make us forget each other, but do I really want him to leave? I have been waiting for Caio since February and planned to wait for him until September. The masked man and the guy in the bookshop appear in front of me—in my imagination, of course—as I look at the city lights through my balcony. I think that plan is gone.

*

Caio has never been a person to apologise; rather, one must see his generous gestures as such. So, I never imagined that I would see him in Kirribilli at 9:00 a.m., in front of the building, leaning against a post, without gifts or flowers.

'Let me make things better for you, for us.'

'Caio, I have to go to Fleur's house.'

'I know. That's why I'm here now. I had a Coke with a banana, like your father once told me. He was right. It's the best hangover cure.' A silence hangs over us. 'I'm sorry, I don't know what's come over me. I love you, I . . . I don't want to lose you . . . Let me walk beside you until you get there, and you can decide if I can come in or not. I bought a present for the baby, for the mother, for the other two children and . . . believe it or not, for the father too.'

I have to hand it to him for his efficiency and thoughtfulness. Besides his anger and him taking it out on me with his sharp edges and self-centredness, there is nothing wrong with him. We'll find each other again, and we'll be able to sort out the problem of his almost adolescent impulsiveness. We walk quietly side by side, separated by a distance that wants to be closed with a light touch of hands, but it remains out of fear. Out of uncertainty. Giving him my hand would mean that I forgive him, when in reality, I am still hurt by the way he treated me last night—and how he came to Sydney unannounced. If I hold his hand, he will understand that I've already excused him, which will add to my irritation at his arrogance and forcefulness.

Caio knows he was wrong and not just this once.

'Sorry about talking about your sailing. You sail very well. I had no right; I know you haven't been on the water for a while. I've seen the wetsuit. You haven't worn it yet.'

It's nice when someone understands you without having to go into a long explanation. We've been through so much together.

'And you know why . . .'

'Yes, I know why.' He stops, waits for me to turn to him. 'I am sorry,' he says, looking deeply in my eyes. 'I don't know what Singapore did to me, but I will fix it.'

I notice a comfort in us. Connection. Real.

'Thank you.'

As we approach Fleur's house, I hold out my hand to him; he takes it, and we enter.

We're the first to arrive, and even against Fleur's initial wishes, we help do what's left to be done for the veggie-barbecue baby shower.

'I've never had a Brazilian friend who isn't half an hour late!'

'Ten minutes at most when it's a party,' I say, and I see Caio smiling.

On our shopping night, I spotted a device that was both an erotic toy and a pelvic muscle strengthener—I imagine she'll need it after three births. Added to this funny gift—judging by her laughter—I brought chocolate, some reusable nappies that were on her list and toys for the older children. She is amazed by the extra gifts Caio brought as well.

Only he and I thought about the older children, and only Caio thought about the father. Soon the guests arrive, and I become the babysitting sensation of the party. The children love me, and their parents offer me various babysitting jobs. I never thought I was good with kids, but these little ones are easy to entertain. Caio is sociable and pleasant and charms everyone around him. It's good to see him like that, in normal life conditions.

It's hard not to fall in love with the idea of settling down after observing Fleur's family. With her husband, Will, their children

Arlo and Zach, and the little one they're expecting, the looks Caio and I exchange become more caring. I know we're thinking the same thing: one day. The two of us and a bunch of smart kids.

Fleur announces that I will be Aurora's or Theo's—name to be decided once the baby is born—godmother at the end of the party. I feel a huge pressure to stay here in Sydney. It's the first step, my invitation to start a different life, without my nomadic tendencies.

I am surprised to think of the masked man right now. Why does he keep coming back to mind? I wonder how far a relationship with him could go . . . No carnal desire can compare to the unconditional love of our future family. September is just a few months away, then life can carry on its flow. I must leave the adventure of these parties and a potential future with the masked man behind, but I can't continue with this long-distance relationship the way it is.

As we leave the party, I start walking back to Kirribilli.

'Where are you going? Let's go home. I have to get my bag,' Caio says while pressing his phone to get a car share back to Bondi.

'Caio, we need to talk.'

'We do, do we?'

'You don't think so? Look, what we're doing is hard.'

'And what are we doing?'

'We're together, but far apart . . . Not everyone survives like this.' I shiver, and it's not from cold. These conversations are never easy. I never had to have one like this before.

'I know, you want to see other people. Open up the relationship.'

'Not really. I wanted us to get to know each other, connect like we used to, you know? Maybe when you come here for good . . .'

'That won't be until November now.'

'November?! You said it was September!' My calmness and hope for our future turns to anger and betrayal. How could I be so in love for *us* again a few seconds ago, and one word is capable of destroying it? 'How can you drop a bombshell like that on me just hours before you leave to go back . . .'

'I wanted to ask you to come to Singapore with me, but apparently . . .'

'Caio, I can't keep running after your career anymore. Waiting for you to decide that I am more important . . .'

We stare at each other until we are both in the same place. We are both right. He knows I'm right. I know he wants me close but not more than his career. We are calm now.

'I'm doing this for us,' he says.

'Me too. I need to stay.'

We embrace each other with the affection he once showed, with the affection he used to give me, now with the added pain of a separation.

'I'll make things better for you, for us. I promise.'

He kisses me, full of hope and fear. His forehead rests on mine. He pauses. He stares at me once again, like he has never looked at me before. I watch our last years go by like a fast-paced movie, unable to connect all the details. It's a termination, it seems; the car arrives faster than we needed it to. Caio doesn't send him away like I hoped he would. He walks, with his back to me, to the corner where the car is waiting for him. Without saying anything else.

'Caio!' I shout, standing still like a statue, waiting for his reaction to decide whether to move or stay there until someone tugs me away.

He turns to me, his eyes filled with tears. I run into his arms, give him a kiss, and one of his tears overflows and reaches my lips.

'I love you. Thank you for everything. I'll see you in November,' I say.

Nostalgic, he returns the kiss, squeezes me like a child would squeeze his favourite teddy when it is taken away from him because he's deemed to be too big to hug soft toys. The car door closes. He's gone. Just like that. Without looking back. Without another nod. Without wiping his eyes.

*

As with all deaths, life goes on. Mum arrives in Kirribilli, and soon we make our way to Bondi together, as she is as excited to see our home—Caio's and mine—as she was with the new wines she tasted and the ephemeral friendships she made over the weekend.

I can't see myself telling her we broke up. She might have figured it out when I ask her to leave her bag at Bibi's, saying we will be back. She doesn't ask me questions, she just follows. She must know. As I see life passing quickly out of the window of the taxi, the thought of him meeting someone else scares me.

What if I never see him again? Caio must still be on the plane, and I have to control myself not to send a message.

Mum is enlivened, praising the flat and Caio for giving me such a beautiful place, until the tide changes. She becomes quiet observing the view. She ponders her movements and her words, looking at the landscape that reflects the typical sunset in North Bondi: the orange-pink light reflecting on the cliffs.

'Is everything all right, Mum?'

'Your father always said that your freedom would take you away from us. But we also shouldn't stop you if, one day, you wanted to brave the world.'

'Thank you, Mum . . .' I pause. 'And Dad.'

I've always prided myself on being a traveller without a destination. I wish I could say I was untethered, but it's hard to let go of the past and of the ones we love.

'I never agreed with him,' she says.

'What do you mean? Why not?'

'I never saw you happy. Wherever you went, it was like a cloud of worry and fear was chasing you.' Her words hurt as much as a punch in the stomach; she's right, I'm not happy, never have been. Nothing really makes me happy. 'You've always managed to have a euphoric, lively life. You're social, you know how to choose who you hang out with, very responsible, you've always sought out . . . I don't know . . . almost transcendental . . . experiences. You dive with sharks; you've camped in the middle of a reserve with lions, hyenas and who knows what else. You stuck yourself in the middle of the Amazon without a way to communicate for twenty days! Do you know how your father and I spent those twenty days before we heard anything from you? You always wanted to get the best grades, you took part in the Olympics, you sail, you run, you swim, you studied in another country, you lived in so many places that I don't even know how many countries you have called home. You speak seven—is it seven?— languages. It was almost as if you were testing life, wanting to give it a chance to take you away like it did your brother. So much anger. And wanting to cushion that pain with awards, euphoria, and experiences . . .'

'Okay, Mum, that's enough. I get it.'

'But you always needed someone to do all this with you. Since you were fifteen, not coincidentally, a few months after your brother died, you started dating, and until now you haven't stopped. You've never been alone; we need to be alone sometimes to get to know ourselves . . .'

'I'm alone, Mum. Do you see Caio here?' My voice changes, getting rude and louder. I've never spoken to her like this, but she doesn't seem to mind.

'No, but you're waiting for him. Why are you waiting so long? The day you die, the next trip, the next boyfriend, the next adventure . . . And today?'

'Enough, Mother! How can you be so happy? I did all this, maybe, maybe to plug the hole, but I did it for you. And Dad. To make you proud, to let you know that you are not bad parents and that Kadu's death was not your fault. Do you think I couldn't hear you talking at night? Do you think I could sleep? Do you know how much I fought insomnia? And yes, dating, sports, awards, all helped me sleep. Maybe, Mom, maybe I was running away, maybe I still am. But I did it to try . . .'

'Living,' she completes my speech, crying as I've only seen her cry at a funeral. Her tears and mine mingle on each other's shoulders, wetting our clothes. Without much explanation, I understand how she manages to go on retreats, to travel alone and not sink into black clothes and loneliness. 'You don't have to please anyone but yourself . . .'

It's been so long since she looked at me like that. I like that look; it's affectionate without asking for anything in return.

'I wanted to forget, to go back . . .' I try to speak between the tears, the sobbing and hiccups.

'It would be nice to have a time machine, but have you thought what a mess it would make in the world? Someone would end up bringing dinosaurs back to life!' The salty taste of tears mixes with my half smile. 'Angel, you'll never forget, and life keeps reminding you . . .' She opens the curtain fully, showing the rocks on the cliffs. 'Of that day, of how you felt, of the pain, the emptiness, the anger, the disappointment . . .'

'He promised that we were going to be together forever, that brother and sister would never separate; he promised that he would always defend me, that he would never . . . How can you live there? Doesn't it hurt?'

'It hurts, it has hurt more, but it still hurts. But wherever I go, he will be with me. Now, they will be with me. I've never lost a brother, so I don't know how you feel, but I've lost a son.'

'Which is much worse . . . I'm so spoilt.'

'Your feelings are your own. I will never understand them, and you, if you are ever a mother, can come to imagine what I feel, but you will never know . . . You don't have to feel my pain to accept it.'

'If I had been there . . .'

'It would have happened the same way. I've blamed myself too much, for too long, and every now and then I still catch myself blaming myself. I thought countless times about the sixteen years of his life, all the things I did, all the things I failed to do, all the fights, all the hugs, my work, the food I made. Maybe the food wasn't enough or didn't have the necessary nutrients. I blamed his—your—father. I don't even know why. I fought with him for not feeling guilty. Little did I know that he was the wise one. We almost split up too, trying to find where I went wrong, where your father and I went wrong.

'And did you find out?'

'No. Sometimes I blamed the freedom I gave you both, I let your imagination run wild and wilfully. Your brother always said he was going to climb that cliff from the steepest side. He never did; he was scared to death. I don't know if you remember, but he asked to take a climbing class. He did, and even after some good practice, he still couldn't climb. It only took one bad experience, one day, one desire to try something new for him to do it. One day when he tried marijuana. A single chance to achieve his dream, and his impulses were greater than logic, reason and security.' She pauses. 'He grabbed a bush to hold on to climb. He fell. He was gone. I disappeared. Your father vanished. You . . . We kept going for you. Freedom without safety can kill.'

'Why don't you say his name?'

'Because it hurts.' I've discovered her limit. 'His face appears in my dreams all the time, while I'm awake or asleep.'

'Kadu. Good and gentle, in Tupi and in life.'[1]

Longing and pain squeeze her insides. The physical and mysterious place where emotions live. Her throat sobs, her body folds on top of her stomach, she touches her own heart, and I hold it all with my own arms. We stay like this for an incalculable time; I realise that I only look at the clock when my feet get cold and our tears dry on our faces.

'Daughter, you are living in the same place, surrounded by the ghosts of him and now your father. Promise you won't blame yourself anymore . . .'

'I couldn't have saved Kadu, but I could have saved Dad . . .'

'Your father was always an excellent sailor! Maybe it was his arrogance or a . . . whale.' And with that word, a giant mammal, we finally manage to rid ourselves of the blame. 'Tainá, you are not to blame for anyone's death. We can neither predict nor prepare for all of life's catastrophes. The only certainty you have is that one day, all of us are going to die. What happens between our birth and death is madness.' I think Mum is getting wiser and wiser. 'Stop inflicting this torture and suffering on yourself.' She points to the cliffs again. 'One sees what the heart feels, my child, and here I think you see the pain every day. Nanú . . .' It has been over a decade since my mother has called me Nánu. 'My child, give yourself the freedom to live!'

We cuddle on the couch again and stay like that for quite a while, until our faces are deflated.

'Come on, I need to take my things to Kirribilli.'

'You're not sleeping here anymore?'

---

[1] Tupi is the native language of a tribe who lived in the land known today as Brazil. Most of their people were decimated by the Portuguese during colonisation, starting in the 1500s.

'No, Mum, I broke up with him this afternoon. We will see each other in November *if* he decides to come here.'

She promptly gets up and helps me put my clothes in my backpack. Smiling. I take the photos I have of Kadu, Mum, Dad and me. I leave all the photos with Caio, although he is in some of them with us. I don't want to erase him. He did a lot for me. We did many things together and spent a lot of time sharing life. I leave a note for him hanging on a photo of us: *I love you. Thank you for the years together.*

We put what little food is left in a supermarket bag. I tidy the bed, and Mum does a quick clean with me so as not to give the cockroaches a chance to get in here. I close the curtains, saying to myself, *Goodbye, brother. Goodbye, Dad.*

As we leave, Mum says, putting her arm over my shoulder and her head on mine as we walk down the corridor: 'You know, daughter, in life the only thing we can't solve is death. For everything else, there are psychologists, lawyers, cooks, architects . . .' She manages to get a smile out of me even at a time like this.

*

Holidays. Nothing better than holidays! And, what's more, a holiday with someone you don't need to hide anything from, someone who doesn't judge you and whom you don't judge. I understand now, finally, how wise my mother is, has always been, and that her happiness—which bothered me so much—was nothing more than her wisdom reflected on her face. It was her coping mechanism for pain and loss.

We remain standing with our backs to the world and our eyes on the sea and my rented boat, with our hair behaving as a nine-knot wind would like. I know I am about to pass through yet another portal of my soul, where emotions of glory, defeat, complicity and grief will surface. With a gesture, I ask for my mother's hand, as I imagine I have asked many times when facing fearful situations in my childhood. I feel that the two of us are the perfect family. I grant that the ghostly presence of Dad and Kadu beside us is a figment of my imagination, since I have never understood supernatural matters, nor do I have the courage to investigate them thoroughly. The amount of clothes we wear proves how much I need to take this medicine and how much my mother loves me; after all, only necessity, passion or love would make someone get out of bed to face a winter day sailing.

'There will never be a better day than today,' she says.

'Ready?' I ask excitedly.

'With you? Always.'

She encourages me with minimal words and maximum strength. Her vote of confidence is strengthening. I conclude briefly that our greatest good fortune is who our parents are. What would have become of me with a different mother? So much could have gone wrong in my life if not for the parents I had. We both embark on the journey of overcoming my own fears. Sailing again. Expelling the ghosts of memory and imagination. And soon, I find out that it is much like riding a bike: there's no forgetting.

From Rose Bay to Manly, stopping at Watsons Bay for a traditional meal of fish and chips, we spend a restorative day.

She remembers skills she had forgotten; I release monsters to leave me for good. The sea and the boat no longer frighten me, and I learn at every second, at every gust of wind that he, my father, will always be with me. The dolphins accompany us for part of the trip, which, according to another sailor we chat to when we arrive back to shore, is unusual at this time of year.

I teach Mum the luxury of a hot bath to warm the bones and spending a night in flannel pyjamas watching TV after we order food. We sleep like children on the night of their birthdays: enchanted, embraced by the magic of the day.

Mum starts the next day off at a thousand miles an hour, with a rented van and GPS attached so we can buy furniture and utensils that seem like me. Luckily for our bank accounts, the flat is tiny, and Bibi already has the basics, like a fridge, dining table, sofa bed and mattress. But she doesn't have a bookshelf, the cupboard is a chest, and, in the bathroom, there's only a small mirror with a shelf. We go to Ikea and have a blast. We spend six hours picking out a wardrobe for the bedroom, a modular bookcase that I can make bigger as I buy more books, a mirror with a cabinet for the bathroom, towel racks, shelves and curtain for the shower, a luxurious wooden tray for the bathtub, frames to put my photos in, candles, pillows, a console to put shoes and keys in by the entrance, decorative lights, and a big vase for a small tree that we still need to buy in the next few days. Tomorrow, we'll buy new sheets because she thinks sleeping must be done in something very luxurious.

'Do you think I'll be here long, then?' I say as we sit exhausted on the sofa.

'I think you will stay as long as you need to. You can sell all this later or even give it to Bibi as a present for letting me stay here for free, don't you think? All this was much cheaper than staying in a hotel! Look how crazy.'

'You don't think I should stay in Bondi, do you?'

'Not at all! Daughter, I can imagine how strange it is to lose someone you shared your life with for so long . . .'

'Mum! Can you *imagine*? And Dad?'

'It's different, daughter. I had no choice; your father passed away. You chose to break a bond; you decided that the security he gave you is no longer as valuable in your life. That causes a lot of uncertainty, a lot of fear.'

I rest my head on her shoulder; I accept her observation. Yes, I am afraid of being without Caio. Like a train leaving the station slowly, I see the countless moments in our lives when he supported me, gave me a shoulder, a lap, affection, support, and, as the train speeds up, I see so many other times that he was rude, demanded my support, put me at a crossroads of choices. I interrupt this train, listening to my stomach.

'Mum, it's time for dinner. We only had meatballs today.'

'Leave it to me, I'll ask the app.'

Her acceptance of new technologies is admirable; she is definitely not a quasi-sexagenarian like my grandmother was and like so many others are. Sometimes I see a girl, a younger adult than me, someone extraordinary, someone the world should know more about.

I kiss her forehead in a long, tight kiss, the kind that says, *Thank you for everything, I love you, don't leave me, I'm sorry for leaving,*

I'm sorry for not being everything I could have been, everything you deserve for me to be. All in a single kiss.

11

Despite my resisting seeing the date of the party this week, not only did the bookshop guy turn up like an angel, but my mum bought the paper. So, as much as I've avoided it and genuinely committed myself to being with Caio, the universe won't let me get away from the party.

It's time to take at least one piece of advice from my mother and allow myself to live. She will have tonight all to herself while I go out. I thought about not meeting my masked man, but how can I? I missed last week because Caio showed up by surprise. Mum, despite me offering to go out together, asks to stay at home because she needs to sleep.

After our saga cleaning our souls with the sea, and preparing the house for the future, today we are buying new sheets, plants and trying to take care of us. Facials, massages and new clothes, like we haven't done since my fifteenth birthday, when we tried to erase the sorrow, pain and grief in an intervention of happiness. Very different from now, when we can finally enjoy life, understand where we are and how to live, even though we've had a few pieces of ourselves removed.

'More colour, Nanú, clothes that match you, fabrics that are more *you.* Let's ditch that work uniform of yours!'

And so, we spend the day buying clothes that don't resemble my boring, practical work uniform: black trousers, white, black or grey blouses and black jackets. We have a few fights during the day, as mothers and daughters will always have, but they are more the result of tiredness than of a lack of admiration for each other. She likes to spend money on clothes for me; I don't, except for my masks and my dresses. She ends up buying a lot more than I need, which irritates me.

Tonight's party will be different. I have no more boundaries with Caio. I am officially single. Mum is particularly happy to see me going out with my friends—she doesn't know it's just one. After we have our early dinner at 5:00 p.m., on the small balcony facing the opera house, she helps me get dressed and do my hair with feathers that make my head much bigger than usual. My dress is another new addition to my wardrobe, another gift from the fashion producer who loved the new closet I designed for her.

I wonder how long I'll keep getting expensive gifts and when this won't be a problem at work. Floor length, the back of the tight dress opens in a V. A small, braided cord runs down the neckline, and at the end there is a small pearl pendant. The front is closed with a kind of poncho attached to the dress that covers the breasts and the long sleeves. Without that detail, it would be quite ordinary. From the knee, the feminine silhouette opens up into more fabric, creating a flowing skirt that touches the floor. Standing in front of the mirror, I associate the poncho with the wings that were still attached to me. I put on my necklace, the one he recognises me by.

'My goodness, Tainá de Oliveira Drummond! You're a knockout! Is that what kids say these days?' She enthusiastically compliments me. 'I've never seen you in red! This deep red is so beautiful on you! That's it, my daughter, open yourself up to life, and life will enter you like a bolt of lightning!' she says, ignorant of the party and who I'm going to meet today.

My wool and cashmere coat keeps me warm. I take my mask and put it in a foldable bag in the hallway outside the flat while Mum gets ready to talk to her friends, binge watch a series and go to sleep. A lightness comes over me; life can flow at last.

*

I'm back where I met him, in the row of terraced houses in the Rocks, the magical place with gardens and an incredible view of the bay. I've been looking for my masked man for almost an hour now, and I still can't see him. My hands sweat and tremble. I realise I'm starting to crack my fingers, a habit that comes back from high school. My stomach shrinks, and I question if my dizziness is the dress's fault—it is quite tight—or if it's not finding him. Maybe he won't come. I walk up to the mezzanine looking, but my inability to spot him in the crowd makes me regret going out to dinner with Caio last Friday. I should have come; I disappeared the week after that night with the ropes. What would he think? That I'm not interested, obviously. No, maybe he has an appointment; maybe he's wearing a new outfit and my hurry is making me blind. He has every right to have his own setbacks. Only when I start to descend the stairs to the mezzanine do I bump into him. Wearing a different mask and a different outfit, I can only recognise him by the invisible link that exists between us. Call it pheromones, electromagnetism or soul; the fact is that when we meet someone, we find ourselves in the field of the incorporeal.

'I didn't think I would run into you again,' he says.

I wish I could say that I'd thought about him the whole time, that Friday was awful, that I felt like I betrayed both of us. I wish I could say that all I want to do is hug him, but I don't. I just smile and give an evasive reply: 'I had some setbacks. What happened in my absence?'

'Nothing. I gave myself two hours to find you and went home.'

'You went home? All that effort . . .' I gesture, indicating the hard work it must be to get dressed in his elaborate clothes. 'And you went home?'

'Yes, I looked incessantly for you. I must have scared a few people by staring. I waited for you to fall into my arms during a couple of dance rounds, and being unable to find you, I imagined the ropes might have been too much, that I crossed the line, I felt a . . . And I walked away.'

His reticence needs reassurance, an answer, so I make sure to soothe his worries: 'You have not crossed the line. I'm here. Let's dance.'

Tonight, something is different. Our eyes remain glued to each other, we follow the choreography like everyone else, but the real dance is happening between us. Only us. The focus of love may be silent to the ears but never quiet to the senses; much is said by how—and which parts of us—we move and touch;

passion is fuelled in the space between us. Feeling free to be with him tonight is more thrilling than all the enchanted atmosphere of the party with the coordinated dancing, the orchestra and the magical lights. We slowly come to a stop by the large window, still in the last dance position: he holds my right hand while resting his own hand on my lower back. We remain quiet, observing our souls passing, the movement of the candlelight flickering over our masks. It's changing colours, reflecting what we are inside, what is happening to us, as we wait to find the perfect time to make the leap to be us.

If he has good hearing, he might mistake the low, deep sounds of the orchestra for the beating of my heart. We know that the only place that exists now is here and what prevents us from merging into each other are the layers of fabric covering our bodies. Fabric which could have been incinerated in the ardour that emanates from us—were we not humans. I admit, there's fear too. Who is he? Am I safe? I don't know. I believe I am. Why doesn't he just kiss me? What is he afraid of? I stare at him purposefully telling him, without saying a word, that I want him to end this emotional agony. I want him to understand that my expression is a yes, that the paper-thin distance I put myself from him is a yes. His hand travels up my arm towards my face; he holds it gently; his thumb touches my lip, slowly, opening it slightly. My eyes close. He doesn't move I get closer. He does too. I feel his lips caressing the revealing sigh of my desire for us. For him. I abandon myself. I surrender my past, my fears, my future, my limits, my shame and everything else that kept me from embracing life. He pulls me close. I breathe his relief. Immersed in the freedom of being able to be where we belong. I can't describe where we are going. I don't pay attention to anything else but us, him, the energy attracting us, moving us forward, step by step, hurried steps. All I know is that we see each other alone. Alone at last, between four walls. The long kiss directs us to love each other, entranced and shuffled in sheets, cushions, pillows and masks. Sometimes we seem like inexperienced, clumsy and flustered adolescents, unable to control the internal burning and overflowing desire. At other times, most of the time, we love each other to the sound of moans and grunts of novelty and pleasure. I lose myself analysing his creases and curves, shaped by sport; he seems to forget how long he spends kissing every inch of my body. So do I. We're reminded of the fact that we don't see each other's faces only by the eventual scratching of our masks. An extra touch of excitement. We are armed only with freedom and curiosity, dipped in an ocean of trust, living and reliving each other, creating tale-worthy memories. At some point during the night, we merge into each other's skin, falling into a deep and contented sleep.

The winter sun wakes me up, and I can observe where we are. Or were. He's gone. My mask hurts a few parts of my face. I'm wrapped in sheets and nothing more. I've never experienced this before. I have never given nor received such an exchange. We were in the same place; we entered a world of our own. It's 7:30 a.m., and although I don't have to be anywhere, Mum must be worried because I didn't sleep at home and I will miss our morning walk. I don't even have my phone to let her know. Why is he not here? Something is bothering me. Could it be the sunrise, the twelve chimes that turn the carriage into a pumpkin?

On the bedside table, there is a drawing, done in ball-point pen once again. An eye whose upper outline is a female body lying down; the lower outline is a male body. The iris is full of detail. In the eye, there are a series of dots arranged like stars and galaxies. My description falls short of the quality of the illustration. Below, in the left corner, a small saying, a small poem:

When you and I meet
You leave yourself in me
I leave myself in you
Merging the universe that exists

After the poem he's written: *Thank you. I hope to see you next week. Your (un)masked man.*

He is here, he left himself here, making sure I would know he didn't simply leave me. I take the pen as a souvenir and smile, satisfied; if I wasn't human, I would have fallen back in slow motion. Where did my masked man go? Is he here somewhere? Will I be able to recognise him in the world outside?

I observe the room: beautiful, sophisticated, serene. The beige and woody tones make it easy to forget that it's winter outside. I feel my spine tremble when I see the posts of the canopy bed. I remember him leaning on them as I discovered the curves of his back, from his shoulders to his feet. Every single millimetre. Trust is essential for the end of inhibition. I force myself to wake up from this dream, quickly getting dressed and leaving this surrealist reality with my drawing, my mask and my wings.

The slamming of the door behind me erases any fear that this place is one of original sins, a pornographic underworld which exploits the female body for the exclusive pleasure of selfish and self-centred men.

The masked receptionist hands me my bag and says that the room has already been paid for. He wishes me a good morning and, together with other humans energised by the love they gave and received last night, I let the morning, the responsibilities of the routine and the last days with my mother take me hurriedly home. To a wise and understanding person, explanations are unnecessary, and my mother is heartened by my not-so-enigmatic happiness.

'What do you want to do today? Do you want to sleep?' she asks, smiling.

'No way! We're leaving! Pack your bags!'

'What? Travelling where? I have to go to Auckland on Sunday.'

'I know, Mum. Don't worry.' As I look at my phone, I discover that the flights I can catch now in the morning are cheaper without a suitcase. 'Forget the bags, Mum. Put a bikini, pyjamas and an outfit in your handbag!'

On our way to the airport, I buy the tickets, hire a car to use at our destination and book a yoga, spa and meditation retreat in Byron Bay for us.

When we arrive back to Sydney on Saturday night, it is as if we have been born again, as mother and daughter. The welcoming warmth that surrounds us makes the world unique;

we are like a bubble; we care for ourselves. We talk about the strange feeling that if this bubble took us high and away, to a new dimension, this world would not miss us, we are so tiny. Even so, we feel grand, as if the whole universe were just the two of us and everything fit inside of us. I joke that if this is how people feel when they try hallucinogens, then maybe I should change my opinion about drugs. We look at each other and know that I will never change this opinion. Life itself can be a trip on its own.

Sunday night comes much sooner than desired, and I feel a huge tightness in my whole being when I think about letting Mom out into the world again. She notices the tears, and this time they are not tears of loneliness.

'One week is so short! You're coming in December, right?' she asks.

'Yes, I'll come visit you in December. I'll let you know if Caio will come. We'll see what happens in November.' She looks at me, a proud and worried mother, her head slightly tilted to the side, as if she's looking at a baby. Her baby.

'Mum, tell me, how are you going to do research in Auckland with your English?'

'Easy—with translators. A fine young man, a student, who is the son of Brazilians, will help me during the research. The lecture will be translated and have subtitles in the presentation.'

'Oh Mum, you are incredible.'

She rolls her eyes, dismissing my marvelling at her independence and bravery.

'If I let my inability to speak other languages get in the way of what I want to do, I wouldn't do anything,' she continues.

I look at her with pride and longing; her look says the same. We are in that grounding place of mutual admiration.

'To new beginnings!'

With our water bottles, we toast to our new projects and new paths. *Good luck, mother. Good luck, daughter.* With her eyes full of tears and the promise of great adventures, she enters the portal that will take her to another world: the airport terminal.

12

This morning's meeting baffles me. It's when I notice Luke's similarities to my masked man: the way he says *coffee*, the broad shoulders, the memory of my skin and the associations in my mind between him and the masked man disturb every moment of my day when I'm not focused on work. Work is a great distraction from the problems of the heart. Of the soul. Every trip to the bathroom, every bite of food, every sip of water and every step until I get home is full of angst as I analyse the similarities between the two men. The eleven-degree winter and the frigid wind aren't even enough to make me forget the odds that my coworker—the expert on all things computers, the guy who has already blindfolded me in front of the entire office—is the same man who sees and touches me every week like no one ever has.

Already at home, a synaesthesia of senses shakes my body as I try to do the most banal things, like cooking. The mechanical and repetitive activity of making food allows the thoughts that take me back to Thursday night to invade my mind and my matter, my flesh, my meat, my body. Alone, I again feel the turbulence that he, the masked man, caused me. Without his body to warm me, his muscles to lift me, his mouth to make me squirm, I feel imprisoned by this memory. Without being able to meet him today and kill these delirious manifestations, I try and fail to expel this desire from me via cold baths, boring reading, horrendous news in the newspaper. Nothing works, and I decide that, instead of fighting against it, I must surrender. For the first time since puberty, without really knowing what to do, I satisfy myself, thinking, under my sheets, of his body on mine and his face between my legs, retracing with my hands the paths that his had taken. A new door opens, and I sleep wrapped up in myself.

*

If Caio and I were a recipe, we would be in bain-marie, waiting to know if we'll become a proper dish or be thrown in the bin because there are not skills to make us a success. I send him a message, confirming that I'm no longer in Bondi, but that I left some of our photos there. He seems confused; he doesn't seem to believe that *we* are no longer *us*. I reinforce that we'll see what happens in November, when he is back to Sydney. No response. I know he gets my messages, but does he read them? Why doesn't he take my calls? I feel an emptiness invade me. Our nomadic life of so many years has made it difficult to sustain good friendships with meaningful ties. Maybe he is lonely too. Lost. I send a voice memo. Perhaps he will hear this one. *We can't be everything to each other. Feel free to expand. If we are meant to be together, we will find the same path again.* He doesn't seem to have liked the message one bit and replies a few hours later, stating how evil I am: *You seem to enjoy watching me suffer.*

I take a deep breath, inhaling the creative air I need to work and the smell of corporate pragmatism to remind me that architecture is ten per cent inspiration and ninety per cent perspiration. I exhale confidence. It is all I need to be able to ignore Caio's comments and focus on my new life.

If only I could. Life is more complicated than that. Maybe it's not life, it is us. It is me. Rationally, I know I haven't cheated, but I doubt if that is true. Did I cheat on him? Am I a cheater? Did I destroy all that we created?

Luke had the makings of a great friend, but the undeniable similarities between him and the masked man torment my mind and my productivity. Now that Luke has been added to the equation, it's all a fog, a charged cloud hovering over my head with the occasional lighting strike electrifying my body and my memory. How small is the world if they are the same person? Could we have a *life* together?

The days that follow our rendezvous see me learning to control my body's reactions when Luke's scent reminds me of the other one, or when I conscientiously compare what I can compare, a most needed tactic so I don't embarrass myself like I almost did at our rendezvous. Could they really be the same person? I need to hear his voice again, Luke's; I need to hear him say *coffee* one more time.

The thoughts of their similarities don't leave me alone. They both like computer stuff, they are physically similar, they sound and smell alike. But are they the same? I ask if Luke wants to go get coffee with me. He agrees. I note the rest of the team's requests: Fleur asks for a noncaffeinated herbal tea, and Tommy wants his usual, a medium latte with no sugar.

'I thought you didn't drink coffee.'

'What?' I heard him the first time, but there was too much background noise for me to properly listen.

'Coffee. I thought you didn't drink coffee,' he says again, and there it is: the shiver running through me. I take a deep breath.

'I didn't sleep well last night; I'm struggling to stay awake,' I lie. I calculate my next question carefully to understand if he has any other connections with IT, since this is another resemblance with the masked man. 'Do you have plans to focus your career on BIM, rendering, IT?' I stare at his face, searching his eyes. He is very evasive; he doesn't look at me.

'I think so. It's something I like, and it ends up paying more than straight architecture. It's an area without many specialists yet, so yeah. I think . . .' As he answers, I pay attention to everything I can: his chin, his height, his jaw, his stubble, his teeth, his lips, his smile, his hands, his skin and his proportions. Am I psychotic?

'If that's your plan, why don't you ask Chris if you can be the BIM manager of the project? It frees you up from doing specs, spreadsheets of doors, windows . . . that boring stuff,' I suggest.

Chris is our lead project architect, our boss, effectively. He is cool. Luke likes the idea and, reciprocally, asks me questions related to my own career goals. A strange feeling, I must say. I'm not sure how—or if—I can answer where or what I want to be in six months. He thinks I'm very qualified. Maybe he didn't hear me well. Maybe he is entranced by all the countries

I've lived in. He gossips that Chris already trusts me and that because I'm charismatic, people like me from the start. Am I really charismatic though? I can't stop comparing this with what the masked man said when I told him I was a photographer. I wait for Luke to ask where my accent is from, but he doesn't say anything. I wonder if I had already answered this on team development day, when Luke blindfolded and guided me through the obstacle course while I was tied to him.

Luke offers to take the coffee tray back to the office. Gentle as the masked man. I never imagined it would be hard to recognise someone just because you haven't seen their face. What about the smell, the touch, the voice? Our conversations are quite easy as well. Luke must also know how to draw. He must—every architect knows how to draw to some degree.

Back in the office, I thank Luke for going for a break with me, and I abandon my obsession for today and focus on work. After all I must leave on time too. Tonight is party night!

*

If I read the poem right, the yellow petunias in the flower beds indicate to me that I must make my way to a mill somewhere. The only one I can find in Sydney is a street called Windmill, and, as usual, I find my masked tribe entering a warehouse. The thrill of discovering yet another party spot is exhilarating. As soon as I arrive, he finds me.

'Thanks for wearing the same mask as last time.' He smiles. 'It makes it a lot easier to find you.'

'There's a small difference.' I greet him smiling as well while taking out the drawing he left for me in the room. 'You can't be an IT guy.'

'How come?'

'A computer science guy doesn't draw this well.'

'Um . . . Elementary, my dear Eva. I don't work in IT.' He pauses. 'Or rather, I grew up in a household of artists who made no money at all and decided to follow a more profitable path, despite my talent.'

'Plausible . . .' I notice his gaze has become a little distant. 'Do you miss it?'

'Miss drawing? Not professionally. Everything we do professionally loses its fun.'

'Oh yeah? I didn't know that.' I laugh.

'Maybe it's more like everything we do because we have to ends up being a burden.' He speaks cryptically. I'm not sure if he is talking about drawing and work anymore.

'A prison, maybe,' I say.

'Inevitably,' he agrees.

'You've never been married, or . . . are . . . you?'

He avoids answering. He pauses in silence. He doesn't find any jokes or reflective thoughts; eventually he gives me what he can:

'It's complicated.'

'Absolutely,' I agree, unable to stop thinking about my pseudo-marriage with Caio for a moment. 'The older we get, the more moments like that we have: the big holes, the big misunderstandings, the big empty spaces. Either we learn to live with them, or we try to cover them up with countless vices, addictions.'

We stare for a few minutes at the dark sky through the arched window. There are no stars to be found in the city. Not real ones anyway. He reaches for my hand and gets close to me, wrapping his arm around my waist. 'I'm not married,' he whispers in my ear.

I smile in relief.

'Come on, let's live like tomorrow doesn't exist,' I say, knowing it is a tacky thing to say, but right now, I don't care how broken my English is; he doesn't know who I am. I can embrace my second-language flaws.

Music. Ringtones. Vibrations. Unusual cramps pinch beneath my ribs. The sweat from our long ballroom dance carries away the nostalgia that lowered our energy.

His body remains attached to mine while he guides me at the rhythm of the song to a fireplace where four people occupy one chair and an ottoman. We stand, leaning on a brick wall. One of the bricks has the ouroboros symbol. The fluidity of the flames creates a golden reflection on his mask. His eyes take on another colour, and I imagine that mine do too. We know where we want to go; there's so much that can be said in silence. Communication is certainly not an exclusive verbal art. We say so much when we don't speak.

'I don't want you to feel . . . obligated to do anything.' His vulnerability shows the fear and the confusion that plagues him.

'Don't worry, I won't do anything I don't want to.' I am startled by my own statement: Could that be true? Yes, here it is, though I'm not sure if it is when I'm in the outside world.

The hypnotic intensity of his gaze empties me of any logic and blends with the softness of his hands, the dexterity of his steps, the smell of uncertainty and the loud music of my heart. I feel as alive as when I was in Salvador in the middle Olodum's drums. I enter our world once again. I reciprocate, tightening my arms around his neck with the same intensity that he pulls my waist close to him. I could ignore all the stares around us and give myself over completely, exploring every line of his body, every groove, every curve; but no, I take my time, as clumsy and rushed love is over quickly and doesn't leave such great memories. Like a good meal, decent love needs to be tasted, appreciated, delighted. Speed, in this case, is the enemy of perfection. I force myself to detach our lips, and I whisper in his ear, 'Follow me.'

Lovers, poor creatures, must not spoil the heat of their affairs when going from the spark moment to their love nests—where they can indeed be free. It is on this path that we find an indoor pool, and lucky for us, there is not a soul around. I sneak a peek at it, inviting him through the double doors. He hesitates. I ask if his mask is made of paper, and this small challenge is enough for us to stay and try something new. The freedom of no one knowing who we are gives us certain privileges, like not worrying if someone will come to complain about our inappropriate nudity. Granted, it took a bit of juggling to keep those masks and our headgear in place, but being immersed in a warm pool with a person who reciprocates your every caress and does so not out of obligation but out of a desire to pleasure you is an unparalleled experience. He likes it when I respond, when my body responds. A man has never, ever loved me like this.

We vibrate on the same wavelength. The warm water holds us like a force field, though I am unsure if the field is made of water or pheromones. I wrap around him with my legs while he stays strong with his feet on the bottom of the pool.

'Where have you been all this time?' He squeezes me, revealing a little of who I am to him. At least for tonight.

'I don't know, maybe working alongside you?'

'I thought you were a travelling photographer.'

'I am, but when I'm not, I work in an office, doing . . . amazing things.'

'What kind of amazing things?'

'If I tell you, you'll know I work beside you. Then we will be over, and we'll have to put our reality masks back on.'

He smiles, agreeing.

'You're pretty smart. I like the way you think. Do you think that's why I never found you in . . . real life? Because when we're out there we hide who we are?'

'Maybe. How can I know who you are when you are not here? Do you think you would recognise me if you saw me having lunch on the Martin Place steps?'

He agrees, and our conversation ends when we hear people entering the pool room.

'Quickly,' he says. 'To the sauna.'

Skilfully, he had already discovered the button for the dry sauna, which has some towels for hotel guests to use.

'Have you been here before?' I ask, impressed by how he manages to cover our bodies so quickly.

'Only with my other masks . . .'

Other masks. How many masks can one person wear? While the anxiety of these people arriving settles down, I wonder what he does to have been somewhere like this during the day. A businessman or the place's manager. The other people don't wear masks, which leads me to believe that we are somewhere we are not meant to be. We have fun with their odd stares; there's no reason for us to be embarrassed about being wrapped in towels, wearing sophisticated masks in a sauna with a glass front. If the masks weren't here, we would probably be a lot more well behaved. He asks me to cross my legs slightly, and under the towel, his hand travels to every curve I own. I squeeze my towel until I dig my nails into my thighs and bite his lips to avoid releasing the instinctive sound I can't keep from coming out of me. Only then, he stops. The pool water on my skin is replaced by sweat caused by the heat from the sauna and the heat inside me. He smiles and kisses me. I don't know how to reciprocate, but I suggest we continue in a private room only with us. He refuses, saying nothing else needs to happen tonight. The novelty of his words surprises me. He wants nothing in return?

As we get up to leave, he gently holds me with my back against the glass wall, one arm next to my head while the other one travels towards the part of me that has just been played with. Orgasmic enjoyment in life is anticipation, and he seems to know this because he deliberately decides to interrupt what he has started.

'I want to make sure you come back next week,' he says in his most seductive voice and kisses me slowly.

'I will come back.' I am certain my smile is silly enough to embarrass me if I didn't know he knew so little about me. After all, he thinks I'm Eva, the travel photographer. I feel loved.

I go home. He goes home. We both believe no one in the pool has seen us doing what we did, but we secretly want them to have noticed something. After all, who cares if they saw anything? I finally understand why voyeurism can be the thing for many people. When the cold and the emptiness of my apartment finally pull me out of my enchantment, I doubt my dignity, my values, my morals, and most of all, I question if the life I was living was living at all. I agree with myself that continuing to go to these parties may cause me to lose my mind. Certainly, I will have to end Eva at some stage, and I wonder what will become of me when she vanishes. I find comfort in my mother's words: *In life the only thing we can't fix is death. For everything else, there are psychologists, lawyers, cooks, architects . . .*

Wise mother. I will resolve the death of Eva when the time comes.

*

A beautiful, cold day, with a dry, deep-blue sky framing my walk to work. A passer-by crosses my path in the street and greets me with an energetic 'Good morning!' I reply cordially and realise that I was smiling spontaneously. I must have been daydreaming about last night and didn't realise.

I barely recognise myself in the days that follow. I notice I have become a bit more obsessive about Luke: I ask for his help whenever possible, I make weird statements and ask questions trying to discover if he is the masked man. I don't even know if

I want him to be. I catch myself wondering what I would do if they were the same person. My productivity plummets, and I go out and buy expensive noise-cancelling headphones—an action that estranges my colleagues.

On the bright side of things, Chris officially makes me the team leader, which is a huge win for me and adds to the positive things that are happening in this new chapter of my life. In the same manner, Luke is appointed the IT lead for our project, effectively managing the modelling and the 3D file. I'm proud that my little obsession has paid off in our professional lives. After the announcement, Luke comes over to thank me in the hallway as I come out of the bathroom.

'Thank you, Tainá,' he says, a little closer than social norms dictate. 'How can I repay you? If it wasn't for you, I wouldn't have got this . . . promotion.'

'You don't have to repay anything.' I step back a little, away from him. 'I've also become a team leader, right? I wouldn't have asked Chris if it wasn't for your suggestion, so I need to thank you too. We are even.'

Not every man thanks a woman for helping him. He could be the masked man. I swear there isn't a single drop of flirtation in what I say, but we have an uncomfortable moment. His distance and stare are a bit odd, closer and longer than other teammates would have allowed themselves. Why is he doing this? What if he knows I'm Eva? My breathing changes, and my heart beats faster. He can't know anything; he is Luke, not the masked man. I take another step back. What I crave at our parties makes me uncomfortable now. I thought he was still married. I stay slumped where I was, lost in my thoughts, as he walks back to where he came from.

Personal complications aside, I need to make sure our project will succeed, and in my experience, communication is key.

'Luke!' I call out to him. 'Can you put a time in our calendar every Friday? We will need discuss the next week's goals.'

He waves, as the masked man did at the party at various times. I must be imagining things. The similarities are suffocating me.

When I arrive at my desk, I already see the request for a recurring meeting every Friday at noon. Right before lunch. I schedule a recurring meeting with Chris at 2:30 p.m. to discuss some problems and strategies I will go over with Luke. The acceleration of my heart at the thought of spending time with Luke alone bothers me. What if they are the same person? I need to know. I need to end this doubt. I need to see if he can draw.

'Luke, can you do a quick perspective of the entrance?' I hand over my pencil.

'By hand? No way! Better ask Fleur or Bec. I can do a rendering, but not until tomorrow. I can show you a draft by lunchtime, but the final would be ready by Friday. How many do you want?' he replies, and so as not to look like a useless request, I ask for just one image of the building's entrance in the early morning light, given that it is an east-facing façade. I spend the rest of the day completing the concept design of that area so he can work on it next day. I know he and everyone else thinks this was a dumb request. Why would anyone create elaborate 3D perspectives that are highly time consuming at such an early stage of the concept design? I'm making a mess of the programme; I will need to fix it next week.

Friday morning arrives, and we end up spending a lot of time together discussing what I want for the perspective he is doing on Revit.[2] He seems to flirt with me from time to time, mentioning things that sound out of context but relate to me and the masked man somehow.

'I reckon we should propose a sauna overlooking the city.'

'A sauna?'

'Yeah, don't you like saunas?'

'Sometimes,' I answer, suspicious.

Despite the occasional awkwardness, I feel comfortable being around him. He is so enthusiastic about computer stuff, he has this energy about making the image better, he doesn't settle for the easier solution, he wants the best. I travel in my thoughts, wondering why anyone would leave such a kind, good-looking, intelligent and passionate guy? He probably doesn't make a lot of money, but who cares? What could have happened between him and his wife? Could we be together in real life? I have to snap out of it and go back to actually listening to what he is telling me.

I leave the meeting with him in search of Fleur. I feel paranoid and lost. Despite his physical appearance, the excitement for all things technology, the intelligence and the kindness, I can't be sure if Luke is my dancer, my lover. Can I

---

[2] Autodesk Revit, commonly known as Revit is a software used by architects and engineers to design buildings in 3D.

call him that? Lover. L-o-v-e-r. I need to give my masked man a name.

'Fleur, have you noticed anything different about Luke?' I speak quietly, almost whispering.

'No, but I noticed something different about you!'

'Me?' I try to control the agitated voice by breathing deeply. Am I *that* transparent? What if the flirting is coming from *me*?

'Yes, you! Look at your loose, beautiful, long hair!' She emphasises the *o* in *long*. 'While everyone else is hibernating in their grey-black-white colours and thick woolly scarves, you seem to be coming out of your cocoon.' Can she be right? 'You have the button of your blouse open; you are wearing vibrant combinations of colours and some patterns; and that smile that shows your white teeth like a wedding dress shining in the desert is constantly brightening up our days!' Am I smiling that much? 'The only thing missing is make-up and some bling jewellery, but I have a feeling that's not really you.'

Shy and confused I reply: 'Thanks, Fleur, you are funny. I don't wear make-up in the daytime. It damages the skin.'

'And there's more: if I noticed how you changed'—she gestures with her head and hand to the men in the office—'they noticed it too. They just can't say anything, or they will be on the harassment list.' She smiles with her lips closed, looking at me, wanting to say something more. 'I wouldn't be surprised if your boyfriend becomes your ex-boyfriend soon if you decide to come out of your hiding place at night.'

I should tell Fleur about everything that has happened between Caio and me. But not about the party. I can't say anything about the party.

Later in the day, when I realise that Luke isn't staying for Friday night drinks, I decide to make my way to a nudist yoga class I found on the Internet earlier in the week. Something that will take all the men out of my head. I take the train, as it isn't walking distance from the office. In fact, it is a few suburbs away.

The track lights illuminate an arch on the feature concrete wall of the yoga room, reminding me of the Lapa aqueducts.[3] The ambient song is voiceless; the olive-green mats are already laid concentrically towards the teacher's space in the middle. Yoga blocks and white towels are already in place, one per student. There are no mirrors or windows. The tall, dark, deep-green vegetation is placed in charcoal-and-white pots in the corner. The final touch is the heated engineered timber floor. All the elements combined give warmth to the otherwise hostile concrete box. Just before the class time, two teachers enter the room in robes just like us. A male and a female body. Unusual. After turning on the candles in their spot, they walk around smiling, offering us hot tea. The class is diverse: teenagers, adults and elderly mix in the nude, not judgemental of each other. No one wears a mask. Figurative or materially. There are no mysteries here; the only secrets are each person's stories, those scars that cannot be seen even when the clothes come off.

As the class goes on, I enter a sublimely meditative state where everything passes through me. Some memories are still cutting, but others come by to make sure the healing is happening. Opening and closing. Pain and healing. The losses in my life: my brother, my father and my grandmother. The

---

[3] Lapa is a neighbourhood in Rio de Janeiro. Its aqueducts are iconic in Brazil.

cities I didn't know and the buildings I didn't build because I left a place; I left way too fast. The days I don't spend with my mother, with my friends; old boyfriends, Miguel and Caio. The doubts around Luke spend time on me; I am not sure what they are. I can't find the answers now. Do I like him, or do I pretend to because I want him to be the masked man? I feel a weight in my body, my legs heavy as steel, my hands and arms like iron swords. I say goodbye to all of these memories and thoughts, I let them pass. When the cloud of the masked man arrives, I let it stay, as I do when the lifetime laughing with Bibi and the recent memories with my mother embrace me. They are like soft, comforting clouds. The heaviness starts to go away, I feel light, and I enjoy the fluidity of my body as I move, guided by the teachers.

I am free now, like a bird. Light as feather but not faithful enough to be left to the wind's whims; the strength of my muscles seems to ground the notion I have of myself. A beautiful dichotomy of solidity and fluidity; of material and immaterial, of strength and vulnerability. In my mind, the horizon is close to me. I am touching it; I touch them, my dad and my brother. The taste of a tear shows me how much is inside of me, desperate to come out. I feel lucky to have the person I call Mother: affectionate, loving and wise. I thank the years of partnership with my exes, mainly Caio; I thank the technology that makes the distance from home not such a burden. My favourite places are as clear in front of me as if I was there: my bookshops, my beaches and the many corners I call my own around the world. I end the night feeling whole. Alone but supported by a good life. Good luck. I wrap myself up to face the winter outside, which tries to penetrate my skin and break the summer inside me.

*

When I look at my phone in the morning—a mistake—there's a message from a common acquaintance I had with Caio, a woman in London. She can't believe we broke up; she found out through Caio's social media—and he has plenty of those. I try not to click on the links she shared with me, but curiosity is a hard impulse to control. I create an account of my own, without any photos, and start following Bibi—as I promised her. It takes me time to find a name for it. *EvaInSydney.* It makes sense. I was never one to look at his photos, and now I realise how much he was doing without me. There are photos of parties at flats, nightclubs and restaurants. Mostly with other men. The dates on most of the posts are from when we were together. I read what he wrote in all of the descriptions. There's nothing about me, expect for one. It's a photo of Singapore taken from a penthouse or a tower *Sometimes, the ones you trust are the ones who hurt you the most. To a new life. To a free life.*

I see the date of his posts and link them to weekends and sometimes even weekdays. In his latest photos he has more people with him. Faces touching, him carrying women in his arms. One of them seems to appear in more posts than others. A new girlfriend perhaps?

I can't say it's jealousy any more than relief if he has found someone else—I have too—but our relationship is different. I can't see him whenever I want. How could seven years together have ended so quickly? Or has it not ended fast at all? When was the beginning of the end?

There is a reason I never wanted to have these social media accounts. I delete my account. I send a message to Bibi apologising for not having created the account yet to follow her. She understands. I thank her again for the flat. I go out for a run around the Lower North Shore; lots of hills to make my legs and my lungs stronger. Suddenly, I come across a rather unexpected real-life 3D perspective—Luke, and he is facing me, walking towards me.

He said he lived in Tamarama, so what is he doing here? He waves from afar; I reply in the same way, but then he changes his route towards the park. His wife or ex-wife and his children wait for him with a picnic setup. I stop my run and look at them. Luke waves again and tells the children to wave. She doesn't wave. Not so bubbly today. Jealous? I wave back. I go on with my life. I have no intention of ruining a family.

While I run, I talk to Mum about her week with the research group and if everything is ready for her talk today. I ask if I can watch it remotely, and she says she'll send me a link, but that it might not work, *you know how these things are, right?* She refers to the quality of the videos and the internet connection. *There's still a lot to improve, don't you think?* I agree with her just because I don't want to start an argument; internet is pretty good these days, and I know she thinks that too. She is just a bit worried about presenting on video. I go home to get ready to try and watch her live.

In the bath, the feeling after yoga last night and my nights with the masked man erases any worm of toxicity that was starting to enter my head. I think about the man who desires me, how his body responds differently to my touch and how mine responds to him, so unashamed. I can't even say that it's sex, as it feels more like a place we go together to experience a carnal and spiritual evolution. This sounds so tacky, but it shouldn't be the most sublime feeling. Maybe we need new ways of describing such moments in time. How different it is to love with him. I wonder if this ecstasy is because he doesn't know who I am and I don't know who he is. Fantasy fuels our desires after all. Does the lack of inhibition make love more intense, or are we a true meeting of souls? I heat the water to almost burning, enough to relax my tense muscles. I take longer than necessary under the water. Who measures what is necessary and what is superfluous? When I get out of the shower, I write in my notebook: *It is the shame of what people will think of us that prevents us from loving.*

Mum's talk is a hit; there are so many questions about the impacts of neuroscience and our psyche. Another good example of what is tangible and what isn't. The instruments can tell how our brain turns on and off when we feel, but does it really explain what it feels? She inspires so many people to think differently. Now I know how she can produce so much and do so much: it's the way she can deal with the pain of her loss. She heals by adding more of what she likes in her life: pleasure. I check the newspaper in the little shop on Broughton Street on Thursday. The party is on Thursday. It was good to see Luke with his family today; somehow, I don't seem to believe he is the masked man anymore.

Monday. Neurology or psychology, I can't keep myself from observing Luke's hand. There's no wedding ring. Is he or is he not married? Not that people need to wear a ring, but make it clear for us! Or stop flirting with me. Could he take his wedding ring off to come to work?

I take the first opportunity, when everyone is a bit quiet, to ask Fleur how long she has been married and what the secret to a good relationship is. My hope is that Luke will overhear it and answer, but he says nothing. I wonder if the lack of a wedding ring is a sign of divorce, and if so, I'm an insensitive cow. We joke around with some marriage and couple's jokes; Chris joins the conversation, and Tommy comments that his social life now revolves around gay weddings. Since the legalisation of same-sex marriage, he says that the number of gay weddings is growing at the same rate his couple friends are breaking up.

'It's a strange thing. The people who always wanted to get married and complained they couldn't are breaking up,' he says, and we all laugh.

'We all want what we cannot have.' Luke finally speaks.

Work carries on as usual, ten to twelve hours a day. The good thing about our profession is that it's hard to get distracted by things other than work when we are working. It's so intense, so tedious, so polarising, with so many consultants, clients and internal teams.

Throughout the week, I sometimes catch myself watching Luke sketch on his tablet, but these are rare moments, and his sketches really do not resemble the masked man's drawings.

The problem comes when a coincidence does not look like a coincidence at all. Today, Thursday, the day of the party, both Luke and I say we need to leave right on time because we have to be somewhere.

'I hope it's not the same appointment,' Chris jokes.

'I doubt it, unless he likes solving mysteries and parties.' What's wrong with me?! Why did I say that? I have no filter today!

'I love a puzzle,' he replies, looking at me with a confusing smile; one side of his lips is up, and the other is slightly down. 'But I'm not up for playing today.' He winks.

A wink? What does Luke mean by that? Where is he going tonight?

I reach the edge of sanity. I was so serene during the week, particularly this morning, but now I am calculating what time to leave the office to leave exactly at the same time as Luke. I am ready to go, but I pretend to keep working until he needs to go. Am I going to follow him? Yes, I know I will. Why? I can't do that. We take the lift together and say goodbye outside the building. I get my phone as a distraction and wait for him at a far enough distance that I can be behind him without being seen. It is still 5:47 p.m., and he enters a hotel in the middle of the city. It's not one of the party hotels. I wonder if he's coming here to change. It's 6:10 p.m., and if I don't leave now, I'll be late. I walk as fast as I can. The flower beds are green, which means the party is at a new place.

The green leads you
To a secret place
Where across the cove you see
Only sails of concrete

Sails of concrete must be the opera house; that's an easy one. *Across the cove* can't be Kirribilli, because it's on the other side of a bay and not a cove. The cove to the east of the opera house skirts the botanical gardens, but I don't find any buildings there, just a clubhouse, and I know you can't see the sails from there. I ask the taxi driver to drop me off at the park to the west, under the Harbour Bridge; from there, I will have to walk to find this new secret place. Being five minutes late means there were already several masked guests walking to the party, and it was the easiest location to find. I adjust my ring invitation, leaving the snake's head facing up. I am greeted with a generous smile from the doorkeeper.

Under normal conditions, the grand party serves as an aphrodisiac; mystery has that power over people. And keeping the mystery between two people would be the ideal key to valuing what we can lose at every moment. My masked man and I use the party not only as a game of hide and seek but as a test to see if our souls will find each other again. Week after week, with or without new masks, we get what we were looking for. At every encounter, it's the end of the mundane, it is the rising of the want, of the reciprocity, of the complicity. Tonight, he wants to prevent me from a disappointment next week.

'I'm going away,' he says without much explanation.

'Fair enough. Thank you for letting me know. Thoughtful of you to tell me.'

As I ponder whether I can ask where he's going and what he will be doing, he interrupts me with a surprise:'But I wanted to take you somewhere else on Saturday.'

Another place, outside all of this? No masks? I freeze. Do I want this? Maybe.

'Cat got your tongue?' He smiles charmingly.

'Another place . . . on a Saturday? I thought Saturday was a . . . reality day.' Equally excited and afraid, I picture Luke's face beneath the mask. It's disappointing. Don't I want Luke to be him, then?

But before I can give wings to this thought, he reassures me: 'There's no need to panic; you won't see my ugly face just yet. We will still be wearing masks.'

How can he tell I'm nervous? Am I squinting? Are my lips tense? Maybe it is my breathing. I must have held my breath in.

'I doubt there's any ugliness in you. Where do you want to take me?' I breathe out.

'The opera house.' He points across the water as he speaks. 'There's a work event , and I'd like to take you. It's a fundraiser.'

'But do people know you?'

'Some do, but everyone will be masked.'

'I doubt people will be as elaborately dressed and disguised as they are here.'

'Maybe, but I will be; people won't recognise me. I can use a fake name. You know, someone you know might be here. Say, a work mate . . .'

'Work mate?'

'Yeah, a teammate. Possible, don't you think?' he says, having a sip of his drink.

I stare at him silently, giving him a cue to continue, but the person who continues is me:

'There's a guy who looks like you . . .' The words hang in the air again as I try to fish out some reference, but it seems futile to try and find Luke in him.

'He might look like me, but does he think like me? Does he want you like I do?'

Shy, blushing, I realise words do have a huge power.

'Not that I know of . . .' I'm sure my voice is trembling. 'What about me? Is there anyone who looks like me in your life out there?'

He shrugs, making fun, smiling and shaking his head, saying no. He holds me close, our masks almost touch, we stare. There's a bit of suspicion in the air, from both sides perhaps. I wonder if he is an actor. I feel uneasy with this possibility. An actor would thrive in a place like this; he would know how to fool me, and I wouldn't be able to tell.

'I doubt there's a woman like you at my job . . .' He turns me around by the waist. 'People there only know how to talk about money and video games.' He pulls my body even closer, wrapping his arms around my waist tightly, fitting his embedding his hips against mine, whispering in my ears: 'No woman out there has that universe inside of them; if they do, they know how to hide it, and the best thing about you is that you don't hide it from me.'

His kiss is too bewitching. Perhaps because it is accompanied by words that incite the mind and ego, but even if he were mute, his body and his lips always kiss me with affection and desire. An eagerness to have me, but with the seductive delicacy of affection. His kiss, or should I say our kiss—since one does not kiss alone—is the perfect combination of two opposites. It's like going out on an adventure knowing I have a home to return to, a home that will wait for me and be better than when I left it.

'Tell me something I don't already know about you,' I say.

He looks around, ponders and asks me to wait where I am. He goes towards the musicians and talks to one of them. As soon as the current song ends, he, holding a microphone, starts singing and dancing to a musical number that, although familiar, I have no way of remembering the name of now. It is lively and romantic at the same time. Soon the guests become the audience, making room for his number. Those who know the choreography join him, and those who can't sing or dance clap to the rhythm. I'm in that second group. He pulls another woman up to dance and twirls with a few others. I watch him, I know his eyes and his body could never be exclusively mine, but I admit to feeling a spark of jealousy and a small injury to my vanity. I have an uncontrollable urge to have him to myself and get him out of here. He finishes the number, stopping in front of me. I am the last one he pulls close to him, and it is me he kisses. From there we set off for the rest of our night between four walls.

*

Lying in his arms, with the sun still so low in the horizon that it feels like night, encased in the scent of the two of us, my body reacts to remembering last night. He notices. He accepts. He respects. He responds. When I remember how he took a deep breath as he found the line between my neck and my shoulder, I shiver, lifting my shoulders, and he kisses them lightly. When I remember how his left hand held my hip from behind while his right hand gently tugged at the rope of my dress, I arch my back, and he massages me along my spine. When I remember his two hands running down my shoulders and turning me just before the dress fell to the floor, he takes my lips and runs them along my chest and belly, making me believe I am his greatest gift. His tongue runs through me and knows me more than I have ever known myself. Last night, after his musical show, little time was lost discovering each other among the others; we came to one of the beautiful rooms in the high tower overlooking Sydney, my city of love. Who knew Paris could lose its throne? We willed each other onto every piece of furniture in the room, and even after we tired our bodies, he continued to love me with every part he knew how to make use of. From head to toe, he taught me that a man's climax doesn't have to be the end of our lovemaking. Enthusiastically, we only stopped when I asked, because, exhausted, I finally needed to recover my nervous system, which clearly couldn't continue receiving so much stimulation. Clearly, it was a very special night. He also brought two sleeping masks that covered most of our faces. They are made of silk, undoubtedly much better for sleeping than our party masks.

The rays of the sun warm our bodies; I imagine them illuminating our synchronised movements. My responses to his touches prove that it is possible to love someone whose face you've never seen if the desire is mutual. He keeps my mask on but takes off his, guiding my hand over it so I can see his face with my fingertips. I decide to give him the pleasure of being loved by someone who will not use sight to know him. Every part of my body merges into another part of his body, my nails running down his back become one of the reasons for his soft growling. I imagine the surprise of delighting in this exploration was indeed the last straw for his pleasure. As always, he holds me tight. I sleep once more, and when I wake up late, I am accompanied by one more drawing and a poem.

Who am I if not the who
you let me be?
Despite all that can be hidden
The truth lies in you and me

The drawing shows two merged bodies, one in front of the other, dancing a contemporary dance. On them is a projected image, just like they do with the light shows in the city during winter. From the two sharp bodies grow arms and legs like a strobe photograph of a dancing couple, where you can see what they did before. How can he draw so well and so quickly? The paper has the hotel logo, so he cannot have brought it from home; he must have stayed up longer than me.

I walk to the window and watch the urban forest across the water, the boats and ferries moving from side to side, the cars and trains on the bridge. Where are they going in such a hurry? Where did he go in such a haste?

I realise that it is almost 8:00 a.m. and I still need to go home to change for work.

The grey of the office is lighter, not as oppressive as it used to be. Perhaps because of the winter sun coming in through the narrow windows, or maybe because I don't mind its dullness so much anymore, or because I decided to notice the white desks and the reflected lights on the floor. Luke is particularly cheerful this morning, his gestures are more open and his posture slender. Something good happened last night to him. Where did he go?

He asks to move our meeting to 9:30 a.m., and I grant his request. In the small meeting room, he compliments my hair. Odd behaviour for him. I don't think it's sensible to say its crumpled and wavy beauty comes from the salt overflowing in the sweat of last night's encounter, so I just thank him. Then he goes on erratically until he finally tells me he's travelling next week. Personal issues.

'Sorry for letting you know—so short notice.'

'Not a problem at all! We will survive without you for a week,' I reply lightly.

One more coincidence with the masked man is enough to bring my mild obsession back, as much as I try to fight it and tell myself they cannot possibly be the same person. My trembling legs and my tight stomach don't let me lie. How I wanted to ask where he was last night, and if he's going to the opera house the following Saturday! Agony!

He looks a bit off. Was I rude saying we will survive without him? What is going on? I want to ask but how?

As my anxiety takes over my hand, I see myself changing from tapping my pen to fidgeting with my necklace. My necklace! I didn't take it off this morning! I purposefully try to draw his attention to it as I talk; if he can recognise my necklace, then he will know who I am, and the secret is no more. Do I want the secret to be exposed? Can I respond to Luke's flirtations? Am I seeing things? Is he flirting with me on occasion? How would we start dating? *Here, I have a relationship with someone. I don't know who it is. If you are okay with that, we can start* . . . No! Maybe . . . maybe? Focus, Tainá!

We are both quite distracted today, but we eventually complete the work and resources planning for when he will be away next week.

Tommy is chosen to take over part of Luke's job, mainly because he is good at it, not because he wants to. Not many people like doing what Luke does. Tommy is quite verbal about giving Luke his condolences because he will miss my birthday celebration on Friday night.

'I didn't know it was your birthday. When is it?'

'The actual day is next Saturday, the fourth.'

'Why don't we celebrate on Saturday, then? I'll be back by then,' he says, lively, but quickly changes the tone to a more doubtful one. 'Oh no, I've got something in the evening.'

Really? In the evening? Are you going to the opera house? Just ask, Tainá! Just ask! I don't ask; instead, the rubber bands that normally sit in my pen holder are abused as I squeeze my anxiety through the knots I tie in them.

'I also have to be somewhere in the evening on Saturday.'

He could ask me. Ask me, Luke. Ask where I'm going!

'Where are you guys going? Maybe it's the same place and you can celebrate together anyway.' Fleur appears from the silence of her work to make me feel awkward.

He says nothing.

I get up from my desk and ask Fleur if she can come help me. An excuse, of course. Once in the printer room, I pretend to have issues with the printer and try to casually ask her what she is trying to do.

'Fleur, why did you say that?'

'Tainá Drummond, I ask you, what's going on between you and Luke?'

'Nothing, why?'

'Why? Everyone's already noticed that there's something going on between you two. Bec is so—excuse my French—pissed off! She's been waiting for him since forever; it's pathetic, but you come in and take that chance away.'

'He's married. I saw him with his two small children and a woman who is clearly their mother.'

'Okay, gossip time just to clear out the air. He's not married anymore. Looks like they've completed their divorce. Woman, you have to be more in sync with what is being said in the corridors,' she whispers, and we continue talking in that confidential tone.

'Really? But what about the children? They're so little still!'

'Better two happy houses than an unhappy one,' she says. It doesn't take time for me to agree. 'Nothing is happening between Luke and me. And I. Between Luke and I.'

'Don't worry, I won't correct your English!'

'I didn't know he was getting a proper divorce. They seemed kind of happy when I saw them.'

'It happens, in the best families.'

'Dear Fleur, for your information: he is still out of the equation for me. I am not rebound material, and I have no intention of being a . . . stepmother!'

She laughs.

'Watch out, then, you *know* how charming he is . . .' She emphasizes the word *know* and continues. It's a dangerous thing when good looks, sensitivity and intelligence meet in a man. It's temptation overload.'

'Well, there must be something wrong right? If he's all that, why is his wife leaving him?'

'I don't know, maybe he didn't do the dishes!'

We both laugh and go back to our work.

Fleur leaves at half past five sharp, dismissing our envious faces by saying that we are the lucky to be able to work late as we don't have to carry 14kg in our bellies and we can manage to stay awake until nine o'clock at night.

Tommy, Bec, Luke and I keep going. Chris comes back from his meetings around 5:00 p.m., and instead of going home, he makes time to sit down with the three of us, answering questions and guiding us through what we can improve in our presentation. Pre-delivery nights are never early. Around 7:30 p.m., he orders some pizzas and makes sure we eat in the kitchen—not at our desks—and demands that we take a break for twenty minutes. The clock keeps ticking, and despite being at work at 10:00 p.m., I don't feel exhausted. There is a great connection between us all, but we miss Fleur's funny energy. Chris tells everyone to do all that we can until 10:30 p.m. and leave. We can finish on Monday, but he also advises us to arrive at 11:00 a.m. then. He thanks us for our monumental effort and wishes us a good weekend. I need to be the last one to leave as the documents need to be uploaded and sent prior to the meeting, so I wait for Luke to finish rendering his last image. It takes time. Bec has no reason to be here anymore; she could have left with Chris, but she keeps going doing who knows what. After the conversation with Fleur this afternoon, I can only imagine she has stayed to try and hit on Luke. She sticks around until 11:30 pm, when the lack of sleep has—as she puts it—fried part of her brain.

I see that we're alone in the office, Luke and me. I really don't know what could be more clichéd than that. I avoid getting close or into personal conversations, and I keep answering emails to keep the distance, but he becomes quite chatty.

'What were you doing in Lavender Bay the other day? I thought you lived in Bondi.'

'I used to live there, but I'm in Kirribilli now.'

'You run to work?'

'No. It's not far enough to justify changing clothes, showering, that sort of thing, but I walk.'

'Why did you move?

'To be closer to work.'

'Cheaper as well, I imagine; your street in Bondi is not for everyone.'

He must be referring to the cost of rent. People here seem obsessed with how much things cost, particularly rent and houses.

'Um . . .' The truth is that in Bondi I was living rent-free since Caio's company was paying for it, but I don't think that fits in this conversation, so I agree, partially. 'Yeah, sort of. And you? I thought you lived in Tamarama.'

'It's my parents' house. I used to live in Crows Nest, with my wife . . . ex-wife . . . and my kids. I'm at my parents' for a while until I find a place my kids approve of. They are very specific about where they want me to live.'

Now I know, from him, not from gossip.

'They know what they want!' I say.

'Yeah, they're full of demands, but you know how Sydney is; it's not easy to find a decent place to live.'

'Yeah, I heard it's pretty hard. I've been lucky so far.' I pause. 'So, your kids know what they want. How about you? Do you know what you want?' I can feel the dual meaning of my question: partially trying to help him understand himself, partially assessing if he has any interest in me.

There's a heavy silence in the air, maybe he is not ready to look into the future just yet. I try to stop being selfish by acknowledging that things must be difficult for him right now: 'I'm sorry about the divorce.'

'Thank you, me too. I thought we were happy; I don't know what I did wrong.'

I let what he says sink in for a while; I ponder it while pretending to write emails.

'Luke, sorry to be nosey, but as far as I know, there's never a single culprit; it's never the one thing that went wrong. It would be nice and easy if it was that simple.' A wise insight.

He breathes in deeply—probably unaware of it—tilts his head to the side; I get a sideways closed-lips smile. I must have made him feel good. Did I? He doesn't look at me.

'You said it all.' He still clicks away on his machine with no eye contact 'Anyway,' he continues, 'I've sent you the final images now. You can put them in the preso—aka presentation—and press that button; we are finished!' He has an awkward enthusiasm. Must be the soup of exhaustion, tiredness and pride that follows any met deadline. Positive and negative all mixed together at once. Or it could be that I have poked a place in him I shouldn't have. I shouldn't have said anything, but how could I let someone feel guilty when they shouldn't have to carry all this weight, all this burden alone? No one can break up a relationship by themselves, right? It's always the two . . . the three, four . . . all parties involved, isn't it?

He comes around the desk towards me to see how the presentation is coming together, and his left hand touches my back. I freeze. Air is stuck inside of me. I move forward on my chair; and as we detach, the air leaves my mouth in a sigh.

'Sorry! Missed the back of your chair,' he says nervously.

'Oh, not a problem, these chairs are a bit wobbly,' I almost stutter, and in my anxiety, I start fidgeting with my necklace again.

Luke must think I'm an idiot.

'You can go if you want; you don't need to stay,' I say. It's true, he can go.

He brings me a glass of water without me asking, only because he went to get one for himself and brought one for me too. Kindness has the power to turn water into elixir. I drink the water, forcing myself not to fall in love with someone who will be my coworker for the next two years—if we win this project. I finish the presentation, transitioning between my imagination and the pragmatism of what I need to get done. I find more and more similarities between the two of them; we talk about issues and themes related to architecture, urbanism, politics, buildings we love, buildings we hate, new technologies, an apocalyptic future and so on. We agree, laugh and diverge on every topic. Why would anyone leave him?

Seduction is much more interesting when you have nothing to lose, such as your job or your reputation. I could evolve this moment into an unexpected night, I could be the one that takes away his sorrow about a failed marriage in exchange for him ending my agony. I would know beyond a shadow of a doubt if they were the same person, but I can't. I can't get myself to. What if Luke is just Luke? What will happen to us as colleagues, to my job, once he is back from his leave next week? Similarly, what if they are the same person? Am I as attracted to Luke as to my masked man? Am I going to give up the mystery of our weekly dates to openly become the stepmother of his kids? No. Between truth and magic, I choose magic. I don't want to know.

I don't look at him as I know quite well that once the souls meet through the eyes, we would be on a path that's hard to return from. I press send on my keyboard.

'Done! It's over!'

'High five! Great teamwork!' he says tiredly, euphorically raising his hand. We clap our hands together, relieved, but, to my despair, he doesn't let me escape his eyes. 'Tainá, look at me.' And when I look, he thanks me profoundly.

The world is different when you feel heard, when you feel seen, when someone else acknowledges your existence. It's naïve to believe this individualistic story that we don't need anyone else. We are everyone else. We are what happens between us and the other.

'You're welcome. It's my job,' I answer slowly, attempting to give back what he has given me: acknowledgement.

'Don't underestimate yourself. It's hard to find people like you. Great work and . . . great company.'

He says *great company* slowly. Is he flirting again?

'You're welcome. Thank you too. Holy crap! Look at the time!' I change the subject and quickly pack up my desk for tomorrow, putting what I owe in my bag.

'I can take you home; it's almost midnight, it's late.'

'No, you don't have to. I'll take a taxi,' I reply, denying myself what I want: to continue our conversation, to keep working on this bond we've just created, but I must wait. I must wait for him to heal from his divorce on his own; I want my job and my reputation. So, I go home alone. Distance can do wonders for impulsive decisions.

'Are you sure?'

'Sure, it's not the first time I've been alone at night.'

'All right, then. Can you just text me when you get in? It's not safe for women to be on their own so late,' he says caringly.

A sad reality.

'Thank you, I'll let you know when I get home.'

His kindness doesn't seem to have any other intention but pure, genuine attentiveness. It does seem to be inherent in him. Luke writes his phone number on a piece of paper that he grabs from the reception desk as we wait for the lifts. Once on the street, he pulls out his mobile phone to call the ride-share, and we begin a small competition over which vehicle will arrive first: taxi or ride-share.

'Why don't you use an app? So much faster.'

'I've used it, but I don't like it. I don't think it's safe . . .' I stretch out my arm, waving to a taxi from a traditional, reliable and certified company. 'And normal taxis are much quicker. See?' I smile, and he opens the door for me. He asks me to roll down the window—like the masked man.

'The company will pay for that taxi. Get a receipt.'

'I will. Good night.'

'Text me when you get home.'

'I will. Have a good time next week.'

He steps back from the car and waves as the taxi drives away from the kerb.

'I bet next time you see each other, a kiss happens there,' observes the taxi driver.

'What? Not him! No . . . we just work together.'

If the taxi driver noticed Luke's inner desires, I couldn't have been wrong. He *was* flirting with me.

'The blind person is the one who chooses not to see. That guy who put you in the car is crazy about you. Enjoy life, girl! You're still young.'

I thank him for his advice, then I change the subject, asking him how his life is and where he is from, which is enough talk until I get to my house. I remember to get the receipt as Luke said. The dark streets of the residential areas in Sydney quickly make me regret not letting him bring me home. I also doubt if it was necessary to ask the taxi driver to drop me closer to the door; after all, what are the chances of a random taxi driver becoming a stalker, particularly in an apartment building? Sure, it's a small building, but still, how could he know which flat I live in? Paranoia. I walk hurriedly, relieved only when I close the door of the building behind me and even more when my empty, cold flat welcomes me. It would be nice to come home to someone. There's no message from anyone. Alone. I'm alone. I'm free, really: I have no one to answer to. I text Luke as promised. *I'm home. See you soon.* He must have his phone in hand as I get his reply almost instantly: *I'm glad you got home safe and sound. Sleep well, thanks again for the work and the company tonight. See you when I get back. Good night!* L

I wish I could stop dwelling on my decisions. I can't sleep. I reflect on whether it would have been truly disastrous to bring Luke here—or carry on in the office—and give wings to the energy that surely is between us. Is he thinking of me? Life without masks is a great diplomatic game; it tests our patience. Do I really choose the magic of mystery, or will Luke and I eventually get together? Why is it so hard to choose? Do I really have anything to choose from?

I get into a hot bath, the kind that makes your skin red where the water touches it, the kind that moves your blood faster through your arteries to warm your feet and the tips of your fingers, your extremities. That kind of transitional bath where you can transport yourself to a new part of your day. There's no job or reputation to save in my imagination; the only battle is against my inner critic, the shame she puts on me. I don't give her much thought. I let my mind flow wherever it wants to. I stroke the bath salts across my body, replacing my hands with those of the masked man. In my memory, of course. Luke's face enters the scene in a synaesthesia of neurological, emotional and imaginative connections. The body, the voice, the scent, the memory of one man and the face of the other. One completing what is missing on the other. The perfect threesome. I discover yet another way to make my body and my mind as light as a feather. There's a discharge of guilt when you can live your fantasies without boundaries. More than a necessity, my bath is a pleasure. It is inevitable that we'll stifle what moves us; sooner or later, awake or in a dream, our desires always resurface. I sleep without a fight, snuggled into my sheets and duvet, warm inside and out.

13

Saturday arrives, as does my run; as I pass the park on Lavender Street, I remember Luke with his ex-wife. I text Fleur, offering to treat her to a lunch without kids. She can't make it; weekend lunchtime is her time to catch up on some sleep as her husband takes the kids to his mother's house.

My phone beeps with a message from Caio that was clearly meant for someone else: a photo of him posing shirtless. I reply with a question mark only, and he quickly confirms that he sent it to the wrong person. He hasn't been in touch for days, and I wonder how he could have misdirected a message to me, since my phone number shouldn't be the first one in his inbox. Maybe it wasn't an accident, maybe he did on purpose. My phone rings. It's him. While I'm thinking about whether to drag the green button or the red one, the call ends. I call back, and to my surprise, he answers.

'Hi, you picked up . . . ,' I say, surprised.

'Yeah, people change . . .'

He is angry; he speaks with sarcasm.

'Caio, why did you call? We'll sort it out in November. If we want to . . .'

'I want to sort it out now. I can come over this weekend, spend your birthday with you.'

'No, we need distance.'

'It was the distance that separated us; we need to be together, in the same house . . . Tatá . . .'

'Don't call me Tatá, please. Distance can also be good; it gives us the space to find out what we really want . . .'

'I want you! I want us, the way we were!'

His voice increases in volume, desperate and pleading. *The way we were* rings in my head, and I hold it in my throat to avoid unnecessary talk. What is that way? Was I happy the way we were?

'I'm not going to solve it over the phone, Caio.'

'I'm coming over this weekend; I don't care how much it costs. I'm coming! I want you, Tatá.'

I fit so many words into my mouth. Words of anger and indignation but also soft words of longing, affection and love. It's complicated when your life is so intertwined for so long. It's been seven years, and the memories of the good things get tangled up with the feelings of entrapment. These memories then get overlaid by the moments of enjoyment of my new life now, my work, my choices, my new friends and, yes, without a shadow of a doubt, the enjoyment of my body; but above all, the pleasure of my freedom. Perhaps I am selfish, perhaps I don't know what I am losing yet, what good is so much freedom if I return to an empty house like last night? This soup of contradictory emotions does not find a clear path through words, so they remain stuck in my chest trying to implode it. Lucky for me, this crowd of feelings and thoughts finds an effortless escape valve through the tears that flow through my trembling voice, which gives away my conflicted interior—to those who want to listen, obviously.

'I already have plans. Don't come. There's no need to be desperate about it, we'll . . .' I'm about to say that we'll talk about us and our future together in November, when his work isn't more important than us, but I'm interrupted.

'How can you throw everything away? It's been seven years! Seven years, Tainá. Fuck! I'm a wreck! Look what you've done to me!'

I don't like the tone he uses, aggressive. *Look what you've done to me.* He wants to try to blame me for how he feels. Did he ever think about how he made me feel coming unannounced, asking me to move all over the world, to quit my career and start over every time he got a promotion. Has he ever thought how he treated my body to satisfy his most primal feelings? I've never felt better than I do now. I wish I knew the new me then.

'Caio, everyone has a process, a time. Go and have fun. For this photo and for your photos on Instagram . . .'

'You have Instagram now, do you? You've changed!' he mocks me.

'Everyone changes. I did it to help Bibi, and I've deleted it.'

'What have you been doing?'

'Working.'

'As if anyone's hit on you yet.'

'Caio, don't hurt yourself for nothing. What we do or don't do is none of anyone else's business. We'll talk in November, okay?'

'Tainá, don't hang up . . .'

'I have nothing more to talk about. The flat in Bondi is empty; let the company know, but there are pictures I left for you there.' He is silent for a few seconds. In our seven years together, there were only a handful of times that I saw him taking time to answer, only a few times that I saw him reflecting.

'I promised you that I would make things better for us.'

'That's not how you're going to make it better. I'm going to be late; I need to go back to my run.'

'I miss you.'

'Bye, Caio.'

I hang up without giving him a chance to say anything else and set off running as fast as I can, annoyed with myself for letting him know what I am doing now. He doesn't need to know what I am or am not doing. Maybe it's habit, and there's nothing harder to end than a habit. Each step a pain, each pain an anguish released. The anger comes out my calves, the disappointment through my thighs, the pain of mourning what we could have together is thrown out of my head, but the weight in my chest is compassion for Caio's pain, which soon transforms into remorse for being the one who destroyed seven years of our life together. I need another tactic to expel the guilt and relieve the tension in my shoulders—and in my soul. After appreciating the blue sky, the sun and the winter day, I take a slow shower, washing my hair. I eat a toasted sandwich of melted cheese and ham that reminds me of Grandma's house, and I make way to my favourite bookshop. I read a book on Brazilian modernism, bringing back a lot of nostalgia. I think about my friends, scattered all around the world. After going to the cinema, I get the newspaper to check the date for the next party. I don't know if I'm going; I will decide when I have to.

On Sunday, I sign up at a sailing club, and I'm kindly bombarded by compliments on my story of *almost* being an Olympic athlete. They invite me to talk about it in one of their classes. Sometimes what we think is our own failure is already a great victory to others. A big knot has been untied inside me. I invite Fleur to go shopping with me, but she cannot. She says she would change her son's little friend's birthday party in a heartbeat, but she has already arranged with her husband that she would take the boy. It would be so nice to have a more meaningful life like Fleur's and her family's, but before I allow myself to be crucified for breaking up with Caio again, I remember her ongoing struggles for time and self-care. And then, her advice on long-distance relationships and how she says she envies my life a little. I then listen to what I said to Luke, that no relationship ends because of one person. I mean it, and my guilt is gone. I still want to see Caio happy and free like me, but I can't do that for him. I know that in a few months we'll meet and accept that it was better this way.

*

I allow myself to go to work at eleven in the morning, but at nine Chris calls to apologise and asks me if I can arrive as soon as possible. He saw a small spelling mistake in the presentation and wants me to try to fix it as he can't manage the software;

but also, he decided it would be good for me to come to the pre-presentation meeting to defend the project internally before we go to the clients this afternoon.

My wardrobe has seen an exponential growth in the number of new blouses and work dresses. It has become harder to choose an outfit; it was easier when it was all black, white and grey. I put a couple of options on the bed and video call Bibi to help me choose quicker, but when I see the time, I remember that it is already midnight in her European time zone. Mum is my salvation, and she answers with the same exciting glow in her voice every time I ask for help.

'Wear that silk scarf you got from Denise. The one from the botanical garden in Rio, remember? And mix it with some new clothes, like the orange blazer we bought together, with that brownish blouse that borders on cream.'

I thank her for her bold help without debating, but deep down, the orange might be too exuberant for me. It draws too much attention, but I know that at some point or another I'll have to wear it. I can't throw away the money she spent on it. I lay the outfit on the bed. On one side I have the orange-cream combination, and on the other, I have the black-and-white traditional corporate uniform. I change into the orange and feel that I am not daring enough to wear it, but that I should. I search the internet for other orange jacket image references, and, seeing countless beautiful combinations, I feel more empowered to mix colours. As a safety measure, I put on the black jacket and trousers from the bag.

I arrive at work forty minutes later, aware and conscientious of my radical wardrobe change. Is it too much?

'It's gorgeous! Go get them. Win this project for us! I don't feel like looking for another job.' Tommy laughs as always.

Everyone in the boardroom is in black, and I, despite wanting to be the orange dot, feel like a firework. No one mentions anything, no little jokes, no compliments, and I need to tell myself that no one cares, that I should be confident in what to say, just like Tommy said. We need to win this project.

It will be a few days until we hear if we won the project or not. Chris sits with me to strategise about resources while we wait for a result. We finish our meeting at 5:20 p.m., and he lets me go home. I go back to the nudist yoga place instead.

Romance has nothing to do with cliché imagery; it has everything to do with listening. Caio is not listening. There's a huge bouquet of flowers on the door of my building when I get back. I don't have the energy to call or pretend to say thank you. Why can't he disappear for a while? Leave me alone, give me space? He won't heal if he keeps thinking of me so obsessively. Is he obsessed?

Spending the week without the distraction of Luke and the masked man brought me a great focus for the things I like to do: work, friends and books. I woke up in the middle of the night to talk to my friends from uni in a group call; we had a great time, while practicing my Spanish and my Catalan, which is always fulfilling. I completed my portfolio by adding a summary of the fashion magazine project and watched some series that I haven't had time to see while I've been so distracted about masks, clothes, dresses, men and all the other stuff that has been going on. This week saw me contented, peacefully calm, and I didn't anticipate going to the party tonight until now.

Until thirty minutes before it starts. Sitting on my couch, I ponder. Would I prefer to spend the night refraining from asking Caio to stop with the flowers again or should I go get changed? Why shouldn't I go?

I dress faster than a bullet train, grab a taxi and I'm outside the warehouse just after seven o'clock. The dancing is amazing, the conversations with other people energising. I feel like a desirable woman and with the enviable privilege of saying no to the advances of the other guests. The only one I feel tempted to say yes to is a mysteriously seductive woman, dressed in a red dress with a corset layered with black lace, making her torso seem small compared to the bulging floor-length skirt. She wears a golden mask that shines just like her confidence and a smile that showcases the liveliness inside of her. Her eyes are aligned with her intentions; there's no oblique, subliminal motives. It flows, it's real, it's here, it's an invitation rather than an ultimatum. It is disheartening that we don't experience such a sense in our daily lives. It's sad to know that one can spend an entire week without looking their family, colleagues or friends *in* the eyes. Worse perhaps is knowing that most people don't see you without the expectations they have over you. Some strands of lush, tight white curls fall down to her collarbones from the top of her head, creating seductive shadows on her neck. Her fishnet gloves, usually associated with prostitutes and considered vulgar, are the opposite of what she is. I don't reciprocate her desire beyond our seductive games as we play amongst all the other guests. It's time to go home, not because of the masked man, fear, stigma or prejudice, but because I don't want to give more. Because tonight, this is enough for me. I am satisfied with my night; it was so me.

I wake up writing in my notebook: who do I betray the most when I repress so much of what I want, just to satisfy someone else? Saying no to others is sometimes saying yes to myself, despite not knowing what I missed out on last night by saying no to her. I am happy. Even more so when I see that the flowers Caio sent me last night, which I carefully placed at one of my neighbour's doors, have been taken. I created some magic from an otherwise annoying instance.

*

There's an extra reason besides this month's birthdays for today's celebration at work: we won the competition. We won! Two—maybe three—years of design for the office. It's massive—as they say. Chris gives credit to the whole team for making the presentation a success. Being recognised by him in front of the entire office is as uplifting as winning the project; it is a Band-Aid—not a solution—for any low self-esteem or self-doubt. Luke unfortunately isn't here to receive the accolades, but it seems that someone has recorded a video and will send it to him. I text: *We won, and he thanked you in front of everyone! Well done!* I only notice the exclamation marks once the message is gone. I don't mind. Today I don't mind; it awkwardly feels okay, light, the exclamation mark makes perfect sense. Our director jokes that if we want to win projects, we just need Fleur to get pregnant, because everything she touches when she's pregnant turns to gold. They won a big award during each of her pregnancies. I didn't know that. Tommy also gets his fifteen seconds of fame, and in this spirit of celebration—my birthday and the project—I am taken by Bec, Tommy, Martha, Michael and Fleur to a restaurant-nightclub for a proper dinner party.

Fleur, who stupendously manages to stay up until 7:00 p.m., receives a message from her husband saying their two-year-old son fell off his bunk. He called the ambulance, but she doesn't need to go home; everything seems fine, and he will keep her posted. She ignores his advice and rushes home in a taxi, but not before ordering dessert to go and promising me that my present will arrive tomorrow at lunchtime; I'll need to be at home because she's going there to deliver it in person. I try once again to reassure her that I don't need a gift, but she insists.

'Someone warmed the chair for me!' Luke—who else—appears as Fleur gets up to leave. The timing so perfect that it sounds as if it were scripted.

She gives two kisses on his cheek, saying excitedly that she is glad he could come. She winks at me from behind him. Only I see that. Fleur, the dreamer matchmaker.

'How was your week?' Bec asks.

'It sucked . . . ,' he says loudly with good humour, and everyone laughs. 'I missed working late.' This second part was directed at me; his eyes found and stuck on mine until the end of the sentence; his voice is lower, and he is closer to me. While they exchange greetings, I get up to say goodbye and apologise to Fleur for making her miss her son's fall because of me, even though I'm glad nothing more serious happened.

'Come on, woman! There will be many more falls to come. At least hubby called the ambulance,' she comforts my guilt and leaves graciously, hiding her worries for her son in her high energy.

Incidentally or intentionally, Luke hugs me as soon as I finish saying goodbye to Fleur. He wishes me happy birthday, borderline whispering in my ear. My body gives me no signs of unusual excitement. The hug is familiar, not a stranger's hug, which makes sense given that we have been quite close in the last little while. He hands me a present, a box sized something between A4 and A3 and thick enough not to be a book. It is also very light. Is it common here for people to give gifts to someone you barely know? I thank him.

'Open it!' shouts Tommy.

'No, let her guess!' says Michael.

'Let her imagine . . . ,' says Martha.

Bec doesn't say anything. I secretly hope it's a mask and I can move on with my life without this romantic puzzle.

'Take your time,' Luke says in the same tone as the other one.

Be a mask. Please be a mask. I open it carefully, as I need to control my reaction. What will I do if it is? Kiss him? Shout in relief? Pretend I don't understand so I can keep the masked man as he is? Would I be able to pretend? What do I want?

There are two martini glasses, a cocktail shaker and a packet of coffee beans.

'For you to baptise your coffee.'

I can make good use of the glasses. But the coffee . . . I wonder if he has ever noticed I don't drink coffee. Maybe he assumes I do from that *one* day that we went to get it for everyone. I never have a coffee cup in the office—or anywhere.

'Thank you. That's a beautiful present, and thanks for thinking of me, you didn't have to.' This is true.

'I wanted to, my partner in winning a competition! You deserve it. We deserve it! Let's put them to use; come with me.'

As we walk to the bar, I wonder why he gave me martini glasses? I only drink mocktails in those glasses with the masked man; Luke has only ever seen me drinking caipirinhas in much less sophisticated glasses.

'I know you don't drink coffee,' he stops and tells me, looking at me, 'but I am hopeful that one day, you will come to the dark, caffeinated side of life . . .' There's his charming, endearing smile. In this undefinable light, they look even more alike.

How bad would it be if I kissed him now?

'Thank you, that's very thoughtful of you,' I say in his ears to avoid shouting due to the loud music. An excuse, of course. I want to breathe his perfume. He answers too quickly for me to recognise it.

'You're welcome; you deserve it.'

We are disappointed at not being able to have coffee martinis with my glasses. Something to do with liability for a broken glass or something. It certainly is a country of many rules, and perhaps that is why everything works well compared to where I've lived before.

The night goes on, and I am once again surprised at how much fun we can have by talking and doing silly things; although we don't have masks to take away our inhibitions, we have alcohol. Not quite the same thing, but they can have similar effects.

I smell pot. I didn't think it was legal here. It is unlikely that it is. It's so faint, so far away, yet it is enough to trigger cracks in the concrete wall of my invisible pain. I look up as the tears start to force their way through, just waiting for a blink to finally make them overflow. Here in front of everyone. I look back and away, as if movie is playing in front of me. But it's not a movie, it happened. Far away. A long time ago. I hear offers, laughing, random words: silly, not here, not mine, let's go, somewhere else, no photos please, nothing will happen, share, just one. Just one. Just once. Once is all that it takes sometimes. It all depends on a mixture of safety and luck. Luck. He didn't have luck. We didn't have luck. I was unlucky. How do we know how we will react when we are numbed to the reality of safety? How can we control what will happen when luck is all we have? Shit. Why did Kadu have to die? Get out of my head! I shout silently.

'Are you okay?' Luke asks, placing his hand on my shoulder; he must have realised what a mess I am.

'Yeah. Just . . . memories.'

'Sometimes they're ghosts,' he says. I agree, and he continues, 'Do you want to talk? Was the present what caused your paralysis?

'Oh, it wasn't the present at all! Why would that be a problem?'

'I don't know. You don't drink much, so maybe—'

'No! There's no alcohol problem in my memories. No, you can chill. No bad memories with coffee either.' I'm back to the present, my mouth not as dry, my eyes not teary.

'Good! Now that this is cleared up,' he says awkwardly, 'can I get you a . . .'

'Passionfruit mocktail.' I give him an intentional hint that I am Eva. To the outsider, I am calm and decisive, but internally, my blood has left my hands and feet and is now concentrated around my vital organs: my lungs, my heart, and my torso. 'What do your parents do?' I ask as we wait for the drinks.

'They are artists. My mother paints, and my father is a sculptor.' I watch him as he talks about them and shares some fond memories of childhood. I notice every gesture that could bring me closer to discovering if they are the same person. After careful consideration I have no proof that he is the masked man. Or that he thinks I'm Eva. My blood spreads more evenly again, and I find a serene place where I can appreciate him as Luke without agonising over the overlapping glances and comparisons. The only way to truly know would be to take our masks off in front of each other, and then love each other in the same way as before. Would we be able to do so without masks on? Would we be able to fearlessly surrender to one another, to give and receive if we knew who we are?

'Your life sounds fascinating but not very easy,' I say.

'That's life—lots of ups and downs, but we were happy. I think we were happy. And your parents, what do they do?'

'Engineering and neuroscience.'

'No wonder you're so sharp, then.'

'Sharp?'

'It's not every day that intelligent women like you are found.'

'What does that mean, that women are dumb?'

'No! Not at all! It's so hard to know what to say these days . . . It's suffocating sometimes.'

'We are all in the same boat to some degree, but I'll give you the chance to explain yourself and make amends . . .'

'Okay, I'll try. Most women and men I know are very shallow. Unfortunately, my sample size, and I know you know what sample size means . . .'

'What student has never studied probability?' I prove, jokingly, that I know what sample size means. He smiles charmingly, impressed perhaps.

'My sample size has more superficial women than men.'

By the looks in his eyes and how he rushes to explain himself again, I must have made an astonished face after this statement

'Really!' he continues. 'Blame it on society or the little bubble I live in, but you're different. You're more . . . you. We can have conversations that are not so dramatic, not so polarised. You're not afraid of unresolved conversations . . .'

'Well, thank you, I think. But I can say it's the same about men.'

'Some men don't talk; most do though.'

'Not to women,' I say, and he rolls his head back. We both agree this is a forever discussion. 'You know what? It's architecture, you know how we are . . . superior to others,' I joke, making fun of a collective feeling that surrounds our tiny community.

We return to the table with the other guests, who now want to dance and embarrass me by singing happy birthday. It's not hard to keep Luke away from me because Bec does me the favour of getting in his space. I hold on to Tommy's side to ward off the worms that try to get close to me. These evenings really irritate me; no one seems to want to have fun but rather to count the perks that satisfy their primal instincts and validate them as beings worthy of love. Or pride. Adventures to tell their small tribe and create a legend for themselves. Most of these creatures are leeches in human form, parasitic worms in search of fresh blood to fill them up with numbers and the souls of the other without giving anything in return. Or worse, they believe they are gifting them the honour of their choice, but little do the victims know: it's not about them. It's the man's ego only. Solely. It's very hard to find the event amongst the sample size of these environments. For me, dinner, laughter and these minutes at the bar with Luke have been enough to bring me excitement and peace at the same time. I like the idea he is someone else, that he is Luke and only Luke. There's something between us: identification, admiration, trust—gained by the exchange of confidences—and attraction, all necessary ingredients of passion and, who knows, love. Maybe. He knows and I know. We are both cautious for reasons for reasons we haven't confide to each other yet. We both avoid this knowledge. Sort of. We camouflage our inner restlessness in the darkness of the dance floor, where we can hide our frequent exchanges from others and arrive in a place of our own. He looks, he smiles, he moves, and for all the times I notice him noticing me, I respond in kind as a form of recognition for his attention.

'Tainá.' Bec's abrupt drunk appearance right in front of me breaks our magic moment.

The bridge Luke and I were building collapses; our gestures disintegrate; they dissolve into the dynamics of the surroundings as our shyness, fears and circumstances decide they are not resolved yet to make a move forward.

'Leave Luke to me. You can have *any* man you want; I've been crazy about this man for years!' she continues, leaning over me.

'But he was married. How could you want to be with someone . . .'

'I know, I know! That's why I've never done anything, but now it's my turn. Go with Tommy somewhere else, please!' she begs, exposing her weaknesses, humiliating what little self-love she has left inside her.

I obey. I have no reason to feed her agony when I know the pain of their mismatch will hurt enough. I don't need to put myself in her cursed prayers as if I am the impediment to her loving happiness.

'Good luck, Bec. Enjoy.' I smile, look at him and mouth, *Goodbye, see you on Monday.*

Tommy takes me to the door; we say good night with a friendly hug.

It is still early, and I am going home by train. I call Bibi on the way to reduce the fear of walking alone at night and to keep away those who might inhibit themselves from mugging or harassing a woman on the phone. She tells me about her adventures, her love affairs, her failed recipes, some financiers who want to see her in more revealing clothes, fans who love how she discusses politics and serious issues over food. When I get to the door of my building, I see a box addressed to me. It is from Caio. At least it's not flowers. I know I should find it beautiful. Who wouldn't like to receive a present every day? I wouldn't. Not from him, not now at the stage that we are. He could have given me this attention months ago. I notified him I wouldn't reply to him, and I won't, so he must stop. Can't he leave me alone? How much more can I do? Respecting me is proof of someone's love, and repeatedly doing what I asked him *not to do* is not a sign of respect. Around half past ten, after I finish watching a new episode of *Friends*, I check my phone, and there it is—in the middle of other messages from Mum, about general issues and the futilities of life, and from my uni friends. Caio is asking if I like the present. I don't open his message; I can only see the first few words, but it's a complete question. *Did you like the present?* I don't read it in full. I leave it there. I need to cut off communication, or else I'll keep feeding his behaviour. Maybe he will finally get the message from my silence and leave me alone. Why do we need to end in resentment?

Time evolves a passion to love, and, as the clock ticks forward, the beauty of love turns into true friendship. I no longer believe this. It would be simple if the problems of the immaterial could be understood in such linear and generalised terms. Love can become a habit, an addiction, and like all addictions, it eventually makes the addictive destroy the addicted. Unless the addicted destroys the addictive first: eliminate the temptation, instead of controlling their own urges.

True love is what sets you free. That person who is happy for your happiness, and vice versa. True love is reciprocated, even if shown in different forms. Distance has proven that Caio is not ready to be happy for me. He was always good at helping when there was a problem, comforting my sorrows and providing the support I needed, but what about my successes? Would he have enough courage and love to be happy with my achievements? Dealing with life's shortcomings and filling them with adventures is easy; it binds us even more to the people we share with. What happens when we no longer need relief from my distress? What happens I am free from his support? Can we walk side by side?

I go to sleep with many unanswered questions, irritated by the little green ball on my phone: the message I leave unread. I want to read it, but I don't want him to know I read it.

The next morning, I stay away from the phone, busy with my body and my mind. I cycle to Balmoral, I run up the hills, then walk down the hills a few laps. I rest on the sand, letting the sun dry my sweat and the cold water cool my feet. Looking at the entrance of the bay on the horizon, I feel as if I were home. How I long to be transported there now. Transported with a click. I replace North Head with Santa Cruz Fortress and South Head with the Sugar Loaf. The ferries change colour and I see an oil platform. The boats become fishing boats. I close my eyes and replace the smell of the sea from here with the smell of the one there, the place where I grew up. I look at my bike; it's still here, no one stole it. A different place, where some things are better, others, much worse. A flash of birthday cakes and parties quickly flies by in nonchronological order.

When I get home it's almost 1:00 p.m., and my phone has a few new messages. Most of them are birthday ones. It's comforting to know people still remember it despite the lack of a social media reminder. I call Mum, but it's too late in Brazil; she answers in a sleepy voice, and despite her efforts to chat, I insist she go back to bed. We will chat tomorrow, her time. I reply to the other messages, except the one from Caio; instead of a little green ball with the number 1, there are three messages. He must be wishing me a happy birthday; I give in to my curiosity and open them. I was right: *I know I shouldn't send you anything, I'm sorry.* It's the first time he's ever apologised using words. *I wish I could spend the day with you today. I hope you have a happy day, happy birthday. From your Caio, forever.* I don't know what to think, but I open the box he sent last night; it is a present after all. There are no flowers, just a hand cream, a body moisturiser, an essential oil and two kinds of chocolate. One of them is a biscuit with a layer of chocolate on top saying, *Happy Birthday. I love you.* The other is a small package with chocolate-covered almonds. It's been many years since I broke up with anyone, but I don't remember it ever being so difficult. I reply with a simple and polite message. *Thank you. It's a different birthday, but thanks for remembering and for the present. I'm happy.* He sends another one straight away: *What are your plans?* I answer out of respect for his care: *I'm laying low. We celebrated yesterday already.* That's it. Last message. No more. I have to move on to my new reality, what I want for my future, and I let go of this past. I wish I had received a message from Luke, but nothing. Had I made up what we talked about last night and the time we've spent together in the last month? Maybe he and Bec are together today? Well, it doesn't matter.

Fleur's message apologises, saying her house is upside down and that she will arrive at half past two at the latest. *No problem. I'm home,* I reply and go get myself out of these exercise-sweaty clothes: shower, eat and read.

I delight myself with my own birthday present: a toy made exclusively for me to experience pleasure without pain when my real man is away, unreachable. Close to the window, on my couch, covered only by my robe, I imagine he is here again; the wind coming through the window via the trees is fresh, cool, as it should be in August. The contrast is reinvigorating; I know there are windows that neighbours can see me through, but it doesn't bother me.

Fleur arrives just after 2:30 p.m. while my glow still shines. Her family quickly makes my apartment feel like a shoe box. There's so much life, we can't move around. I let them go everywhere. They apologise consistently, and I stop them. I love having them here. I entertain the children with the biscuit Caio sent me. I cut it into smaller pieces so that no one can read the message on it. I make some hot chocolate for the kids, tea for the adults, and I share the packet of almonds. While her husband watches them with the chocolates and choking hazards, she takes me into my bedroom to give me my present, locking the door behind her.

'Go on, try it on,' she says, gifting me with a white box.

I shake my head in appreciation and embarrassment; she doesn't need to give me a present, and I know it will be one expensive one.

It is an off-white spring-summer party dress that looks like it came off a runway. I put it on carefully, as it is very delicate. The shoulders and top of the back are covered by pure white feathers that fall down the arms. The semitransparent pleated organza that covers the breasts, leaving the chest exposed in a deep V, goes down to the floor, tightened by a band around my waistline; the skirt part is lighter, more transparent and very flowy with openings, cuts that let the leg come through as I walk. There's some light-beige underwear in a soft, unrecognisable fabric—maybe cotton with some elastic—that fits like beach volleyball shorts at the bottom and goes high enough to cover up my belly button. Audacious, seductive, revealing and beautiful.

'Wow, this is so generous! So stunning! Fleur, you didn't have to!'

'It's nothing! One day you will find a place and someone to wear it with. I have no doubt about it!'

I know where and when I will wear it already. The kids start knocking on the door, calling for her, a million *Mummys* per second.

'Just a minute!' she says to them. 'Now, go change back. I need to make these kids go for a run outside, and I'm sure you have more interesting things to do on your birthday then spend the afternoon with us.'

'I don't. I love having you all over.'

I put the dress on the bed and leave the room with her, but before letting them go, I thank her with a foot massage on the couch, as I read that every pregnant woman in her third trimester is in desperate need of one. She refuses at first, embarrassed perhaps, but it doesn't take long for her to give in. I use the cream Caio gave me, the kids go crazy on my pens and pencils, she sends Will downstairs for a little alone time around the block and we spend a pleasant hour or so together. I give the remaining portion of Caio's present to her, which she happily accepts after I tell her where it came from.

14

We meet in front of the fountain at the end of Macquarie Street. The taxi drops me off exactly where I need to be. He's already waiting, and, despite being allowed to use our phones tonight, he doesn't kill time looking at it. I check the time on mine; I'm five minutes early. I ask the taxi driver to wait as I see two children getting close to him, wanting to see his mask. He bends down, they touch it and he does a simple magic trick. As I watch him, his calmness, his charming nature, and the transcendence I feel seem to be more than reason can explain: an ache of emptiness, because it is useless to try to deny that I am in love with this man, and yet I have no idea who he is. I look at myself using the camera on my phone.

My right side has a large butterfly wing sculpted in golden coated wire and mesh going from just under my jaw line up past the top of my head by about ten centimetres. The body of the insect is on my nose, with its antennae a central detail in front of my forehead. Under it, a hard blue base covers my nose up to my hairline and from ear to ear. The sculpture fades to pointy, smaller butterflies, twigs, and dots balanced asymmetrically. I look like lapis lazuli in a forest.

I take a deep breath, pay the driver, and walk towards my masked man smiling, ignoring the broken hopes for a maskless future. He realises that I have seen him and says something to the children, and they disperse onto the large esplanade around the opera house.

'I had a slight suspicion that you were a magician. A wizard with a few tricks up your sleeve . . .'

He also looks like one. Despite my lack of education in men's clothing, he is well dressed as always. He is composed, carefully colour and pattern coordinated, his clothes ironed with crisp edges and a lot of layers. I wonder what we can do with his tie. His mask unfolds rays of sun to the right—sunrise—and a waxing crescent moon fused to the mask covers his face from the lip up in a gradient, from gold to warm grey.

He greets me serenely in silence, with an affectionate smile as he raises his moon arm for me to hook mine in. We walk side by side. Like a couple.

The night is beautiful and cold. The crispiness of the air cut my skin, particularly from my knees down, as they are exposed through the curtains of my dress with every step I take. If it wasn't for my long gloves and my thick scarf, I would feel inappropriately dressed for the weather. Our feet are coincidentally—or magically—synchronised. Our new masks expose our faces more than the others, the fruit of our mutual desire to slowly peel off this mystery—us—or not. Maybe we're wearing smaller masks because we are going to eat.

'How was the trip?' I ask.

'Lucrative and boring, like most business trips.'

'Lucrative is good, no?'

'Yeah, but nothing we didn't already expect. How was the party this week?'

'It was great. I didn't plan to go; it was a last-minute decision . . .' Why did I say that? He doesn't need to know this.

He remains silent for a few more steps and then stops and turns to me, still connected by our arms.

'Did you not plan to go because I wasn't going?'

'The truth?'

'Yes, always.'

'I've had some problems I had to resolve for a while now, and it was draining me. Does that worry you?'

'I don't know. I . . . I don't want to mislead you . . . ,' he says.

He knows my feelings for him, and I know his for me, otherwise we wouldn't be here.

'Neither do I . . . Don't worry, I went anyway. I had a great night. I met people I probably won't recognise again.'

He stares, mute. What is he thinking?

'How does that saying go again?' I continue, 'Some people come into your life for a reason, some for a season and some for a lifetime. I don't think we will be able to spend our lives wearing masks . . .'

'So, we better enjoy the season. Is that what you are saying?'

'For now, yes, unless . . .'

'For now, a season.'

Not surprisingly, it hurts to know that is how he thinks; maybe I said the wrong thing. What a stupid saying to say.

'I was once told about the moon, how happy it is to orbit earth . . .' I try to fix my mistake, referencing something he said when we first met.

He smiles, and his eyes sparkle. We are back. I take him to see the most fascinating thing about the opera house: how they built it. The small bronze sculpture outside, in front of the main entry on top of the stairs, shows how they sectioned a sphere to be able to build its concrete sails in a modular, factory-friendly manner. Technology was invented just for this purpose, evolved by the poetic architect's mind. Emotional and rational, together: human perfection. He has been here countless times before and never noticed the statue, much less wondered how they built it.

'Can I see your photography skills in practice?'

'I only have my old phone.' I know it will look like rubbish.

'Challenge accepted.'

I fiddle with the settings, not letting him see the screen. I put my bag on the ground to support it. The bridge is in the background, the big sail with people arriving at the dinner party walking in the foreground. Thirty seconds later, the photo is finished. Everything that was still is in focus; everything else is blurred.

'Here, proof that time never stops for those who live.' I turn around, bumping into him standing, moving down to meet my lips.

'You are fascinating.' The gentle breeze of his whisper on my lips makes my mouth open to meet his. Our kiss is cushioned, smooth, wet, delightfully safe and reciprocal. 'You almost had me convinced. A good photographer does it like this . . .' He takes the phone from my hand and takes a selfie of us. 'Now, that's photography!' He hands over the phone to me, grabs his own from the internal pocket of his jacket and takes another one.

'That's against all the rules!' I slap him lightly on the arm, jokingly.

'What rules? There are no rules here. Keep it for when memory fails.'

We enter the hall; he asks me to wait just behind him as he hands over his invitation to the receptionist. She checks his name against a list. His real name is there, right on that list. Do I want to know? What is that about *there are no rules here*?

As it turns out, we are at a fundraiser for children with cancer. In fact, it is a cocktail party where waiters wearing small masks around their eyes pass between the guests offering drinks, canapés and other more elaborate foods that are not so easy to eat standing up. We are by far the most elaborately dressed couple here. Most of the other guests can easily be recognised. So much so that everyone greets everyone with great enthusiasm. As we are offered a tray of drinks, he freezes.

'I don't know what to get you when we are allowed to drink alcohol.'

'Champagne before a music performance is always a good choice, madam,' the waiter suggests.

'Champagne it is,' I agree, and my man reaches for it, grabbing one of the same for himself.

This is all a preamble to the symphony orchestra's performance.

'Do you recognise anyone?'

'Yes, some people. Not everyone here seems to be from work. That woman over there is one of our accountants, single, no kids; all she talks about is men and how she has no more patience for them, but she always gets a new one. That guy over there is one of the richest guys I know; he's only thirty-four years old. He cheats on his wife with the new intern, which is that woman in the red dress on the other side. If you watch all three of them, you'll see a soap opera. The whole office knows; no one knows if the wife knows.'

'I will keep an eye on her and will let you know what I think. Do you think anyone recognises you?'

'No, or they would have come over to me by now.'

One woman and two men approach us to compliment our outfits and make small talk. My masked man introduces himself as James; I introduce myself as Eva. I sense an unease coming from him. Could it be that this is his real name, and he knows my name is invented? Does he feel unsettled about me knowing more about him? I don't know if he is in fact James.

'How long have you been together?' asks the woman.

He turns to me, with that charming smile of his, with that look that is just mine, just for me, that wants me to reply, that look that freezes time for us. The woman is waiting for an answer.

'A thousand years,' he says, still reading the core of my soul. He knows I feel the same way.

He excuses us from this trio and walks me to the pianist, whispering something in his ear.

'Come, let's show them real magic.'

We manage to connect in the space that is ours alone, where I can ignore the world around us and feel welcomed and energised once again. I want to confirm his name, but I decide not to destroy the moment with questions.

'I . . .' He leans against my ear but stops as soon as he starts talking.

'Yes . . . James?' I reply, smiling.

'You're very quiet today . . .'

'This is your world; I don't want to ruin it.'

'That possibility doesn't exist . . . I like you here. Some worlds should be mixed.'

'I like being here . . . too.'

The applause starts as soon as the song ends. He invites everyone over, but people keep talking, telling stories, truths and lies about themselves.

'They . . . can't be real even in masks,' I say.

'They don't know anything.'

We go to find our chairs for the concert.

His hand remains on top of mine throughout the concert, something couples do. As we leave, uplifted by so many notes and changes today, we walk aimlessly along the Circular Quay waterfront.

'Thank you for inviting me tonight; it was different.'

'Absolutely. Thanks for coming.'

'May I call you James?'

'I guess so, no?' He makes fun of my accent, but not in a bad way.

'I'm going to treat it as a fake name. I think it suits you, and since I've never given you a name, let's use James. If you want.'

'James is fine. I like James.'

'Why did you want to bring me here?'

He hesitates; his answer comes after a long silence: 'I don't know. I guess I didn't want to go two weeks without seeing you.'

I'm not quite sure why, but I waver between feeling offended and flattered. Tonight was only a coincidental substitute for the party; it is not a move forward to us. But why do I care? Why does it bother me? I don't particularly want to take our masks off.

'Do you have a child, children?' I ask.

A big breath, his head tilts down toward the floor, his hands in his pockets. He is shrinking.

'Not alive.'

'Oh my God, I'm so sorry! I didn't mean to . . .' I notice my eyes filling up with tears.

'Don't apologise. How would you know?' As always, James is polite.

'I'm here if you want to talk . . . or cry.' I offer an ear and my hand, but he stays as he is for a good while, moving forward step after step. I simply follow by his side, in the wake of his silent pain, feeling the ghostly night air I've just conjured up.

'Gabriel,' he eventually breaks from his grief, using the name of his angel. 'His mother said only an angel could have come as fast as he did. He came and realised he was in the wrong place, that he could do more for us from afar, in the realm of the sixth sense. The doctors said he'd live for just a few hours after birth; he defied them and lived two days.'

'The worst days of your life, I imagine.'

'No, the best, because every hour we felt hopeful that the doctors were wrong. Forty-eight hours and thirty-two minutes were enough for him, and defined the rest of our lives . . .'

'And the mother?'

'After a while, we separated. Staying together was too painful for both of us. She still had to recover from giving birth—from giving birth to a baby we knew might not even be born alive. It wasn't easy. I have enormous respect for her, but we couldn't stay together . . . I think I've already said that. We tried again, but it was agonising for her.'

'I don't know what to say. For Gabriel and for both of you. A separation because of a lack of love is easy, but when it's due to grief, it's almost impossible to overcome. It's like mourning someone who still exists.'

'You're right, thank you.' He reaches under his mask, clearing a tear. 'What about you? Kids?'

'No, I couldn't . . .' I pause, scared of what I was going to say.

'Why couldn't you?' he asks me, perhaps expecting some bizarre medical condition or my life story.

'I can't lose anyone else.' The words catch in my throat, opening the valves of my tears, but I quickly look up.

'Anyone else? I have an ear and a shoulder . . . ,' he offers, returning my gesture from earlier.

'My parents know what you've been through. I think. I can imagine. They lost my brother when he was sixteen. A completely preventable accident. And my grandmother died of grief for him; she never admitted it so as not to make me upset and worried, but it's very clear to me now how the sadness invaded her, and she couldn't live anymore.'

He hugs me tightly.

'What they and you have been through is a wound that can't be healed. Send my condolences to your parents.'

'My father can hear you.' I undo our hug to answer. 'He's been gone for almost a year, in an accident with my old sailboat, but I'll pass the message on to my mother.' My voice trembles; it's impossible to control.

Hard and fast, his hug nests me into his shoulders, deforming the sculpture of my mask; his arm moves, then it circles my waist again; I see his mask in his hand. I close my eyes, nervous that he will take mine off.

'Before I open my eyes, why did you do that?'

'I wanted to say that I no longer have any secrets with you. You know me better than any of those people we just saw. You don't have to look at me. With or without a mask, you know me better than anyone.'

I can't process such a compliment, such trust.

'I don't know if I . . .'

'You don't need to. What else would I know about you if I knew your name or your face?'

'Nothing important. I don't even have a social media account. You couldn't even stalk me.'

James laughs, puts the mask back on.

'That is a pity. I want to see the beautiful and useful buildings you will design one day.'

'You didn't fall for the photographer talk, then?' I release myself from his shoulders.

'I believe you take pictures very well, but no, I don't think that's what occupies your forty or so hours a week.'

'Apparently I can't hide what I do.'

'One never hides what makes one . . . vibrate. Passion is *unhideable*.' We laugh by his invention of a new word.

'You're not a computer guy.'

'Yes, I am! My parents lived in the theatre, and I lived with them. But there was always something missing at home; even when the piano broke, we couldn't fix it. I had patched uniforms, given to me by the neighbour; we shared the biscuit packet, the bath, light, food—everything was rationed. There was no lack of books or schooling. Education was the most important thing, apart from jokes. My father is a great joker.'

'You're not very creative, then,' I say sarcastically.

'I really am not creative. I can sing, dance, draw, but without an inspiring muse, nothing comes out.'

'I fear the muse is me.'

'Of course it is. Who else?' He laughs, I laugh, and we walk together with his arm around my waist. He gives me a kiss on the top of my head, where my mask ends. We arrive at the taxi line.

'What now? Where are you going?' I ask.

'It depends. We can say goodnight, and I'll say I'll meet you on Tuesday, in case you forgot to get the date today. Or I can ask for your number, but I get the impression it's not time for that yet.'

I agree with a nod to the phone number: 'We're a bit emotional to make a big decision like that . . . It's better to wait.'

'The third option is to go for dinner. You must be hungry.'

'Is there a restaurant open now? It's past ten.'

'I know one that stays open twenty-four hours.' He opens the taxi door, and I get in without hesitation. Five minutes later, we arrive at the place.

'We could have walked.'

On the twenty-third floor, the room has a magical view. The whole city shines down there, like a living model, and in the distance, looking east, I see the darkness showing the entrance to the bay and the horizon in the background. The beauty of the city lights, the cars, buses, the train passing over the Harbour Bridge. There are millions of people living their lives every day, and me here, living this tale, this film. My lover's embrace from behind is soothing and seductive at the same time. It would be nice if we were without masks, not so I could know who he is, but to feel his full face.

'They're little fireflies, don't you think?'

'Yes. In a concrete forest,' I reply. A knock on the door interrupts our conversation; it's our dinner. 'I figured that was the twenty-four-hour restaurant.'

The mask bothers me; it's not comfortable. He places the trolley with the food on the small round table and serves it like a waiter: 'You got the best view in the restaurant.'

'Thank you. It's a lovely dinner. I love pizza, dips and cheese and sweets.'

'My pleasure.' He sits in front of me, placing the fabric napkin on his lap. 'Tell me what kind of genes it takes to get this combination of olive-reddish skin with blue eyes?'

'You managed to discover my profession but not my accent?'

‘I’m not sure I know enough of the world to pick up that many accents. I’m not a linguist.’

Fun drowns out the emotional moments we had earlier. My mask bothers me so much that I ask if he has the oversize sleeping masks he had the other night. He does, and I suggest a culinary guessing game. He cuts a small piece of something on the table and puts it in my mouth. I’m terrible at it. I’d rather play something else.

Soon enough, the dessert sweetens my chin as it drips down the spoon amidst my laughter; his tongue finds it and cleans it with enough pressure to make me contort in the armchair. I hear ice clinking, and as I make a move to get up, his arm stops me, holding me fast to the chair. A chill under the bottom part of my dress surprises me. As he kisses the skin where the V-neck is, he unties the band around my waist and hides his head where the ice is melting. Warm. Cold. Frozen. Hot. Liquid. Solid. Shapes. Rough. Soft. He undresses between movements; his mask is off. I reach for his shirt; it’s not there anymore. He doesn’t let me touch him; my wrists are bound. His tie?

‘What is our word?’ I feel his belt open. The buckle touches the back of my head as he leans in to whisper in my ear.

‘Coffee.’

‘I won’t stop until you say it.’

I agree, nodding.

A sharper texture—the belt?—secures one of my legs to a leg of the armchair. What feels like a sheet tightens my other leg to the other leg of the armchair, leaving my legs slightly open and immobile. My hands are stuck together. I am very, very limited in my movements. He moves away in silence. Where is he? What will he do next? I sense the lights being dimmed. I have the urge to remove the mask since my hands can reach it. He holds my wrists, stopping me; he was just there. I don't hear the curtain closing; we can be seen by whoever is exercising their voyeurism from another apartment building. He kisses the corner of my lips; he lets me kiss him back slightly but stops. I put my arms around his neck, guiding him to where I want him to go on me. I feel my breathing change, and there, unable to move, I give myself up completely. I have nowhere else to go, and our passion needs to be satiated. I taste different and exorbitant sensations in me. Every inch of me, a physical, tactile experience. Fear and surrender at once. It's easy to give my body away when he gives back so much pleasure. He slowly loosens the knots, caressing each one as it is undone. He carries me in his arms, my legs around his waist; he leans me against a cold surface; it's the window. The fear from falling makes me disentangle myself and lower to my knees on the floor. Facing the window, he lets himself be carried along in my rhythm, which will be the last taste of the night. I enjoy his grunts, his muscles contracting, but he surprises me with a question: 'Do you want to continue?' He kneels in front of me, kisses me tenderly and passionately and takes me to bed in a tight hug. We knead each other in the sheets, in the clouds. He tells me I can take my mask off as he has put his own. I take the offer and go have a shower. I feel full. Alive. He is sleeping when I come back. Who are you, James?

In bed, I lose sleep, wondering if I missed the opportunity to know who he is. Should I have looked when he didn't have his mask on? Would lust have swept through me so intensely had I known who was next to me? How much do we need to see in order to recognise? The old man at the mask shop knows me. Every time I buy a new one, he knows exactly who I am, what I have bought, and, by my choices, he guesses life has been good for me since we first met. I know James enough to miss him instead of resenting him for not responding to my text. Observing him, the man who changes physiognomy every week, just like me, sleeping under the dimmed light, I let out a thread of sound: *I love you, I love us.* For how long can secrecy hold its aphrodisiac powers? He has no reason to tell me the truth about anything, but how well can we lie or pretend to be who we are not? James. Your name is James. What we have is too special to spoil with the details, the compromises, the inconveniences of life. We are too unique to mess up with the judgement, the prejudices, the poison of expectations and, dare I say it, the predictability of monogamy. James. It's nice to say your name. Why do you trust me? I could take your mask off while you sleep, but you know I won't. I could check your wallet for your driver's licence, but you know I won't. You know me, or what matters of me. You have a wounded heart just like mine. I could wake you up, and we could decide to see each other's faces, but nothing good comes out of mixing a life decision with the emotions of helplessness and loss. I know that I'd rather be your outlet of pleasure, the inspirational muse than the warehouse for your open wounds. Patience is a virtue. Tomorrow, curiosity will have passed. As for love, we will have to love each other when we are together and live knowing that jealousy is nothing more than mere vanity. I interlock myself between his neck, chest and arms, my legs over his. I breathe out contentment, being in the place where I belong

I wake up with my eyes closed, feeling the silk of the mask wrapping my face from the hairline to the upper part of my jaw, feeling the heat of the sun on my feet, expecting to be alone and accompanied by his beautiful illustration and honoured by his written words. Groping the other pillow and listening to the silence coming from the bathroom, I confirm I'm alone and free to show my face. I look around, and I can't find his drawing. Has he forgotten? My phone reminds me that it's Sunday, and I feel a slight disappointment that he didn't stay. He could have let me see him drawing. Could it be that all romance is like that? It lasts a short time, and as the routine starts to stick, the noble and transcendent little rituals fall into disuse? Caio persevered with his rituals, as cliché as they may have been, but they were consistently there over time. Could that be why I stayed with him all this time?

Wrapped in the soft sheet, standing by the window, I can see my flat in Kirribilli—small in the distance. I look around the city, examining the bay the same way the angels look at people from up high. It's a wonderful place. What a beautiful city, so feminine, so gentle in many ways. I imagine the lives under the water that no one can see but that we know are there. I'm twenty-eight years old. Life is good to me. I settle down in the armchair where I was seized by sensations last night and delight—even without a drawing or a poem—in remembering the path we walked from the moment I got out of the taxi at the opera house. We got so much closer. I have nothing to do today; I don't even know how long I have been sitting here contemplating life. After a few minutes, I am surprised by a knock on the door. 'Room service,' they say. I put on my dressing gown, open the door and see a breakfast trolley lushly presented with a variety of finely cut fruit, French bread, butter, spreads and cheese. A martini glass with a small tag saying it's passion fruit juice. In the corner, there is an envelope: *I didn't forget, I went looking for paper. See you soon.* He didn't forget; the magic has not ended. I take the trolley in, and after a couple of satisfied sips on my juice, I open the envelope. The woman in the drawing looks to the right. Behind her is a succession of girls growing up, each one in a different phase of life, each one with a wound, a cut, a pain, a tear, leading to the woman with flowing hair and a serene countenance. Among the girls, there is a chain that links them all, but it's clearly breaking, freeing each girl and woman from that which brings pain.

15

It's been almost three days since we last saw each other. Work has not been proven to be enough distraction from last Saturday's dinner. I wonder what will happen tonight, whether we will move forward in the intimacy of our confessions and more details of our lives, or whether we will go back living to playing in that place where the real world doesn't matter much.

Luke goes back to being the normal guy he was before; the similarities with the masked man may even exist, but the differences and recent events are enough to create a clear distinction between the two. Luke is nothing like James. I am free of the obsession that I shamefully admit to having cultivated over the past few weeks.

I call Bianca on my way to the party. I tell her about my affair with James, without going into details about how I was invited to Illyria.

'That's wonderful! Everyone needs this magic combination of the poet and the adventurer! The guy who nurtures the heart, who sees the divine in you, and the guy with his feet on the ground, you know? The one who makes things happen and doesn't depend on you,' she answers enthusiastically, as always.

'I don't know what will happen though; I don't even know what I expect.'

'Even better! We never know, hun; we pretend to know what we want, creating certainty around uncertain matters because we are obsessed with feeling safe. Love always evolves. If it doesn't it's not love; it's passion, horniness, ego or itchy trousers!' Her answer is always very authentic, funny, light, objective and at the same time sincere and profound. 'Friend-sister, enjoy life! You deserve it!'

'Maybe you are right.'

'You don't need to expect anything; keep going until it's not good for you anymore. If he does the same, then you will always be on the same page. Talk to him, maybe—maybe not. See how you *feel!*'

What I feel is that every week I get a few millimetres taller and my lungs get a little less full when I enter the magic portal of this new routine of celebration and passion.

A petal holds as many colours
As the garden in front of it
Where the birds and children
Are as botanical as it.

I bet on Sydney's most famous garden, the botanical gardens, and discover with a quick online search that there is a conservatory in it near Macquarie Street. I assume this is where children are supposed to learn music. It is the taxi driver who sees the first people like me—with masks on—walking down the street, and he stops as soon as we can. I see them going into a historic building across the gardens and the music school. I'm proud to have found the right place again. I'm beginning to think these poems are too easy to decipher. If I can figure these locations so quickly, anyone could, right? I hardly need to look for James; my poet is at the bar, waiting with a passion fruit mocktail.

We talk more than usual about all the things we don't need to hide. I tell some tales about the places I've lived; he somehow discovers that I am a descendent of native Brazilian Indians—and I end up telling him the full story. I realise that his ex-wife is in many of his stories. Out of curiosity, I ask if he minds telling me how long they were together. Ten years. I have a feeling they have not split that long ago. Am I the rebound girl? Woman? Am I the healer of his pain? I can't go down this endless spiral. I should either ask him, telling him about my restless doubts, or move on to the present and enjoy what we have tonight. Feel grateful to have one more night together. After all, who knows if we will ever meet again?

While James goes to the toilet, another man invites me to dance. A simple instinctive matter of competition, the male bird is showing off his feathers to see who wins. The prize is pleasure—very different from the reproductive motives of the jungle. I accept solely to tease the man I want to be with later, hopeful this will act as an aphrodisiac. He, the other man, extolling his own ego as the winner of this battle, takes my hand. A couple of songs have played when James gently takes me from this other man who, without a fight, accepts the loss graciously.

Of course, this is not a normal party. He moves slowly towards my ears and speaks with a voice overflowing with desire, passion and possession.

'Your dress is tease enough.' He follows the line of pearls from my shoulders to my lower back with the tip of his fingers, pressing buttons only he knows how to press. 'You didn't have to go dancing with that little guy . . .'

'I was just having fun while waiting for you,' I say, melting like the wax that drips from a candle.

'*I* will amuse you.'

Determined, with passion and possessiveness, he leads me through the arched corridors of the building's central atrium towards the vintage lift, which has a door like an accordion. There's no glass in it, since it was built before glass was used for this purpose. As we wait for it to arrive, he stands behind me, his hands wrapping around me, holding my hands. A sweet image for those who see from afar, but a far more intense moment to anyone who could hear him describing what he will do to me in the lift. I try to remain composed, controlling the impulses created by my imagination in order to prevent a public embarrassment. Pride is a dangerous thing when wounded; in my James's case, my restrained artist, hurt pride is pleasurable. When the lift finally arrives, he pulls open the antique accordion door and charmingly denies entrance to the other guests on the queue, who have been waiting for as long as we have, with a polite sentence: 'It's a party of two.' The lift ride is too short for him to fulfil his promises, confined seconds earlier to me, but it doesn't stop him from starting: keeping an elegant composure, he unzips the zipper that runs down my back; his fingers know how to provoke the imagination and the senses, making it hard to control my response. The assertive touches, as he knows how to turn my buttons on, a slight bite to my right ear, leaving the skin wet and more sensitive to the mild breeze from his sigh of pleasure. Voyeurism. He likes that people can see I am in his hands. I don't know how much they actually notice, but it's the idea that counts more than the reality. The beep of the floor arriving gives me one last pinch between my legs, in the void that is now filled with desire for him to continue with what he promised. We have another set of lifts to go up to our room in the sky, and he certainly keeps the desirable tension by being purposeful in what he says and where he touches, where he kisses and when he stops. It's a blur, a passage that's almost impossible to describe; he is a formidable magician who incites the right hormones and turns off any inhibition-causing preconceived ideas. He carries me with the desire of a teenager and the experience of someone his age. Somehow, I am being carried with my legs around his waist, his hands sweeping up to my back from underneath my spine. I lower my head, and like contortionists, we kiss a succulent kiss until we reach our bedroom. His promise to amuse me in ways I have never conceived is executed with precision, culminating in synchronised moans followed by two blissful sighs.

We delight in each other's presence, studying the curves, the freckles, the hair, the lines, the forms, silent in our thoughts, generous in our caresses. The curse of any architect is not being able to ignore the surroundings; we notice each colour, defect, button, light switch, and for that reason, I discover a piece of paper on the bedside table that says: *Welcome to the Experiment*

Room. Underneath it, a paper not much bigger than a card with clear instructions on how to place the two rings—one mine and one his—in a recess on the wall. One more detail to add to this dualistic saga of so many secrets and so many truths. The snake rings work like keys: the wall opens as double doors swing towards us, revealing a large illuminated walk-in cupboard brimming with gadgets, props, games and books to be studied and used privately. Standing next to each other—me in a hotel robe and him wrapped with a sheet around his waist—we are intimidated so much novelty at the same time as we are curious about it.

'Experiment Room,' I repeat.

'I think that's what they call research material . . . ,' he says while reading a booklet with comprehensive instructions on how to use the mini-room—safety measures and cleaning procedures for our own benefit. Enticing.

'Where should we begin?' I suggest, surprised by the lack of inhibition. James smiles and wraps his arm around my shoulders tightly, bringing me closer to him and giving me a quick kiss on the top of my head. He's pleased.

The first thing I pick up is an illustrated Kama Sutra with gold edges and a leather cover. I have seen simplified versions of it before, but I can't remember when I actively felt inspired by it. The mini-room has everything one can imagine for an introductory—or maybe an advanced—course in the art of the erotic: from historical books on love and sex, like a reproduction of the Arabic work *The Perfumed Garden*, to latex masks, chains and items that help those with physical impairments. For the good listeners like us, it doesn't take long to conclude that love and pleasure are mysteries the world has been trying to unravel for centuries, if not millennia. Would the world be a more peaceful place if everyone had access to the teachings from this room and the lab partner I have? After all, he who loves does not kill.

The feeling must be the same for a child in a toy shop; choosing is harder when there are too many options. We follow our individual curiosity and try as many options as we can; our *to be cleaned* box is about to overflow, so we stop, promising to come again to this room. Our trial-and-error approach turns out to be more for educational purposes. The pleasure comes after intimate laughter that arises from trust. Trust created by the complicity of shared experiences. Energised by inspiration, he collects the blankets scattered on the bed plus some extra duvets hotels always have.

'Get dressed. Come with me.'

He takes me to a place I thought nobody would have access to. In the open sky, illuminated by the artificial lights of the buildings around and below us, with the brutal melody of the innumerable vehicles that insist on entering and leaving the city at this time of night, he nurtures our adventure by laying all the pilfered bed linen on the bitumen roof.

'How did you . . . ?' I start to question his initiative, but he stops by closing my lips with his finger.

'Don't overthink it.'

We fit together perfectly, in a place between the past and the future, where our fears and our certainties meet. Nestled under my hips, his rhythm is complicit with mine; together we culminate in the heat of desire, in the choice to leave ourselves on each other, and as our souls leave our bodies to meet in the air, we sigh—we merge.

I feel like I have wings: light and strong, able to fly purposefully wherever I want to go. I look at him half asleep, delighted. What are the secrets you hide? When will we get ugly? I get up to go home. He notices me moving, grabs my arm and pulls me to him under the covers.

'I love your perfume.' I know he means my natural scent as I do not wear any chemical ones. 'Do you want to go back to our room?'

'No. I'm going home.'

'Don't go. Why are you leaving? Have I done something wrong?'

'You snore,' I reply, laughing as I dress, and he gives me a crooked, suspicious look, but good humoured, demanding another response. 'I wake up too late when we sleep together. I'd better go.'

I want to say that couples sleep together, and we're not a couple. Do I want to be a couple? Do only couples sleep together? Can we not be a couple for the night?

'Wait for your drawing, at least.'

I nod happily.

'Where are you going to get a pen and paper from up here on the roof?' I ask, and he pulls a small pad from his jacket, with a pencil of the same length attached to it. 'What else have you drawn there? Can I see it?'

'No!' He giggles as if his art is badly done. 'You can only see the completed works.'

'I like to see the process; the value of anything can only be measured by how it was created.'

'Are you brave enough to sit on the edge?'

'The question is do I trust you enough to sit on the ledge of this building?'

'I hope you do.'

'I do.'

We lose our words while we find ourselves in each other's eyes. I sense he wants to remove the masks. Can he know I fear losing what we have? We can say so much in silence.

'I've jumped from ledges more dangerous than this one.'

He stares, mute, and then sighs. 'I'm not ready.'

I don't know what he understood from my cryptic sentence, but it has to do with us, with our masks. Maybe I was right: he does want to get them off.

It's okay. I don't think I'm that ready either. It's what I want to say, but what comes out is the response he deserves: 'Take *your* time. I will be here. Waiting. I'll be waiting.' I paraphrase him; he's already given me so much space to be what I needed to be.

His smile is appreciative; his eyes are once again shiny and enchanting.

'It's getting cold,' he says, sitting back to draw me.

There is something extremely vulnerable and powerful about exposing yourself for someone to draw you like this: it is not just the seduction that comes from doing something unique and prohibited—I am sure we are not allowed on this roof—nor simply the sensuality of James drawing me while I am half dressed on the cold roof of a skyscraper after spending hours immersed in love, pleasurable sensations and novelties. It's the stillness of being here while life continues at full speed at all levels between us and the street. People working, sleeping, partying, going places, fighting, loving. Animals hunting, hiding, copulating. All of that while we are here, unknown to everyone, still, in our own world. Life seems rich, special, elegant, profound. When we value something that much, it's almost impossible not to fear losing it. I force myself to stop ruminating about our love: how it will not evolve into partnership beyond these parties, how our future has an open ending, an unknown deadline—a stressor for any project—I don't know how long we can maintain this passion and these masks.

'There!' he says. 'Open it at home.' He puts the folded drawing in my hand, closing my fingers over it; he closes the zipper of my dress and adjusts the collar, sliding his finger over some of the pearls.

Should I really be going home? Will he let me go that easily? Why doesn't he insist that I stay? This is the problem of love: trying to find answers to questions I have not yet asked.

'Do you want me to stay?' I say after inhaling deeply for courage.

'Always, but it's up to you. I respect your decision,' he says while putting a duvet around my back to warm me up. 'You're right, I wake up early because I need to work, and before you make assumptions about last Sunday, I . . . chickened out. I had already arranged to go sailing with some friends, and yes, I was allowed to cancel, but I couldn't. Too much of a big jump. It wasn't because I didn't want to wake up with you or spend time with you; it was because I don't know if I can jump into a relationship, especially when I know neither of us has been looking for that.'

'I totally understand. I'm scared too.'

'I want to take off these masks and see if I've imagined the face I've drawn so many times in my mind, in my *unpublished* work,' he says with a giggle. 'The face I have been looking for in the crowd as I walk, as I eat, as I live. I want to ask for your phone number and send you messages. I want to give you birthday presents. I want to meet your mother and give her my condolences for the death of her son. A mother never forgets. I wanted this to be reality; I want to know your real name. I want to comfort you when you need it. Eva, this is the dream. We are not kids anymore; we know well enough that every dream disappears when we wake up. It's with a lot of pain and ambivalence that I don't ask you to limit yourself to me; there are other needs that a person must satisfy. I can't be everything for you, and I can't demand that you be everything for me.'

I remain mute, in shock, for a while. I don't think he has ever spoken this much. I curl up in his arms, and we remain silent, suffering the pain of losing what we haven't had yet, the pain of not living what we know we can live, just because of fear. We let these raw open wounds—past, present and future—bleed, not forcing any decision that may make them hurt more. We have time. We will heal.

'I don't know what to say, but I think you're ready for a monologue.' I try to lessen the insecurity, but to my surprise, he doesn't react with the humour I expected. He is serious, and I respond with the due respect he deserves again.

'Sorry for the joke. Thank you for saying all that. I wish I could be eloquent like you; I wish I could reciprocate, but I don't want to lose what we have. I also look for you when we are not together. I . . .' Should I tell him about Luke? 'I obsessed about someone who vaguely reminds me of you.' I can't believe I just said that. 'I am always wondering if it would be possible to live day by day with this awakening of the senses, this adventure that we have and the complicity of friendship and the welcome of love. Is it possible to sustain the coexistence of antagonistic things for long?'

'I thought you were not *that eloquent*.' We both laugh. 'It's a big question. I don't know the answer; maybe it's how much we work to make it work,' he continues wisely.

The cold wins out. Once back in our bedroom, he tidies the bed, gets his ring off the wall-door and asks me to stay, reminding me how dangerous it can be to go home at four in the morning.

'See you next week.'

'See you, then.'

I know it's no use caging you
That the world belongs to you
It's enough to know that to my arms
You are back to comfort and pleasure.

He's drawn me with huge angel wings, sitting naked on the parapet, the folds of the dress spread like stars in the dark sky. I am looking and smiling at him, with the wind stirring my hair, which covers my face, just like the mask.

I set the clock to seven in the morning, turn out the lights, close the curtains and take off my sleeping mask.

*

The enchantment soon fades as I leave the hotel, reading messages from Caio, who's notifying me that he's coming to see me. He is at the airport, waiting for the plane. *I can't stand being away from you any longer.* He insists on going to lunch with me at work as soon as he arrives.

Today is Fleur's farewell. She's going to have the baby any day now. Today is not a good day. You should have told me you were coming. Let's have dinner. How about somewhere in Bondi? I will meet you on the corner of Hall Street and Campbell Parade at 6:30 p.m.

Caio doesn't reply to my message, so I imagine he's okay with my proposal, but I'm wrong. Like an uninvited ghost, he waits for me in the lobby of my office, where he's been charming Lynnette since 4:50 p.m.

'Look who came to see you!' Lynnette says, infatuated by his grand gesture, not knowing we have broken up.

I walk over to say hello, still intending to leave at 5:30 p.m., when work finishes.

'Caio, I asked you not to come here.'

'What's the problem? This way we get more time together. I'm not staying long in Sydney.'

Of course not. Why would he stay?

'I thought you said you couldn't bear to be away from me. Isn't that what the message said this morning?'

'And it's the truest truth. I want us to start again. I can't come to Sydney yet; they need me in Singapore.'

'I'm not going to live in Singapore.'

'They want to make me permanent there, which means our Australian visas can be revoked because I will no longer be employed by an Australian firm.'

'Yeah, that's a big problem! For me. Not for you.'

'If it's your problem, it's mine too.'

'Caio, let's discuss this somewhere else, not here.'

'I'm calling the taxi. I'll wait for you downstairs.'

I apologise for leaving early, but Chris doesn't make a fuss; in fact, he encourages me to leave earlier. I save my files and, raging, I go downstairs. Maybe I'm too enamoured by last night, but what rights does Caio have to . . . invade my life like this? In the car, I realise that the anger is not only mine.

'Why didn't you tell me you were sleeping in Kirribilli?'

'I did. We broke up, Caio. I had the right to stay in your flat. I didn't want . . .'

'We broke up . . .' His mood change is abrupt; he sounds like an angry animal.

'Yes, we're done—'

'Who are you staying with in Kirribilli?' he interrupts me, looking out of the window. His hand on his lap is closed in a fist, another sign of anger. 'Your mother left ages ago.'

'No one. I'm alone.' I try to be calm and understand where he is coming from. 'It's closer to work, and it didn't feel right to be in Bondi after we broke up.'

'We didn't break up.'

'Yeah, we did. Where were you?'

'Tainá,' he looks at me now. He's desperate. 'I said I was going to make things better for us. Would I make things better if I knew you were going after someone else? Like a bitch in heat wanting to breed?'

'You have no right to insult me like that. I will not talk to you when you are this angry.'

He remains silent, staring out the window away from me, one arm on the windowsill, the other on his hip, taking up space in the back seat. His legs shaking in anxiety, his jaw clenching, his fingers snapping. I'm glad he's not his dad. He calms down by the time we arrive in Bondi; he walks to the cliff's edge. It's already dark; the ocean has lost its enchantment; I feel an alarming chill on my spine.

'You have changed,' he says quietly, without affection, without tenderness.

'You too.'

'Come on, let's go upstairs. I've got something to show you . . .' What can possibly be there? An engagement ring? I am not moving to Singapore.

The opening of the door reveals to me another side of him I didn't realise he inherited. There, on the table that held so many of my lonely dinners, there's proof of a side of me he didn't know I had: the book, the drawings, the poetry, my diary and an open jewellery box, with an opulent engagement ring inside. My chest is invaded by a wildebeest stampede. The door closes behind him, and he walks slowly, purposefully, to the other side of the table.

'I'll ask you one more time. Are you cheating on me?' His eyes show hurt pride.

'No, we haven't been together for a few weeks now. A month, if I'm not mistaken.'

'Okay, okay, clearly I, the asshole, understood it all wrong. I was meant to believe we broke up.'

'We did break up.'

'Okay, I give that to you.' He stares at me; flames are shooting from his eyes. 'Before that, did you cheat on me with someone else?'

'No. How did you get all this? When and how did you get into in my flat?' I am more shocked by not remembering giving him keys to Kirribilli than by any accusation he is making.

'I can't believe . . . I can't believe you're going to play the victim!' He puts both hands on his head and then punches the table.

He has been angry before, earlier, before we met, never towards me; his hurt pride is indeed a dangerous thing.

'What do you want me to answer? What will justify your anger? You broke into my house! I can put you in jail for that,' I say calmly after a couple of deep breaths.

'The truth. I need to know . . .'

I realise he doesn't have the courage to complete the sentence, so I do it for him:

'. . . if I betrayed you.'

'Yes,' he agrees, looking down, evading my eyes, looking out the window to the beach. He is restless.

'Will my answer make any difference?' I say, getting close, massaging his shoulders. 'You won't believe me if I say no, but if I say yes, I'll be lying. So, I ask you, what is betrayal to you?'

His words are vulgar, his actions animalistic fuelled with anger. I can't recognise him, this is not the Caio I know. This is not the man with whom I shared my life with for so long, who made me feel loved under so many skies, over so many lands. Images of our past that were once calming become stained with red. Red of anger, not love. How can he throw away all that we had?

'No! My answer is no,' I say, my tears held in by the shock of how he's behaving. What have I done to my life? Why was I with him? 'I didn't do any of that while we were together, or when we were apart. If you think I'm capable of that, you've just betrayed all the years I've given my life and my body to you.'

Quiet. He is staring immobile at the world of people below us on the beach, and in the absence of any reaction, I continue: 'But you don't believe me. Why?'

He blinks. I don't think I've looked at him so intensely in years. He has little wrinkles next to his eyes, his lips, his neck that I've never noticed. What's going on in your head, Caio? What do you want to tell me?

'If I say yes, how could you be certain that if I cheated once, I wouldn't cheat again? Won't I be punished to the end of our days for a yes or a no, regardless of the truth?'

'Yeah, you cheated on Miguel with me. I'm an idiot for thinking I'd fix you, that I'd be *the* guy . . .'

'I didn't cheat on him with you. Miguel and I had a very open and free relationship; we knew how long it would last. He got upset because, well, who wouldn't?'

'I trust you.'

He speaks quietly. I can see his anger is almost gone, opening space to his sadness, his insecurities.

'We've been apart for a long time, and it's normal to feel like we are strangers. It's normal to look for what we don't have, right? But we can fix it. If you did or if you didn't, we'll work it out. But I need to know the truth.'

'Why do you want to stay with me?'

Answer me, Caio. Tell me what I need to hear.

'Because you are my life, my friend, my partner. Because we've been together for seven years! Living apart, having adventures. Because you left him for me! Because I am better with you, because you motivate me, because I do everything for you, because I need you.'

'Caio, you were my best friend, my best lover. I still admire your work, your energy in getting things done. But I don't live to serve you . . .'

'Tainá, that's not what I said! Don't twist things.'

'Caio, I'm not offended. But none of your reasons are about me. They're all about you.' I breathe before saying what I am about to say, 'Ask your mother. She will know how I feel.'

'Tainá, leave my mother out of this. Stop analysing everything like she does. I love you! I want to be with you! The idea of not being able to touch you, to kiss you, to have you by my side . . .'

And there it is. I finally see him cry again, maybe for the third time since we've been together. I don't feel the same arrow of angst go through my heart, but I feel that yes, it's over. There's nothing to save, there's nothing to build in the future for us. It's all about him.

'It hurts me too, Caio. I miss you too. I miss us. I imagine that if it's not you, who will it be? Everything we've been through . . . But . . .'

'No buts. We'll manage. I'll find a way. Tell me what you need, tell me what you want, I'll do it. Is it drawing you need? I will learn to draw! I will learn poetry. Is that what you want? I'll give it to you, Tainá—stay with me. Stay.'

'I don't know. I don't know if it's fair to you. I don't know if you or anyone can replace what I have.'

'What do you mean?'

'I have learned to be free. I won't be able to accompany you in your life anymore. I like being alone, discovering new things. It is impossible to get what I need with you or anyone else I have to take care of, serve . . .'

'You never had to *serve* me! What do you want to discover? I'll go with you; what do you want? I have enough money . . .'

'Caio, I . . . I don't want to have to tell you what I need. I need you to *want* to find out. For you to see me as I am, not as what I do for you or what you provide me.'

'Who is *he*? I will talk to this guy. I'm not angry with you. I left you alone, and that's fine. It was my fault you cheated on me.'

'I didn't cheat on you!' It's like being trapped in a spiral.

'Out of respect for everything we've been through together, don't play me for a sucker. Tell me the truth.' He squeezes my arms and brings his body close to mine.

'I am!' I convince myself that I'm not lying because I know I'm not leaving Caio for James. I don't want a relationship or a life with him. I'm trading Caio for my freedom, my peace of mind, for not having to hurt him. 'I have no way of overcoming your paranoia. It's useless trying to convince your imagination.'

'Imagination?! This is not my imagination!' He throws everything on the table to the floor, including the ring he got me. 'Or do you draw yourself? Don't make a fool of me, Tainá!' he shouts my name louder.

'There is no one. I've said it several times! *I* am the other one, the one I cheated on you with, if you want a name. I'm free, and I don't have to worry about you or anyone. There's only my Mum and I left in my life, and she is happy. I would be lucky to be like her.' I start making way to leave, reaching for what is valuable to me on the floor.

'Your mother is fine because she is an ingrate. She takes for granted everything your father did for her, and now she uses his money travelling the world.'

'Caio, you've crossed the line! Money from *my* father? Is this how you see our life together? *Your* money, *your* house, *your* future wife?' My compassion is now liquid anger; the drawings start to get wet from my tears when everything goes blurry.

My forehead hits the floor. Hard. I touch it. It's swollen. I stand up stunned, holding on to the nearest thing—the chair, I think. I manage to stammer out a few words, perplexed, confused, in pain. I need to leave.

'What did you . . . ?' I stagger to the door, feeling my phone in my front pocket. The door I am trying to open slams shut in my face, the pressure on my back too great for me to overcome. Screams in my left ear seem to deafen me; they ring like bells in my head; the screams are muffled.

Bitch . . . slut . . . all I did . . . give . . . give . . . give . . . ungrateful . . . bitch . . . slut . . . cow . . . daughter . . . how could you? . . . deserve. I feel the bed under me. I think he's thrown me here. I must have blacked out. Everything is cold; I think my clothes are torn. I come back to myself feeling a burning cut across my chest.

'I was going to give you that; I came here to ask you to marry me!'

Did he scratch me with a diamond ring? My mouth bleeds; I can't see out of my left eye. It hurts . . . Everything hurts. I'm in bed, with my blouse torn, my legs cold, my chest burning, and, if that wasn't enough, he's managed to take pleasure in making me suffer.

'Bitch! I should have done this a long time ago so you could see who's boss here!' Thanks to my blurred gaze, Caio blends in with the photos of us that still hang on the wall. 'I want to see what poetry he's going to make for you now!'

Lying there, unable to move, tears and blood stream down my face, falling in drops, bloodying the sheet. I no longer know what is sweat from fear and what is despair. I think that of all the risks I've taken in life, this is what will take me away. My mother doesn't deserve for me to be that failure. What would my father think? What will Kadu say when he sees me arrive broken? It seems ironic that all this dedication, the cherished hugs of the past will become the weapon that will get me out of here.

'You lied to me too.' It's all I manage to say.

I hear the zip of his trousers close.

'Me?' His voice is angry, hoarse, unrecognisable. 'How did I lie to you, you bitch?'

He pulls me by the leg, and I hit my head on the floor. I can feel the softness of the duvet that has been accidentally pulled along with my languid, weak body. My mind goes to the duvet on the roof; the way I felt with James nourishes me, giving me hope.

'Did I lie? How did I lie to you, bitch?'

It's thanks to an angel that I find the strength to speak, to fight to the end.

'You're just like him.'

Certain words are more hurtful than the stronger punches. I fight him as well as I can. His whole body, animalistic until now, turns helpless, a frail boy inhabited only by the pain of his youth. He sees his father and is possessed by his own insecurity and the conditioning that tortured his nights during the years he was transforming into a man. Or now, a monster. He fought so hard to give me a life that was different from his mother's that he forgot to confront his own fears. I pride myself on having no pity. After this verbal punch I've given him, his brain seems to see me as a human being again, his heart starts beating again, and I see the Caio I knew, who promised to never make a woman suffer like his mother did. He holds his face in shock, comes close to me, whispers, 'I'm so sorry, I can't believe I did this to you,' and I hear the door close.

16

The beeping of hospital machines wakes me up. I vaguely remember seeing two paramedics in blue uniforms burst through the door after I fell asleep on the floor, but everything else is a blur, a mix of dark snippets of time and some imagery in colour. A nurse soon arrives to check my heartbeat. I see a plastic bag with my phone, my work bag and the pieces of clothes I was wearing on a chair next to my bed.

'Don't worry about it.'

'What happened? What is that?' I point to the plastic tube that's connected to my vein.

'It's to keep you hydrated. Don't worry, you're already going home with some prescriptions for painkillers. Do you have a family?'

'No. Not here. My mother lives in Brazil.'

'Friends?'

'My best friend is about to have a baby; she doesn't need this.'

'Do you have anywhere safe to go after here?'

'Yes. He's no longer in the country.' Coward.

'Okay, honey, you rest. We had to open your wallet to look for your identity card. Your health insurance company has already been contacted; a representative will come over just before we discharge you to see if there is any payment remaining. I doubt there will be.'

'That would be good. Can I have my phone?'

'Here, I'll get a charger for you, but don't look at yourself. We took pictures for the report and forensics. We need to contact your work and hand over any necessary documentation. You are safe here. Now darling, you get some rest. Your mother must be worried; call her. You can use the hospital wi-fi. Here is the password.'

'Thank you . . . Amanda.' I read her name on the name tag. 'How did I get here?'

'An anonymous call, maybe from a neighbour who heard the noise. It happens a lot.' She is very kind; she has that look on her face. This happens *a lot*.

The nurses come and go, give me food, and unplug me from the drip, giving me less aggressive analgesics. As soon as I am more awake, social workers and some police officers come to talk, to find out what happened, saying that I was very lucky that someone called an ambulance, that if another few hours had passed, I could be in the cemetery. I want to go home, away from here, to the place I never should have left. At the hospital, I get to know some other women in states just as deplorable as mine, and with every story we share, we become stronger. The swelling in my face is going away, and I don't seem to be at risk for internal bleeding now. Now I've got to deal with the bruises and the scar across my chest, which, compared to some other scars, are nothing to worry about. The next day, I get an unexpected visitor, Stephanie, the HR woman from work, who's ready to take me home.

'I wanted to offer that you can stay at my place—don't worry, there's no man in sight.'

'I don't hate men, just one.'

'Or ask permission to go to your flat and see if it's clear—if he is not there. The cops showed me the pictures of the flat in Bondi . . .' Steph cries, and cellular memories make my body ache again. 'I'm here if you need to talk,' she says, sobbing and hugging me.

Back at the flat, she asks me to wait outside, but I go around her and am faced with another violation. Everything is broken and overturned. Even the mattress. My dresses are dumped, tossed, and have shoe prints all over them. The black dress I wore at the first party, which Caio loved so much, is ripped. All my masks are destroyed. My body is still weak, but I am strong enough to bear the memories. I can't tidy up the place by myself, so I ask her to help me; she accepts happily. Very quickly, everything is back in in its place. I just need the bruises to vanish.

17

From a distance, I can already tell where he is. There are two masked women attracted by his charm. He spots me after I've been observing him for a while. He walks that walk I love so much but that I am in no condition to enjoy tonight. That walk through the middle of the crowd, coming in my direction, as if I am the only one he wants to see. He must be feeling my negative energy; his smile disappears as he approaches me.

'What happened?'

I can feel his worry.

'I just came to say that . . .' How much it hurts to say I'm not coming back, that *we* won't exist anymore.

On his own initiative, he takes me to a quieter place at the party. He wants to listen to me, as he always wanted to.

'I'm . . . going back . . . ,' I say, knowing that somewhere inside me, the desire to be with him would be more powerful than my recent scars. 'I'm not coming back anymore.'

'Back where? Back home? Has something happened? Is your mum okay?'

'Mum is fine. Nothing happened to her. It's me. I might not come to another party. I wanted to let you know, set you free from me.'

I look away as his silence paralyses me. He takes my right hand, and with his left one, he holds my chin. I tremble. I push his hands away from me, turn away; the memory of the pain hurts too much.

Uncontrollably, the tears swell my eyes and leave my masked man mute. His trembling hands holding mine make clear what he cannot say. I turn away, fleeing for a few steps. The memory of the pain hurts too much, the prospect of losing him too.

'Did I do something? Did I hurt you? Because I didn't want to . . . You know I didn't want to hurt you, right?'

'I know. It wasn't you; you didn't hurt me—on the contrary, you made me see who I really am. It was the rest . . . Everything that I founded my life on has crumbled. No more masks.'

'I don't understand. I want you the way you've always been and the way we've evolved . . . together.'

'Remember me . . . how we were.'

'Is that what you want or . . . are you afraid?'

'Maybe I'll come back. Don't forget me . . .'

'Never! I can never forget you. Please let me help. Is it a visa problem?'

I stare into his eyes but soon turn away. The latency inside me has multiple causes: bruises, disappointment and fear. Will I ever be able to trust someone? I turn my attention to the floor; I want to leave, but I can't.

'Please don't go. We can fix this. You know me better than anyone.'

'Do I? You don't know my name; you wouldn't recognise me if we worked alongside each other.'

'Of course I would recognise you. No, I don't know your name, but I would recognise your voice, your ideas, your values, your smell, your lips . . .'

I take his hand off my chin.

'Let me kiss you,' he pleads.

'I can't,' I say shakily, reflecting my will, my love and my fears. He does not insist. He would not insist.

'What has he done to you? What happened?'

'It's over. It won't happen again—you don't need to worry. You're the dream; you're the untroubled life, the holidays, the childhood, the happiness, but life woke me up. All of this . . .' I turn my head toward the party. 'And you helped release who I really am from inside of me. I will remember you forever, but a fantasy doesn't last. It is, by definition, impossible, unreal, ephemeral. What future do we have if we live locked away in our own fear of living? At some stage, the party's over. One day the truth will knock on our door. I'd rather remember you for everything you gave me, not for what you weren't. If that makes sense. I need to go. Thank you for everything.'

There is an emptiness, the floor is cold, the air is heavy, the music is muffled.

'Please tell me what happened? Tell me your name, take off your mask, don't go away.'

'You're desperate, afraid you won't see me anymore. You'll find someone else. Don't worry, it's better to keep our memory.' I take off my necklace and place it in his hand, folding his fingers over it.

'I've had my heart broken outside of here too, and I'm scared too . . . You know . . .'

I breathe. It's hard to put this in perspective.

'Do you know what the difference between you and me is? If someone breaks your heart, if someone takes it in their hand and squeezes it, taking away all the love and goodness that lives there, if someone tells you how shitty you are, the only thing wounded is your pride. Which you fix with a lot of time, therapy and someone else. No one is going to beat you and leave you to die after finding the beautiful drawings and poems you got from someone else.' I notice my voice rising in tone. I can't stop; he needs to know. 'A stranger. A stranger. I am alive because a stranger called an ambulance. A few hours more, and I would have rotted on the floor, with so much love, so much blood consuming me and suffocating me inside. Wherever I touch myself today, tomorrow, next week, a year from now—it hurts! It hurts on the inside, and it hurts on the outside!'

'I'm sorry, I never thought, I never wanted to . . . I didn't know you had someone else, I thought you . . .'

'Thought I what? It is my fault now?'

'No, not at all. What can I do?' His hands move closer to mine. I let him touch them. 'Do you have somewhere safe to go? I'll set up a security guard for you. Are the police helping? I don't know what to do, but we'll work it out. Please don't break it off; we'll work it out.'

He lowers his head, trying to look into my eyes. I turn the other way. The weakness of my body shows in my slumped shoulders and aching neck. I notice gum on the floor. When did I become such a mundane person?

I turn my back, slowly, then wind around to look at him.

'You were the spring of my winter.'

'Tell me your name, your real name.'

'What's the point? I don't need you to look after me.'

'How can I find you?'

'In your memory, in your heart, in your body. Eva is over. She exists only for you, and you, my nameless masked man, or James, my golden bird, I will forever fly because of the wings you helped me find.' I hold his face with both hands. 'I'll miss what we were, but we can't last forever here, nor in the real world.' I kiss him lingeringly, imprinting his texture, his coffee taste, his scent of desperation mixed with his old scent of desire, his touch on my waist, which is delicate and fearful today, not wanting to hurt me. 'You're special, I will miss you.'

'You are special too. I will always remember you. I will miss us. Don't leave me—come back. Take your time. I'll be here week after week. Waiting for you all night, until you come back.'

I feel the distress of losing myself in his hands as they try to hold me, comfort me, touch me, but he perceives my trembling. He puts his hands on his mask in order to take it off, and I stop him.

'Let's not spoil our magic with desperation . . .'

'Maybe it's desperation, but who wouldn't be desperate when the love of your life, the person you admire most, slips through your hands like . . . like . . . dry sand. I wish I could stop this hourglass, stop time and heal every open wound that's there. I want you with me. Not for me—you don't belong to anyone—but I want you by my side. I want to be by *your* side. I want us to fly together. Come back, please—come back next week. I want to tell you that I love you, but you won't believe me. If you don't believe my words, believe everything we've experienced.'

'Always. Don't worry about this . . .' I smile, placing my thumb on his lips and my hand on his face. And after our last exchange of glances, my face red from crying, fear and the pain of a lost love, I turn to leave, my legs soft as concrete being poured. Wanting to go back in time to our night at the rooftop.

His mask appears on the floor beside me, splayed out like a rope . . . an entanglement that I have the freedom to choose whether to accept.

'Eva!' He tries once more to pull me back. 'Please tell me your name; you are so much more than what we experienced together. Please, tell me your name; you deserve your real name. Please stay and let me prove you don't need to be scared . . . of me.'

Everything that leaves his mouth is beautiful; my heart tells me to trust, but how can I know? I don't know if I can trust my love decisions again. I look at the mask next to me. I can see him, I can look at him, I can start something new. I shake my head in denial and, not looking at him, not discovering the rest of his face, I say: 'I love you, for all we experienced together, my James, my masked, golden . . . bird. I will remember you forever.'

18

The week ahead is a mix of appointments and responsibilities. I have a few conversations with people at work who notice something is wrong with me, my plummeting energy level; they try to relieve me of commitments and my workload without knowing why I have been absent. I enjoy working. I exercise like crazy to compensate for the nightmares from the night Caio became dead to me; they wake me up systematically, leaving me exhausted the next day. The spring is arriving, and it's warmer every day; the midday sun can already give us a tan.

The government gave me a temporary visa, independent of Caio. They claimed that being dependent on his visa would no longer be in my best interests; an email marks my official separation from a man I no longer recognise. A good solution, as I have plenty of time on this temporary visa to decide what to do while still being able to work, a dream for many people. I don't need plenty of time though. I appreciate the opportunity, but I want to go home. I apologise in my mind to all those who need a visa like this to escape from wars. I want to go home. The home where memories no longer torment but strengthen me. The office offers me a pay raise if I stay. I politely refuse, but I ask for a day to go to Fleur's house and see her baby and her children, which they kindly give to me.

She invites me to stay at their house for as long as I want. I accept on the condition that I'll take on the housework, as I don't like to see my friend without a minute to herself. The little ones treat me with such affection, give me their attention, laughter and play, and I can't help but wonder where we go wrong in the process of life that some children turn into horrendous adults. The laughter and unconditional love of these small, pure creatures are capable of anaesthetising even the scar that burns in my chest. Because of all this strength, instead of running away, I decide to return to the party once again and hear what James has to say. He deserves a better sense of closure; I do too.

It has been a good week, without drama with men. Except for the police, who say they still haven't located Caio. He's likely left the country long ago.

I arrive at almost eight o'clock without fearing that he will be gone because he said he would wait for me all night. The delay is not on purpose; I have decided to disconnect myself from many things that hold me back, including time. I know a delay of this magnitude won't become my routine, but I'm slower than usual, and each day I feel like I live at a different pace. I don't quite understand it, but I imagine it's a way of dealing with trauma. As I approach the party venue, I see people emerging;

some are screaming, guided and huddled by the security guards outside.

'Code Red,' I hear someone say. I'm walking faster towards the house when the masked security guard says, 'Code red.'

'What?' I can't believe it.

'Code Red,' he repeats.

'Did someone die?'

'Yes, madam,' he says, keeping his composure, guiding me with monumental calmness to where the other people are. Stunned would be the best word to describe how I feel. How could anyone have died?

I move out of the way but stand by the side of the house, waiting for my masked man to come out.

'Miss, you need to go. If you were not here before, I suggest you leave as soon as possible. This is a crime scene now; the cops are on their way.'

I nod and walk at a turtle's pace, as if the world around me moves a thousand times faster than me. My eyes, focused like an eagle's, search for James. Yes, someone has died, and all I can think about is him. If I don't see him now, I will never see him again. Everything is a bit confused; I imagine the killer has already left, but what's all the agitation about? Surely the policemen will interrogate everyone. I am relieved that I wasn't inside. Sometimes, being late has its advantages. From a distance, in the shade of a dense tree, without my mask on, I see the faces of the people who, one by one, are obliged to take off their masks by the interrogating police officers. It's over. I stretch out my arm and hail a taxi to go home. James and I are over.

Someone has been murdered, and I have no idea who it was. There is nothing I can do but to look for news in tomorrow's paper. I can't make myself feel guilty thinking about my life, about these men plaguing my mind and my time while someone died just a few hours or minutes ago. Guilt only exists when we know we should have done something we didn't. I left before the police arrived; my number was not registered. I remain anonymous. Maybe not, maybe now our files will be opened, and we will be at the mercy of the police for interrogations and I don't know what else.

I come home to Kirribilli to finalise packing. The reflection of the opera house, the boats and the city lights twinkling on the water and through my window give me a calmness I've never had before. I feel as if I have chosen the right door and that there is a new path open to me. A path to be made with myself.

Luke. Even if he was James, on a day-to-day basis, he hides behind many masks. There is not the same freshness, the same connection, and so I don't see any sense in adding myself to his already complicated life. Caio took from me not only him, the future and my peace, but also our past together. He took my life, he took all the generosity I had, and he made me feel like an idiot. A warrior, that's true, but an idiot for letting myself be blinded and manipulated by gifts and compliments mixed with contemptuous attitudes that little by little undermined my confidence.

My golden-nosed bird, my James, my faceless lover, was spring in my winter. Perhaps the only true romance I have ever experienced is somewhere in this city, and I will never find it again. It's best to end it this way so that our love is eternal, trapped in the memory of an unchanging time.

*

I wake up satisfied to see Sydney in front of me. There are no more horizons at my window, but there is something concrete: a city that gave me nature, culture, work and freedom. Looking ahead, I know my days from now on will be balanced without the nostalgia and melancholy of the horizon that kept taking me to my past and to a future that could not exist. A line that characterised me so much, for I didn't even know who I was. An imaginary line of myself, lost between the sky and the sea, waiting to be seen by someone who cared to look long enough for me. I did not exist. I take my time in front of the mirror. I see me. Perhaps for the first time. No shields, no masks; just my skin and my soul aligned. Both of which I am sure will change, as there's no more armour to contain me. Now, I not only exist, but I know how to feel the bumps, stumbles, my own mistakes and, most importantly, the glories of what it is to live. I alone am now, finally, more complete.

The end of last week's party doesn't have a terrifying effect on me. I've been through worse things. A death, or a secret murder, since nothing seems to have made it into the news. Someone died, and I found myself glad it wasn't me. I, who used to live to tempt death, realise that the choice is always to live. I feel lucky to know that my impulses, my drive, my will, my desires, and my unconscious managed once again to make me use logic, reason and security. I am luckier than many. I will never be able to erase what happened to me, but I live, between bad memories and terrible ones, enjoying what should be celebrated. Bec, Luke, Tommy and Steph spent the week saying their goodbyes to me. Beautiful goodbyes—meaningful cards and useful gifts. Delicious and long lunches, confessions made only to someone who will soon be gone and may never return. Compliments and reference letters to keep with care, in case one day I want to come back to Sydney.

I say farewell to Fleur by going with her little ones to the playground at the end of Blues Point Road for a picnic they've prepared for me themselves. My nephews of the heart, the big sister I never had. I feel devastated leaving them.

I leave my bags open on my bed, hoping to say goodbye to the city and get souvenirs for some of Mum's friends. I'll be home in a month's time. The key and the box I never managed to return bring a smile to my face. I admire the box's details with my hands one more time before placing the key and ring inside it, protected by a handkerchief, an accidental souvenir inherited from James. They will forever make me think of Sydney and the Secret Society of Illyria. This afternoon, before heading to the airport, I will hand over the keys to a young woman who will come to live in the flat until Bianca returns. Now, in the morning, I cross the bridge on foot, on my favourite walk, in no hurry and with nothing weighing on my conscience or on my shoulders, thanks to the beautiful handmade fanny pack that I bought in Spain but never used because Caio always complained about it. Thankfully I've kept it and carried it around the world.

I search for the tracks that, at the beginning of winter, led me to a path with no return. There is nothing. Everything has been removed. The mask shop is empty and now has a floor-to-ceiling sign across the window saying, *New attraction coming soon.* There is a gap between the sign and the door frame. I look, snooping, and there is not a single mask for sale. I can't help but think of the blind gentleman who is now out of a job. What could he be doing now?

The flower beds and flowerpots are colourful. Looking at my phone, the last verse is clear. The path is my own to follow:

And the day the colours are too many
Know there's nowhere to go
Just go it alone
The path that is yours to own.

The cage with the date, removed. The mailbox is open, with nothing inside. The brick on the wall at Suez Canal no longer has the ouroboros symbol. They are just normal bricks. Without the newspaper and without the flowers, there is nothing left, in fact; something tragic happened to this person who went to seek a night at freedom and ended up lifeless.

After all this wandering around, I sit in a café on George Street in front of the MCA and send a message to Mum, confirming that I will see her in a month and that I will send daily photos documenting my time as Bianca's assistant camerawoman. I am full, breathing this free and light air, eating alone and reading, just like old times.

When I am ready to leave, I notice a vase of pink petunias placed amidst the colourful flower bed. It has a key just like the one I have hanging from a small piece of paper, like a bookmark. I have a feeling that this vase is for me. James wants to see me.

I propel myself to take it and read the label when it occurs to me that he could be anywhere around here. I pretend to take a picture of the museum and adjust my camera's focus so that the paper is in the foreground. I can read it clearly; the poem is much larger than any he has made for me. There is a small drawing at the end of the poem, the outline of a woman rising in the waters, looking at the moon—the image from my necklace pendant once again.

Beyond the surface you saw me
And I met you
Let me in your story because in mine
You are already
I wait for you every day
Every day
Until you notice
That you and I together must stay
Every day
Until you come back.

I leave the flower where it is. I take a photo to add to his poems, to know that he wants me, that I will stay in his memory, in a good way. I hope in a good way. He's waiting for me at the Horizon's Edge, every night at seven o'clock. I'm glad it wasn't him who died.

I call the restaurant; they are open to the general public now. 'We are booked every night! You won't regret it!' says the receptionist enthusiastically. I want to ask if there's a reservation for James, but I know there is.

I take a deep breath, the air rushes into my satisfied lungs and I walk back to bid farewell to yet another of my favourite corners: my little cottage in Kirribilli.

I take a deep breath; the air enters my satisfied lungs, and I set off walking to my little corner, my little flat in Kirribilli.

In the taxi, on my way to the airport, I conclude that yes, it is possible to love someone I have touched, smelt, heard, tasted but never seen. And it is possible to love someone in this way, deeply and intensely, as I love myself, as I desire myself. My being does not need to subtract itself from anyone else, and this is true for others who live with me. We are all protagonists of our own stories, and in mine, only those characters who understand that it is by giving that one receives will be allowed to enter. Reciprocity is the fundamental clause of love, whatever kind of love it may be; and freedom is nothing more than the courage to choose what you want. Freedom is not running around searching for the next new thing. This is just a distraction. Freedom is knowing where your fears are and knowing when to face or run away from them.

There is always a world to be discovered in the finitude of where one is. There is no use in a beautiful fruit tree if it can't put its roots in the ground; it will die. My ground is my family, my friends, my language. I'm leaving not because I don't have the courage or the patience to stay, but because I have a lot of blossoming to do and a lot of fruit to pick from myself.

The end.

Or is it just the beginning?

Acknowledgements

Support and encouragement manifest differently for each person, and here I'll try to show my deepest gratitude for each person who contributed directly or indirectly to making this book come true.

I thank my beloved editor, Julia M. Metello. Without her endless readings, revisions, critiques and motivation, this book would still be in my head and in countless notebooks. Thank you forever.

My existence would not be possible without the intrinsic duality between my father's critical and humanistic reasoning and my mother's unlimited creativity and free spirit. I can never thank them enough for making me, raising me and setting me free in the world.

To my brother: together since always in creative endeavours, and to whom I always resort when doubt hits me.

I thank my female friends with the fullest heart, the ones who are forever bound to me through the glue of shared experiences that have left deep marks of strength, joy and courage. You know who you are.

To the secret, imaginary or real lovers who have passed through me. The good marks are in this book, as well as the bad ones.

I thank my psychoanalyst, Tereza, and my physiotherapist, Pamela, who worked tirelessly to align my mind and body, respectively.

I will be forever grateful to all the women and men who shared their stories of domestic violence and contributed enormously, allowing me to be able to write and give them a voice in the world of stories.

I thank the reviewers who pushed my story forward for the better.

I would like to thank Charlotte Rowland and Ana—whose last name I don't know—for their patience and generosity in connecting me with the great energy that surrounds us to clear my doubts and fear, and to open paths for this book to materialise.

My children, it would be impossible to list everything I am grateful to you for, but for now, accept my gratitude for being my fuel for life, for inspiring me every day to become a child again, and never forget that the world is magical.

It is necessary to thank my other family from another country, who raised an amazing man, my life partner, the one who helped me and helps me to heal the wings that were hurt during my trajectory by the simple fact that I am a woman.

And last but not least, I thank him, my eternal companion, who, the universe brought me in a blessed synchronicity, the one who listens to me, calms us down, and it is through him that we continue together in the great ups and downs of life. Of many lives.

Thank you. I am because you are all part of me.

CPSIA information can be obtained
at www.ICGtesting.com
Printed in the USA
LVHW031044120522
718524LV00012B/488

9 780645 293012